SECUTOR

THRACIAN

Sand of the Arena

SAND
OF THE
ARENA

A Gladiators of the Empire Novel

By James Duffy

McBooks Press, Inc.
Ithaca, New York

Published by McBooks Press 2005

Gladiator illustrations: Angus McBride
Cover photos: Alamy Limited, UK
Book design and cover photo illustration: Panda Musgrove

ISBN: 1-59013-111 8

Library of Congress Cataloging-in-Publication Data

Duffy, James, 1955-
    Sand of the arena : a gladiators of the empire novel / by James Duffy.
      p. cm.
    ISBN 1-59013-111-8 (alk. paper)
    1. Rome—History—Nero, 54-68—Fiction. 2. Gladiators—Fiction. I. Title.
    PS3604.U378S26 2005
    813'.6--dc22

                            2005009064

Distributed to the trade by National Book Network, Inc.
15200 NBN Way, Blue Ridge Summit, PA 17214
800-462-6420

Additional copies of this book may be ordered from any bookstore or directly from
McBooks Press, Inc., ID Booth Building, 520 North Meadow St., Ithaca, NY 14850.
Please include $4.00 postage and handling with mail orders. New York State residents
must add sales tax to total remittance (books & shipping). All McBooks Press publica-
tions can also be ordered by calling toll-free 1-888-BOOKS11 (1-888-266-5711).

Please call to request a free catalog.

Visit the McBooks Press website at www.mcbooks.com.

Printed in the United States of America

9 8 7 6 5 4 3 2 1

To Greg, Kris, Nina, and Bill
You are my life.

Acknowledgements

I am extremely grateful to Alexander Skutt and his staff at McBooks for their tremendous support and enthusiasm for this book and series. A special thank you to my editor, Jackie Swift, for her on-the-mark comments and suggestions, and for being such a pleasure to work with. To my agents, Loretta Barrett and Nick Mullendore, for their guidance and reassurance. To editor extraordinaire Patrick LoBrutto for being the first to see merit in my manuscript. To John Maddox Roberts for his historical notes and words of encouragement.

To all those who assisted with my research, especially the master of ancient sources, Sander Van Dorst; Graham Ashford and all the members of Ludus Gladiatorius; John Ebel, Mike Catellier, and Al Barbato of Ludus Magnus Gladiatore; Mike Bishop with the *Journal of Roman Military Equipment Studies;* and Dr. Marcus Junkelmann for his outstanding experimental archeology and boundless knowledge of all things gladiatorial.

To all the friends and family who provided such valuable input and feedback on the manuscript, especially Greg Duffy, Ted McKeever, Larry Casella, June Poole, Mike Schafer, Margaret Torok, Buck Brinson, and Laurie Vid. And of course, my thanks and love to Mom and Dad for their never-ending support and genuine enthusiasm for every project in which I'm involved.

And finally, to Kristina—my wife, best friend, soul mate, and business partner, all in one lovable package. You are the best in-house editor and idea generator any writer could hope for.

INTRODUCTION

A FEW WORDS before you immerse yourself in the grandeur, action, and pomposity of ancient Rome . . .

From its founding as a tiny shepherd's community in 753 BC to its growth as the largest empire the world has ever seen, the story of ancient Rome is a lesson in survival, absolute power, and corruption. Its expansion provoked one of the most dynamic periods in world history—at times violent beyond belief, yet also offering its inhabitants decades of peaceful, happy lives.

The old adage "Rome wasn't built in a day" is important to remember here. Many assume that icons such as the Colosseum, known in its day as the Flavian Amphitheater, always existed. Actually, it was inaugurated in AD 80, thirteen years after the story in this book ends. Therefore, the logical question "Why aren't these gladiators fighting in the Colosseum?" is answered simply: Because it didn't exist yet.

The largest arena in Rome during the setting of this book— AD 63 to 67—was the Amphitheater of Taurus. As with all amphitheaters prior to the Colosseum, it was constructed primarily of stone and wood, although still of massive size. There are conflicting reports as to whether this amphitheater was destroyed in the Great Fire of Rome in AD 64. For the purposes of this story, I have assumed it survived, or at least was rebuilt, providing the characters a suitably imposing setting for their lethal battles.

Amphitheaters existed across the expanse of the Empire, from the northernmost provinces of Britannia to the southern reaches of the Roman outposts in North Africa. The action of this novel takes place in many of these smaller arenas. Although their geographical placement within the story may not mesh with current archeological excavations, provincial arenas did exist in or near virtually every major Roman settlement, a testament to the immense popularity of the games.

One of the most hotly debated aspects of gladiatorial games protocol revolves around the sentence of death to a fighter. Many scholars feel the commonly recognized "thumbs down" gesture is more a whim of movie directors than a result of historical research. The only mention of this practice in ancient writings is the term ". . . with thumb turned." This has been interpreted by various historians as a thumbs up motion, a thumbs down motion, and even a thumbs sideways motion. Many agree on the waving of white handkerchiefs to signify mercy. For the purposes of this story and the sake of clarity, I have elected to use the traditional "thumbs down" gesture to signify death and the waving of white handkerchiefs to signify mercy or *missio*.

Another common misconception about gladiatorial combat is that one of the fighters always died. In fact, most bouts ended with both fighters surviving. The primary reason for this was simple economics. It took a long time and a great deal of money to train a gladiator. The *lanistae*—the owners of the gladiators—were not willing to lose half their investment at every arena event. The games *editor*, or sponsor, knew this and often had to pay extra for each gladiator condemned to death, so the majority of the vanquished fighters were spared. Of course, those gladiators who put on a poor performance or showed any sign of cowardice rarely left the arena alive.

Another point worth mentioning involves the training of gladiators. There were numerous fighting styles in which the gladiators were trained. The five most common were:

- Thracian: A lightly armored fighter carrying a small square shield *(parmula)* and curved sword *(sica)*. His helmet crest often bore the image of a griffin fixed to the front.
- Hoplomachus: A gladiator who worked with a small round shield *(parma)*, a large helmet with a high crest and feathers, and either a short straight sword *(gladius)* or a spear.
- Retiarius: A nimble fighter who used a long trident, a net *(rete)*, and a small dagger *(pugio)*. He was the only gladiator to fight without a helmet. Instead, he wore a high shoulder guard *(galerus)*, which also protected his neck.
- Murmillo: A heavily armored gladiator, who fought with a large rectangular shield *(scutum)*, a short straight sword (gladius), and a helmet with a high crest, usually topped with feathers or a plume.

• Secutor: Another heavily armored fighter, similar to the murmillo. Since he usually fought the retiarius, his helmet was smooth so it would not get snagged in his opponent's net.

Most gladiators also wore quilted fabric pads on the arms *(manica)* and legs *(fascia),* along with metal greaves *(ocrea)* that protected the legs. Often the sword arm would be additionally protected with a metal sleeve.

There were many other variations of fighters, which grew in number as the fickle mob demanded more variety in fighters. The key to the variations was its inherent system of checks and balances. For every positive, there was a negative; for every strength, a weakness. It was what kept the games interesting.

A few points on gladiator training . . . The correct term for a gladiator trainer is a *doctor.* This is not to be confused with a healer and practitioner of medicine, who was also a prominent figure at gladiator training schools. To differentiate between these two important positions, I have added an "e" to the trainer's title *(doctore)* and I refer to the medical doctor as the "physician."

A common misconception is that all gladiators were either condemned criminals or prisoners of war. Actually, not every fighter in a gladiator school *(ludus)* was there against his will. There were some who actively sought the gladiator lifestyle and joined a ludus voluntarily. The reasons were many— some craved the fame and glory, others a chance at riches, and some sought the adventure of facing death head-on to prove their mettle.

The question often arises, "Were women ever trained as gladiators?" The answer is yes. Although not a common sight, there were female gladiators. Most fought only other women, but you are about to meet a female fighter who was good enough to face the toughest male challenger.

Lastly, there are numerous references to money and Roman currency. I use the *sesterce* as the common monetary unit, since that is how most items and services were priced in ancient Rome. It is impossible to equate the value of "a sesterce" to modern currency, due mainly to the dramatic difference in the overall cost of living. Rather, to give you an idea of its value in ancient Rome, it would cost about one thousand sesterces per year to support a lower-class husband and wife. Typical military pay was nine hundred sesterces per year for a legionary. You will see the value of a gladiator was substantially higher than that, and a good gladiator could actually earn much more than a regular soldier in a year's time. Yes, gladiators were paid for their fights, usually in gold coins, but sometimes in valuable trinkets and even livestock and villas.

I hope this book will open your eyes and minds to a side of the Empire you never knew. If so, and if you'd like to learn more, please visit our website: www.GladiatorsOfTheEmpire.com. There you'll find additional information, links to Roman and gladiator-related sites, and an annotated bibliography of reference materials used in my research for this novel.

But for now, let us escape to a glorious and exciting ancient world.

JAMES DUFFY
June 2005

SAND OF THE ARENA

I

May AD 63

THE PERSIAN CAPTAIN stood at the prow as his war galley sliced through the choppy waves. The long black-and-white plume of his helmet crest blew back like the tail of a horse at full gallop. Spray mixed with sweat and made his golden armor glisten with theatrical brilliance. Behind him, two rows of slaves pulled on the long oars, the synchronicity of their labor insured by the muscular madman prowling the gangway, whip poised. The fifteen-meter ship glided forward with each stroke. Two more Persian galleys kept pace on its flanks, creating a formidable wedge driving toward the three Greek warships coming at them.

Quintus Honorius Romanus awaited the cataclysm. His leg bounced with nervous anticipation as he marveled at the dignified bravado of the ship leader. A gleam drew his attention from the confident captain to the long metal spike of the corvus secured to the ship's mast, ready to crash down on the enemy's deck, locking the warships together and working as a gangplank for the assault troops.

A splash off the port bow caught Quintus's eye. In the crystal clear water he saw one battle was already under way. The streamlined fin of a shark sliced the surface, then disappeared in a frenzy of white water as the four-meter fish plowed into its prey. The black leather back of a crocodile sprang from the water as the shark grabbed its hind leg and thrashed side to side. The reptile turned at a speed that defied its bulk and snatched the shark's head in its jaws. The croc rolled over and over, until it wrenched the head from the body. The clear waters turned cloudy red as the crocodile gulped down chunks of the defeated shark, oblivious to the warships gliding by. Within seconds, five more gray fins broke the surface, followed by the distinctive "V" wakes of more crocodiles converging on the scene. Quintus knew this watery nightmare awaited many of the ships' crews.

A wave of sound—the shouting of thousands of voices—snapped him from his trance. He looked up to see the enemy warships closing fast. The large white eyes painted on the Greek bows stared straight ahead. He almost expected them to flinch as the massive battering rams of the Persian galleys drew closer. The Greek ships had giant weapons of their own: directly above the painted eyes protruded two colossal spears, like twin devil horns. Although this was his first naumachia sea battle, Quintus knew he was looking at the face of death.

His attention was grabbed once again by the Persian captain. Quintus sensed valor in the man's stoic face as the captain stared into the eyes of the Greek war vessel. His helmet crest whipped sideways as he turned and shouted to the twenty marines huddled behind him. Quintus could barely make out the words over the commotion of the thousands of voices. A warning shout from a marine near the port bow interrupted the captain's commands.

"Shields up!" The powerful order reached Quintus's ears over the din.

In a single motion, twenty green-and-gold shields clanged together to form a solid roof on the deck of the ship. The nervous bounce in Quintus's leg increased. From the phalanx of Greek ships came a strange cloud. It took a few seconds for him to recognize the sight of a hundred arrows in flight. The dark shape undulated like a living thing as it arced up from the Greek ships. Again the roar of voices swept across the water, pushing the cloud of arrows on to its mark.

The clattering of arrow tips against wooden shields was ungodly. Many of the tips found soft flesh rather than wood. Screams of agony rose as five, then seven, Persian marines fell to the deck. Some lay motionless. Others wrenched arrows out of their own arms and legs.

Quintus did not know where to look next as orders came quickly, barely audible over the chaos.

"Stand by to ram!"

"Make ready the corvus."

"Stand firm, men. Victory may mean freedom for the best of you today."

Quintus scanned the faces of the men about to clash in mortal combat.

Some had a hard look, determined to be victorious. Others had eyes wild with fear, not unlike a horse on its first cavalry charge.

The impact came with a violent, sickening crunch. The Persians' bow spike pierced the iris of the port-side eye that had glared at the enemy ship throughout its approach. Wooden beams as thick as a man's leg splintered like kindling, throwing shards across the water's surface. Quintus froze in morbid fascination. His leg stopped twitching. Without realizing it, he stopped breathing as he saw one of the monstrous spears above the eyes of the Greek galley rushing directly toward the head of the Persian captain. Quintus gasped and yelled a warning, knowing it was futile at his distance. With the lance only inches from impact, the captain finally ducked, the sharp point creasing his helmet crest. Quintus watched him shout an alarm to the troops packed behind him, but the chaos of the engagement, mingled with the incessant distant voices, drowned out the captain's warning. The giant lance skewered three marines like small morsels of food. Their armor had little effect against the three-meter iron spearhead pressed forward by the tonnage of the war galley. The violent rocking of the ship lifted the screaming soldiers off the deck and suspended them over the water. Quintus tried not to wince as their final heartbeats pumped streams of blood down their legs. No sooner had the first drops kissed the water's surface than the shark fins and reptilian bodies began circling.

Quintus glanced back at the captain to see his reaction. It seemed the warrior could not tear his gaze from the three men writhing in agony, even with the chaos of battle growing around him. No longer did he have the bold look of a valiant battle hero. Suddenly the man's face reflected horror, his earlier confident expression replaced with a mask of uncertainty.

The Persian troops did not wait for further orders. One marine swung his sword against the thick rope that held the corvus. The heavy boarding plank slammed onto the enemy galley, pinning one of the Greek fighters to the deck with its iron spike. The marines moved quickly to board first and gain the advantage.

But Quintus's eyes remained locked on the Persian captain. The man seemed oblivious to the frenzy around him. He simply continued to stare at the three men dangling from the giant spear. His head tipped slightly to the side, and his face took on a sense of wonder. Quintus was mesmerized by this insignificant personal drama developing amid the growing bedlam of the naumachia. He wondered what was going through the captain's mind. What suddenly drove this brave warrior into a trancelike state? The sudden jerk of the captain's head made Quintus jump. He flushed as the captain seemed to look right at him. The sea warrior's face was defiant again, but his anger was not thrust upon the Greek fighters. Instead he jumped to the top of the bulwark, his black-and-white helmet crest billowing across his face. He screamed with all his might. For an instant, Quintus felt the man's rage was directed only at him. But he quickly realized the man was shouting at the scores of faces watching the battle. The words were unintelligible in the pandemonium, but the intent was unmistakable. The captain was boldly defying the thousands of spectators who had gathered in the Amphitheater of Taurus to enjoy the sea spectacle.

"What's he on about?" came a voice next to Quintus.

"Lead your men, you dim-witted ass!" another screamed at the ship's commander.

Quintus watched the captain's face turn brilliant crimson as his rage grew. But as quickly as it had begun, the captain's tirade subsided. His head dropped, and he looked down at his side. Quintus followed his gaze. An arrow was buried deep in the captain's waist just below his breastplate. A stripe of red grew down his white tunic and leg. Quintus turned to where the shaft pointed. An archer crouched in the stern of the Greek ship, another arrow already nocked on a taut bow string. The archer released his grip and the shaft flew from the bow. Quintus turned back in time to see the arrow strike the Persian captain just above his left eye and burrow deep into his head. The force knocked him backward into the raging waters. In an instant he was torn apart by the sharks and crocodiles.

"By the gods! Did you see that?" Quintus yelled over the rising crowd noise at no one in particular. "A perfect head shot. And now he's fish food!"

The stranger seated beside him did not seem to hear. His gaze was riveted on the crocodile attempting to snag the dangling legs of the three soldiers impaled on the giant lance. For a moment, Quintus felt an odd sense of loss for the captain, but the sea warrior was soon forgotten as the boy's attention refocused on the hand-to-hand combat developing on the Greek ship's deck.

At fifteen years of age, Quintus Honorius Romanus was a connoisseur of the arena. His understanding and appreciation of gladiatorial combat rivaled that of spectators twice his age. His father had taken him to the gladiatorial and hunting events on many occasions, but this was his first naumachia. From his seat in the middle tier of the Amphitheater of Taurus, alongside the other wealthy merchant families, he had a perfect overview of the sea battle. But he could tell that viewing the naumachia would take some getting used to. With so much going on at the same time, how could one possibly savor everything? Especially when he also had to keep an eye on the activity around him in the seats. He took a minute to scan the spectators in his section to be sure his father was not nearby. Although he and his father often enjoyed the arena spectacles together, on this day Quintus was supposed to be with his private Greek tutor in the atrium of his villa. But today was the naumachia. How could he possibly miss it? Feigning illness and slipping out the window of his bedchamber bought him a few hours of arena excitement. He just hoped his father was not seated close enough to spot him, and his mother didn't check on him in bed. The bundle of tunics under the cover would not withstand a close inspection.

"By Neptune, they're boarding quickly," Quintus said, his attention now fully diverted from the red foam that was once the Persian captain.

"Not as quickly as you're going to move your ass back home."

Quintus froze, recognizing the voice.

"Hello, Father." His own voice quavered a bit. He turned to look into the stern face of Caius Honorius Romanus, seated directly behind him.

"I spotted you from across the aisle, so I thought I'd come join you," Caius said with more than a touch of sarcasm. "What's your mother going to say when she checks up on you? You know what a worrier she is."

"With this sea battle going on today, I'm sure she'll figure it out pretty quickly," he said with a sheepish grin. "Besides, how could I concentrate on my studies knowing I was missing this? It would have just been a waste of everyone's time." He noticed the corners of his father's mouth begin to turn upward and detected a gleam in his eyes.

"Well, then, I guess we'll make the best of it and both take our lumps when we get home." The face softened and showed a broad smile. All along, Quintus had sensed that his father was as disappointed as he over his mother's insistence that tutoring not be interrupted by "those horrid games." This one look confirmed that suspicion. Quintus was relieved that he'd be allowed to stay to witness the dramatic end to this battle.

"By the way," his father said as he reached behind him, "I got this for you at one of the stalls out front. You were supposed to get it tomorrow morning, but as long as you're here . . . " His hand slid forward, holding the most beautiful miniature boat Quintus had ever seen.

He looked up into Caius's hazel eyes as he took the boat and cradled it carefully in both hands. His fingers traced the rich detail that made the terra-cotta warships prized souvenirs of the naumachiae.

"By the gods, it's beautiful! Thank you, Father."

A roar from the crowd turned their attention back to the flooded arena. In an instant, all thoughts of tutors and angry mothers left Quintus's mind.

"If the Persians can take the Greek ship intact," Caius explained, "it can be turned against the other Greeks. They'll be outnumbered four ships to two."

"The herald said they were recreating the Battle of Salamis. Did the Persians outnumber the Greeks there?" Quintus asked.

"Not necessarily. The Greeks won a great victory in that battle, but the outcome here could be much different. It all depends on the prisoners and gladiators playing the parts of the Greek and Persian fighters."

Quintus's hands tensed as one of the Greek ships backed out of the main battle. It was pursued by a Persian ship that had failed to drop its corvus. Many of the sharks followed, seeking their first decent meal in a week.

"It was amazing to watch them flood this arena," Quintus said. "Were you here for that, Father?"

"I've been here all day. They diverted water from two of the aqueducts to fill it. Half of Rome was without water for most of the morning. That's one of the reasons the naumachiae aren't held often. They're a lot of work and very expensive. All these ships had to be built, the fighters had to be trained in naval tactics, all the Greek and Persian armor and weapons had to be made, and the sea creatures had to be transported here."

"I'll bet the naumachiae on the big lakes are really something," Quintus said.

"They have ten times as many ships as this, but from the shore it's hard to see what's going on. Here in the arena you feel like you're right in the action because you're so close."

Greek archers lined the starboard rail of the retreating ship. They lowered their arrow tips into brass urns, bringing a deafening cheer from the crowd.

"The Greeks are fighting back with fire," Quintus shouted.

"This is always spectacular," his father yelled back. "The boats have been soaked with pitch, so they'll ignite quickly. Be wary of the arrows, Quintus. Many a flaming shaft has found its way into the crowd."

In one perfectly coordinated move, the Greek warriors drew their bows and fired. It surprised Quintus that their first volley was not toward the pursuing Persian ship, but directly at the Greek galley, which had already been boarded by the enemy. A dozen balls of hot orange flame burst from the tar-soaked deck and sides of the wooden ship. The reflection of the blaze danced across the surface of the water in the dimming afternoon light. The crowd shouted its approval at the strategic move, as the smoke and scent of charred wood quickly reached Quintus and Caius.

"Smart move," shouted Caius. "They'd rather sink their own ship than have it used against them."

The next swarm of flaming arrows flew over the burning Greek galley and onto the deck of the Persian warship. As Caius had predicted, two of the flaming arrows glanced off the wood surfaces and flew into the lower tiers of the cavea. Senators and other ranking officials scattered.

Caius chuckled. "I don't think I've ever seen Senator Marcellus move his ample body so quickly."

Within seconds the deck of the Persian galley was a holocaust. Both Greeks and Persians had to choose whether to die in the fire or take their chances in the water. Most chose the water, their capes and tunics already aflame as they dove overboard. The lucky ones were grabbed quickly by the sharks and crocodiles, dragged under, and drowned. The less fortunate struggled to stay afloat in their heavy armor, only to endure the torture of having a leg or arm ripped off by the beasts.

For almost an hour the ships waged battle in the flooded arena. A second Greek ship was sunk, sending its archers and oarsmen over the side and causing another feeding frenzy. The two remaining Persian ships converged on the last Greek vessel from both port and starboard.

Quintus tensed for the collision. "They've had it now. There's no way they can outmaneuver this charge."

"Could be," his father yelled back over the growing din of the crowd. "But Greeks never give up without a fight. Remember the three hundred Spartans at Thermopylae?"

As the words left his mouth, the Greek archers dropped behind the bulwark. They reemerged a second later, arrows glowing with flame. They split into two groups—one defending their port side, the other their starboard. In unison, the arrows flew and once again the wood ignited. One of the Persian galleys was engulfed quickly. The crew of the more fortunate ship managed to douse the flames on their deck with vats of water and continue their charge. They maneuvered alongside and dropped their corvus. Even before its spike pierced the deck, the marines were charging across the narrow bridge. The clank of weapons brought more screams of approval from the crowd.

"Now you'll see some swordplay, my boy," Caius said.

"There's no room for them to fight on that deck. I doubt we'll see any finesse in this bout," Quintus replied.

Flames from the burning ships reflected off the polished swords, throwing streaks of orange light across the arena. Quintus's assessment was correct. There was no finesse to the battle, only forceful, desperate blows for survival. Although the Greeks were better archers, the Persian marines were the physically stronger force. This balance of power was carefully calculated into the planning of any arena spectacle. If an opponent had a strength, he must also have a weakness. It was what kept the games interesting.

The Greek archers could not load and fire quickly enough. They were soon overwhelmed by the brute force of the Persian marines. Within minutes, the deck was awash in Greek blood. The Persians spun, looking for more opponents, but none were left alive. They raised their weapons and unleashed a piercing battle cry, which was overtaken by the bellow of the crowd, Quintus's and Caius's voices among them. Persia had rewritten history this day.

Persian rowers manned the oars of the vanquished Greek galley and positioned the ship in front of the royal podium. In unison, the marines raised their swords in salute to the heavyset Emperor who cheered with as much enthusiasm as the mob.

Nero's plump face was flushed with excitement. He raised his hand to quiet the crowd. Quintus watched, entranced, as Nero awarded laurels of victory and small bags of gold to each of the fighters. The oarsmen received smaller laurels and no gold.

"I wonder what it feels like to stand in victory like that before the Emperor," Quintus murmured, more to himself than anyone.

"I wonder more what it feels like to become, as you so eloquently put it, 'fish food.'" His father smiled at him.

Nero again raised his hand to quell the cheering crowd. In a booming voice that matched his ample size, he announced a special final event to this spectacle. Workers lowered a towering wooden plank similar to a giant corvus across the water. It spanned the arena from one side of the stone wall to the other. Three thick support beams mounted under the span acted as trestles, resting on the arena sea bottom and holding the bridge secure a meter above the water's surface.

As the sun began to set, the glowing embers of the half-sunk ships bathed the arena in an eerie red cast. Though dim, the light was enough to see shark fins still slicing the water's surface and the slinking tails of crocodiles circling the enormous pool.

Nero nodded to the praecone, the game's narrator, who stood to introduce the participants in the final event.

"Citizens of Rome! Our esteemed Emperor, the great Nero Claudius Drusus Germanicus, gives you a final gladiatorial contest of epic proportions. Two of Rome's finest swordsmen shall meet as pontarii, bridge fighters in mortal combat on the Bridge of Destiny. The Emperor Nero gives you Gordius the Thracian . . . versus the undefeated champion of Rome, Spiculus the Magnificent!"

The roar of the crowd rolled like thunder across the now calm waters. Quintus and Caius were again on their feet.

"After his last battle Spiculus was given a villa by Nero," Quintus shouted over his shoulder to his father.

"I know. I was here. Remember?"

Quintus scanned the entranceways, searching for the gleam of armor. These were the bouts that got his blood running. Although mobility would be restricted on the narrow wooden bridge, these athletes were trained in the *art* of combat. He was always more anxious to study the moves and strategies of the top gladiators than simply see blood spilt by mediocre fighters. It was the product of his own self-defense training with his bodyguard, Aulus, combined with years of attending the games.

The two gladiators finally emerged from entrance tunnels on either side of the cavea. The wooden seats shook as the crowd grew even louder. Most of the women were in their own special frenzy—the kind Quintus noticed whenever the bigger, broader gladiators were in the arena. Some bared their breasts proudly in tribute to their heroes.

The fighters mounted the bridge and cautiously approached the center. The narrow span bounced slightly under the weight of the combatants. Each wore the traditional subligaculum loincloth held in place with a wide leather-and-gold belt. But the armor and weapons were different, again giving each fighter the strengths and weaknesses that made the bouts exciting.

Spiculus fought as a murmillo, wearing a visored helmet with a high angular crest, a white plume, and two white feathers projecting upwards from side sockets. His right arm was covered with a white padded sleeve called a manica. In his left hand he held his scutum, a large rectangular shield which protected most of his body, but could become a disadvantage due to its weight if the fight went on too long. His legs were covered with white pads called fascia and his left leg also bore a metal greave protecting the shin. In his right hand he carried the lethal short sword called the gladius.

Gordius fought as a Thracian. He had less armor, but his lightness afforded him speed. A metal sleeve covered his right arm and shoulder. From his right hand protruded a sica, a curved sword of Etruscan origin. His left hand held a small rectangular shield, almost square, called a parmula, lightweight and easily maneuvered. Both legs bore metal guards that rose from his ankles to his thighs. A visored helmet, crowned with the traditional thraex griffin, covered his head.

"The crowd is for Spiculus, but I think Gordius has the advantage on that narrow bridge," Quintus observed. "I wouldn't want to have to work that heavy shield on such unstable ground."

The cheering reached a fever pitch as the fighters met at the center of the bridge. Spiculus made the first move, a series of fast strikes followed by a single thrust toward the chest, all parried with Gordius's small shield. Gordius struck next with swift blows alternating from left to right. Although he blocked Gordius's attack with the scutum, Spiculus teetered off balance on the narrow bridge from the weight of the heavy shield.

"I told you so. Now Gordius will force him to swing that scutum back and forth to keep him unstable." Quintus's running commentary aroused the interest of others in nearby seats.

"The boy is right," yelled an old man seated behind him. "A murmillo can't win on that bridge. Look! The crocodiles are already beginning to circle."

Again Gordius charged, alternating his thrusts to force his opponent to swing his shield. Spiculus struck back with a flurry of hard blows, all fended off with the parmula and sica except the last, which caught Gordius on his unprotected left shoulder. Blood ran from the deep gash, agitating the crocs and sharks further as it dripped from the bridge. The crowd reacted with more turmoil. Shouts of *"Hoc habet"*—"He's had it!"—rang out across the cavea. The lonely clanging of the weapons could hardly be heard over the crowd.

"That's a good move for Spiculus," Quintus yelled to his father. "It might shake Gordius up enough to make a mistake. But if he doesn't do something with that scutum soon he's going to knock himself right off the bridge."

Ignoring the blood streaming down his arm, Gordius kept his opponent unbalanced, forcing him to work the shield back and forth. Spiculus's helmet turned slightly as he appeared to glance at the reptiles circling under the bridge.

Quintus could tell Spiculus was up to something. A seasoned fighter would never look away from his opponent like that, even for a second. Gordius capitalized on the distraction and charged his opponent.

Quintus sensed it before it happened. "This is it! Watch!"

Gordius's charge was at the point of no return. Spiculus's left arm snapped forward. The heavy scutum was loose. It flew the short distance between them with the speed of an arrow. Its weight struck hard against Gordius's right arm.

The sica flew from his hand and splashed into the water, followed by Spiculus's scutum. Gordius seemed stunned by the impact. His left foot was half off the bridge. He looked up into the facemask of Spiculus, who had closed the distance right behind his shield.

"He's fish food!" yelled Quintus.

With a single thrust Spiculus's gladius pierced his opponent's stomach, and Gordius toppled helmet-first into the water. As if sensing it was the last meal of the evening, a fight erupted under the bridge that rivaled the one which had just taken place above it. The water quickly turned to red foam.

But all eyes were upon Spiculus, arms raised in triumph and a fierce bellow booming from his throat.

Quintus was in the same pose on his wooden seat, the terra-cotta boat raised like the victorious gladius on the bridge. "That was genius! He turned his weakness into his most effective weapon." He looked at his father who seemed as entertained by his son's antics as he was by the arena battle. "*That* is the difference between skilled gladiators and a mob of slaves playing marines."

Nero once again waved the crowd to silence so he could honor his favorite gladiator. As Spiculus approached the end of the bridge under the Emperor's podium, a hefty bag of gold coins and a silver palm leaf struck the wooden planks in front of him. He retrieved his awards and gave a final victory cry. The crowd's frenzy reached the boiling point.

Quintus was loudest of all. His eyes closed and his boat thrust skyward in triumph, it wasn't hard for him to picture himself, instead of Spiculus, standing on that bridge.

"That's quite a young man you have there, Caius," said the old man seated behind them. "I think he should be teaching these fighters instead of watching them."

"What a job that would be!" Quintus said with excitement.

His father gave him a disapproving look, then smiled and tousled his hair. Being referred to as a "young man" always got Quintus's attention. To most people he seemed older than his fifteen years, both in wisdom and stature. His close-set brown eyes and round handsome face framed by short wavy black hair gave him a look of natural intelligence, which was validated by exceptional school work. His broad shoulders spoke of good physical conditioning.

Nero bid the crowd good evening, then requested those with special invitations to stay seated while the others left the arena. Quintus gathered his green wool pallium. He had shed the overcloak in the heat of the afternoon sun. Even his short white tunic was damp with perspiration after the day's excitement.

"What's your rush?" Caius asked. His teal pallium still lay crumpled on the seat beside him. He scratched casually at his close-cropped beard. His hazel eyes twinkled and scanned the amphitheater. A slight grin grew on his thin lips.

Quintus looked around and saw most of the patricians in their section heading toward the exit tunnels.

"Are we not leaving?"

Caius smiled as he slipped his hand under the teal pallium and withdrew a small rolled parchment. "Not while I'm holding a special invitation to the Emperor's banquet. Care to join me? I can bring a guest."

His smile turned to a laugh as Quintus's jaw dropped open.

"Really, Father? We're going to a royal banquet?"

"Actually, we're already here. Wait until the arena clears out and see for yourself."

Quintus watched the drab brown and olive tunics of the poor and the slaves in the upper seats moving toward the exit tunnels, hoping to catch a glimpse of Aulus.

"So, what did you think?" Caius asked. "Was the naumachia what you expected?"

"Well . . ." It took Quintus a moment to get his thoughts together. "I liked it. But it was hard to focus on the individual fights."

"But that's not what the naumachia is all about. It's about working as a team to overcome your adversary."

"Oh, I understand that. It's like the chariot races. You need to work with your horses as a team. But when gladiators fight it's man against man. Each has total control over his own destiny. There's no dependence on the horse or the oarsman or the ship's captain. Life or death is totally up to you, and you alone."

"Well, I guess I expected that," Caius said. "But still, I thought the pure spectacle of a ship battle would overpower the lack of subtle combat strategy for you."

"Don't get me wrong, Father. I did enjoy the show. That final fight was amazing!"

Caius showed a broad smile as he cuffed the back of his son's neck. "Well, I'm happy our esteemed Emperor was able to salvage the show for you."

It took another twenty minutes for most of the cavea to clear. Many of the best seats closest to the arena wall remained occupied by Senators in their white and purple togas. Mixing with them were a few military legates in their dramatic red capes. In addition to Quintus and Caius, there were another forty or fifty merchants and noblemen in their mid-level patrician section.

A fanfare of trumpets interrupted the quiet talk. The water swirled as the Gate of Life opened once again. Four massive barges floated through the opening, pulled by a hundred workers manhandling thick ropes along the arena wall. Set upon each raft were dozens of deep red banquet couches grouped in multiple square arrangements. Sheer canopies of blue and white silk embroidered with gold billowed above the boats, held aloft by Corinthian pillars. Typical of Nero's fondness for the theatrical, he had each barge dramatically lit by hundreds of torches anointed with oils burning in shades of green, red, yellow, and blue.

On the final barge sat Nero himself upon a gold and red throne surrounded by thirty of the most beautiful dancers in Rome. Enthusiastic applause broke out among the dignitaries, partly to show their appreciation to the Emperor and partly in anticipation of the exotic dance performance for which Nero's banquets were so well known.

Quintus stared, speechless, as the workers maneuvered the barges into place and secured them alongside the arena walls close enough to form one continuous floating platform. "By the gods . . . I can't believe it! He's having the banquet right here in the flooded arena. How did you get invited to this feast?"

"Quintus, my boy, you don't give your old man enough credit. Our business has grown into one of the largest in Rome. Success brings privileges, you know."

Although Quintus had always known his father was a hard worker, he never really considered the elevation of their social status as the years had passed by. Since they moved into their new villa three years ago, life had been good. But royal banquets were another matter. Now their improving social standing was becoming obvious even to someone of his young years.

The workers laid gangways from the arena wall to the first barge. Nero nodded and the herald bellowed a welcome to the few hundred special guests.

"His Excellency, Nero Claudius Drusus Germanicus, bids you welcome and invites you to join him aboard his royal barge for food, wine, song, and other delights. Let us feast!" On cue, a billowy white curtain was drawn aside revealing a band of ten musicians. An upbeat melody flowed from panpipes, double flutes, cithara harps, and a hydraulic organ, as the girls surrounding Nero rose and led him to his special couch.

The crowd moved down the cavea aisles and climbed the stairs that had been set against the arena wall. Quintus looked over the side as he crossed the gangway in time to see a huge shark swim by with a human arm grasped in its jaws, the frozen hand still clinging to a sword. Thankfully, the smell of death and offal was masked by the somewhat pleasant scent of charred wood from the smoldering galleys.

Many of the Senators had already taken up residence on the choice couches closest to Nero's. Caius and Quintus respectfully moved toward the secondary barges.

The opulence was far beyond anything Quintus, or Caius for that matter, had ever witnessed. In keeping with the nautical theme of the festivities, gargantuan trays of shellfish were scattered throughout the couch enclosures. Quintus had to smile at the thought of the earth-dwelling creatures consuming the sea creatures on the barge, while the sea-dwelling creatures devoured the earth creatures below the barge. Serving girls snaked their way through the growing crowd with silver trays of eggs, cheeses, and fried dormice, a delicacy favored by the Emperor.

"Caius! Caius! Over here!" The call came from the next barge. Caius and Quintus worked their way through the rows of couches and very carefully stepped across the half-meter of open water between the two rafts.

"I thought that was you, you old sea witch," said an elderly man, clasping hand and forearm with Caius.

"Hello, Marcus. How's Neptune treating you?"

"Fair winds and fair seas I'm happy to say. And look at this young man. What's it been, Quintus? Five years?"

Quintus was speechless, primarily because he didn't have a clue who the man was. The windswept face, wrinkled but still soft and friendly, was only vaguely familiar to him.

"You don't remember Marcus Didius, do you?" his father asked. "I believe it *has* been about five years now."

Quintus smiled and shook hands as a hazy recollection formed in his mind. But he was more interested in the food trays than in recalling past acquaintances. Marcus invited them to join him on a nearby couch. The traditional position of eating while lying on one's stomach across the communal couches made it easy to enjoy the company of friends.

"I was your father's boss many years ago." Marcus looked at Caius with the pride of a victorious tutor in his turquoise eyes. "He was one of the best sailors I ever trained. That's why he worked his way to first mate so quickly."

Obviously embarrassed, Caius looked down and began prying open a shellfish. Quintus enjoyed seeing his father squirm in these situations, for although Caius was tremendously proud of what he had built for his family, he was also quite unassuming about it.

"And look at you now, with your own shipping firm. I heard you just landed three ships in Ostia, hauling grain from Egypt, all in a single week."

"What can I say? Business is brisk for merchantmen with good crews," Caius said, sampling the flamingo tongues. He paused and looked Marcus straight in the eye. "I learned that from a great ship captain once."

Marcus laughed heartily. "True. But with your business sense, I trust you could buy and sell that old ship captain many times over by now. The Romanus family name is becoming one of the most respected in Rome, you know."

"Well, the Viator relations are certainly helping out there." Caius was quick to share the credit with his wife's side of the family. "My wife's brother, Sextus, just opened his sixth textile shop."

Quintus saw the man's eyes light up at the mention of his mother.

"And where is the lovely Politta this evening? Did she allow her two ruffians a day out on their own?"

Quintus and Caius shared a smile. "She doesn't have much of a stomach for the games. And, actually, she doesn't exactly know I'm here," Quintus explained, then crunched another fried dormouse.

"Ahh, so the two ruffians are conspiring together I see," Marcus said with a wink. "You two are peas in a pod. I take it you'll be following your father into the shipping business one day, eh, Quintus?"

Quintus wiped the crunchy residue from his mouth with his forearm. "Actually, I'd rather be a gladiator," he said with a nonchalance that seemed to surprise even his father.

"Ohhh, a gladiator." Marcus glanced at Caius with an amused smile. "You'll have to be a pretty good fighter to earn the kind of money your father makes. Wouldn't it be easier, and a lot safer, to just take over the shipping firm someday?"

"I'd rather fight," Quintus answered.

"Last year it was 'a charioteer' and before that 'a Praetorian guard,'" Caius said, shaking his head. "He's quite the adventurer . . . at least in his own mind."

Marcus laughed and called for another goblet of wine. "So are you making the most of the family enterprises, Caius? I hope your ships are helping to move your brother-in-law's materials."

Quintus was excited to answer. "Absolutely! We're heading to Britannia in just five days with a shipment for them. The whole family's going."

Marcus seemed surprised. "Britannia? That should be an adventure. Why did they settle there?"

"Sextus and his wife, Julia, are good at getting a jump on the competition," Caius said. "There's a new resort town there called Aquae Sulis. Actually, it's a very old resort, but new to us Romans. They say the healing waters in the natural baths are like nowhere else in the Empire."

Marcus picked up on the business opportunity immediately. "So your brother-in-law figures that the waters will attract the wealthy older patricians to the resort town, and he will make a healthy living supplying them their togas, cloaks, and stolas."

"They also wanted a life away from the confines and noises of the bigger cities," Caius continued. "They moved from Rome a while ago to set up their shop in Ravenna on the Adriatic. Then they were in Pompeii for a while. Now Britannia. We haven't visited with them in almost ten years. I know my wife is looking forward to seeing her brother again. And I'm looking forward to taking one of my ships past the Pillars of Hercules and outside the Mare Internum for a change."

For the first time all evening, Quintus detected concern in Marcus's face. "Be wary, my friend," Marcus warned. "I've not traveled that far north with my fleet, but I've heard stories from those who have. They say the winds and weather are much different than what we're used to."

Caius seemed touched by this man's concern for his welfare after so many years. "I've put my best captain and crew on this voyage. I'm sure it will be an uneventful journey."

Marcus made a face as he bit into his first fried dormouse. Quintus was quick to volunteer to finish the portion, which Marcus gladly handed over. "So, business is good for them I take it."

"Who, the Viators? Must be," Caius answered. "They've asked us to bring another one hundred rolls of woolen, twenty rolls of Egyptian linen, and even five rolls of silk with us."

"Impressive. Very impressive," Marcus replied, watching Quintus finish his fifth helping of dormice and swig a large gulp of watered-down wine from his goblet.

The music suddenly grew louder and faster. A curtain on the last barge was drawn back unveiling the thirty female dancers, frozen in a pose resembling Egyptian hieroglyphs. What caught Quintus's attention were the thirty golden trays balanced high in their hands and the sixty bare breasts below the trays. A stuffed blue-green peacock was lavishly displayed with feathers fanned on each of the trays. From a gold belt around each girl's waist hung two long panels of sheer material that perfectly matched the blue-green of the peacock feathers.

Synchronized to another change in music, each dancer in the Egyptian tableau came to life and traced a winding path through the barges, distributing the main course to each cluster of couches. Once the deliveries were made, each dancer remained in the center of her cluster.

"Well, things are picking up, eh, Quintus?" Marcus asked. Caius smiled as Marcus winked at him.

The peacock trays were passed around the couch as hands ripped and tore at the delicate poultry. The dancer in the performance square in front of Quintus wasted no time in getting her group's attention, although her flaming red hair had already caught the eye of every man and most of the women on the barge. From his angle on the couch, Quintus could only see her from behind. But it was obvious through the gauzy green material that she possessed a beautiful, well-toned body.

In a fluid, sensual movement she began to snake her arms in front of her, causing her bare breasts to alternately rise to the right, then the left. She slowly arched her spine backward until her torso was fully upside-down. A broad smile broke across her inverted face as she stared into Quintus's wide eyes.

The others on the couch cheered as she reached over her head to retrieve two peacock feathers that had fallen from the golden tray. Hoots, whistles, and catcalls grew louder as the dancers began their unspoken competition to put on the most outrageous performance of the evening. Those who made the biggest impression always took home the most gold, both from the royal coffers of Nero as well as the private pockets of the Senators and merchants.

Defying gravity, the redhead slowly straightened up, concealing her chest with the two long feathers she had rescued from the floor. She spun gracefully and once more locked eyes with Quintus. He decided that she was even more beautiful rightside-up. Stepping in beat with the music, she slowly approached him, drawing the feathers across her bare breasts with each step. Quintus could clearly see that the sensation of the delicate feathers against her skin was causing her nipples to stand erect.

"Beware, Quintus," came a deadpan voice from Marcus. "The Eyes of Horus are upon you."

His couchmates chuckled, but Quintus was awestruck by the redhead and her perfect nipples, which were now close enough to touch. The tension in his body, combined with the poultry grease on his fingers, caused his metal goblet to shoot from his hand and clang loudly on the floor. Riotous laughter erupted around their square of couches. An embarrassed Quintus glanced at his father, who offered a broad smile and an empathizing wink.

As he looked back toward the open square, he was startled to find the sheer blue-green material that had once draped the dancer's lower body now on the floor. He tilted his head back, slowly savoring the view, and came eye-to-eye with the completely nude redhead not ten centimeters from his face. Her breath was hot and sweet. Perspiration was beading on her upper lip and forehead.

She abruptly grabbed Quintus by the shoulders and rolled him over on the couch like a rag doll. With a quick step forward she straddled his head with her thighs and began grinding herself against his face, never missing a musical beat.

Quintus's arms and legs flailed in shock. He didn't know whether to scream with delight or scream for help. The fact that he couldn't breathe was pushing him toward the latter. But before he could make his decision, he was slid out from under the dancer's crotch and propped up on his wobbly legs.

"Come along, Adonis. I think it's time we go," came his father's voice out of a fog. Caius smiled at the dancer and tossed her a gold piece. "I don't think he's quite ready for you yet, dear. Perhaps another time." The redhead grinned wickedly and moved down the couch to her next victim.

Marcus, who was choking from laughter, smacked Quintus on the ass as his father steered him toward the gangway. "Nice work, my boy! You'll give these Senators a run for their money someday." He looked at Caius. "So long, old friend. May Neptune be with you and your family on your trip to Britannia."

"Thank you, Marcus. Thank you for everything."

They crossed the gangway from the barge to the cavea and Quintus took one last look over the side, hoping for another glimpse of the sea creatures. Seeing only black water this time, he followed his father up the stairs and out the exit tunnel to the wide deserted street that surrounded the amphitheater. The sounds of the party spilled over the high walls and echoed on the stone street. A single torch mounted in the tunnel exaggerated their flickering shadows on the rough stone wall of the gladiator school across the walkway.

"Well, that was some evening. Wouldn't you agree, my boy?"

Quintus stared straight ahead. "I have seen paradise." He broke into a wide grin.

Caius laughed loudly as he threw an arm over his son's shoulder and together they walked toward the center of the street. They stopped short as three shadowy figures stepped from the murk of a second tunnel.

"So you saw paradise, did you?" The voice was almost ethereal against the stone walls of the tunnel.

"Aulus!" Quintus shouted. "I looked for you in the cavea."

The smile that broke across the slave's face told Quintus he was flattered. "I was near the top as always. A mere speck from your seats."

Quintus had a hard time believing that, with Aulus's tremendous size, he would be a mere speck when viewed from any seat. He and the two smaller bodyguards approached Quintus and Caius and, although the street was deserted, formed a protective barrier around them.

Aulus Libo was the biggest of the Romanus household slaves, standing a full head above Caius. His short light brown hair and blue eyes hinted at his Celtic-Hispanic heritage. Under his drab green tunic, his broad chest was scarred from years of arena battles, the most serious of which had brought him to the Romanus family. As with most top gladiators who were severely injured in the arena—yet spared by the crowd for an outstanding performance—he was sold to the upper class as a personal bodyguard. Aulus was on the auction block the day Caius entered the slave market looking for a protector for his newborn son. Caius had paid a hefty sum of ninety-five thousand sesterces for him. Quintus had often heard his father say it was the smartest money he'd ever spent.

Although Aulus was a slave, his relationship with Quintus was a special one, and because of it, he was treated differently than other slaves. Quintus, Caius, and Politta all saw Aulus as more of a big brother to Quintus than a household slave. Aulus repaid this affection with a commitment to the Romanus family that was equal to the commitment he had made twenty years earlier to his gladiatorial family. He would just as willingly die to protect them as he would have died with honor in the arena under the eyes of the Emperor and the gods.

"We should go now," Aulus said. It was a two-kilometer walk to the Romanus villa, which stood on Clivus Orbius between the Palatine and Esquiline Hills. While their neighborhood was a wealthy fashionable district, some of the streets between there and the Campus Martius, which housed the Amphitheater of Taurus, were less than safe.

"Tomorrow, can we work on some of the moves made by Spiculus and Gordius this evening?" Quintus asked.

"Absolutely," Aulus said, his head swinging back and forth, scanning the street as they began their walk.

Caius looked at Quintus with a smile and a raised eyebrow. "Assuming, of course, you survive the wrath of your mother after slipping out that window today."

Quintus knew well that any trouble they might encounter with bandits this night would pale in comparison to what probably awaited him in the morning.

II

May AD 63

THE MORNING BREEZE brought welcome fresh air through the peristyle of the Romanus villa. The sound of trickling water from the fountain in the rectangular pool usually enhanced the peaceful atmosphere of the garden oasis that made up the rear quarter of the villa. But on this morning the sound of wooden weapons overpowered everything else in the garden.

"Show me how Spiculus landed that shoulder hit on Gordius last night," Quintus panted while engaging Aulus in mock combat. "That was an amazing move."

"That's a bit advanced for your level," Aulus said between whacks from the wooden practice swords. "Concentrate on the basics first. Try the advance and thrust I showed you last week . . . That's better. Now come across hard. Good!"

The sounds of their combat echoed off the colorful murals of hunting scenes that adorned the walls beneath the covered portico surrounding the green oasis. The portions of the walls not covered with murals were painted a deep maroon and trimmed with black and gold cornicing. The mostly white mosaic floor of the portico, which incorporated the same maroon, black, and gold palette into tasteful geometric patterns, was becoming cluttered with the small tables and backless chairs being arranged for breakfast.

"Alright boys, the battle's over."

Politta Viators's voice was delicate, yet colored with authority. She stepped into the peristyle and began rearranging the bread loaves. As she did every morning, Politta personally supervised the preparation of the light morning meal for her family.

"Yes, Mistress Viator." Aulus raised and spun his sword in the quick salute that had become his arena trademark so many years ago. Quintus mimicked the move, though with not quite as much flair as his trainer. As he replaced his sword in the small rack, Quintus watched his mother carefully, trying to judge her mood by reading her body language. She had been asleep when they returned last evening. This was the first he'd seen her since he feigned a fever by hugging the charcoal brazier in his room, then immediately calling her for comfort. Just how mad was she about the ruse?

Quintus pretended to noisily rearrange the wooden weapons on the rack, trying to catch her attention. But his mother did not so much as glance in his direction. He continued to watch for an opportunity to make eye contact, to charm a smile from her. Although she worried too much and was too strict for Quintus's liking, he had always held a deep sense of love and respect for her. As she walked among the serving trays and tables, her belted white tunic flared back handsomely just above her ankles. A red stola draped from her left shoulder, across her front, and wrapped over her right hip. Her shoulder-length brown hair was tied back in a tight bun and held in place with a narrow gold band that stretched from the top of her head to behind her ears. Her face was classically Roman: olive skin and hazel eyes set perfectly astride a delicate, slightly pointed nose.

Quintus could see he was not getting her attention. He slowly made his way across the garden, stopping to retrieve his new terra-cotta boat from the fountain pool. The souvenir had not left his sight since the previous afternoon. He continued his tentative approach, clearing his throat and forcing a cough to gain attention. If his mother heard him, she took no notice. With a few more steps, he stood directly behind her. He leaned over her shoulder and kissed her cheek.

"Good morning, Mother."

Politta continued to arrange the narrow bread loaves on the silver serving tray in silence. Only when the final loaf was placed did she turn to face her son. Her hands went to her hips, and her head cocked slightly to the left. Quintus knew immediately he was in trouble.

"Well, it's hardly a good morning for me, now, is it? I was up half the night worrying about you. All I found was a pile of tunics when I checked in on you. I had all the servants hunting the villa and the nearby streets, thinking you wandered off in delirium from your fever. I finally figured you took off for the arena again." She glanced down at the boat in his hands. "I see I was correct."

Quintus made a point of lowering his head a bit and looking at her through his long lashes. That usually worked to melt her heart.

"Don't give me that look. You know perfectly well that your studies are more important than those games." She turned and resumed directing the setting of breakfast.

"I'm sorry, Mother. It won't happen again." Quintus tried to sound contrite, but inside he simply could not understand why she felt tutoring was more important than the games. He knew if the circumstance arose again, he'd be right back at the amphitheater.

After a few quiet moments, he noticed her glance again at the boat.

"You missed an amazing naumachia," he said, trying to warm the chilled air.

"Oh, is that so?" Her short response was all the encouragement he needed, and he excitedly launched into a rambling description of the sea spectacle, using the toy boat to reenact the battle action. The servants bustled around them as they spoke, arranging the food displays and fresh-cut flowers from the garden.

As usual, Lucius Calidius was jealous. The fifteen-year-old kitchen slave stood motionless, pitcher in hand, half hidden behind one of the Doric columns that supported the portico roof. His eyes were fixed on the toy boat and his attention was more on Quintus's story than on his household duties.

"Are you going to pour the fruit juice sometime this morning or shall I dump it on your head?"

Lucius heard the words, but they did not register. He was too absorbed in Quintus's tale of the epic sea battle.

"Lucius!" His name came with a sharp crack to the back of his head. The kitchen manager continued in a vicious whisper. "What's the matter with you? Pour the juice before I beat some sense into you."

Lucius gave him a long glare then approached the table and began pouring the mixture of pear nectar, apple juice, and honey. While he poured, he strained to absorb every word of Quintus's story.

"Isn't this boat a beauty? Father bought it for me."

Lucius's gaze never left the terra-cotta ship as it passed to Politta's hands. He watched with envy as her fingers traced the intricate details.

"I love the Persian captain standing on the bow," Quintus continued. "That's just where this captain was standing when he took an arrow right in the forehead!"

"Alright, that will be enough of that this morning." Politta put the boat down on the table and began arranging an assortment of cheeses on Quintus's plate. Lucius was still filling the goblets as the toy boat appeared on the table directly in front of him. He inspected the model for a moment, then stepped back toward the column and did his best to blend into the shadows again.

He wondered why he continued to do this to himself. Hearing Quintus tell these stories of gladiator spectacles and other adventures made his insides squirm. A common kitchen slave would never get the opportunity to live life like Quintus Honorius Romanus. That thought ate away at him every moment of every day. Yet he felt compelled to absorb as many of these stories as possible. As much as he hated it, the only adventures he lived were through Quintus.

"And you should have seen the pile of gold Nero awarded Spiculus," Quintus continued as he sat and began his breakfast. "Every gold piece was well deserved. He was cunning as well as powerful, wasn't he, Aulus?"

"That he was, Master Quintus." Aulus's deep voice surprised Lucius when it came from the other side of the column where he hid. He had not seen the bodyguard return to the peristyle.

"By the sword of Hercules!" Quintus shouted as he banged the table with his empty goblet. "We should drink a toast to Spiculus! More juice!"

Lucius knew he should step forward immediately with the pitcher he held in his hand. But his feet did not move.

"Lucius?"

Quintus leaned forward and their eyes locked. Lucius simply could not bring himself to keep pandering to this spoiled rich kid. He knew it could mean a flogging. He had been there before. But his resentment sometimes outweighed his fear of the whip.

"Lucius! Are you awake? More juice here," Quintus ordered.

He simply stared at Quintus. He allowed a slight smile to cross his lips, just enough to let Quintus know he'd heard him. It was his subtle way of standing his ground, of showing he still had a backbone, of showing he still had some pride of his own left. But his personal victory was brief. A solid crack on the back of his head snapped his neck forward and almost dropped him to the mosaic floor.

"What's the matter with you?" Aulus hissed. The bodyguard had stepped around the column and now hovered over Lucius like a titanic statue of Jupiter. "Master Quintus is calling for more drink. Bring it to him . . . Now!"

Lucius stepped forward with the pitcher. Quintus held his goblet up and turned away from the servant boy as he resumed his discussion with Politta, beginning a detailed description of Nero's banquet. Lucius poured the juice quickly. Too quickly. The golden yellow concoction splashed across the front of Quintus's white and gold tunic and puddled in his lap.

"Lucius! Watch what you're doing," Politta yelled.

Quintus stopped in mid-sentence. He looked down at his tunic then up at Lucius. The look in Quintus's eyes told Lucius he knew this was not an accident. Quintus did not say a word. He simply stared at Lucius. But the slave boy didn't flinch. He defiantly returned the stare.

"Get a cloth and clean this up!" the head servant hollered at Lucius. "I am so sorry, Master Quintus. Lucius will be dealt with."

The two teenagers finally broke their glare as Lucius turned to get a cloth.

"No harm done," Quintus said tightly.

Lucius returned with a dry cloth and began patting feebly at the yellow stain that marred the front of Quintus's tunic. While he worked, he kept his gaze locked on Quintus's eyes, doing his best to send the unspoken message that there was no repentance whatsoever. Quintus grabbed the cloth from his hand.

"I will deal with it." He turned his back on Lucius, leaving him standing awkwardly at the table.

Politta helped her son blot the fruit juice from his clothing while the head servant cleaned the spilled liquid from the floor. Politta sent Aulus to her son's room for a change of clothes.

While the cleanup progressed, Lucius saw an unexpected opportunity. As he turned to leave, his arm swung wide and the miniature Persian galley disappeared from the tabletop without anyone noticing. He quietly blended back into the shadows of the portico and began making his way around the perimeter to the villa door at the far side of the garden.

"It's fine. It's fine. I'll change after breakfast." Quintus's voice echoed off the muraled walls, followed by the sounds of utensils on trays and dishes.

"So you were saying that the Emperor knows how to throw a party," prompted Politta. Lucius slowed his walk. He was torn between making a clean getaway and eavesdropping on more stories of the grand festivities.

"It was held on four barges that were easily the length of the war galleys," Quintus continued, "but perhaps twice as wide. Here, I'll show you." Then there was silence. Lucius stopped walking and peered from behind the closest column. Across the garden, he could see Quintus looking under the table and chairs.

"Where's my ship? Mother, did you move it?"

"No. I laid it there on the table."

Lucius's heart began to race. He had meant to be clear of the garden long before the theft was discovered. Quintus called loudly across the peristyle to the head servant who was returning from the kitchen.

"I only removed the wet cloths, Master Quintus. I did not touch your ship."

Lucius had only six more columns to go before he reached the closest villa entrance. Then a quick dash to his spartan slave's quarters down the hall near the utility area. If he stayed back against the wall in the morning shadows, he'd make it for sure.

"Where in Hades is my ship? Search for it, will you?" Quintus snapped at the head servant, who dropped to his knees and began scouring the floor under the table. Lucius smiled as he slipped from column to column and watched the old man crawl on his knees for the young master. He quietly eased past the last two columns and made the turn into the villa doorway. But instead of an open passageway, he walked into a green tunic as rigid as a stone wall. Aulus looked down at him with eyes that burned like tiny charcoals.

"I think the search is over," Aulus hollered across the peristyle. One massive hand snatched the terra-cotta boat from Lucius, while the other lifted the boy off his feet by the collar of his brown tunic.

"Seems someone's a bit upset at not having such a souvenir for himself," Aulus said, as he casually carried his trophies across the garden. Lucius kicked wildly in the air a half-meter above the ground, until he realized his struggle was useless. Even if Aulus dropped him, where would he go?

"Is this true, Lucius?" asked Politta.

"Of course it's true!" Quintus yelled. "He's been eyeing it for himself since I brought it down here this morning. He's a damn thief!"

Lucius could feel his face turn red from humiliation and seething rage. He was not about to hang there quietly and be judged by this bastard rich kid. With a loud yell, he swiped his arm past Aulus's chest and knocked the boat from the bodyguard's right hand. Quintus's face went white as his eyes followed the fragile clay ship. The vessel arced into the air and crashed onto the mosaic tile floor, shattering into a hundred pieces.

There was stunned silence in the peristyle. Lucius looked down on the surreal scene as he dangled from Aulus's thick arm. Regardless of the punishment to come, the look on Quintus's pale face made the entire episode worthwhile. A low moan in Quintus's throat rose to an animal-like growl as he sprang from his chair.

His shoulder pounded into Lucius. The force knocked the boy from the slave's grasp and, together, Quintus and Lucius toppled backward into the garden fountain. Water splashed across the narrow strip of grass and onto the mosaic floor, making the footing difficult for both Aulus and the head servant who tried to get to the boys.

With a scream, Quintus pushed Lucius's head underwater. The slave boy tried desperately to breathe, but his lungs filled only with water. He could vaguely make out the blurred face of Quintus, contorted with rage. The boy's fist dove deep under the surface, seeking Lucius's jaw. Spray flew everywhere.

After what seemed like an hour, Lucius felt his assailant's weight finally being lifted off him. He jerked his head up, gasping for air and coughing up water. Above him hung the hazy outline of Quintus, struggling in the grasp of Aulus.

Lucius stood slowly on wobbly legs, knee-deep in the fountain pond. Neither he nor Aulus were ready for Quintus's last swift kick. His foot caught Lucius on the back of the neck and sent him sprawling into the breakfast table, knocking the three large metal trays across the tile floor with a great crash.

Aulus's voice was surprisingly calm amid the chaos of the brawl. "Settle down, Quintus. We'll get you another boat."

"There *are* no other boats! They were specially made for yesterday's games." He turned his rage again on Lucius. "My father bought me that, you bastard!" Quintus struggled to get free from Aulus.

Lucius was shaken but held to the vision of Quintus's shocked face as the boat hit the floor. It braced him enough to offer a defiant smirk, which provoked another swinging kick from Quintus. Lucius crawled backward to avoid the kick, directly into the legs of Caius who had appeared in the doorway.

"What in the name of Jupiter is going on here?" Caius bellowed in an unusual display of anger.

"Father! This dung-eater deliberately smashed the boat you bought me yesterday."

From his position at Caius's feet, Lucius watched him glance at Politta for affirmation. She seemed visibly shaken by Quintus's violent outburst. With a hand still covering her mouth in shock, she nodded at her husband.

Lucius's brazen gaze met Caius's as the master of the house looked down upon him. Their posture epitomized everything Lucius hated about his life. He quickly got to his feet. Although he knew this man would solely determine the severity of his punishment, he made it a point not to break eye contact and, most of all, not to show any sign of remorse.

Caius spoke to Aulus, but never took his stare from Lucius. "Aulus, let's see if ten lashes across his back will teach this young man some manners in our home. Then send him to Tertia and let her deal with her insolent son."

Lucius had felt the sting of the whip before. As much as the words brought fear, he continued to gaze defiantly at Caius, then at Quintus, as Aulus roughly hauled him from the garden.

• • •

Quintus dropped heavily into his chair as the servants began cleaning the food and debris from the floor. He watched silently as the kitchen master bent and retrieved the largest remnant of the shattered boat. The servant handed it to Quintus with a nervous smile. He studied the miniature figure of the Persian captain who had stood in command of the small ship. The captain had somehow survived the turmoil unscratched. Quintus stared at the tiny stoic face until the sound of the broken shards of terra-cotta being swept into a pile brought tears to his eyes.

"That's one tough ship captain," Caius said, obviously trying to lighten the mood.

"It's not fair, Father. That bastard broke it for no good reason."

"I know, son. I don't know what to say to make things better. But I will say this . . . There are two lessons here. First, always be wary of those who do not have. For they would rather take from those who have, than earn the spoils themselves."

"Well, that defines the essence of Lucius, doesn't it?" Quintus said in a dejected tone.

His father continued as he wiped the tears from each of Quintus's cheeks, "Second, never let an opponent see you upset, either from fear or emotion. It will give him the advantage."

Quintus had often heard this rule from Aulus in his self-defense training. It was habitual among the gladiators, at least those who knew how to properly handle themselves in the arena.

"Of course, when things mean a lot to us, even Jupiter himself can lose his temper," his father continued with a smile. "It's over now. Let's get you changed and see what we can salvage of breakfast. What do you say?"

Quintus stared down at the Persian ship captain in his hand. He didn't want to say anything for fear the tears would come again. He placed the tiny figure into the dripping-wet leather pouch that hung from his belt.

Caius patted his son's head and walked toward Politta. "What are we going to do with that damn arrogant slave boy?"

Quintus caught a glimpse of his mother shaking her head. She called to the remaining servant, "Assist Master Quintus in the back room, Agathon."

"Of course, Mistress Viator."

The servant handed Quintus the tunic that Aulus had brought and ushered him into a back room to change. As he stepped through the doorway, Quintus heard his mother's voice. He waved the servant on and hung back near the portal to listen to the conversation. After today, anything to do with Lucius's punishment he wanted to hear firsthand. The voices drifted down the portico and into the open doorway.

"I don't think I've ever seen him so upset," Politta said.

"That damn slave boy can drive anybody mad. He's grown as insolent as a stubborn mule. It's a good thing for him he's the son of your ornatrix or I would have sold him long ago. Can't you speak to her about him?"

"I've spoken to Tertia. She feels it's a phase that boys go through at his age. But she admits he seems to be getting worse, rather than better, as the months pass."

Quintus could hear his father pacing, the leather soles of his sandals scraping on the white mosaic tile.

"A phase boys go through . . . What a pile of horseshit! Even when he was a little boy, Quintus would have nothing to do with Lucius because he couldn't stomach his constant jealousy and resentment. I'm personally getting sick of this brazen attitude. The only time he shows any initiative at all is during my business meetings. Then he's so underfoot I can't get rid of him."

The sound of sandals on tile stopped and he heard his father sigh.

"Look, we treat Lucius just as well as we treat all our servants. Yet he seems to have a hatred for everyone in this household."

"I think it has less to do with how he's treated and more to do with the simple fact that he resents his position in life."

"Well, that's a fate the gods have chosen for him, not me."

"He has a hard time with authority, that's all," said Politta.

"Well, that's a real liability to someone born into slavery."

The tone in his father's voice made it clear he was surprised at Politta's tolerance. Quintus had to agree. After all the problems they'd had with Lucius, why was his mother still so indulgent?

"Tertia's been a part of my household staff since she and I were both young girls, Caius. We can't just sell her son to strangers. I won't have it."

Quintus listened for his father's response, but none came. Surely he wasn't going to let this matter drop. The silence persisted. He assumed his father was formulating a plan that would work for everyone. He was surprised to hear his mother's voice again.

"I wonder if Sextus and Julia can use any help in Britannia."

The quiet nature of her statement belied the gravity of its significance. Did he hear her right? Was she actually contemplating shipping Lucius off to the relatives in remote Britannia? A smile crossed his face as his father quickly picked up on the thought.

"Now that's an idea. We can take him with us to Britannia, then leave him there with Sextus when we return. It will separate him from Quintus, yet Tertia should find some comfort in the fact that her son will be with someone in our family rather than selling him at auction. Yes, I like the idea. I'll bet some of Sextus's foremen can straighten out his attitude."

The morning's miserable events were quickly fading from Quintus's mind. If a smashed boat resulted in his lifelong tormentor being shipped away for good, then it was a worthy sacrifice.

"We'll be separating Lucius and Quintus, but we'll also be separating my favorite handmaiden from her only child. It's not something we normally do to our servants. You know that."

The remorse was already evident in his mother's voice. He hoped his father would seize the opportunity and push it to its conclusion.

"Yes, but this is not a typical situation either. The boy is becoming a menace to our household. Tertia will have to deal with it. Tell her she can take Lucius with us, but I wouldn't tell her any more until we reach Britannia."

Quintus heard his mother sigh. He held his breath and waited desperately for her response.

"Alright. But we'll have to keep the boys apart during the trip. I don't want to have to worry about them throwing each other overboard."

"Yes. It's going to be an interesting journey."

To Quintus, the gloomy storm clouds suddenly parted revealing a bright blue sky. He wanted to burst through the doorway and throw his arms around his parents. But he thought twice about it and decided to keep his celebration private. He removed the small terra-cotta sea captain from his damp leather pouch and studied the brave face once again.

"You're a good man," he whispered. "You've sacrificed your ship for the good of the battle."

He could not wait to step aboard the *Vesta* and sail to a life without Lucius Calidius.

III

July AD 63

QUINTUS AND HIS FATHER climbed the stairs and emerged from the deckhouse of the *Vesta* after a late afternoon dinner.

"I don't think I've tasted fresher fish than we've had on this trip," said Caius as he rubbed his swollen stomach.

Quintus was ready to claim credit for at least part of the meal. "You can thank my strong hooks and secret bait recipe for that."

He looked up at the orange mainsail and twin triangular topsails, all pulled taut by a stiff northerly breeze. The foresail billowed out ahead of the bow, tugging the ship along from the forward-raked foremast. Beyond the sail, Quintus glimpsed a tall cliff on the horizon. He turned and called to the ship's captain above them on the roof of the deckhouse, which acted as the ship's poop deck. He saw that Aulus had joined the captain on the roof to enjoy the afternoon breeze.

"Is that Britannia off the starboard bow?"

The captain had already been checking his charts and watching the rock mass that was Land's End grow above the horizon. "Yes, Master Quintus. That's Britannia."

Quintus was exhilarated. He thought back to his father's friend, Marcus, at Nero's banquet. The old seaman had been correct. The waters of the great sea beyond the Pillars of Hercules were much different from the calmer aquamarine waters of the Mare Internum. Many on board the *Vesta*, even those who had worked the sea for many years, were feeling the uneasy stomach of the land dwellers. But not Quintus. This was the trip of a lifetime and nothing was going to ruin it.

It had been five weeks since they put out from the port of Ostia. Their route had taken them to the south of Sardinia, due west along the North African coast, and between the Pillars of Hercules, which stood like sentinels at the mouth of the Mare Internum. They then set a northerly course along the coast of Hispania and Gaul to the channel that separated Britannia from the mainland. Their captain planned to round the rugged cape at the southwestern corner of Britannia and head into the port of Glevum, fifty kilometers north of Aquae Sulis.

Although the trip by sea was much more agreeable than the land route, it was still a tiring journey. Quintus spent his time on board working with the crewmen. It made the days seem much shorter than just sitting on deck watching the waves roll by. Once he learned the ropes, he was always first in line to help trim the sails or take the tillerbars to relieve the helmsman for short spells.

The *Vesta* was the flagship of the Romanus fleet. At forty meters long she could carry four hundred tons of cargo, although on this voyage the load was half that. The ship had been specially designed by Caius two years earlier to transport both cargo and passengers. While many ships of the day were outfitted for double duty, few had the amenities of the *Vesta*.

From the relatively spacious servants' quarters on the lower deck to the luxurious master suite, the *Vesta* was one of the finest privately owned vessels afloat. Caius had the preeminent craftsmen in Italia outfit the comfortable family suite with towering bookcases, copper tubs, gymnasium equipment, and a galley that rivaled the Romanus villa kitchen. The rear wall of the suite was ingeniously designed to be folded open against the side walls, revealing a beautiful view of the sea with the white foam of the ship's wake trailing to the distant horizon.

Caius and Politta's bedroom was enlivened with graceful wall murals of the most picturesque ports-of-call for the Romanus shipping fleet, including Alexandria, Carthage, Ostia, and Massilia. These images were in sharp contrast with the murals in Quintus's bedchamber next door, which depicted gladiatorial contests and animal hunts. Throughout all the rooms a beautiful mosaic floor scene of colorful sealife and coral reefs gave the illusion that one could see through the ship's hull and into the ocean depths.

The area forward of the passenger compartments contained the primary cargo hold and the crew's quarters. In addition to ferrying the giant bolts of fabric to the Viator clothing business, Caius was using this Britannia excursion to establish new business contacts. Besides one thousand sacks of grain and three hundred barrels of olive oil, he had taken on thirteen thousand liters of wine in Ostia for a merchant looking to export his finest spirits to the relatively new northern province. The wine was transported in five hundred amphoras, large clay jugs sealed on the top with wax and pointed on the bottom so they could be stacked tightly and secured against the inner hull in tiers four levels high. Caius had personally supervised the loading and stacking of the amphoras into special wooden holders that were cushioned with twigs and branches.

On deck, the sight of their destination got Quintus's heart pounding. "Only one more day to go," he said. "And we have favorable winds. Maybe we'll be in port by morning." As much as he had enjoyed these weeks at sea, he was ready to feel firm ground once again beneath his feet.

Caius studied the sails and ship bearing. "Perhaps, but more likely late afternoon."

The door to the deckhouse swung open behind them. Quintus excitedly pointed to the distant cliffs.

"Look, Mother! Britannia!" he yelled, fully expecting Politta to step from behind the open door. Instead, Lucius's face peered around the wooden hatch, wearing its usual smirk.

"Oh, it's you."

"So what's the big deal?" Lucius said in a low voice. "I don't see why we're going to this barbarian island anyway. Just to visit some relatives you don't even know. Who cares?"

Quintus knew Lucius was goading him into another test of wills. He had successfully avoided the obnoxious slave boy for most of the trip, but it was difficult to totally elude someone on a small ship during a five-week voyage. He took heart knowing Lucius's days in this household were numbered.

He smiled at Lucius with a nod. "Keep it up, asshole. And we'll see who has the last laugh."

"Well, why don't . . . " Lucius's words caught in his throat as Caius stepped from the side of the deckhouse. Quintus's smile broadened. Although his father never used the dreaded beaded whip on his slaves, Quintus knew that Lucius had not yet forgotten the lashing he had received after their brawl in the garden.

Quintus watched with amusement as his father gave Lucius a deadly look before he spoke. "Do you need another lesson in manners? When are you going to realize that Quintus is as much your master as I am? I'll warn you for the last time. One more disrespectful comment out of that foul mouth and, as Neptune is my witness, I'll ship you to my grain barge crews in Alexandria and let them straighten you out. And you won't enjoy their methods. Am I understood?"

Lucius ignored the final question, looked at Quintus, then walked away.

"Just give me a half hour with him alone and I guarantee I'll straighten out his attitude," Quintus said as he watched his adversary lean over the stern rail and spit into the ship's wake. He saw Aulus approach him and drew satisfaction in knowing how the ex-gladiator intimidated Lucius.

Caius looked at Quintus with a smile. He lowered his voice so only his son could hear his words. "I've told no one of this yet, but we won't have to deal with him much longer. Your mother and I have decided to leave him with your aunt and uncle in Britannia."

Quintus thought quickly. He felt it best not to let on that he already knew of his parents' plans. "Thanks the gods!" he said with as much surprise as he could muster. "This is turning out to be a most pleasant trip." His broad smile matched his father's as he looked across the sea at the Britannia coastline with renewed enthusiasm.

Lucius spit into the ship's wake and leaned against the stern post. The fresh air began to settle his stomach for the first time in three days, even though the swells seemed larger now than earlier in the day. He felt a presence beside him and turned to see Aulus hovering over his shoulder.

"You're trying your best to feel the sting of the whip once again," the bodyguard said in a more congenial voice than Lucius expected. "What drives you to this madness? You should consider yourself fortunate that you are a servant in the Romanus household. Caius is a just and fair man. I've seen slaves tortured and killed for less insolence than you've shown his family."

Lucius continued looking out at the ship's wake. "That's the difference between me and you," he said bitterly. "I'll never consider myself fortunate to be anyone's slave."

"This is not your choice, Lucius. This is the fate the gods have dealt you. You were born into slavery and there's nothing that can change that. Perhaps someday, if you behave, you may be granted your freedom at an old age. Or you can learn a trade and earn some money to buy your freedom. But don't think that your life will suddenly change overnight. Any slave who thinks that is a fool."

"Spending your life in the service of others is no life at all," Lucius said. "If we are all men, then what makes the rich ones better than the poor ones?"

"Many are better because they made themselves better. Master Caius was not born into luxury. He worked hard to get where he is today. He saved his bits of gold and invested wisely in himself and his abilities. He saw a path to a better life and he walked it."

"Oh, please," Lucius said with a shake of his head. He had a hard time believing everyone thought Caius was some sort of business genius. "That old bastard doesn't even know how to run his shipping business. He could bring in a lot more grain if he restructured his shipping schedules. Believe me, the man makes money in spite of himself."

Lucius glanced at the large slave and detected a look of surprise on his face.

"I make it a point to serve food during his business meetings," he said, annoyed that he had to explain himself to this lumbering fool. "Let's just say I pay more attention to his fleet manager than he does most of the time."

Aulus seemed like he was about to say something, then stopped.

"And what about Quintus?" Lucius continued. "He just happened to be born to the right parents? Is that his whole story?"

"Well, perhaps that's true. But is that a reason to hate him?"

Lucius turned from the railing and looked deep into Aulus's eyes. "When I have to serve his every whim because that's his lot in life, then in my eyes that's cause to hate him. My father was a Romanus slave who was killed in a shipping accident. He never had the chance to make something of himself. He never had a chance to make a better life for me."

The longer the debate went on, the more Lucius's blood boiled. But he was determined to show Aulus that nothing this oaf of a slave could say or do would ever change the way he viewed the Romanus family.

Aulus finally broke eye contact and glanced down at the deck. "I'm sorry about your father, Lucius. But you can't spend the rest of your life hating the world because your father didn't provide you a better life. Take advantage of what you have. Caius brings Greek tutors to the villa, not only for Quintus, but for you and the other young servants. You've learned to read and write because Caius believes that a well-educated staff is more loyal and works harder. And from what I've seen, he's right. All with the exception of you."

Lucius shook his head and turned his attention back to the sea. "Yes. Well don't expect to see me groveling my thanks to the great Romanus family. They can all kiss my welted ass."

He spit again into the wake then walked toward the deckhouse door, leaving Aulus alone at the stern rail. As he passed Quintus, he could not help nudging the boy's shoulder, pretending his footing was a bit unsteady from the growing waves.

"Hope you're feeling better, Lucius," Quintus called after him. Lucius clearly heard the sarcastic tone. "The sea's picking up a bit."

Lucius glanced back as he opened the deckhouse door. He found both Quintus and his father with wide grins. Caius was fastening a sapphire-blue cloak over his pale blue tunic. As he locked the clasp he looked up into the mainsail, the sea salt glistening in his beard.

"I'm feeling a storm in the air, Captain," he called up to the ship's commander standing on the deckhouse roof. "Better keep a sharp eye tonight."

"Yes, sir," the captain responded.

But Lucius knew the comment was meant more for his ears than the captain's. He knew Quintus and Caius enjoyed seeing him suffer with bouts of nausea when the swells increased. He stepped through the portal that led down to the cabins. He heard the chuckle in Quintus's voice as he closed the door.

"Have a nice night, Lucius."

• • •

Quintus was deep into a dream about a lovely Celtic woman he had yet to meet in Britannia. Her face faded as he was slowly awakened by a loud creaking. He opened his eyes, but in the pitch black cabin, they might as well have stayed closed. He became conscious of the severe rocking of the *Vesta*. The ship had seen some rough waters on this trip but none like this. The creaking of the wooden hull was louder than he had ever heard. He lay in bed for a moment, not sure if he would be able to stand if he tried. A sudden bolt of lightning and a thunderclap jolted him to a sitting position. His head swam with dizziness, and he quickly realized just how violently the *Vesta* was rocking.

He threw his legs over the side of his bed and, holding tight to the edge, worked his way toward the open doorway. His foot struck the twin-handled storage trunk that held his clothes. Normally it sat out of the way at the foot of his bed, but the pitching had caused it to slide into the walkway. He teetered and almost fell as he stepped over it.

Politta called out from the next room. "Quintus, are you alright?"

"Yes, Mother. Where is Father?"

"He went on deck to help the crew through the storm. I pray to Neptune that he's well."

Quintus could not possibly stay below while his father and the ship's crew battled the elements on deck. Without a word, he groped his way across the sitting room toward the main door. A sizeable wave struck the port side, and Quintus was thrown against the large cushioned chair that had slid to the center of the room.

"Are you alright?" shouted Politta.

"Yes, I'm fine. I'm going on deck."

"No! Quintus, you will stay here with me until this cursed storm subsides."

"I can't, Mother. How can I leave Father to fend for himself out there?"

The disembodied voices shouted back and forth in the blackness over the din of the gale that howled through the planking and rigging. Quintus was determined to get outside to see how he could help. He finally felt the latch of the main doorway.

"Stay well, Mother. I'll be back quickly."

He opened the door in spite of Politta's anxious protests. His first sensation as he stepped over the raised sill was numbness in his feet. It took a moment for him to realize that he was standing in four centimeters of cold water. Amid the other noises of the storm he distinctly heard water running, like the sound of the fountain in their villa garden. He sloshed forward, bouncing from one wall to the other in the narrow passageway, until he stubbed his toe on the first of the steps leading up to the deckhouse. Seawater cascaded down the steps like a waterfall, soaking the white tunic Quintus wore as a nightshirt.

Ignoring the bite of the icy water, Quintus began climbing the stairs. The violent rocking made him nauseated for the first time this trip. The sound of the wind, rain, and crashing waves became louder with each step.

Finally he reached the deckhouse door. Water poured through the small gap between the door and the raised doorjamb. He grasped the handle and pushed, but the door barely moved. The force of the wind worked against him. He leaned his shoulder against it and pushed with all his weight until the wooden hatch finally burst open.

Quintus felt he had passed through the portal of Hades itself. A flash of lightning lit up the scene just as he stumbled onto the deck. In that split second, a scene of horror was etched in the boy's mind forever. He saw a towering wall of black water on the port side of the ship. The colossal wave easily reached as high as the mainmast. The orange canvas of the mainsail and foresail was lashed tightly to the yardarms. But the twin triangular topsails were in tatters, the remnants fluttering straight out toward the ship's bow. Sheets of rain dashed across the deck with a force unlike any Quintus had ever witnessed. Between the lightning flashes there was just enough ambient light from the full moon filtering through the storm clouds to make out what was happening.

Holding tightly to the open door, Quintus reached for the wooden rail that ran the length of the deckhouse. He worked his way, hand-over-hand, toward the rear of the structure. He could barely hear voices shouting over the howling wind and crashing sea. A tremendous wave struck the side of the *Vesta*, and she rolled heavily to starboard. Quintus's feet gave way on the slippery deck, and he began to slide toward the open bulwark just a meter behind him.

He clung to the deckhouse rail with all his strength until the *Vesta* righted herself.

"Toss the other anchor! Now!" He recognized his father's voice, but it was strained with an urgency and panic he had never heard before. He slowly made his way to the rear of the deckhouse and found his father, the captain, and the helmsman all struggling to hold the twin tillerbars on some semblance of a steady course. His father still wore the sapphire-blue cloak, although, sopping wet, it did little to protect him from the biting cold of the fierce wind. Even with the limited vision afforded through the driving rain, Quintus could see in their faces that the men were fighting a losing battle.

Four crewmen and two of the larger household servants pushed past Quintus. He could see panic on their faces. Wobbling back and forth they made their way to one of the massive iron anchors lashed to the deck near the bow. They somehow managed to free it, lifted the shank end, and began dragging it aft. A taut thick rope running from the stern post into the blackness of the ocean told Quintus the other anchor was already overboard.

"Come on, men!" yelled the captain. "The one is not holding us. Toss the second. Quickly! There are rocks ahead!"

Quintus suddenly realized the true peril of their situation. Being hurled about by gale winds was one thing, but when rocks were nearby the danger became lethal.

The six men struggled to drag the giant anchor across the pitching deck and under the tillerbars. As they approached the stern post, two others quickly slipped the stock over the shank and secured a thick rope to the top ring. The other end of the line had already been secured to the stern post.

"Put your backs into it, men!" yelled Caius. "Lift the anchor and throw it aft."

The eight men labored to lift the massive iron grapnel. Quintus released his grip on the deckhouse rail and tried to walk aft to help the crewmen.

"Quintus! What are you doing up here? Get below," yelled his father, obviously in no mood for an argument.

"They need help, Father!"

"They'll manage. Now get below." A note of pleading entered his voice.

Quintus watched as the men moved into position to toss the anchor over the side. Without warning, out of the darkness came another huge wave. It broke heavily across the aft deck. Already off balance from the heavy load on their shoulders, the men screamed as they were pitched against the stern rail. The decorative banister buckled and splintered, sending all eight men and the anchor over the side and into the sea.

Caius and the captain looked back in horror. Caius turned to Quintus and their eyes locked. Quintus realized that, had he stepped forward to help hoist the anchor, he too would have been over the side. His father mouthed a single word to him: "Please."

Quintus relented. For all the carnage he had witnessed in the arena, this was far worse. The men in the arena could see their adversary and had control over their destiny. This was a struggle of mere mortals against the god of the sea.

Quintus turned to make his way back down the side of the deckhouse. A bolt of lightning lit up the scene before him like daylight. The sea swells were surreal in appearance, like the background of some overly dramatic painting in a Roman bathhouse. But it was what he saw beyond the sea swells that sent a shock up his spine. Not a half-kilometer off the starboard bow was a massive outcropping of rocks. Behind them Britannia's coast seemed far too close for safety. His head snapped back toward Caius, and he could see the look of desperation on his father's face.

"Hopefully the second anchor will hold," Caius yelled to the captain, still transfixed beside him on the second tillerbar.

There was nothing Quintus could do here, and there was no reason to worry his mother further. He rounded the forward corner of the deckhouse and reached for the door latch. A shout from the bow caught his attention. He could barely make out three figures through the torrential rain. They seemed to be carrying large coils of rope on their shoulders. From their silhouettes Quintus could see that the one in the middle was much taller than the other two. Aulus! Quintus had been so concerned for the safety of his family and their ship that he had forgotten to check for Aulus. He called across the deck.

"Aulus! Be careful! We just lost eight men off the stern."

Another tremendous wall of black water was growing rapidly behind the three men. Quintus could see that in another instant it would break across the bow.

"Watch out!" His warning came too late for the men to find shelter or handholds. The immense wave crashed onto the deck with the force of a thousand bulls. The *Vesta* listed heavily to port as the seawater washed across the deck like a mighty river. Quintus jumped back to the side of the deckhouse as the surge of water rushed past. He could hear the sound of the foremast snapping like a twig. He could also hear the screams of the three men. As the last of the water drained over the side, he looked around the corner to see only a vacant deck.

"No! Aulus!" The thought of his lifelong friend, protector, and mentor being washed overboard was too horrible to consider. He turned and leaned dangerously far over the side railing to look for signs of the men in the dark ocean. The pitching of the ship brought him from sea level to fifteen meters above the ocean in a matter of seconds. There was no sign of life anywhere.

"Aulus! You can't die. *You can't!*" There was no response from the black water.

"Alright, then. I won't die."

The voice made Quintus jump. It was as casual and unflustered as if they were on a pleasure cruise down the Tiber River. Quintus thought perhaps he was dreaming. Or perhaps madness had begun to take hold in this nightmare.

He felt a hand grasp his shoulder. He spun and looked up at the towering bulk of Aulus, dripping wet in his olive tunic. Quintus was stunned and elated at the same time.

"But I saw you get washed overboard!"

"It wasn't me. Perhaps another poor crewman. I've been below, moving the passengers into the cargo hold where there's more protection. You, my good man, should be there also."

He did not release his firm grasp on Quintus's shoulder until Quintus headed toward the cargo hatch amidships. Quintus glanced back at his father, still wrestling the tillerbars with the captain and helmsman. Caius was watching him and Aulus cross the heaving deck toward the cargo hold.

"That's good, Aulus," Caius yelled. "They'll be safer there. Get all the passengers into the hold."

"It's already done, sir. This brave lad is the last of them."

Aulus lifted the heavy cargo hatch, and Quintus squirmed under the edge and felt for the rope ladder with his feet. He looked at his father one last time before descending. Caius's gaze had never left him. Caius managed a tight smile and a nod to his son as the rainwater streamed from his face.

"May the gods watch over you, Father," Quintus murmured to himself and to whatever gods were listening in the middle of this maelstrom. He knew his father was offering the same prayer for him and his mother.

Quintus finally allowed himself to slip over the edge of the hatch and climb down into the cargo hold. Aulus followed and quickly secured the hatch cover despite the small waterfall that followed them through the deck opening.

Politta and what was left of the servants were already huddled in the center of the hold. It was a cramped space among the sacks of grain, barrels of olive oil, and tiers of wine amphoras, but the closeness added a sense of security for the scared passengers. A small lantern suspended from an overhead beam swung like a pendulum from side to side, throwing grotesque shadows against the inside of the hull. All the passengers were wet and cold from the dash across the deck to the cargo hatch.

"How's your father?" Politta asked right away.

Quintus chose his words carefully. "He's working with the helmsman to keep the ship clear of danger."

"Clear of what danger?" came a voice from the darkness. Quintus had not noticed Lucius pressed closely against his mother. Tertia was attending to an armful of Politta's dresses and jewelry that she had grabbed from the storage closet.

"What danger?" Lucius asked a bit louder. Tertia looked at him sternly and put a hand on his leg.

Quintus did not want a panic on his hands. "The dangers of a gale storm," was his measured response. He sought to change the subject quickly. "Are those amphoras secured? The last thing we need is that rack of clay jugs coming down on us."

Aulus answered, "Yes, Master Quintus. I re-tied them myself before I brought all of you in here."

As if to prove the point, another wave suddenly struck the ship. This one seemed more powerful than the others, and the *Vesta* listed far to port, rolling flat on her side for what seemed an eternity. Screams of fright filled the hold as the passengers were tossed into the branches cushioning the clay jugs that lined the port side. All eyes turned to the wooden rack on the starboard side that now hovered menacingly above their heads. The ropes strained and the wooden holders creaked, but every jug remained firmly in place.

Finally, the ship began to right itself. But the smell of smoke alerted the passengers to a new danger.

"The lantern!" yelled Quintus. "It set the branches on fire!" Aulus began splashing the bilge water that had collected at their feet onto the small fire. It was quickly extinguished. Luckily the candle inside the lantern remained lit as it swung back across the hold, the eerily shifting shadows adding to the surreal scene.

"How ironic," Aulus said with a tight smile. "Here we are in a torrential rain storm, and we almost burn to death!"

Quintus returned the smile, but he was alone. The signs of hysteria were becoming more evident, especially among the female servants. The continual rocking to and fro was also taking its toll. Lucius and two of the older servants were doubled over vomiting, the stench quickly filling the dank air in the hold. In a chain reaction, the vile smell caused more and more of the passengers to become sick.

Quintus held his mother, who began to shake violently between bouts of nausea. He wondered how long this would go on. A strong burst of wind brought yet another wave crashing into the hull. But as it hit, Quintus felt something different. There was a loud pop, and the *Vesta* lurched forward suddenly as if a leviathan had released its hold on her. Those seated without any support were tossed backward into the grimy bilge water.

Quintus looked to Aulus. Their eyes locked. They knew what had happened. At least one of the anchor ropes, securing them in place above the seabed, had snapped. This realization was followed by a commotion of voices and feet scrambling on the deck above them.

"What's happening? Why does it feel like we're moving faster all of a sudden?" asked Lucius, panic rising in his voice.

In a trembling voice, Tertia tried to reassure him. "It's nothing, Lucius. It's just the sensation of the wind and waves."

The voices on deck became more frantic. Words could not be deciphered, but the tone was unmistakable to those huddled below. Something was terribly wrong.

Quintus cocked his head to try to hear what was going on. Only one word filtered through the deck planking as clear as a brass bell.

"Rocks!"

IV

July AD 63

THE VESTA BOBBED in the rough sea like a child's toy. Inside the rancid cargo hold, time hung suspended. Quintus looked from one anxious passenger to the next to see if anyone else had picked up on the seriousness of their situation. He saw Lucius's face turn white. The slave boy grabbed at his mother's tunic.

"Rocks! They're yelling of rocks, Mother!"

Before anyone had time to react, a massive swell hit the *Vesta*, tossing all of the passengers against the port side of the cargo hold again. Quintus felt the bulky arm of Aulus around his waist, as the slave used his own body to protect Quintus from slamming headlong into the amphora racks. The young Roman sat up quickly and tried to get his bearings. The ship now seemed to be moving sideways as it traveled up the front of the tremendous wave and down the back side. Suddenly the starboard hull crashed open, throwing barrels and amphoras across the hold. The shining black face of a boulder, partially covered in green algae, pushed its way through the cargo hold, crushing two of the female servants against the amphora racks. Screams and a gush of blood erupted from their mouths as the other passengers scrambled to get out of the way. The dank fish smell of the ocean overpowered the nauseating odor of vomit. The *Vesta* seemed to hang on the rock face and, for a few seconds, an eerie silence filled the hold.

Quintus's mind flashed to scenes of the naumachia with the large battering rams splintering the hulls of the war galleys. His thoughts jumped forward to the scenes of sea creatures devouring the unfortunate participants who ended up in the water. He wondered what would be worse this night, their fate in the hold of the ship or their fate in the sea. He also wondered how his father was faring on deck.

"We've run aground," shouted Lucius. "Let's get on shore before the ship is beat to Hades by the waves."

"No!" Aulus shouted. "We were too far out to sea to be on shore. We've hit an outcropping of rocks."

"Well whatever it is, I'd rather take my chances on something solid than on this damn ship," said Lucius.

Before another word could be spoken, the *Vesta* released her hold on the rocks and began sliding to port. The granite boulder fought its way back out of the cargo hold, splintering more planking and beams, widening the hole as it exited. The gaping void was immediately filled with a rush of cold seawater. The cargo hold was large, but the volume of water surging in was substantial enough to begin filling it rapidly.

Aulus released his protective grip on Quintus and sprang into action. Even in this maelstrom, Quintus felt a sense of relief knowing his trusted body-guard was formulating a plan.

"I can't swim," shouted Politta.

"Nor I," yelled Lucius, hysteria setting into his voice.

"I doubt anyone here can swim," said Aulus. His outward signs were calm, but Quintus knew his mind was racing to plot their escape from this nautical deathtrap. He watched his blue eyes flit from item to item in the cargo hold. He jumped as Aulus suddenly leaped from the waist-deep water and climbed up the outside of one of the amphora racks. The bodyguard pulled a short knife from his belt and slashed at the rope that secured the top tier. Quintus and the others stood mute and watched as the water continued to swirl in around them.

"Stand clear!" Aulus yelled as he pushed the freed amphora jugs from the top of the rack. One by one they splashed into the rising water.

"Quintus, find something heavy. A piece of wood beam. Anything!" Leaping clear of the rack, Aulus followed the last jar down into the water.

Quintus searched quickly and handed him a meter-long section of a wooden rib snapped from the ship's hull by the rocks.

"Good! Now stand back." He lifted one of the bulky amphoras and placed it flat on a barrel of olive oil. With a mighty stroke, Aulus brought the wooden beam down on the pointed end of the wine vessel. The clay tip easily gave way, and dark red wine began pouring out and mixing with the seawater.

Quintus stood in stunned silence, cold water swirling around his chest, wondering why Aulus suddenly felt it necessary to begin destroying the cargo. Then it came to him.

"Yes!" he yelled, grabbing another beam to help Aulus. "The empty amphoras will trap air and float. We can use them like rafts."

The water was shoulder high when Aulus shook the remaining wine from the first jar and floated it toward Politta. Lucius's hand sprung from nowhere, grabbed the makeshift float, and pulled it under his arm. Quintus was about to swing his wooden beam at Lucius when Tertia grabbed the vessel and pushed it back toward Politta.

Lucius's face showed pure outrage. "Why, Mother? Why should they live while we die? They're no better than us."

"Shut up, you sniveling weasel!" Aulus yelled as he shook the second container over his head to dump the wine faster.

Quintus could take no more of Lucius's spineless ranting. "You bastard, I'll kill you myself before you drown if you don't . . ." A change in the sounds of the cargo hold interrupted him. He looked around and realized the neck-deep water had stopped rising. Aulus too had stopped working on his amphora for the moment.

"What's happening?" he quietly asked Aulus.

The sound of rushing water grew louder again. But this time the water drained from the hold rather than filling it. Quintus also noticed that the ship had stopped rocking.

"We're grounded on the rocks at the bottom of a swell," Aulus said. "There's more water inside the ship than outside. Stand clear of the opening!"

But his warning came a moment too late. The suction of the water rapidly escaping the breached hull was too strong. Three of the servants were sucked under and tossed roughly through the ragged hole, their bodies torn to ribbons on the splintered wood.

Quintus felt the powerful current grab at his legs. Before he could reach for a handhold, his tunic was snagged from behind. He looked over his shoulder to see Aulus with an empty amphora in one hand and a fistful of Quintus's white tunic in the other. His legs were wrapped around the wooden rack to prevent them both from being sucked toward the hole.

A woman's scream pierced the dank air of the hold. Lucius's mother, Tertia, floated swiftly past them. Quintus grabbed for her, but she passed too quickly. She screamed again for help as the powerful suction dragged her backward.

"Mother!" Lucius cried. "Grab onto something!"

With no handholds above the waterline, she was helpless to stop her momentum. She slammed against the hull. Her eyes widened in shock as she was impaled at the top of the breach, a sharp fragment of wood planking projecting through her chest.

Politta screamed and then vomited as she clung to the heavy sacks of grain. Lucius held firm to the wine rack but seemed frozen in his own state of shock. Now, only the four of them remained in the cargo hold.

"We've got to get out of here before the next wave fills the hold again," Quintus said.

"You're right," said Aulus. "Once the water begins flowing in again, we may never get out."

Quintus noticed the top of the gaping hole was once again revealed. But the outward flow was still dangerously fast.

"Look! We can gauge the hole better now."

Aulus had seen it too. "Yes. Let's go. It's still swift, so take care to slip through as cleanly as you can."

Quintus and Aulus both looked toward Politta. Her gaze was glued to the ghastly sight of Tertia's lifeless body.

"Mistress Viator, please go first," Aulus said. "Your son and I will be right behind you."

Politta stared numbly at Aulus, then at Quintus. "Promise me you'll be right behind."

Quintus gave her a reassuring smile. "I'm certainly not staying in here."

Aulus pushed one of the amphoras in front of her. "Take a deep breath, grab the handles of the jar, and push through as quickly as you can."

She released her hold on the heavy grain sacks and immediately surged toward the hole.

"Duck down, Mother! Duck!"

They had all underestimated the speed of the flow and before she could take a breath, Politta's head smacked hard into the rough wood above the opening. The force of the water pushed her quickly through.

Quintus was sickened by the sight. "Is she alright?" He struggled against Aulus's grip.

"Let me go! I have to get her!"

"Alright! We're both going."

They looked at Lucius who still held to the far end of the wine rack. The boy continued to stare at his dead mother hanging from the wooden stake. In spite of his deep hatred for Lucius, Quintus felt a twinge of compassion for him.

Aulus swung Quintus around to his front. "Hold tight to my neck, wrap your legs around my waist, and take a deep breath when I say so." Aulus shoved an amphora toward Lucius. "Break this open and use it to follow us out," he yelled, but Lucius seemed totally unaware of anything going on around him.

"Go!" Aulus shouted. Quintus took a generous gulp of air and hung on.

Aulus released his legs from the wine racks and dove low, struggling to keep the buoyant amphora down long enough to get through the hole. As they approached the breach, the sound of another wave roaring into the side of the ship reverberated through the water. Quintus could barely make out the movement of the opening as the ship shuddered under the impact. Aulus held tightly to the clay jar with his left hand and wrapped his right arm around Quintus to offer more protection as they shot through the opening.

The *Vesta*'s shift was enough to cause the amphora to miss the hole and hit the inside of the hull just to the left of the breach. Miraculously the durable clay jar did not break. The strong current forced them swiftly through the opening. But as they began the plummet to the dark water below, they suddenly jerked to a halt. They dangled precariously in the midst of the driving waterfall that spilled from the hull breach above them. Although his vision was blurred by the rushing water, Quintus could see that the amphora remained wedged inside the hull, causing Aulus's arm to bend back grotesquely. But the slave's hand continued to grasp the jug that wouldn't follow. Quintus heard the snap of bone, oddly muffled by the rush of seawater. Aulus screamed in pain, but refused to surrender their only means of flotation. Quintus's heart beat faster as the unrelenting deluge forced the air from his lungs. He was jerked from side to side under the torrent as Aulus struggled to free the amphora. Finally the splintered timber holding the jug snapped free and they both dropped into the churning sea.

As if in a terrifying nightmare, Quintus spun round and round, helplessly disoriented under the black ocean. Finally an arm encircled his waist and he looked into the face of his bodyguard. A swarm of bubbles burst from Aulus's mouth as he screamed again. The buoyant amphora was tugging them to the surface, but was wrenching the slave's broken arm even harder.

They surfaced seconds later, both spitting up large amounts of water. Quintus grabbed the amphora and frantically looked around. Through the torrent of rain he could see the outline of the *Vesta* towering above them, hung up on the rocks. They had surfaced just aft of amidships. From his view at water level, the waves looked double the size they had from on deck. Another tremendous swell crashed into the far side of the ship, throwing up a heavy spray that mixed with the downpour.

"Mother! Father! Where are you?" He could barely hear his own voice over the storm that seemed to have grown in intensity. He scanned the tilted deck, but saw no activity.

Aulus was next to him, scouring the water which was already covered by fragments of wood and other debris. It was difficult to tell the floating wreckage from possible survivors. The bodyguard tapped Quintus hard on the shoulder.

"I want to check something out. I'll be right back."

As Aulus awkwardly dog-paddled his way toward the stern, Quintus continued calling for his mother and father. He kicked hard to maneuver his float through the wreckage. He came across the bodies of three crewmembers and two female servants. If they had not drowned, the grisly cuts and bruises told Quintus they had been dashed against the rocks or suffered Tertia's fate as they came through that cursed hole.

As a swell lifted him high, something caught his attention. He could make out the form of a person lying atop a large curved section of hull. It floated near where they had surfaced, but the body had been blocked from sight until the hull section spun in the rough sea. The body appeared to be that of a woman in a tattered white tunic.

"Mother! Hold on, Mother! I'm coming."

Quintus kicked toward the debris. He felt as if he was on a giant teeter board, for as he went high up on the crest of a swell, the debris would fall low into a hollow between the waves. But he kicked behind the amphora with every ounce of strength in his legs. Up and down the waves the woman's body rode on its makeshift raft, never moving, never acknowledging Quintus's calls.

As he reached the hull wreckage, Quintus began working his way around the side that sloped into the water. Politta appeared to be unconscious. She was bleeding heavily from a wide gash across her forehead. In the distance, Quintus could hear Aulus's voice shouting to him. He reluctantly took his eyes from his mother's injured face to see why Aulus was calling. The bodyguard was near the stern, paddling frantically toward Quintus. Behind him, the clouded sky was obliterated by a massive wall of water. This was not a rounded swell as most of the waves had been. Whitewater along the crest and the unmistakable arch told him that this wall was about to collapse on the *Vesta* and everything floating around it.

He scrambled to reach his mother before the wave did. But it was a race he could not win. The massive breaker pounded down on them like a titanic hammer, pushing him and his clay float deep underwater. Although partly filled with water, the amphora continued to do its duty and tugged Quintus back to the surface quickly. He shook the water from his face and looked up at the hull section. The water cascaded down its curved face to reveal a clean and empty piece of wreckage. Politta had been washed from her life raft.

"*Mother!*" Quintus was frantic. Holding to his float with one hand, he ducked his head underwater and opened his eyes. The salt stung him, and the black depths denied him any real visibility. He felt a hand grab his arm. His mind raced with hope. It was Aulus. He had already dove beneath the surface, trying to retrieve Politta.

"Where is she?" Quintus was panicking now.

"Stay on the surface before you drown. I'm looking for her."

Aulus dove again, quickly disappearing from view in the inky water. Quintus could only wait and watch. The bubbles floating to the surface were the only trace of life beneath the waves. He hoped at least some of them were coming from his mother. He rode the swells, kicking to remain in position. It was taking too long, he thought. Surely he must have found her.

The water boiled with bubbles. Something was happening. Aulus's head suddenly broke the surface. He loudly gulped air into his depleted lungs.

"Where is she? Did you find her?"

Aulus shook his head as he recovered. He increased his labored breathing and disappeared again.

Quintus floated alone on the rough ocean. This couldn't be happening. This was all a horrible dream. He was actually asleep in his bed in the grand suite of the *Vesta*, warm under his blanket. A loud crack brought him back to reality. He heard it again coming from the deck of the ship. The mainmast, a single timber as thick as a man's waist, was giving way. He could only watch in stunned silence as the force of the gale pushed against it until it buckled and fell forward across the deck of the *Vesta*. The yardarms snapped as they straddled the girth of the ship, the orange mainsail draping over the sides like a banner on a funeral urn. The force of the crash shook the *Vesta* free of the rocks. Quintus watched the ship slip beneath the waves.

The water beside him began to foam with bubbles. Again his heart leaped with anticipation. Aulus's head broke the surface once more. And once more he was alone. His gasps for air were short now. Quintus could tell the man had no strength left. For the first time he also noticed Aulus's left forearm flopping uncontrollably and the white bone protruding where his elbow used to be. A steady stream of blood poured from the gaping wound. Without a word Quintus looked into his eyes. And without a word, Aulus told the boy that his mother was gone forever.

Quintus's head dropped to the clay jar that continued to hold him afloat. After a second, he gasped loudly and jerked upright.

"Father! What about Father? Did you find him?"

The expression of Aulus's face did not change. Quintus could see the slave's eyes were wet and red from more than salt water.

"Yes, Quintus, I found him. He too is gone."

A piercing cry shot from Quintus's lips and mingled with the wind and thunder. Aulus reached for him and held him close.

"Aulus, are you sure?"

"When the anchor rope snapped it cut down all three of the brave men at the tillerbars. Your father was one of them. I found him when I swam to the stern. I'm sorry, Master Quintus."

Quintus felt as though his heart had been ripped from his chest. All he could hear now was the sound of the howling wind.

"Why, Neptune?" he whispered. "Why have you taken my parents from me?" His voice grew stronger as he lifted his head. "They were all I had. Do you hear? They were all I had in this world." He threw his head back and the rain battered his young tormented face. His voice yelled strong and clear and the wind carried it above the waves. "*Damn you!* Damn you, oh great god of the sea!" He spat the title contemptuously. "You've taken a man who devoted his life to you. And a woman who devoted her life to her family. Why? How did these people offend you?" His voice trailed off as his head sunk back to his float. "Why?" Aulus placed his good arm across Quintus's shoulder and together they wept.

Quintus heard Aulus's voice whisper close to his ear. "I swear by all the gods that I'll get you through this, Master Quintus. If it costs me my life, I will get you through this." It was little relief for the tremendous loss he had suffered this night, but at the same time Quintus realized that Aulus was now his only true companion in life. He held Aulus's shoulder and stared wearily at the roiling waves. Through the blurred vision of his tears, Quintus saw a bubble rise to the surface. Then another. And another. In a moment, the water beside them boiled as it did when Aulus had surfaced. He watched dumbfounded.

"Mother," Quintus said quietly. "Mother!" He began to yell.

Just as Aulus turned, something big broke the surface with a speed that startled them both. The heavy object struck Quintus hard in the left temple. The last thing he saw was a blurred image that took flight a full two meters into the air. Then everything began to spin, and his vision went black.

• • •

The sound of seagulls faded up slowly in Lucius's ears. His eyes fluttered open, and he squinted in the harsh glare of a new day. He rolled his head to the side and saw Quintus lying motionless next to him, a large knot caked with dried blood evident on his left temple. Beyond Quintus was a turquoise ocean that lay as smooth as a lake. Debris floated everywhere, most of it wood planks and sections of hull intermixed with the olive drab tunics of dead servants and the pale blue tunics of dead crewmembers. He winced as the horrors of the previous night came flooding back to him.

The image of his mother dangling from the wooden spike would be etched like a horrible scar forever in his memory. He remembered the sudden gulp of seawater that broke him from his trance, then the realization that the ship had flooded and sunk. He remembered breaking open his own amphora as a float, but his recollection of finding the breach was hazy. Then there was a burst of speed. He was suddenly being pulled through the water as if by a team of chariot horses. Then a feeling of flight, then of being laid upon a hard wet surface. Now, in the calm light of morning, he wondered if it had happened at all. Another scan of his unfamiliar surroundings told him this was no dream.

He slid from the hull section that had been their life raft, and his bare feet touched the warm sand of the deserted beach. He took a step and stumbled over a large body half submerged at the water's edge. He grabbed the green tunic at the shoulder and rolled it over, revealing a large puddle of blood. A crab that had been picking at the festering wound on the man's arm skittered across the red-stained sand and back into the sea. A moan, barely audible, came from the man's throat. Lucius recognized the face and smiled.

"So, Aulus . . . the tough gladiator is now food for the sea creatures. Some bodyguard you are." Lucius suddenly remembered how he had ended up on the large piece of wreckage. But he refused to acknowledge the fact that this man might have saved his life.

He looked out to the ocean and distant rocks, cupped his hands, and shouted.

"Hellooo? Is anyone there?"

Only the seagulls answered his call. He stood for a moment staring at the debris that littered water and sand. He looked back at Quintus's body lying on the wreckage in his torn white tunic, and his mind began to race. A smile crossed his lips. But his thoughts were interrupted by another moan from Aulus's swollen and cracked lips.

"First things first," he said to the unconscious bodyguard. With considerable effort he rolled the heavy body back into the ocean. Lucius's heart skipped a beat as the sudden splash of water on Aulus's face seemed to revive him. But from his floundering motions, Lucius could tell the large slave was severely incapacitated by his broken arm and loss of blood. With a vicious cry, Lucius jumped on the man's back, forcing him facedown into a half meter of water. With surprising strength, Aulus fought back, pushing with his good arm to raise his head above water. Lucius feared he had underestimated the amount of life left in the ex-gladiator. He grabbed the dangling remnants of the man's broken arm and twisted as hard as he could. Bubbles streamed from Aulus's mouth, his scream muted by the seawater. Lucius drove a knee into Aulus's back and pushed his head down into the sandy sea floor with all his might. Finally, he felt the resistance subside, and the body underneath him went limp. Lucius thought for a moment, then jerked Aulus's head from the water, leaned forward, and spoke directly into his ear.

"Today my life changes, gladiator. And there's not a damned thing you can do about it. *You* might have been happy being a slave your whole life, but not me. I am a slave no longer."

He slammed Aulus's head forward again with a splash and held it under another minute to be certain his work was complete. Then he stood and scanned the beach to be sure they were still alone. He walked from the water and moved toward the hull section. He grabbed the front of Quintus's white tunic and roughly pulled him to a sitting position. He was startled when a low moan came from the boy's throat.

"So you're still alive too, rich boy. I thought you'd gone to the gods with your bodyguard."

There was no response from Quintus as his head rolled from side to side. Lucius released his hold, and Quintus dropped back onto the wooden life raft with a thud. He moaned again. Lucius continued to speak as if his adversary's unconscious mind could hear every word.

"So, where's your protector now, rich boy? There's no one here to fight for you. We're all alone now."

Lucius reached over his own head, grabbed the back of his wet green tunic, and pulled it up and off his body. He then yanked Quintus forward and grabbed at his white tunic. As he worked, he spat his words passionately into Quintus's ear.

"There's something I want you to see before you die. Let's see who's the master and who's the slave now."

He threw the rough and ragged green clothing over Quintus's head and pulled it down around him. He then put Quintus's white tunic over his own head and let it drop into place. He ran his hands over his chest. It was the first time he had felt smooth soft cotton against his skin. He felt his entire disposition change with his clothing. He grabbed Quintus by the shoulders and began shaking him violently and slapping his face.

"Wake up, you bastard! I want you to see yourself as a petty slave just once before you die. I want you to see me as the rich orphan I'm about to become. Come on, wake up!"

He gave Quintus's face another hard slap but still got only a moan in response. He drew back to swing again and suddenly heard a voice. It had not come from Quintus but from the water behind him. He froze. Had the meddlesome bodyguard managed to revive himself? It couldn't be.

"Hello! Is anybody there on the beach?"

Lucius spun quickly and spotted a small, green fishing boat with a white and red sail secured to the short yardarm. It was just clearing the rocks that jutted out from the beach a hundred meters to his right. The boat was manned by three ragged fishermen, two of whom were propelling the boat through the debris field by oar. The third, an older man, was salvaging boxes and other items that looked to have value.

They waved at Lucius on the beach and called to him. "Stay put. We're coming for you."

Lucius noticed the Brythonic accent of the Celts. He waved to the boat, then thought fast. He had planned on hiking inland to look for help. But that was to happen after he was done with Quintus. Now these provincial fishermen had ruined his plan. He looked around quickly for a weapon to finish off Quintus. But the two fishermen rowed with speed, and the boat was approaching too quickly. The older fisherman called out as they neared the beach.

"Are you injured?"

"No, I'm alright," Lucius answered.

"We came upon your wreckage on our way out of Glevum this morning. We were searching for survivors when we heard your voice."

Lucius hunted quickly for a story. "My bodyguard was injured badly last night during the storm. He lost a lot of blood and died this morning. I was praying that the gods look after him on his journey."

The bow of the fishing boat lightly touched the shore.

"What about the other boy there?"

Lucius looked down at Quintus's inert body and paused for a moment.

"He's dead, too. He hit his head on the way off the ship. It looks like I'm the only survivor."

The fishermen looked at him with pity.

"Well, come aboard, son. We'll get you to the harbor."

Lucius stepped into the water just as another low moan came from Quintus.

"Did you hear that?" one of the rowers asked excitedly. "I think that boy is still alive!"

"By the gods, it's a miracle," Lucius said in the most sincere voice he could muster. "I checked his breathing myself just now and he appeared to be dead."

"Climb out and get him," the old fisherman ordered. "We'll take him as well. The physicians can have a look at him."

The two rowers secured their oars and waded ashore. The boat owner looked Lucius over as he climbed in and sat on the well-worn bench near the stern.

"That was a rough storm last night," the fisherman said. "I wouldn't want to be caught on the waters during one like that."

Lucius sat motionless as he watched the two men maneuver Quintus off the beach and lay him atop the fetid fish scales and offal that littered the bottom of their boat. His head rested on a trunk they had salvaged from the wreckage.

"That's quite a bruise he has there," said the old fisherman. "I'll bet he'll be alright. Nothing a few days of rest won't fix."

The two men shoved the boat into deeper water and manned the oars once again.

"You sure were the lucky one," the fisherman said. "What's your name, son?"

Lucius looked down at Quintus lying at his feet.

"My name is Quintus Honorius Romanus, son of Caius Honorius Romanus. And this is my personal slave, Lucius. We were on our way to visit my aunt and uncle in Aquae Sulis."

V

July AD 63

QUINTUS'S MIND SWAM in a whirlpool of pain and confusion. He was once again on the deck of the *Vesta* in the driving thunderstorm. A bolt of lightning etched the form of a demon in the black sky. He could see the deck pitching violently, but felt no sensation of movement. He saw his father, the captain, and the helmsman struggling with the tillerbars. A wave built behind them. He tried to shout a warning, but the words would not come. He attempted to run to them, but his feet would not move. "Beware! All of you! Beware the wave!" His mind thought it but his lips refused to speak the words. The wave struck. He saw the stern post buckling. He heard the rope attached to it singing under the strain of the anchor embedded in the ocean floor. "The rope. Watch the rope!" He felt weak. He could not mouth the words. There was a loud pop. The ship lurched. The broken rope recoiled across the top of the water. All the strain that had held the *Vesta* in place now converted to reflex energy. The rope flew at superhuman speed as it cleared the stern rail. "Watch the rope!" He was paralyzed. Helpless. He saw the snaking rope, now suddenly gliding slowly, gracefully. The wind became chimes in his ears. He felt he could count each raindrop as they fell with the leisurely grace of snowflakes. He could hear every drop as they splashed at his feet, which seemed melted to the deck. With a repulsive crack the rope struck the three men.

Images froze in his mind like pictures from a ghastly mural: the captain's head lobbed from his shoulders, the tillerman's outstretched arms removed from his body, his father's torso severed at the waist. Still wrapped in the blue cloak, the top half of his father's body fell to the deck and began to wash overboard. The lifeless head turned to Quintus. The eyes sprang open. The mouth formed a single word.

"Beware."

"No. No!"

The villa's slave quarters were normally quiet. But this was the third time the boy had let out a piercing cry from his long, restless sleep. This time his eyelids twitched and his head rocked back and forth, first slowly then more quickly.

"I think he's coming to," said an old kitchen servant as she moved to his bedside.

The voice sounded like an echo in Quintus's ears. His eyes fluttered open, and he stared for a moment at the drab ceiling lit by a single oil lamp hanging in the corner. He could hear the voice and other noises, but nothing was familiar. Each sound brought a stab of pain in his head. He gently turned his neck and looked toward the heart of the small room. The fuzzy images began to clear, but the dimly lit surroundings were foreign to him.

"Where am I?" His voice came in a hoarse whisper.

"Well, it's good to see you awake after so many days. That was quite a nightmare you've been having." The old woman's voice was friendly, if a bit curt. She placed her hand on his forehead. "Looks like your fever is gone."

He sat up slowly. Any quick motion caused dizziness. Her hand brushed his left temple and he winced in pain.

"That knot has gone down quite a bit," she said as she stood and walked across the room. "You should have seen yourself a few days ago when they brought you in here. You were not a pleasant sight." Her voice had an unusual accent to Quintus's ears.

He took in the sparse surroundings. The room was modest but relatively clean. Besides the straw bed in which he lay, there were two other beds, each with a small box at the foot. The old woman rummaged through one of them. A younger man hung tunics on three wooden pegs protruding from the far wall. The drab olive and oatmeal hues of the clothing told Quintus they belonged to the household slaves. Their tattered appearance indicated outdoor labor.

"Where am I?" he asked again.

The woman spoke with the young servant, then went on searching through her small box of possessions. Quintus was not used to being ignored.

"Will you answer me, woman! Where in Hades am I?" His voice rang loud with authority. He threw the bedcover aside and began to stand up. But something caught his eye and, coupled with the sudden spell of dizziness, it drove the thought of rising from his mind. He sat back hard on the straw bed.

"Why am I dressed in a slave's tunic? Where are my clothes? What's going on?"

The two slaves stared at Quintus.

"Why don't you answer?" The words were more a threat than a question.

The old woman looked stern. "You may have received a nasty bump on your head, young man. But that doesn't give you the right to speak to me in that tone of voice."

Quintus was dumbfounded. He looked toward the young man holding the tunics and saw another pair of glaring eyes. He began to wonder if he was still in his dream.

"We saw no other clothes. You were brought here wearing what you now have on," the male slave said. "And why do you show such disrespect to the woman who helped nurse you back to health?"

Quintus thought for a moment. He would not get answers from these two unless he calmed down.

"I'm sorry, madam. I meant no disrespect. But my mind is cloudy. Can you tell me how you found me and where you have brought me?"

The woman's face began to soften. "You are in the villa of Sextus Livius Viator near Aquae Sulis in Britannia."

For the first time, Quintus felt a sense of relief. He had made it to his destination. The woman continued to speak.

"Word came to the villa four days ago that two boys had been found along the coast after a shipwreck."

Quintus interrupted. "Two boys? Is that all? There were no others rescued?"

"No. Just the two. He said he was from the Romanus family and was traveling to the Viator home when the storm hit. Master Viator sent a wagon right away and his servants brought both of you from Glevum. I've been minding you ever since."

Quintus's relief turned to depression. His mind again flashed through scenes of that horrible night. His mother sliding from the wreckage and drowning. His father's body floating in the waves. And what of Aulus?

"Was there not an injured man found with us? A large slave called Aulus?"

"There were no others," the woman said, a look of pity crossing her face.

Quintus lowered his head into his hands, despair weighing on him like an oppressive force.

The old woman sat on the edge of the bed and held him close. His shoulders quivered as he cried. After a few moments, he looked up and wiped the tears from his cheeks with the back of his hand.

"I need to see my uncle. Please bring me to him."

The male servant turned and looked curiously at the old woman. She seemed equally puzzled.

"I don't understand, boy. What uncle?" she asked.

"My uncle . . . Sextus Viator. I need to see him."

The woman looked toward the male slave and shrugged. The slave's forehead was wrinkled with confusion. Quintus stared at them both, his impatience growing again.

"Do you hear me? I need to see my uncle," he repeated slowly and deliberately. He was beginning to wonder why his uncle would put him in the slave quarters to recuperate with these dense servants rather than in a villa guest room. He grew weary of the bewildered looks.

"My mother's brother . . . *Now!*"

The old woman nodded toward the slave. He tossed the rest of the tunics in a pile on the bed and left the room.

The cold mosaic tile under his bare feet reminded Quintus of his walk down the corridor of the *Vesta* four nights earlier. Now he was being ushered down a much wider passageway, a beefy slave on either arm, partly to steady him and partly to push him quickly along. Elaborate floral displays on narrow tables seemed to blur as they passed by. He was led past door after door along the lengthy east wing of the house. Finally they stopped at a large wooden doorway, ornately carved with scenes of running horses. A loud knock by one of the slaves was answered with a short grunt from inside. The slave pushed open the door and motioned with his head for Quintus to enter. The boy scowled up at him as he passed.

The square room was dim near the entrance, but well lit at the far side by tall bronze lampstands, each holding four hanging oil lamps. A heavyset man sat behind a large desk, writing briskly with a feathered stylus. Quintus stepped to the front of the desk.

"Are you my uncle?"

Sextus Viator stopped writing and looked up.

"Well, I'm somebody's uncle . . . but I doubt yours." His tone was abrupt.

Quintus could not understand why he was being treated so rudely by everyone in the household, his uncle included.

"But . . . we were coming to visit you. And then the storm hit and my parents were both . . . "

"Yes, yes. We've already heard the story," Sextus interrupted him, annoyance evident in his voice.

Quintus was now totally confused. "But I am Quintus, your nephew!"

Sextus simply stared at the boy, just as the two servants had done in the slave quarters. After a moment, the silence was broken by a new voice.

"I told you to beware of him, Uncle."

Quintus spun around. Emerging from the shadows near the entrance door was Lucius. He continued speaking, the smirk never leaving his face. "This one is crafty. He's been a problem in our family for some time now. Why Father never sold him is beyond me."

Quintus was speechless. The last time he had seen Lucius, the boy was sitting in a state of shock, staring at his dead mother hanging in a flooded cargo hold. Now he walked from the shadows like a demon returning from the grave.

Quintus was finally able to get his lips to move. "How dare you, Lucius! What gutless scheme are you trying to pull now?"

Sextus chuckled and folded his arms as he watched the scene unfold. "Well I have to say you predicted this to the letter, Quintus."

Quintus's head snapped back to Sextus. He fought back the dizziness and nausea the quick movement induced.

"Quintus?" He first whispered the name as a question. Then he shouted it. Even through his clouded mind, he saw Lucius's plan with crystal clarity.

Lucius continued, his voice conveying a sorrow Quintus knew to be false. "Of all the good people who could have survived this nightmare, it had to be this wretch. My parents died, yet he lived. Sometimes the gods have no sense of justice."

The fire in Quintus's stomach burned hotter than the oil lamps. "You bastard." The words came slowly through clenched teeth. "This will never work."

Quintus turned and leaned across the large desk. Sextus pulled back, obviously shocked at the intensity in his face. "Uncle, do you not see *he* is the slave, Lucius, and *I* am Quintus? I am your sister's son!"

Sextus regained his composure and leaned forward, coming nose to nose with the boy. His words came in a low steady voice. "What I see is a boy dressed in a servant's tunic, who my staff tells me has done nothing but rant and rave since we nursed him back to health. You have also managed to interrupt a memorial gathering for my sister, which is taking place in my courtyard while I'm sitting here wasting time with *you*. Now I suggest you go back to your slave quarters and use this night to get your strength back. You will be put to work beginning tomorrow."

Quintus was incensed that this ludicrous plan was actually working. He noticed that Lucius was wearing one of his short white tunics. "The tunics . . . He must have swapped our clothing at some point."

There was a laugh from Lucius. "Oh, that's correct, Uncle. In the middle of an awful storm and shipwreck I started swapping tunics with other people on the ship." He stepped forward with as much conviction as Quintus. "My only concern was to help save my parents and get off that ship."

Quintus snapped. Hearing Lucius talk of Politta and Caius as his own parents was too much to bear. He vaulted across the study with a yell and landed on Lucius. They tumbled in a heap on the floor. Fists flew and bodies rolled from side to side. The two large slaves who had accompanied Quintus jumped to separate the boys. But before they could reach them, the fighters rolled toward the corner and into one of the bronze lampstands, sending it sprawling across Sextus's desk. Burning oil spilled from the lamps and in a second the desktop was aflame. Sextus pushed back his chair, but it caught on an imperfect mosaic tile and tipped backward, sending the stocky man flat on his back. The slaves refocused on the new problem. One beat at the flames with his hands while the other helped his master to his feet.

"Get sand, you idiot, before the whole room is in flames!" yelled Sextus. The second slave ran from the study and headed to the kitchen, yelling for help.

The sound of grunts, yells, and fists hitting flesh filled the room. The brawl was more evenly matched this time as it traveled back into the center of the study. Quintus didn't have the advantage of holding Lucius beneath the fountain water as he had in the garden back in Rome. Plus the struggle was causing his head to feel as though it were splitting open. And Lucius now had more to fight for.

The house was in an uproar with screams of "Fire!" echoing through the hallway. Three more slaves burst into the room. They seemed baffled by the incongruous scene of the desk on fire while two teenagers rolled around the tiled floor in a heated fistfight.

"Are you going to stand there or help us?" yelled Sextus. It was enough to snap the servants into action. They grabbed the boys and, with much effort, finally separated them. A slave raced through the doors with a large wooden bucket. He poured sand across the desk and beat out the remaining stubborn flames eating at the surrounding books and paperwork.

Quintus still struggled to get at Lucius and another slave moved to help restrain him.

"Enough!" Sextus's voice bellowed through the room and down the hall. It startled his wife, Julia Melita, as she reached the doorway to the study. It finally got Quintus's attention.

"What's happening here?" Julia yelled, smelling the smoke and seeing the scorched desk. "We have a courtyard full of guests wanting to know if our villa is burning down." She looked toward Lucius. "And what happened to you, Quintus?"

"This damn slave boy decided to go crazy," Lucius yelled. "He needs a good beating, Uncle."

"He is not Quintus! *I* am Quintus!"

"Oh, don't start that again," Sextus said, now calming down. He readjusted his pallium over his shoulder. "Take him back to the slave quarters and keep him quiet. Tie him up if you have to."

Lucius watched the two servants drag a screaming Quintus from the room, and Julia began inspecting the charred desktop. "What was that all about?" she asked, lifting a smoking accounting book by its corner.

"Oh, the slave has some mad story about Quintus swapping identities with him," Sextus said. "Quintus predicted he'd try something like this. Apparently he's a real troublemaker."

Sextus looked at Lucius, who was tenderly touching his rapidly swelling and blackening right eye. He moved closer to the boy and put an arm across his shoulder. "It seems everyone on that damn ship has lost something. I've lost my sister. You've lost your parents. And that poor slave boy has obviously lost his mind."

Julia put the blackened papers back on the blistered desktop. "Well, Quintus," she said gently. "Things will be different for you from this day forward." She touched his bruised cheek. "We cannot replace your parents. Nobody can. But you can start a new life with us here in Britannia. Your uncle will get guardianship papers started immediately. You can be like the son we never had." Lucius looked toward Sextus, who nodded in approval.

Lucius had been so focused on creating this new life for himself, doing and saying whatever was needed to make it happen, he had never considered the concept of new guardians. Sextus and Julia could easily give him a life equal to, if not better than, Quintus's life in Rome. They had built the Viator Mercantile business and amassed a sizeable fortune. Profits from their shops in Ravenna and Pompeii, as well as their new shop in Aquae Sulis, had been used to build this sprawling estate in the hills overlooking the river Avon in western Britannia. The funds also helped keep Julia looking remarkably good for her thirty-four years, especially when dressed in the low-cut tunics she designed for herself. Rumors abounded at the villa and throughout Aquae Sulis that Julia was the shrewder partner in the Viator business. That part mattered little to Lucius right now. He simply saw a new life developing that was beyond his wildest dreams. It did not take him long to answer.

"Thank you, Aunt Julia. I would be honored to become a part of the Viator household."

His right eye was beginning to swell shut. With his good left eye he looked at Sextus. "He will be punished for this, right?"

Sextus sighed. "Let's look at it this way, Quintus. Both of you boys have been through an awful ordeal. Let's consider it a consequence of that horrid shipwreck and forget it."

Lucius was not happy but let it go. He had lost this battle but had won the war.

"Fine. But I don't want him near me or around the main part of the villa when I'm here."

"We can arrange that," said Sextus with a smile. "We can always use another stableboy for the horses."

VI

July AD 63

QUINTUS COULD SMELL the horse stables long before they came into view over the rise. Up to that point, the perfumed morning air with its scent of jasmine was a refreshing change to the stuffy slave quarters where he had spent the night. The fresh air also helped ease the headache that continued to pound, though with less intensity than the previous day. As he walked the manicured pathway, he looked across the rolling hills of the estate dotted with beech trees. The symmetrical and orderly vegetable gardens, wheat fields, and livestock pens stood like geometric patterns on an emerald carpet.

But the stables were a different story. As he approached, he understood why the animals were housed well away from the open-air villa.

The tall slave foreman who accompanied Quintus finally said his first words of the morning. They came with unmistakable loathing. "Listen, boy. I've been assigned as overseer of the Viators's new horse-breeding venture. It's not a job I love, and training new slaves to clean stables is my least favorite responsibility of all. So shut up and listen."

They entered the open breezeway that ran down the middle of the first stable building. The stench was overpowering to Quintus. The foreman smiled.

"I can tell by your wrinkled nose that you have no experience with this job whatsoever. Well, kid, you've got your work cut out for you."

Horses' heads emerged from the stalls to investigate the voices. Two grooms arrived and began setting up to shoe some of the horses.

"Hasn't anyone cleaned this place lately?" Quintus asked, trying to breathe through his mouth.

The tall foreman looked down at him. "Nah. The last stable boy got kicked in the head by one of the stallions. He's dead now."

Quintus's jaw dropped. The foreman and grooms broke out into loud laughter. Quintus couldn't decide if the story was true or if the man was just tormenting him. The foreman tossed him a heavy wooden bucket.

"I'm only going to say this once, Lucius, so pay attention."

"I'm not Lucius. Don't call me that."

The irritation was clear on the foreman's face. "Fine. Start at the far end. Lead each horse out of its stall. Tie it to the hitching post. Take the bucket and fork into the stall. Load the shit and dirty straw into the bucket. Dump the bucket loads into that cart. When it's full, pull the cart over that hill to the dung heap and empty it. Then put down fresh straw. I want this entire stable smelling like roses by the time I get back. Now get to work."

Quintus's exasperation grew with every word. He looked down the long row of stalls. He estimated twenty to twenty-five horse heads hanging over the low doors on each side of the building.

"But that's impossible! How can I get all this done in a day?" Quintus tossed the bucket against a stall door. The bang made the horses jump and begin to stir. The grooms stopped setting up their bench to see what was happening. "I shouldn't even be doing this. Just because that little bastard convinced my uncle that he's me, I'm out here cleaning stables. Well I won't do it. A Romanus does not clean horseshit!"

The foreman stood with his arms folded, nodding as Quintus raged. When the boy was finally done, he continued nodding. Then, in the blink of an eye, his right hand flew from under his left arm and cracked Quintus across the face, knocking him to the ground. He grabbed the dazed boy by the front of his olive tunic and pulled him right to his face. The rotten smell of fish on the tall man's breath overpowered even the stench of horse manure.

"Look, you little prick, I don't care who you think you are. Neither does anybody else around here. But guess what? Now you're a fucking slave just like the rest of us. And I don't want to hear another word about what you think you should and shouldn't be doing. I'll tell you one last time. Clean up this stinking stable."

He dropped Quintus back into the dirt like a sack of spoiled vegetables.

"Now get to work!" He kicked the bucket back at Quintus on his way out of the stable building.

Quintus looked to the grooms for some sign of support, but they ignored him and went back to work. He wiped the blood dripping from his nose and picked up the bucket. As ordered, he started in the farthest stall.

The foreman returned at nightfall. Quintus was only halfway done, but the right side of the stable building looked noticeably improved.

"You've given me one of the Twelve Labors of Hercules to complete here." Quintus was physically and emotionally exhausted. "There's no way to finish this job in one day," he said, the words panted out slowly one at a time.

The foreman smiled. "I know that. And now you do, too. But I got a good first day's work out of you, didn't I? Come along."

Quintus slept well that night. Even the scratchy straw in his thin mattress didn't keep him awake as it had the first night. Morning came much too soon and he was back in the stables again. When he finished the first building there were others to clean. He worked mostly alone, but sometimes others were nearby, shoeing and saddling the horses, training the animals for various duties, or repairing the tack used by the horses to pull the carts and carriages. He spoke to the other slaves at every opportunity, trying to convince them he did not belong there and he was not who they said he was. All turned a deaf ear. They had their own work to do. He began to believe what the slave foreman had told him earlier. Nobody cared.

One week into his new life as a slave, Quintus began settling into a routine, although he took every opportunity to let those around him know he was unhappy about it. As he worked, his mind raced, attempting to make sense of his plight in Britannia. It appeared he was not going to convince the Viators that he was the real Quintus. While he lay unconscious those first few critical days, Lucius had had plenty of time to worm his way into the hearts of the family through sympathy and compassion. By now, Quintus was sure the fiend had cast a spell on them that was unbreakable. And his own hot temper and stubbornness in completing his slave chores were alienating the household staff, who were growing tired of his complaining and his constant insistence that Lucius had stolen his identity. Since he refused to allow anyone to call him "Lucius," the slave staff concocted a new name for him. They called him "Grumbles."

Although keeping the stables clean continued to be Quintus's main responsibility, he was soon assigned to work as an assistant to the grooms. He spent his first morning at the new job preparing the Viator family coach for a trip to town. Quintus had seen the carriage on the grounds before but had not been able to appreciate its workmanship from afar. Growing up in the city, Quintus had rarely ridden in a coach, as the laws of Rome prohibited most horse-drawn vehicles on city streets during daylight hours. But here in the country, he could see the necessity of owning such a vehicle.

He helped push the carriage out of its shed and onto the bridle path, which led from the main house to the regional road about a kilometer away. The morning sunshine lit up the vermilion sides of the coach and glinted off the gold trim that edged the roof and outlined the geometric "X" pattern on the two sides. The carriage could hold six comfortably, though only Sextus, Julia, and perhaps a close friend or two ever occupied it. Quintus imagined that Lucius would now also be seated upon the soft couches in the luxurious interior.

"Where is the family off to so early this morning?" Quintus asked the grooms as he helped steer the coach backward.

"Master Viator has expanded his mercantile shop at the baths," answered one of the junior workers. "He and the family are attending the opening this morning."

"Grumbles! Watch what you're doing!" The voice came from Dida, the head groom. "You're going to run the coach into the garden."

Two of the larger horses were led from their stalls. One set of grooms maneuvered the matched pair into place while another began hitching them to the carriage. The mare on the left shifted forward and back to shake off the groom's hand. Quintus held tight to the bridle.

"Hold her, Grumbles," Dida said. "I need to cinch her backstrap."

"'Grumbles'! That's great." The words were followed by a forced laugh. The voice came from behind the carriage. Quintus leaned out to see around the horse's flank, though he knew by the voice who it was.

Lucius peered back with his perpetual smirk. Sextus and Julia stood behind him next to the rear wheel. Julia moved her hand to Lucius's shoulder, preparing to restrain him. Their wardrobe was dazzling, backlit by the low sun. Sextus wore a beige tunic and dark brown pallium, which blended beautifully with the rich green tones of Julia's stola and palla, the small cloak that covered her shoulders. But it was the sight of Lucius dressed in a long white tunic and red pallium that took Quintus by surprise. It was the first time he had seen the slave boy dressed in formal garments of the patrician class, and the sight left him speechless. Lucius looked at least three years beyond his age of fifteen.

"Let's be off," said Sextus. "There are still some preparations that need to be made before the customers arrive." Sextus prodded Julia and Lucius toward the step at the carriage doorway. Lucius gloated as he stepped into the sumptuous coach while his former master held the horses steady. Quintus had to look away. The sight made him physically ill.

The head groom stepped up to the driver's seat. Quintus released his grip on the straps. He dared not look up for fear of what he might say or do. Another beating at the hands of the tall foreman was not something he wished upon himself. The whip cracked and hooves clattered on the crushed stone path. As the wooden wheels began to roll, he heard Lucius's voice.

"Back to work, Grumbles." The laugh that followed trailed off as the carriage rode down the bridle path. The servants dispersed and Quintus stood alone.

That laugh lingered in Quintus's ears for the rest of the day. When night came he could not sleep, for each time he closed his eyes he saw Lucius in his red pallium standing before him, laughing. Although three other slaves slept only a meter from his bedside, he could not have felt more alone. His frustration began to give way to hopelessness. He wallowed in self-pity as he lay there with tears running down his face. Reality was beginning to set in. No longer were his strong father and compassionate mother there for him. Nor was Aulus. He was now truly alone, for the only family members still alive had forsaken him. His loneliness grew to desolation.

The more he tried to ignore his sorrows through sleep, the more his brain refused to allow it. His father's warning kept floating back to him. *Be wary of those who do not have. For they would rather take from those who have, than earn the spoils themselves.* He spent the late-night hours considering what he could have done differently to heed the warning and prevent this repulsive situation. How did this happen? Was it his fault? After hours of self-judgment and deliberation, he finally came to a conclusion that allowed him some welcome moments of peace. He decided that, under the bizarre circumstances, he could have done nothing to ward off his dilemma.

The relief was almost physical. He felt as though a mental fever had broken. The hours of self-analysis and painful catharsis had finally cleansed him of the guilt he felt at letting Lucius win. Now his father's second piece of advice came to him. *Never let your opponent see you upset, either from fear or emotion.* His thoughts were becoming much clearer now. He set a course for himself. It did not take long to determine that two things had to be done. First, he must confront Lucius alone. He must let him know this new life for both of them was only temporary. Second, he must begin plotting his escape. Being a stranger in a strange land, he needed to bide his time. But when the opportunity arose, whether in a week, a month, or a year, he would make good his escape and pursue a new survival plan. It was time for him to choose his own life rather than have others choose it for him.

His mind was finally at ease. Sleep came with only a few hours of darkness left.

Quintus dedicated the next few weeks to changing his attitude. He found solace in the thought that life sometimes takes strange paths and this was his current avenue, albeit a temporary diversion. With a more positive outlook, he noticed the servant staff began treating him better. He was the first up every morning and did his best to appear anxious to get on with his chores. He never again mentioned the identity theft and ceased all whining and complaining. Unfortunately, much to his chagrin, the nickname "Grumbles" was there to stay.

The weeks passed quickly for Quintus as he threw himself into his work, even offering to help others when his daily tasks were completed. The first of the new duties for which he volunteered was well-calculated. Being in and around the stables got him more comfortable with the horses. He watched some of the younger grooms exercise the animals each morning, riding them through the pastures and along the bridle paths. With the villa in its remote countryside location, he would need some form of transportation to get anywhere an escape plan would eventually take him. He had to learn how to ride.

The head groom welcomed his request and was more than happy to train him, since they barely had enough stableboys to exercise the dozens of horses on a regular schedule. Quintus's first few outings were tenuous at best, but he caught on quickly. Having spent little time atop a horse before coming to Britannia, he marveled at the feeling of power he got being on horseback. Virtually everyone in Rome walked within the city, so occasional romps through a country field on a family outing had been the extent of his horsemanship in Italia. But here at the villa, he was handling the mares with ease in just a few weeks. The feisty stallions took a while longer.

As he had hoped, with his new duties and better attitude, his freedom at the villa increased. This allowed more access to areas and materials that might help with his new objective. He learned the layout of the family's winged corridor house, although under Sextus's order, he was still kept away from Lucius whenever possible.

His first real opportunity to put his new plans into action came with an errand to the equipment shed. Alone in the dim, hazy shack, he was able to pocket a sharp blade and a broken handle from an old gardening tool. These he buried inside the third stable building. His grooming work with Saturnia, his favorite mare, allowed him enough time each day to slowly fashion the pieces into a formidable knife. Tough strands of horsehair from Saturnia's mane helped hold the blade securely to the handle. He considered smuggling the weapon into his quarters, but with only the small box at the foot of his bed as a hiding place, the knife could be too easily discovered. He decided to leave it buried in the corner of Saturnia's stall.

His second opportunity came a few weeks later.

• • •

"Grumbles! You're needed at the house this morning," one of Julia's hand-maidens yelled down the narrow corridor of the slave quarters. Quintus was just finishing his breakfast of bread and cheese. He jogged out of the cramped room and ran to the servant's entrance at the rear of the villa home. The tall foreman met him just inside the kitchen.

"Master Quintus did not feel well last evening. His chamber pots are more than full."

Quintus tried his best to hide the smile of guilty pleasure that was growing on his lips. The effort did not escape the tall man. He broke into a smile of his own as he continued.

"He has personally requested that you clean it up."

For an instant, Quintus felt his hatred for Lucius swelling. But he was determined to keep his temper in check.

"But, sir. I have been told to remain clear of Master . . . Quintus." It was the first time he had used his own name when referring to Lucius. The effort was painful.

"Master Quintus is outside the villa getting some much needed fresh air."

Quintus wanted to punch the wall, but kept calm. He decided to look at this unpleasant duty as an unexpected opportunity. He relaxed and bowed slightly. "Then I am at his service."

The foreman almost looked disappointed at Quintus's eagerness. "His room is the second door on the left in the east wing corridor. Get to it."

"Yes, sir."

Quintus grabbed a handful of cleaning rags from the wash basin and walked from the kitchen. He passed a few servants in the wide hallway going about their household chores. He remembered his last time in this hallway, he had been dragged kicking and screaming by two large servants back to the slave barracks.

He came to Lucius's room. He could tell it was the correct room from the stench of waste that reached him before he opened the door. He pulled at the handle, and the foul odor that assaulted his nose was worse than his first day in the stables. He walked quickly to the window and threw open the shutters, remaining there to catch a few breaths of fresh air. In the distance, by the banks of the river Avon, he could see Lucius and Julia sitting under a tall tree, the leaves beginning to turn shades of autumn gold. It could have been such a beautiful scene, he thought, if it weren't for the rubbish seated next to his aunt.

He tore himself from the freshness of the outdoors, back to the reek of Lucius's room. Three large pots were filled with a vile combination of vomit and human waste. What wasn't in the bowls was splattered on the white mosaic tiles.

Quintus began by tying one of the rags around his lower face. He preferred the musty smell of the damp rag to what was in the pots. One by one, he walked the pots down the hall, through the kitchen and out to the waste trough that was dug behind the villa walls. He rinsed the pots at the well, then returned to the room to clean the floors. He worked quickly in order to leave himself enough time to explore Lucius's quarters. He casually pushed the door closed as he wiped the floors near the entranceway. He took the cloth from his face and tossed it on the pile of used rags in the corner.

The room was large, almost the size of Sextus's office. Quintus assumed that his aunt and uncle had given Lucius their biggest guest room as his own. The bed was placed near the window. It was moderate in size with a low headboard and footboard decorated with tortoise shell. He sat on the violet blanket and sank into the wool-stuffed mattress. He hadn't realized how much he missed a bed that was not stuffed with straw. He ran his hand over the small pillow. It had taken him many weeks with a stiff neck to get used to sleeping without one.

Above the headboard was a polished marble shelf bearing a statuette of Neptune. The water god looked down on the bed like a sentinel, his trident raised in glory. Quintus wondered if the effigy had been in the room before Lucius's arrival—or did Lucius seek to honor the deity who had given him his new life? The thought rekindled Quintus's rage over the loss of his parents at sea as this god looked on indifferently. He lifted the hefty bronze figure, spat in its face, then replaced it on the shelf.

He rose and walked across the room to the large upright chest. A tug on the hand-carved walnut doors revealed a colorful assortment of clothing, including the bright red pallium Lucius had worn to the Aquae Sulis shop opening. Sextus and Julia had filled the cabinet with an incredible assortment of garments, perhaps twice the number Quintus had hanging in his Rome villa. There were certainly advantages to owning your own mercantile business, he thought.

Quintus quietly closed the cabinet and glanced out the window to be sure Lucius was still by the river. He was. He turned his attention to the small trunk next to the bed. As he approached it a glint of recognition crossed his mind. He knew this trunk with its distinctive twin silver handles. This was his storage box from the *Vesta!* But how could it be here? Some of the wreckage must have been salvaged by the fishermen, he concluded. He grasped the twin handles and slowly raised the lid. The once-full box was now only half filled with clutter. His neatly folded tunics had been removed, probably ruined after sitting for days in the seawater. What remained were two pairs of sandals, a drinking horn in the shape of a small deer head, a game of bones, the small flute he had never learned to play, wax writing tablets, a stylus, and a small bronze urn in which he kept his mementos. Each item brought a flood of memories. He knew exactly the last time he had used each article. But the bronze urn struck the deepest chord inside him, for he remembered the last keepsake he had placed inside. His hand began to shake as his fingers slowly tipped back the lid and entered the narrow neck of the container. They stretched deep, probing the few small trinkets within. He touched leather and his heart jumped.

"Yes!" he whispered out loud.

Snagging the small strap, he slowly lifted his hand from the urn. His eyes welled with tears as he stared at the small leather pouch that hung from his hand. Although stiff and crusted by salt water, it was the loveliest thing Quintus had seen in weeks. He pulled at the top rim and unveiled the precious relic inside. He gazed at the miniature terra-cotta ship captain that lay in the palm of his hand. It was like rediscovering a long-lost friend. In this tiny figure he saw his father enjoying the naumachia again. He saw his mother admiring the craftsmanship of his boat in their garden. And he saw Aulus rescuing the captain and his beautiful ship from the hands of an infidel. He closed his fingers around the figurine and clutched it to his chest. He vowed that this token, the symbol of those he had loved so much and then lost, would never again leave his possession.

Voices in the hallway broke his trance. Two servants passed by without opening the door. But Quintus realized he was spending too much time in the room. Someone might soon be looking for him. He placed the captain back into the pouch, reached up under his olive tunic, and tucked the pouch inside the band of his undergarment. Then he silently closed the trunk and rose to the window. Lucius and Julia were walking along the riverbank. He pulled the shutters closed and threw the latch to secure them. He froze a moment, studying the simple latch and the slight gap between the two wooden shutters. He slowly raised the metal hook on the right screen out of the small eyelet on the opposite screen. Slowly and carefully, he released the hook and noticed how it remained pointing upward. He tapped lightly on the shutter and the hook immediately fell sideways, its point seating into the eyelet.

"Grumbles! Are you finished yet?"

Quintus jumped. The voice came from the slave foreman who was standing in the now open doorway. Quintus wondered how long he had been standing there.

"Yes, sir. I aired out the room. I was just closing up."

The foreman made a face. Quintus was unsure if it reflected a sense of disbelief or a sense of unhappiness about something in the room.

"The stench still lingers. Bring in one of the floral displays from the hallway and put it on the cabinet. Perhaps the scent of flowers will work some magic in here."

"Yes, sir. Right away." Quintus was relieved. He scurried past the tall man and sought the fresh flowers.

When he finished inside, Quintus left through the kitchen servant's entrance and walked the long way back toward the slave barracks. He carefully counted the windows as he passed the outside of the east wing.

The cool night air was a welcome relief after another long day with the horses. But on this night, adrenaline kept Quintus awake. He lay staring at the dark ceiling for hours until he heard the loud snoring and heavy breathing that told him the three other slaves in the room were fully asleep. He rose slowly, careful not to rustle the straw mattress, and tiptoed down the hall.

As with all trusted servants, there were no locks to keep him inside the slave barracks at night. Quintus was soon moving across the villa grounds, keeping to the shadows and out of the pale yellow light cast by the full moon. He made his way to the stables, where he dug in the corner of Saturnia's stall for his knife. Despite the midnight intrusion, his favorite mare remained silent.

"Good girl," he whispered in her twitching ear. "Go back to sleep now. I'll be back shortly." He tucked the dirty knife securely into the belt at his waist and left the stables.

He walked quickly along the whitewashed wall to the main house, then made his way along the east wing. He re-counted the windows, knowing that Lucius's bedroom was behind the fourth set of shutters. He quietly approached his target, looking right and left for any late-night wanderers on the villa grounds. He was alone.

He slipped the knife from his belt, then hesitated. He thought for a moment about the prudence of this act. If he was caught breaking into his master's chambers with a knife, his punishment would be far worse than a beating. Given his past encounters with Lucius, chances were good he would be arrested for attempted murder. But he knew he had to do this. It was part of the new decree he had written for himself. He thought of Julius Caesar's words as he crossed the Rubicon to secure his own future a hundred years earlier: *The die is cast.*

He stood from his crouched position and the center of the window came to eye level. He carefully inserted the knife into the gap between the two red shutters. With steady hands he slid the blade upward until he heard the delicate metal clink as it struck the interior latch. He applied a bit more pressure and heard the hook uncouple from the eyelet. He guided the blade slowly higher until in his mind's eye he could see the hook standing up on end. Cautiously he gripped the shutter frame and gave a gentle tug. It opened easily and quietly. He took one last look around the grounds then hoisted himself through the opening.

The full moon spilled just enough light into the room to allow Quintus limited vision. He checked the latch hook and saw it was still balanced straight up on its tiny hinge. He stood at the foot of the bed, savoring the moment. Lucius lay on his side, facing away from the window. His shallow, labored breathing told Quintus he was still feeling the effects of his illness. With the knife firmly in his grasp, Quintus approached the bed.

In a swift, carefully calculated move, he was on the mattress with his hand tight over Lucius's mouth and the knife point aimed at the back of the boy's neck. Lucius twitched violently and his eyes sprang open. Quintus pressed the cold metal tip of the blade against the nape of Lucius's neck to let him know this was no dream. He heard Lucius whimper as he leaned close to his ear.

"I should kill you right now, you lying bastard."

Quintus spit the words into Lucius's ear and felt his captive shudder as he recognized the voice.

"But that's not why I'm here. That would be too quick for you. I'm here to let you know that the tables will turn once again. Every day of your life, no matter where you are, you should be looking over your shoulder. For on one of those days, I will be there to avenge what you have done here. This I swear on the souls of my mother and father. Do you hear me? *My* mother and father!"

Quintus tightened his grip on the boy's mouth to help make his point. Lucius was obviously having a hard time breathing and pulled at Quintus's hand. Quintus enjoyed watching him squirm. He leaned closer to torment him further.

"On second thought, perhaps I should take my revenge right now by plunging this blade into your neck at the base of your skull." He pressed the blade a bit firmer, but was careful not to break the skin. "Do you realize that's the quickest way to die, Lucius? It's the way a gladiator kills his foe in the arena." Quintus smiled as he felt the tremors increase in Lucius's body. "Or perhaps I should just slice your back wide open." He removed the knife from the nape of Lucius's neck, but instead of placing it at his back, he laid it aside and reached for the statue of Neptune on the shelf above the headboard. He positioned the water god's trident firmly against Lucius's spine halfway up his back, which sent a visible spasm through the boy's trembling body.

"Now, you're not going to scream like a baby, are you?"

Lucius shook his head in a short burst under Quintus's hand.

"Why don't you tell me—quietly—how you managed this deceit so cleverly."

Quintus slowly eased the pressure off Lucius's mouth. There were long gasps of air as Lucius filled his starved lungs. Quintus glanced at the bronze statue and wedged the bottom firmly against the soft mattress, freeing his hand to once again grasp the knife. Lucius had gulped enough air to begin pleading for his life.

"Don't kill me! What do you want to know? I'll tell you anything. Just don't kill me."

Imperceptibly, Quintus began slipping from the bed.

"Why don't you start at the beginning? A false move or a loud cry and this knife will find the back side of your heart." Quintus jostled Neptune's trident to help make his point.

"It was on the beach . . . near the shipwreck. After you were knocked out I changed our tunics. I just wanted to feel fine cotton for once in my life. But then some fishermen came. I was afraid . . . Aulus . . . He . . . He was already dead. I panicked. I . . . I didn't know what to do. You can understand that . . . Can't you?"

There was silence.

"Can't you understand how I was confused?"

There was silence again, then a slight tapping and the frail sound of a small piece of metal falling.

Lucius did not know what to do. Did Quintus want him to continue? Why wouldn't he answer? Without moving his head, he strained his eyes to see Quintus crouching behind him. He feared the blade's incision if he dared turn around. So he laid paralyzed with fear and waited. But still there was only silence.

"Look, what do you want of me?" He worked up enough courage to turn his head a bit. The point of pressure lessened against his back. He seized the moment and jumped from the bed.

"An intruder! Help me! He has a weapon!" His muffled cries echoed through the hallways of the east wing. The servants who lived in the main house were the first to be roused. Julia shook Sextus awake. Within seconds of his call, the heavy door to Lucius's room was thrown open and in stepped two of the household slaves.

"What is it, Master Quintus?"

Lucius sat shivering in the corner, too frightened to move in the dark. "An intruder! In my room! He's armed!"

A kitchen worker arrived with an oil lamp and they began searching the room. Julia and Sextus pushed past the small crowd of flustered servants gathered in the doorway.

"What is it, Quintus? What's happened?"

"It was Lucius! That scheming slave boy! He held a knife to my neck as I slept!"

"What?" Sextus yelled.

Lucius rambled on as Julia led him back to the bed. She held him close to settle him down. "He grabbed my mouth. And then he put his knife to my back and said he'd kill me!"

Over Julia's shoulder, Lucius saw the slave with the oil lamp look toward Sextus and shrug. "Master Viator, there is no place to hide in this room. No one is here."

Lucius was outraged. "He's here I tell you!" he screamed at the slave.

Sextus walked to the window shutters, paused, and then moved toward the foot of the bed. Lucius heard his voice from behind him.

"He had a knife like *this* against your back?"

Lucius felt the tip of the knife on his back once again and jumped with a holler. "Yes! Yes! Like that!" Lucius turned to see the statue of Neptune in Sextus's hand.

Sextus smiled. He took the oil lamp from the kitchen servant and dismissed the staff.

"You've had a bad dream, Quintus. Probably from your illness last night. It's nothing."

"No, he was here, Uncle. I heard him."

"Ah, you *heard* him, but did you see him?" Sextus smiled at Julia, who still held the boy tight.

"No. The room was dark. But I know his voice."

"Look, the window shutters are still latched from the inside. If he had used the door, someone would have seen him running through the house, no? Where else could he have gone?"

Lucius could not answer. Sextus nodded to Julia and she laid the boy's head back on the pillow.

"We'll leave the lamp for you for the rest of the night," she said gently. "Try to go back to sleep."

They shut the door quietly as they left. Lucius watched the single flame flicker against the walls. The words were still clear in his head. Too clear to have been heard in a dream.

Every day of your life, no matter where you are, you should be looking over your shoulder.

They were said with an intensity he would never forget.

For on one of those days, I will be there to avenge what you have done here.

Lucius knew this was no dream. And he knew beyond any doubt that Quintus meant what he had said.

VII

August AD 64

AS THE TREES DROPPED their leaves and the snows came, Quintus soon felt how much colder the northern provinces could be. But even for Britannia, the year-end freeze was far worse than normal. The charcoal-burning braziers throughout the Viator house and slave barracks did little to relieve the bitter cold. Quintus and the other grooms spent many bone-chilling nights in the stables minding the braziers that were lit to warm the horses. A few of the older and weaker slaves died, but the horses all survived the season. Each of the villa residents, from the master to the youngest slave child, was happy to welcome the warmth of spring and summer back into their lives.

It had been over a year since Quintus had arrived. As if to further isolate him from the life he once knew, news had reached the villa in early August of a great fire in Rome. Three of the city's residential districts, including most of the Palatine and Esquiline hills, had been completely destroyed in a holocaust that burned for a week. Rumors were rampant that Nero himself had set the blaze to secure land for a new palace. But that mattered little to Quintus. The Romanus family home was situated in the middle of the ravaged neighborhood. The house itself had been sold by Sextus and Julia, although they held on to his father's shipping fleet to augment their textile business. The selling of the house was one thing, but the thought of his childhood home, with all its memories and possessions, now lying in a smoldering heap brought Quintus to tears. It was another cold reminder that life as he knew it would never be the same.

The news reinvigorated his determination to put his plan of escape into action and get on with seeking his new life. But how? Throughout the spring and summer, Quintus had kept a watchful eye for the right opportunity. On his early morning rides to exercise the horses, he had often considered simply jumping the low fence that surrounded the villa and riding off across the green hills. But where would he go? Though there were few physical barriers between him and freedom, many obstacles still blocked his path. He knew the punishment for runaway slaves was death, often by crucifixion. So where he went and how he hid once he left the villa were far more important than simply planning an escape route across the villa grounds. He considered the lives of the street urchins who were so plentiful in Rome. Was a life of begging and scrounging for every meal any better than what he had now? At least at the villa he ate relatively well and slept with a roof over his head. He had come to think of it as "The Pleasant Prison." No, he would need to find a better life than that before he risked an escape. But, in over a year, that last elusive component had never presented itself.

As he did most mornings, Quintus shoveled grain into his cart before making the rounds of the horse stalls. Down the hill, he noticed the family coach already on the pathway with two mares in place. Each had a feed bag strapped to her face and a groom was wiping mud from the carriage sides. Quintus thought it odd that the coach had been out on the road so early.

The head groom led a small caravan of assistants, each loaded down with heavy tack and harnessing gear, past Quintus toward the stables.

"Hurry up with the feed this morning, Grumbles," Dida called out as he passed. "We'll be needing quite a few of the horses shortly. We'll also need you to help pull three more wagons out of the shed."

"Right away, sir." Quintus thought he detected an unusually cheerful tone in the old groom's voice.

Quintus's strength and stamina had blossomed dramatically in his sixteenth year. To his mind, it was the single positive aspect of the manual labor to which he was now so accustomed. He was usually one of the first slaves sent to manhandle the heavy wagons from their shed. But three, he thought, in addition to the family coach, was a lot for a single morning.

He finished his feed rounds quickly then ran to the shed to help pull the cargo wagons out. These were smaller and easier to handle than the family coach, with flat cargo beds in the rear enclosed with wooden poles that held the payload secure. While Quintus began leading Saturnia and the other horses out to be hitched, the head groom cleaned the dirty straw from the back of the wagons and pitched in fresh-cut green hay. Quintus noticed a distinct smile on his face.

"What's all the activity about, sir?"

"Games, Grumbles! Games today!"

The word didn't sink in with Quintus. Games? What sort of games?

"Our kind master has selected his most loyal servants to accompany the family on this trip into Aquae Sulis. And I've been chosen." His smile grew wider and a gleam was evident in his eye. "This old slave has not seen the games for many years."

Games! Now he understood. It seemed like a hundred years since he had last thought about his favorite pastime.

"There is an arena at Aquae Sulis?" Quintus was astonished. He had never considered that provinces so far from Rome would house an arena and host their own games.

"It's a short distance north of town on the Corinium road."

The old groom returned to his work. Quintus's mind raced as he helped hitch the mares to the wagons. He had to devise a way to be included in this outing.

"Who will watch the horses during the games? Surely they can't be left alone."

"There are no lack of hands willing to hold onto bridles outside the arena for a few sesterces."

Quintus scratched at Saturnia's nose the way she loved. He spoke to the horse but aimed his comments at Dida. "Yes, but they wouldn't take care of my beautiful Saturnia and her helpers like I would. Would they, girl?"

The old groom looked from behind the cart.

"Grumbles, we have twelve servants going, four to each cart. Where would you even ride?"

He had never seen the groom in such a friendly and benevolent mood. But Dida's negative responses were beginning to irritate Quintus. He wanted to shout: Put me anywhere, you fucking old bastard! Just let me go to the games! But he knew he had to keep his temper in check.

"I could hang from the back or along the side." He jumped up on the foot peg used by the driver to climb into the high seat. "Look. This would be fine." He hurdled the seat and landed in the new green hay that filled the back of the cart. He looked Dida directly in the face with the pleading eyes he used to flash at his mother when he sought a gift for himself as a boy. Inside, he was a seething mass of impatience. "Please, sir. I've not been off the grounds of the villa since I arrived last year. You know my work and attitude have improved. I'll mind the horses and keep them watered and safe through the day."

The groom stared at him for a moment. "I have to say your attitude has improved since your rather unfortunate beginnings here. I'll check with the foreman. If it's alright with him, it's alright with me."

Quintus was concerned since his relationship with the tall foreman was tentative at best. But he had hope that he would finally see something of Britannia. It would also give him the opportunity, even if somewhat limited, to look for refuge outside the slave barracks of the villa.

Within an hour, the sun cleared the tops of the beech trees along the barley field and the morning chill dissipated. The wagons were put in line to leave. Although the beds were packed tight with human cargo, the close quarters did not seem to dampen the spirits of the chosen few. Quintus stood, anxiously holding Saturnia's bridle. He still had not heard a final decision on his inclusion in the group.

Dida and three of his senior assistants walked from the nearby stable accompanied by the tall foreman. Quintus could overhear their last-minute instructions for the trip. He watched the head groom mount the driver's seat on the family coach and the other three climb into the seats on the cargo wagons. They took the reins and got ready to nudge the horses down the bridle path. No one said anything to Quintus. His chin dropped to his chest. The foreman waved to Dida and walked to the last cart where Quintus waited, still holding Saturnia's cheek strap. The foreman stepped on the foot peg and pulled his lanky body up onto the bench next to the driver. He glanced down at the horses without acknowledging Quintus. After a moment, he spoke out casually.

"So, Grumbles. Are you just going to stand there looking sorry for yourself or are you going to climb aboard?"

His words were like a ray of light on Quintus's soul.

"Climbing aboard, sir!"

Quintus reached for the handhold to pull himself up on the foot peg next to the foreman.

"Not here. This cart is already overloaded," said the foreman. "I believe there's room next to the driver on the family coach."

Quintus was stunned. Not only was he being allowed to go on this excursion, but he would be traveling atop the family carriage. He decided that the villa was a distinctly better place when the overseers were in a good mood.

"I expect the horses and carriages to be well looked-after today," the foreman called to him as he ran forward.

"Count on me, sir," Quintus yelled over his shoulder.

He grabbed the handhold at a full gallop and his momentum carried him up onto the driver's bench. Dida still retained his smile.

"So, a trip into town on one of the best seats in the house. Must be your lucky day."

Quintus smiled at him. "Thank you, sir, for putting in a good word for me."

The old groom winked at him. Their attention was drawn to Julia, who was approaching the side of the carriage. She was guided into the vermilion coach by one of the assistant grooms. Sextus and Lucius were nowhere in sight.

"Is the master not attending the games?" Quintus asked the groom in a low voice.

"Master Viator and Master Quintus are already in Aquae Sulis. I drove them in earlier this morning. They had work to do at the textile shop. We'll be going by there to pick them up."

The notion of Lucius working his way into the Viator family business made Quintus wonder what miserable scheme he was now formulating. He pushed the depressing thought from his mind. This was a special day and he refused to allow thoughts of Lucius to ruin the mood. Besides, he thought, the stop would be a bonus. Not only would he get to finally see the Britannia countryside, but he would also visit the town of Aquae Sulis. The only thing left was to catch a glimpse of the games. And of course stay alert for a place to conceal himself after his escape.

Dida snapped his reins and the caravan slowly rumbled down the path toward the villa entrance. They crossed a wooden bridge over a small stream, and the dirt-and-crushed-rock pathway soon gave way to an impressive wide avenue capped with smooth paving stones.

"This is a nice road. Better than many in Italia," Quintus said.

"Yes," Dida answered. "It's the main regional road. It passes the walls of Aquae Sulis then goes on to Corinium and Glevum, the port city where you were brought in by the fishermen."

Quintus decided the province was much more beautiful than its reputation throughout the Empire implied. Yes, the winters were cold, but spring and summer brought a pleasant warmth and a vibrant green cast to the landscape like he had never seen. The road followed the path of the river Avon for many kilometers. Willow trees bent low along the bank, which was interrupted from time to time by a small stone bridge that allowed access to another country villa. The rolling hills reminded Quintus of the Tuscan landscape where he had traveled with his parents many years ago. The happy memory brought a smile to his face and enhanced the feeling of freedom as he watched the pastoral vistas pass by.

About an hour outside the villa they topped the crest of a hill on the edge of a deep valley. The silver ribbon of the Avon snaked across the valley floor. On a small peninsula created by a horseshoe bend in the river stood a town of clay-tiled roofs and lofty temples encircled by an impressive wall.

"Aquae Sulis," proclaimed the old groom. "The baths here are remarkable, you know. They say they've been used for thousands of years by the locals. The Romans are just beginning to recognize their powers."

Quintus could see that the settlement had already leaped beyond the town walls and filled the balance of the peninsula. Its location at a vital crossroads was evident from their high vantage point, where the sun-bleached rock beds of five converging roads were clearly visible.

The three cargo wagons of the caravan waited outside the town walls as the passenger coach entered through the south gate and rode north toward the massive bath complex. The majority of foot, horse, and carriage traffic was headed out of town, probably to the arena, Quintus figured. It had been over a year since he was immersed in urban life. While the activity in this town was far different from the commotion of Rome, it was heartening to see people going about their daily lives in jovial freedom. But it made the isolation of enslavement that much more oppressive.

Dida pointed to the impressive building just ahead. "That's the Temple of Sulis-Minerva. It honors both the Celtic god Sulis and Minerva, our own goddess of wisdom."

The main entrance to the baths was adjacent to the temple. Steam from the natural hot springs produced small white vapor trails that rose into the blue sky. Quintus spotted the Viator sign painted on the wall in red letters above a well-appointed shop. The business was on the ground floor of the massive stone building that housed the baths. A row of thirty Corinthian columns lined the covered promenade around the building. The Viator shop commanded the premium location just off the main road, first in line on the promenade. The constant stream of people coming and going through the doorway, all carrying large parcels and bolts of fabric, reflected its success.

"Take the reins while I go and summon the master," commanded the old groom. He climbed from his seat and disappeared through the shop door.

From his roost atop the carriage Quintus studied the people on the street. They appeared to be a mixture of Roman, Briton, and Celtic heritage. Most were well-dressed Roman patricians enjoying a day at the spa. He overheard many discussing the day's games. Some were placing bets.

He wondered how he could blend into this crowd. His dirty, olive drab wardrobe marked him as a slave. Or a pickpocket. Or at best, a street beggar. He knew of nobody in this town to whom he could appeal for help. Besides, he also knew the penalty for harboring a runaway slave was the same as for the slave himself: death. His mind worked to devise a storyline he might be able to feed one of these families—not now, but in a few days or weeks, once he made his way back to town on his own. He wondered if he would not be better off heading to Glevum, the port town. At least there he might be able to find passage back to Rome as a stowaway or ship assistant.

From the storefront emerged Sextus and Lucius, followed by the head groom. His uncle was dramatically dressed in a royal blue pallium over a short white tunic. Lucius wore his bright red pallium again, this time wrapped over a short cream-colored tunic. Quintus wondered how long Lucius had practiced folding the toga-like garment alone in his room to appear comfortable wearing this upper-class fashion.

As Lucius approached the carriage, Quintus considered turning away so he would not be seen. But deep inside he wanted Lucius to know that, in some small way, he too was gaining a bit more power and freedom. He wanted to show that he had risen to a higher status than Lucius ever had as a slave. Mostly he wanted to show that this slave life was not beating him. He decided to remain exactly where he was.

As Lucius glanced up for the handhold, his gaze met Quintus's face staring down at him. He jumped back as if struck by lightning. Quintus smiled with satisfaction at the look of shock on his adversary's face. Obviously the whispered threat from the bedroom incident still echoed in Lucius's mind.

"What is he doing here?" Lucius shouted. "Why is he not in the stables? Who allowed this imbecile to leave the villa?"

"He is here only to mind the horses and carriages, Master Quintus," Dida explained with a nervous smile.

Sextus quickly said good-bye to one of his customers, then ushered Lucius into the carriage. His voice carried out the window and reached Quintus perched on the driver's seat.

"Will you stop worrying about him?" Sextus said with some irritation. "You're obsessed with that slave. He has responsibilities on our staff, you know."

Quintus was pleased that he still had such a negative effect on Lucius. The old groom climbed back up in his seat. He glanced at Quintus and shrugged, then expertly turned the horse team around and drove them back out the south gate. The three other carts merged in behind as they headed north on the Corinium road toward the arena. Progress was slowed by the throng of pedestrians and the hundreds of carriages and carts that clogged the road. The shutters on the Viator coach remained open to the fresh air. Quintus watched the countryside pass by as he eavesdropped on the conversation between Julia and Lucius.

"Business is growing better each week, isn't it?" she asked.

"It is, Aunt Julia. But I would think you could do even better with a more diverse inventory. Frankly, I think you need more colored fabric. This is a resort town. I'll bet more colorful palliums, like Uncle wears, would sell very well for you."

"First of all," Julia began, "what I want to hear is 'sell well for *us*,' not 'sell well for *you*.' This business will be yours some day, Quintus. You should start thinking of it that way. Secondly, I couldn't agree more. It's such a shame we lost all the inventory that was aboard your father's ship."

Quintus bristled at the reference to *his* father.

"We haven't been able to get another supply of silk from the Far East," Julia continued. "There's no telling when another shipment may come our way."

"How about Egyptian cotton?" Lucius asked. "I overheard some of the customers saying how much they miss the feel of Egyptian cotton. Can we get that?"

"I think we can. What do you think, Sextus?"

Before her husband could answer, Lucius was speaking again. Quintus was astonished, not only at how much Lucius had learned about the textile industry, but at how involved he was becoming in the Viators's business. This was a side of Lucius that Quintus had never seen.

"Why don't we dye it?" asked Lucius. "I thought the Celts were supposed to be good with dyes here. That would give us the colors we're looking for."

Julia seemed energized by Lucius's enthusiasm. "That might work. I know the people of society here would prefer the Egyptian cotton over the standard grades, and they certainly can afford it. We could charge triple our cost, including transport and dying expenses. Don't you agree, Sextus?"

"Sure, dear, whatever."

Quintus casually glanced back at the side of the vermilion coach to see Sextus staring out the window. His uncle seemed uninterested in the conversation as he watched the morning sun glisten on the river.

"I'm glad to see you taking this interest, Quintus." The intensity and determination in Julia's voice was unmistakable. "It's good to think about the future. There are great things in store for you. We're well known in the equite class, so you're in the right circles to make a political move." There was a brief pause, then she continued. "Your uncle missed his calling a number of years ago. But you're still young. You have the opportunity to do more."

"I missed no such calling." Sextus's voice was strong, but Quintus noticed he never looked away from the passing countryside. "The voice called to you, dear, not me." Quintus sensed that his uncle had had this discussion with Julia before and did not wish to have it again. But his aunt seemed determined to keep the conversation going.

"Face it, Sextus. We could have done so much more with our social standing. Even now, our friends push you to climb the political ladder here in Aquae Sulis and still you refuse."

"I'm very happy with our business and our standing in life. It's you who wants the glamour of high society, not me."

"Yes, because that's what it's all about, isn't it? Class is everything in the Empire. You know that as well as anyone."

"Yes. And that's exactly why I chose to move from the environs of Rome," Sextus responded. "High society and political office were not my aspirations. Nor are they my aspirations in the provinces."

Quintus glanced back in time to see Sextus break his gaze from the scenery and address Julia head on. "That was something *you* aspired to through me. I wanted no part of it and I have no regrets."

The silence coming from the coach told Quintus the discussion was over. While he had come to know Julia as a determined woman, he had never before heard her lock horns with her husband. He was intrigued by his aunt's political plans for Lucius. And knowing how fierce Lucius's ambition could be, Quintus had no doubt the scheming wretch would embrace and expand those plans.

The amphitheater was only two kilometers north of the town center, yet with the congestion it took almost thirty minutes to reach the site. The Viator coach and carts were waved through the outer ring of security by legionaries in polished armor. Wealthy families, merchants, and political figures were allowed to station their horses and carriages at secure positions near the arena walls. The groom steered his team to a shaded spot under a large oak tree. The slave carts followed.

Quintus's heart began pounding. He could feel the energy in the air. He felt alive again. Though this facility was half the size of the Amphitheater of

Taurus in Rome, he discovered that the excitement of an arena on game day was the same, whether in the capital or in the provinces.

Quintus and Dida jumped down from their bench and opened the coach door. Julia stepped out, followed by Sextus and then Lucius, who made a point of ignoring Quintus. The family headed for the main stairs, followed by the chosen servants at a discreet distance. The servants' anticipation was evident in the animated hand gestures and loud laughter. The old groom was the last to go.

"Keep a good eye on the horses, Grumbles." He then glanced up into the immense oak tree above the coach. "You know, you do have another eye. If I were thirty years younger I might use it to watch the games from up in this tree. Looks like a pretty good view." He smiled, then made his way to the entrance stairs.

Quintus was way ahead of him. He had not only scrutinized the tree, but had already selected the branch on which he would spend the rest of the day. He first checked all four sets of reins to see that they were secured to the lower branches. He grabbed two buckets from the cargo carts and trotted down to the river's edge. He wanted the horses well watered before he climbed the tall tree. He decided to spend a few minutes brushing down the mares and cleaning the mud from the side of the coach, just to show he was mindful of his responsibilities. But the deeds came to an abrupt end with the blare of the trumpets. In a moment, Quintus was ten meters in the air, comfortably situated in the crotch of two thick branches.

The view was magnificent, if a bit higher than Quintus was used to. He noticed the arena floor was about ten meters lower than the outside ground level, indicating the reason this site had been chosen for the amphitheater. A natural depression in the earth was exploited to allow more tiered seating without having to build a towering structure. The ten thousand spectators climbed a staircase outside the arena, which brought them in at the top tier. The servants, slaves, and poor jostled for seats in the upper rows, while the patricians and politicians worked their way down to the best seats near the arena wall.

The soldiers of the Second Augusta and Twentieth Valeria Legions in their crimson tunics were seated along the mid-level rows. Their grouped presence produced a wide red band that ran fully around the arena, creating a visible separation between the upper and lower classes. Without their games, especially in these remote provinces, a cohort of legionaries could become a disgruntled lot.

Quintus scanned the arena and spotted Sextus in his royal blue pallium. The family was still making their way down the aisle toward their seats, stopping every few steps to greet a friend or customer.

Lucius trailed behind as Julia and Sextus proceeded through their usual lengthy entrance ritual. He glanced with trepidation at the sand-covered floor of the arena. He wondered how close to the death and carnage they would be sitting.

"I see it takes you a while to get to your seats," Lucius said, attempting to keep the growing nervousness out of his voice.

"Not to worry. Our seats are secure," Julia answered between hugs and false kisses. "You know, being seen at the games is as important as seeing the games. It's not often that so many influential people are gathered in one spot like this. Why not take advantage?"

Sextus worked a few jokes into his conversation with a wealthy older woman, as Julia and Lucius descended another few steps down the stairway.

"Oh hello, Macro. Let me introduce you to my nephew, Quintus." Julia looked over her shoulder at Lucius. "Macro is one of our best customers. I think he would be interested in the Egyptian cotton we were just discussing." She spun back with a smile toward the handsome young Macro. "Quintus was suggesting we import a few bolts and have it dyed locally to create some colorful palliums."

"An excellent idea, Quintus," Macro said with a cheery smile. "You can count me in for a few of those. This town could do with some more color. Too much white everywhere for me."

Lucius nodded and smiled tightly. "I'll let you know as soon as they're available, Macro. Enjoy the games."

Julia gave Macro a wink, then turned her attention to finding their seats as they continued down the steps. The closer they got to the arena wall, the more nervous Lucius became. Having never been to the games in his life, he had never considered how he would react to the violence. He did not have the benefit of being hardened to the bloodshed and gore at an early age like the male children of the patrician class. Now, as they took their third row seats, he wondered how much of the carnage he would be able to stomach at such close quarters. He jumped as the trumpets blared again, announcing the parade of the gladiators.

"What is it, Quintus?" asked Julia. "Don't you enjoy the games?"

"Of course I enjoy the games," Lucius snapped.

Julia smiled. "Well, to be truthful, I don't like them much either. Entirely too bloody for my taste. But it's important to be seen here, so let's make the best of it."

VIII

August AD 64

QUINTUS'S HEART SKIPPED A BEAT as the arena tunnel doors swung open to reveal the blazing silver and gold of ceremonial armor. A deafening roar went up from the crowd. Within the confines of the horse stables, he had forgotten the pageantry of the pompa, the parade of the gladiators. The hunters and fighters entered the arena and circled close to the wall, allowing the spectators an intimate view to whet their appetite. Polished bronze and silver helmets adorned with plumes of purple and red covered the heads of some gladiators. Most had left their helmets off, looking to be recognized and cheered by their pockets of fans. Their bodies were impressive to men and women alike, their muscular physique accentuated by golden shoulder armor and leg guards glistening in the sunlight.

Behind the fighters walked slaves carrying the weapons of the day. At the head of the column a slave carried a bright yellow banner proclaiming Familia Gladiatoria Petra, indicating these were gladiators from the familia of the lanista Petra. There was not the military precision seen in Rome, but any gladiatorial contest with seasoned fighters was worth watching.

"Well, Master Petra," Quintus said out loud to himself in the tree branches, "I hope you've trained your hunters and fighters well."

"Why aren't you inside?"

The second voice in the tree startled Quintus. He hadn't noticed the small boy who had climbed up behind him and now sat a few meters away.

"What?"

"Why aren't you inside the arena? Why are you sitting in this tree?"

"I'm minding our horses."

"Oh. I'm cheering for the one with the big red plume on his helmet. I like his armor."

Quintus smiled at the cute little boy, with his dirty face and bushy brown hair. He looked to be about nine or ten years old. Judging by his soiled brown tunic, Quintus assumed he was either a poorly treated slave or a homeless guttersnipe who managed to keep a step ahead of the slave traders.

"A colorful plume is no way to pick a hero. Do you know how well he fights?"

"Nah. I just like his armor."

Quintus returned his attention to the arena. "We'll see. Perhaps you're right."

"I'm Decimus. What's your name?"

"I'm Grum . . . I'm Quintus." He hadn't said his true name in over a year. It felt good to introduce himself.

"These are pretty good seats, eh, Quintus?"

Quintus smiled at him. "Yeah, they're great."

"I've never seen a gladiator fight before."

"Well, you're in for quite a show. Of course, this is much smaller than the games at the Amphitheater of Taurus in Rome . . . "

"You've been to Rome?" the boy interrupted. "My mother used to speak to me of Rome. She said it's the biggest city in the whole world."

"Well, your mother was right." Quintus wondered how the boy survived if he spoke of his mother in past tense. Before he had an opportunity to question him, the crowd's cheering grew and the trumpets blared again. The participants had lined up in front of the games' editor, the local magistrate who was sponsoring the games. He was an older, thin man with a sickly face. Quintus counted thirty fighters. They raised their weapons in salute, then filed out of the arena as the attendants known as harenarii smoothed the sand for the first event.

"My mother didn't like the arena," Decimus said. "I remember she used to call the gladiators 'the dregs of society.' What's a dreg, anyway?"

Quintus was sure now that the child was an orphan, and one who longed for his mother. He knew the feeling well.

"A dreg is a not-so-nice person. Maybe she was right in some cases. But I've known gladiators who were some of the smartest and best men I've ever met. I'll show you a different side of these fighters before the day is out."

The trumpets announced the first event.

"Which gladiators will fight first?" Decimus asked.

"Actually, the gladiators won't fight until this afternoon. First there will be the venatio, the animal hunts. These can be just as exciting, although I don't know how good the venatores in this province are."

The boys watched from their perch as a tall, lean young man entered the arena alone. He was naked except for a red and white beaded choker and a small red loincloth that provided a trace of modesty. His oiled black skin was dramatic against the light arena sand. Braided hair hung to his shoulders, held clear of his face by a thin headband. He carried the long bow of the sagittarii, the archers. Attached to a wide strap slung across his chest was a quiver filled with arrows, their bunched white feathers looking like a small bird at his side. Based on the rousing reception from the crowd, Quintus assumed he was a local favorite. As the hunter reached the arena center, a door next to the entrance tunnel was thrown open. Out ran three large black boars.

"Whoa! Look at the tusks on those things!" Decimus shouted over the crowd.

"A boar can be one of the most ferocious fighters in the arena. If they feel trapped, few animals can match their aggression." Quintus was always happy to provide a commentary on the games to anyone who would listen. Here he had a captive audience.

The African hunter carefully watched the wild pigs sprint across the sand, one behind the other. They were large, easily reaching his waist. His eyes never left the beasts as he nocked his first arrow. He took aim and let fly a missile that struck the ground not three centimeters in front of the galloping pigs. With no chance to stop, the first pig tripped over the arrow, causing a rear-end collision with the second and third. The crowd roared with laughter. The lead boar spun and ran off in the opposite direction. The hunter fired again and did precisely the same thing.

"He's toying with them," Quintus explained. "He's a very good shot."

As if to prove Quintus's point, the venator began firing in rapid succession, herding the wild boars back and forth, zigzagging them between the obstacles he was planting precisely where he wanted across the arena. The crowd was on its feet, none cheering louder than the legionaries. The venator responded by turning his back on the enraged boars and taking a deep bow.

"That's a dangerous move," Quintus said. "An enraged and frustrated animal is very unpredictable."

The hunter seemed to sense the charge even though he could not see it. He dove to the right just as the giant maddened pig reached his back, tusks flailing up and down. The hunter rolled once and came up with another arrow nocked and ready to fire. Only the lead pig was attacking. The two others were holding their ground about ten meters behind. The boar halted its charge and stood defiant, staring down the hunter not three meters in front of him. The furious animal threw back piles of sand with his front feet in a threatening display, expelling a loud menacing grunt with each toss. The venator smiled. His white teeth flashed brilliantly against his black skin. He lowered his weapon and hunched over until his hands touched the sand.

"What's he doing?" Decimus asked. Quintus could not answer because he had never seen a venator perform like this before.

In a mocking motion, the hunter also began tossing handfuls of sand behind him, imitating the grunts of his adversary. The crowd went wild with laughter. The grunts emanating from the hunter were identical to that of the animal. Even a venatio novice could sense the confusion in the animal's movements. But survival instinct reigned and the boar charged. It took only a second for the animal to close the three-meter distance, but it was enough time for the hunter. From his crouching position he leaped straight into the air as the boar passed underneath him. At the apex of his flight, the venator re-nocked his arrow. The boar spun and continued its charge, head and tusks thrashing wildly from side to side. The hunter rolled forward as he landed and came up on one knee, facing the charging animal. He sighted down the shaft and fired. The metal point pierced the giant pig directly between the eyes, and the animal dropped dead at his feet.

"Wow! What a shot!" Decimus yelled.

Quintus did not hear him over his own cheering and that of ten thousand others.

The two remaining boars had been content to stand back and let the aggressor of the herd do the fighting. But seeing the animal now dead on the ground incited them to action. Remaining on one knee, the hunter spun in the sand to see the double threat coming at him from across the arena. Rather than attempting an evasive move, he sprang forward and ran directly at the two pigs charging him side by side.

"This venator is amazing," Quintus yelled over the rowdy crowd. "He does the opposite of what the animals are expecting him to do."

The open space closed quickly between the three adversaries. Just as the boars lashed with their tusks, the hunter vaulted. His legs pumped wildly, as if running on thin air, until his bare feet landed squarely on the animals' backs. His momentum and pumping legs drove him down the boars' spines and off the tail end in a split second. The animals were as shocked as the spectators. The boars continued racing forward, gaining speed for another pass at their prey. They turned in a wide arc near the arena wall, looking much like an equine team pulling a chariot at the Circus Maximus. They passed in a cloud of dust directly in front of the Viator seats.

Quintus glanced from the charging animals up to where Lucius sat. He noticed that Lucius's attention was fixed on the blood pouring from the forehead of the twitching dead boar. Quintus smiled when he saw that Lucius's face bore the same pallid look as the days he spent seasick on the *Vesta*.

The hunter's voice brought Quintus's attention back to the arena.

"So you stay together always, my friends?" the black venator yelled at his two remaining adversaries. "Then together you will die!"

He drew the last arrow from his quiver. He seated the nock around the taut string and raised the bow. The boars had circled the arena wall and were now headed back in his direction. The hunter wavered for a moment then began running along the wall, this time away from the charging pigs. His legs became a blur. His long braided locks flowed out behind him. His speed seemed inhuman. Although he ran ahead of the boars, his confidant air indicated he was leading the animals into a trap rather than fleeing in fear. His two legs tore through the sand faster than their eight and he gained a substantial lead. But the boars were relentless.

The hunter began a war chant as he ran. The repetitive sounds were taken up by the crowd. The faster he ran, the louder the crowd's chanting became.

The boars continued to charge side by side showing no indication of tiring. The hunter's chant grew louder. He was now almost directly across the arena from the charging boars. But the animals hugged the wall in their blind rage and did not see the shorter angle of attack.

The hunter's mantra turned to a high-pitched cry as the crowd pumped their arms in time to the chanting. His cry suddenly ceased as he froze, took aim, and fired. He led the swift animals by exactly the right amount. The arrow passed completely through the inside boar and penetrated the overworked heart of the outside boar. Both animals dropped dead in their tracks.

The chanting of the crowd turned to a howl of pandemonium, the archers among the legionaries cheering the loudest. It was one of the finest displays of precision archery they had ever witnessed.

"Two with one shot!" cried Decimus.

Quintus was equally amazed. "That was quite an opening act. This venator belongs in Rome. He's too good for the provinces."

The hunter moved to the arena center, his bow raised high in victory, as the animal carcasses were dragged through the portal by the attendants. The editor waved him forward. The old magistrate's voice was weak, and at a distance Quintus had a hard time hearing what he said. He tossed the African a bag of gold and the crowd cheered vigorously as he exited through the tunnel.

"I missed the herald's introduction. What did he call him?" Quintus asked.

"I think he said his name was 'Lindani,'" the young boy answered.

"Well if the rest of the hunters are as good as ol' Lindani, this will be quite a show."

Five more hunt events followed the African's performance. Some hunters fought alone, others fought in pairs against a wide assortment of beasts. The final hunt pitted two venatores with long spears against a lioness, an unusual adversary in the northern province due to the scarcity of the over-hunted local lions and the expense of importing them from Africa. One of the hunters was mauled and had to be saved by his partner. Quintus felt none of the hunters showed the skill of the thin African.

As noontime arrived, there was a short break in the action. Quintus climbed down to water the horses once more, then shared with his small friend a loaf of bread Dida had given him for lunch. The sound of the trumpets called them back to their perches.

"Prepare yourself for some violent combat, Decimus," Quintus warned. "If you've not seen a gladiatorial contest before, it can take some getting used to."

"I've seen men's throats cut in the street for a few sesterces."

Quintus believed him. Life on the street was not easy anywhere in the Empire.

The grating at the tunnel doors opened and once again came the yellow banner proclaiming Petra's familia, followed by the gladiators. Quintus paid special attention to their movements and how the crowd reacted to each fighter.

"Look at the legionaries," he pointed out. "You can tell by their yelling who has wagered the most on which fighters. But you can also see there is respect for the skill of these arena warriors, even from members of the best-trained army in the world."

Rather than the gold and silver ornamental armor of the first parade, the fighters were now dressed in their fighting armor and held the weapons they would use in their matches. Some waved and posed for the crowd as they continued around the arena wall. The mob responded with cheers for their favorites and taunts for those they had bet against. From his viewpoint hovering above the arena, Quintus had a new perspective on the spectacle, one he had not seen while caught up in the frenzy from his seats in the Amphitheater of Taurus.

"It's interesting how so many people think of gladiators just as your mother did—the dregs of society," he said to his treemate. "Yet once inside the arena they are worshipped like gods. The dregs suddenly become the heroes. They are idolized by everyone, from the house slaves to the wealthiest business owners to the most powerful politicians."

The horns gave the signal to clear the arena and within minutes the first match was under way. On the sand, a retiarius with his net and trident dodged the blows of a secutor. A trainer stalked the outer edges of the sand acting as a referee. The long wooden rod in his hand assured that his fighters would put on a good show. Quintus could see the excitement in Decimus's eyes as he witnessed his first gladiatorial combat.

"The retiarius is a special type of fighter, different from every other gladiator," he explained to his novice companion. "He has almost no armor, so he can move quickly, but he is also the most vulnerable. The secutor fights with the gladius, the short sword in his right hand. That's where they got the name 'gladiator.' Also, look at the secutor's helmet. The eyeholes are tiny. That's to protect against the points of the trident, but it's also part of his disadvantage."

"His helmet is too plain. It has no plumes or designs."

"That's so he doesn't get it caught in the net. If his helmet was snagged, he could easily be pulled into the trident."

The crowd reacted with a cheer as the retiarius tossed his net. It missed its mark but the rope tied to his wrist allowed a fast retrieval. The secutor saw an opportunity and attacked, lunging with his gladius while remaining covered by his large shield. The first thrusts were knocked aside by quick parries with the trident. When the thrusts came too close and too quickly, the retiarius fled. The secutor was hot on his heels, although the heavy shield hampered his mobility.

"Why does he run? Why doesn't the crowd taunt him?" asked Decimus.

"Because that's the accepted fighting style of the retiarius. It's the secutor's job to chase him down."

The pursuit wound its way across the arena. When he sensed the secutor tiring, the retiarius spun and tossed his net again. This time the cast was more accurate and he ensnared the secutor.

"Good cast!" Quintus yelled. "He has his fish in the net!"

"I don't think the chaser sees it that way!" Decimus answered.

In a split second, the secutor had his fighting arm free from the net and turned the successful cast against the retiarius. Swinging his large shield, which was caught under the net, the secutor began dragging the retiarius closer toward him. With the net rope tied firmly to his wrist, the retiarius was helpless to avoid being pulled in toward the tip of the gladius.

"Use the pugio!" Quintus was torn between yelling his advice to the participants and explaining the match to his treemate. "The retiarius has a small dagger called a pugio in his belt. He should toss his trident and cut the rope to free himself from the net."

By the time Quintus explained the strategy, the dagger was in the fighter's hand, his trident stuck deep in the sand next to him. But the secutor had anticipated the same strategy. He sliced at the dagger hand each time it was raised to cut the cord, preventing a quick escape by the retiarius. The two combatants were quite literally locked in a life-and death-struggle. The secutor began spinning, causing the retiarius to run circles around him or risk being knocked from his feet, the final step before a death blow. Just when he seemed about to lose his footing at top speed, a desperate slash of the pugio released him from the net. The sudden lack of tension on the rope caused the secutor, still partially wrapped in the mesh, to fall backward. The retiarius used the speed he had built up to snatch his trident from the sand at a dead run and straddle his fallen opponent before he could recover. He raised the trident high and brought it down on the man's shoulder, pinning him to the floor. A scream of pain echoed through the arena until it was drowned by the cry of the mob.

"That's it! The secutor is a dead man!" Decimus yelled.

"Not necessarily," Quintus responded. "Look at the crowd. They recommend life because he fought an aggressive battle."

All around the arena white handkerchiefs were waving, the sign of mercy. The editor stood and made a show of looking about the stands. He then dramatically withdrew a handkerchief from a fold in his white toga and waved it twice before his chest.

The retiarius released his grip on the long trident handle and raised his arms in victory. The crowd responded and the editor tossed a palm frond and a small bag of coins to the champion.

"I thought they always killed the loser," Decimus said, sounding disappointed.

"Actually, less than half the fights end in death. A good battle is rewarded on both sides. That's called a missio. One walks away with the palm of victory and a bag of gold. The other walks away with his life. Assuming of course he can still walk at all."

Arena attendants helped the secutor up from the sand, the trident still projecting from his shoulder. The barbs would need to be cut from the points protruding from his back before the weapon could be wrenched from his body.

"I doubt we'll see him fighting again anytime soon," Quintus said. "But this lanista, Petra, should be proud. He trains his men well. I wonder where his school is."

"I've heard there is a school near Glevum," Decimus said. "That might be his."

"Near Glevum? The port town at the end of this road?"

"Yes."

"How long has it been there?"

"I don't know. I've just heard when some of the Celts and Britons have been arrested, they've been sentenced to the school at Glevum."

Quintus had assumed these fighters were brought in from a much bigger settlement, such as Londinium, or from across the channel at the schools in Gaul. He had never considered that there was a gladiator school here in southwestern Britannia.

The bouts went on well into the afternoon. With every hour, the grow-ing heat from the summer sun took its toll on gladiator and spectator alike. Attendants were kept busy carrying unconscious bodies from both the sand and the packed arena seats. No sooner did a seat empty, than it was filled again from the line waiting outside. Quintus and Decimus were happy for their cool, uncrowded viewing spot, although a few others had discovered the tree seats and joined them in the branches.

Throughout the day, Quintus had kept an eye on Lucius in the cavea next to Julia and Sextus. Even at a distance he could see Lucius's face grow paler as each geyser of blood stained the arena floor. He could not help feeling elated that, between the heat, the blood, and the growing stench of death, Lucius was not stomaching his first games well.

Quintus continued to teach his young companion the intricacies of the con-tests as hoplomachus fought thraex, provocator faced provacator, and thraex battled murmillo. Some ended in death, others in missio. To Quintus, each bout further reinforced how much he loved the games.

The final battle of the day had a muscular, seasoned Thracian facing a broad-shouldered hoplomachus. The struggle began with unbridled intensity as the two traded blow after blow without a break. Early on, the hoploma-chus's gladius cut a deep gash through his opponent's right arm, turning the white of his padded manica to a wet crimson. But the thraex fought on without faltering.

"These men fight well," Quintus said. "I ask you . . . who cannot admire these warriors?"

The metallic sound bounced through the amphitheater as sica met shield and gladius struck parmula.

"Whether they choose to be there in the arena or not, they face each other bravely for our enjoyment."

The hoplomachus slashed wildly at his opponent. The thraex was more calculated, each blow measured to deliver death.

"They're ready to give up their lives, yet they seek only the admiration of the crowd and a few coins of gold."

The hoplomachus lost his small round shield. The thraex pounded mercilessly with his sica.

"This is the ultimate test of courage before you right now, Decimus."

The hoplomachus stumbled and fell backward.

"Where else is there such courage?"

The Thracian was on him with sword at throat.

"Who else combines such courage with discipline and cunning?"

The thraex received his instructions. Thumbs were turned. He lifted the hoplomachus by the crest of his helmet, pressed him against his own thigh, and plunged the sica into the back of his neck, severing his spinal column.

"That, Decimus, is what it's all about."

The thraex tossed down his sword and ripped the helmet from his head, revealing a bearded face, red with intensity. With arms stretching to the sky, he let out a piercing cry. Quintus was sure the roar of the crowd could be heard two kilometers away in Aquae Sulis. But he did not cheer. He simply watched the victorious champion standing alone in the sand of the arena.

Quintus's voice was suddenly a whisper. "That's me. There is my destiny."

IX

August AD 64

A NIGHT SEEMS ENDLESS when you cannot sleep, thought Quintus. He continued to stare at the dark ceiling of his slave quarters, waiting for the first streams of sunlight to find their way through the small window. The plan was set in his mind. All he needed was light.

He thought back to the end of the gladiatorial match at Aquae Sulis, when his future had suddenly laid out before him like a voyage track on a sea chart. It had been a sacred vision. He saw his new purpose, his new life, his new family. The gladiator school in Glevum. That was where he belonged. A part of Familia Gladiatoria Petra. The games he loved all his life would now give him back the life that had been taken from him.

He had considered leaving right after the bout, in the confusion of the crowd, catching a ride to Glevum on the gladiator carts. But that was not the time to approach the lanista, Petra. Besides, the Viators would have raised an alarm immediately. They would have spread the word of a runaway slave right there among their friends. The image of his crucifixion had flashed in his mind more than once throughout the night. But he had pushed it aside and plotted the details of his plan carefully. Now, he was ready. He needed only the morning sun.

He closed his eyes as he waited and another, more pleasing, image came back to him. He remembered watching Julia fan Lucius with her handkerchief as the games came to a close. The blood gush from the final death blow had proved too much for Lucius. He had passed out in his seat. Quintus smiled in the darkness as he replayed the scene over and over in his mind.

His next recollection was of being shaken awake, just like every morning, by one of the three slaves in his room. He sat up with a start and saw that the room was bright with sunlight. He couldn't believe he had actually fallen asleep just before sunrise. The most important day of his life and he had fallen asleep! He cursed himself as he threw on his work tunic and bounded down the hallway for breakfast. There were more people milling about now than his plan had anticipated. The thought crossed his mind that he should postpone his plans until tomorrow, but he quickly pushed it aside. Just one more day of the status quo would be unbearable now that he had seen a whole new life before him.

He deliberately slowed his eating so he could be alone in the meal room for just a few minutes. Once the last slave left, he tossed the leftover bread, cheese, and fruit into the small bag he had fashioned from a fragment of horse blanket. The bag's only other occupant was the small terra-cotta statue of the ship captain. He tucked the bag under his arm and casually walked to the stables as he did every morning.

He was glad to see no activity at the third stable building. He filled a bucket with grain, poured some into his cloth bag, and walked directly to Saturnia's stall. The mare welcomed him with a grunt and a shake of her head.

"Good morning, girl," he said quietly as he scratched at her nose. "We're both going to have an adventure today. I hope you're ready."

He placed the oats on a stool in front of her, then stopped as a new thought came to him. Although taking Saturnia was part of his plan, it suddenly occurred to him that he could lessen the chance of Sextus ordering a pursuit if he took one of the older, well-worn horses rather than a prized mare like Saturnia. He knew the value of a strong, well-trained draft horse far outweighed that of a common slave, especially when the horse was half of a matched pair.

He turned and dug in the corner of the stall until he retrieved his hand-crafted knife, which he placed in the bag with his food. He pushed Saturnia's head out of the way and grabbed the bucket of oats. She snorted loudly at the interruption.

"Sorry, girl. Change of plans. Keep well."

Quintus moved a few meters down the walkway and entered the stall of Ceres, one of the older mares used to pull the farming equipment. He placed the oat bucket on her stool and began gathering her bridle and riding blanket.

The horse whinnied at the unexpected early breakfast and her nose disappeared inside the bucket. Quintus worked quickly and quietly as he tossed the blanket up on her back.

"Why is this old nag going out first this morning?"

The sudden voice startled Quintus, but he kept working to present a picture of normalcy. He glanced over his shoulder and saw the tall foreman watching him from the passageway.

Quintus thought quickly. "Well, I figured since some of the others had a long pull into town yesterday, I'd give them a day off from exercise."

The foreman watched as Quintus slipped the bridle onto the horse's head.

Quintus kept up his cheerful façade. "You're ready to go, aren't you, girl? You're up for a little trot around the pasture, aren't you?"

As he turned to lead the horse from her stall, he saw that the foreman was gone. It was a safe bet he went to discuss the change in the workout schedule with Dida, the head groom. Quintus would need to move fast.

He secured his small bag around his waist, then walked Ceres a few meters down the bridle path. He scanned the surroundings to see who might be in the area with further questions about his actions. Deceiving a fellow slave or even an overseer uneducated in the keeping of horses was one thing. But he knew he would not be able to lie his way past the head groom or one of the senior stable hands. He also harbored a more personal reason to avoid the head groom. He had grown to like Dida, who was more easygoing than any of the other overseers at the villa. It was he who unknowingly gave Quintus the push to make this bold move by allowing him to go to the games. He felt he was betraying the old man's trust and benevolence. And he knew Dida would be seriously reprimanded for this escape, since Quintus worked under his dominion. The concerns weighed on Quintus's mind, but not heavily enough to alter his course.

Seeing no one in the area to challenge him, he grabbed a tuft of Ceres's mane and swung himself up onto the black riding blanket. He took the reins and nudged her gently with his heels. He wanted to keep the mare at a walk for the first few minutes so he did not arouse suspicion.

He thought back to the first day he had volunteered to exercise the horses and used it as an excuse to learn to ride. He knew someday the skill would help him with his dream of escape. As he kicked Ceres up to a trot, he realized that day was finally at hand.

He kept his gaze straight ahead to avoid eye contact with the few workers he passed. His peripheral vision told him that most never glanced up. The few that did went back to work without a question. Up the first hill he rode, past the barley field, and down into the small glen by the stream. He kept his ears open for the raising of any alarm. He heard none. Around the bend they moved, past the fenced cattle pasture. He was now into an area of the grounds he never used to exercise the horses. In fact, Quintus had been on this entranceway only once before, but Ceres knew the path well. She seemed happy not to be pulling heavy equipment and trotted along briskly. Quintus recognized the small bridge over the stream from yesterday. He realized he had only a few hundred more meters to the paved regional road. The horse's hoofs on the wooden bridge seemed excessively loud. He worked up the courage to look behind to see if anyone was following. He was alone.

The horse and rider cleared the tall poplar trees that lined the first hundred meters of the villa's entrance path and suddenly they were on the paved road. He pulled the mare to a stop. He listened again for any sign of alarm at the villa. He heard only the sound of birds and water rushing in the small stream.

"It's done," he said to his unwitting accomplice. "I'm free. We're both free. I can't believe it."

It all seemed too easy. The regional road was clear and he tugged the reins to the right. They stood for a moment facing north.

"Alright, girl. Once again the die is cast. I ask Minerva to grant me wisdom along this path."

He leaned forward and dug his heels into Ceres's side with a whoop. She bolted into a gallop. He wanted to howl with joy as the wind brushed his face and drove back his dark shoulder-length hair. He couldn't decide if it was the early morning sunlight or his euphoria that made the road ahead look paved in gold. As they galloped on, Quintus never looked back, for behind him lay a lost, dark year of his life, one of submission and servitude. Ahead of him lay the bright promise of a new family and a life of adulation and glory in the arena. His only hope was that Minerva had heard his prayer. Together he and Ceres disappeared over the first of a hundred hills between them and Glevum.

They reached the valley of Aquae Sulis after traveling for only a half hour. Without the cumbersome carriages and the road congestion from the games, they were able to make good time, much better than the day before. Although Quintus wanted to reach Glevum by nightfall, he slowed Ceres to a trot. He did not want to attract attention in this area where Sextus and Julia had so many acquaintances. The sight of a slave boy noisily galloping past the town gates would be too vivid a recollection once the questions and searching began. He passed the length of the town wall and continued north at the intersection, keeping Ceres at a slow trot, striving to look like a slave on an important errand.

In another few minutes they passed the arena. Workers were still piling and burning the refuse left behind by the previous day's crowd. He cast a proud eye on the structure and the large oak tree alongside. This was the place where his life had taken yet another unexpected turn. From here on, it was uncharted territory.

The surroundings soon changed from an open valley to a sparse forest. The road twisted and turned to follow the natural path cut by thousands of years of animal migrations. They passed a variety of intersections, some branching to smaller paved roads, others to dirt trails, but Quintus stuck to the main road. About twenty kilometers north of Aquae Sulis, they stopped at an isolated stream for water and a quick lunch, then pressed on along the dark forest road until they came to another wide valley. In the center was the small town of Corinium. As he passed through the outer reaches of the town, Quintus again noted that the settlement had been established at a crossroads. Unfortunately for travelers unfamiliar with the area, none of the six roads were marked. There was a fair amount of horse and cart traffic at the junction, and Quintus shouted to two men riding side by side toward Corinium's town center.

"Can you tell me which road leads to Glevum?"

The men eyed Quintus suspiciously. "What would a slave boy traveling alone want in Glevum?" asked the larger man with a gruff voice.

"I have a message from my master to deliver to a ship's captain there. Now, which road do I take?" Quintus tried to appear annoyed that these men were impeding his important mission.

The two riders looked at each other and pulled their horses to a stop.

"Well, we wouldn't want to interfere with your vital duties, now would we? Keep heading north on that road there. But even if you hurry, I doubt you'll make it before nightfall."

The second rider began to laugh. "Yeah, you'd better watch yourself around here after dark, boy. Especially with a horse."

Ceres snorted, as if addressing the man's warning. Quintus leaned forward and scratched at her mane. "Let's go, girl." He gave the men a quick nod of thanks, then kicked the mare into a trot toward the northern road. Behind him, he heard the laughter of the two men fade away as they continued their ride into Corinium.

The pink sunset was a welcome relief from the summer heat and humidity. Quintus had plodded north for another two hours with no sign of Glevum. He began to wonder if the men had deliberately misguided him. Perhaps he shouldn't have been so curt, he thought. The combination of the ten-hour ride and the lack of sleep the night before was taking its toll on him. Ceres, too, was showing signs of weariness.

The next clearing revealed a small lake. Quintus decided it was a good place to spend the night. He rationed out some of the oats in his bag for Ceres. Once the mare was fed and watered, he cut a few slices of cheese for himself. The two shared an apple for dessert. He laid back in the tall grass, listening to the night creatures, and stared up at the starry sky.

"We may not have a roof over our heads, Ceres, but tonight we both sleep free. No chores, no overseers, and no cleaning up after you and Saturnia and your other friends. Go ahead. Shit all you want. I don't have to clean it up!"

Quintus laughed out loud at himself. It seemed like years since he had heard the sound of his own laughter. Ceres's ears twitched and she neighed. With a clear mind and high spirits, sleep came easily for Quintus. His dreams put him in the center of the Arena of Taurus in Rome where he did battle with gladiator after gladiator, vanquishing each with his mighty gladius of gold.

• • •

The sound of rustling came to Quintus's ears a split second before the sharp pain in his side.

"Come on! Get up, kid."

His eyes sprang open to see the shadowy figure rear back for another kick. He rolled quickly and avoided the second blow. Jumping to his feet, he reached behind and was relieved to feel his homemade knife still in his belt. Even in his drowsy state, Quintus had the presence of mind not to reveal the weapon. It might give him the advantage of surprise.

It took a moment to focus on the two figures in the dark. The smaller man, whose greasy pointed nose reminded Quintus of a weasel, stood laughing in front of him. The burly one held tight to Ceres's bridle a few meters behind.

"Settle down, kid. I just wanted to see if you had anything else of value before we rode off with your horse."

"I know you. You're the two from the crossroads at Corinium."

"The same," said the larger bandit holding Ceres. "You should watch who you take directions from. We couldn't help noticing your lovely mare here. She'll fetch us a few sesterces in Glevum."

The weasel reached for Quintus's bag, which lay where he had been sleeping. In a blur of motion, Quintus pulled the knife from his belt and flipped it end over end directly into the man's left hand, pinning it to the ground. The man let out a howl that startled the other bandit.

"What happened? What is it?" The burly thug had not seen the blade fly.

Quintus dove at the weasel. In a single fluid motion, he wrenched the weapon from the back of the man's hand, sliced upward, and came up facing the large man holding Ceres. He scanned the two bandits, waiting for another attack. But the weasel was preoccupied watching the thin red line that ran the length of his forearm slowly split open, revealing the tendons and bone underneath.

"He cut me! The son of a bitch cut me!"

In a frenzy, the weasel charged Quintus, who spun and prepared for the impact. A large hand grabbed Quintus's right wrist, yanked him out of the weasel's path, and twisted his arm up behind his back. Quintus hollered in pain. As the weasel's charge ended in the lake, the large bandit held Quintus tightly and used his free hand to pry the knife from the boy's fingers.

"Well, you're quite the fighter, aren't you?" he said menacingly into Quintus's ear.

The weasel's arms flailed as he tried to disengage himself from the sticky brown mud in the shallow lake. "Did you see that? He sliced my arm wide open. I never even saw the blade move!"

Quintus struggled to get out of the bandit's arm lock. Although he was strong for a boy of sixteen, the large bandit had him at a severe disadvantage.

"You won't get away with this. When my master finds his horse, you'll both be thrown to the lions. Better still, I hope they sentence you to the gladiator school. I'd love to meet you both again, face-to-face in the arena."

"Ohhh, I see. We have a gladiator on our hands here."

Quintus realized too late that he should not have mentioned the gladiator school.

The weasel, dripping wet with a vine draped over his shoulder, approached Quintus. He used his right hand to hold together the skin of his left forearm, but released it just long enough to deliver a hard blow to Quintus's stomach.

"Well, I say we turn our thumbs down and sentence our little gladiator here to death. How about you?" the weasel asked.

Quintus was doubled over in pain and gasping for air. Above him the thieves debated his fate.

"Hold on," the larger bandit said. "I wonder how much the gladiator school at Glevum pays for slaves with good fight in them."

"He's not big enough for gladiator school. I say we stick his head in that mud for a little while."

"Every gladiator isn't a giant, you know. And based on that slice he put in your arm with this little homemade knife, I'd say he can handle weapons pretty well."

The weasel jerked Quintus's head up by a handful of hair. Although still wheezing heavily, Quintus stared him down. An evil grin crossed the weasel's face.

"Yeah, alright. There's nothing I'd like to see more than this little asshole getting his prick sliced off in the arena by some barbarian."

X

August AD 64

WHAT DO YOU MEAN he's gone? He just took one of our horses and rode away?"

Lucius watched Sextus's face turn as red as the distant sunset out the window behind him. The knees of the head groom, Dida, visibly trembled as he stood before his master's desk. An all-day search had turned up no sign of the missing slave boy or the horse. There had never been a runaway slave from the villa before and Sextus seemed to be taking it as a personal insult.

"I'm very sorry, sir. I take full responsibility," Dida responded. He had not been present during the conversation between Quintus and the tall foreman that morning. But when the foreman had refused to take the blame, guilt fell automatically to the head groom's position.

Sextus grumbled something unintelligible and sent the groom away. He looked to Julia and Lucius seated on the backless chairs next to his desk.

"That boy was actually turning into a pretty good stable hand," Sextus said. "Why would he risk death as a runaway when he had a perfectly good life here?"

"I told you he was a strange one, Uncle. It's just as well he's gone." Lucius tried to hide his relief. Now he could stop worrying about Quintus returning to his room at night to place another blade at his back.

"I still can't believe he stole one of our damn horses," said Julia.

Lucius was quick to respond. "I wouldn't worry much about it. That mare was an old hag anyway. We have others that are getting up in years and can be put to work pulling the farm equipment. I say good riddance to the both of them."

Lucius studied Julia's elegant face as she glanced at her husband. He wanted desperately for them to give up the notion of a search for Quintus and the horse. He watched her expression change from aggravation to mild bemusement. After a few seconds she looked back at him.

"So what's your recommendation for making up the losses, Master Quintus?" she asked with a grin.

In that instant Lucius knew he was rid of his lifelong enemy forever. It was as if he had had those extra seconds on the beach to drown him along with his dim-witted bodyguard. Lucius was quick to return Julia's smile.

"I'll need time to consider it, Aunt Julia. But I already have some ideas on restructuring staff assignments for better efficiency. Give me a day or two to work out the details."

The sound of weapons clashing drifted over the tall whitewashed walls. The fighters were hard at work on their morning training when the two bandits arrived at the gates of the ludus gladiatori, the gladiator school outside of Glevum. Quintus sat quietly on Ceres, whose reins were held by the weasel. Although he did not like the circumstances, he was relieved that he was being hand delivered to the front door of his desired destination. He was also happy to see the yellow banner that hung alongside the large wooden gates reading Familia Gladiatoria Petra. This was indeed the troupe that had fought two days ago in Aquae Sulis, just as he had hoped.

The armed guard at the front gate returned. "Dominus Cassius Petra says he is a busy man. You'll need to come back another time."

"Look, we have someone here he's going to want to see. This slave is a tremendous fighter. And our price is reasonable."

The guard reluctantly went back inside through the small door beside the main gate. The façade reminded Quintus of a military fort.

They heard the scraping of a large bolt being drawn back and suddenly the gates swung open. To Quintus it was as if the Gates of Paradise were opening before him. The bandits nudged their horses forward and Ceres followed.

The entranceway led directly onto the main training ground, a large rectangular field forty meters wide by sixty meters long. The field was surrounded on three sides by a tiled colonnade supported by a line of Doric columns. Countless doors and passageways could be seen under the portico. Dominating the far end of the dirt plaza was an impressive statue of Hercules towering four meters over the heads of the fighters on the field. Quintus recognized its significance immediately. This was the personal god and protector of all gladiators. He could not take his eyes off the colossus. The design of the sculpture was exquisite, with the god's head and torso anchored proudly above a massive square block of marble. In his right hand he held a gladius and over his left shoulder was draped the skin of the Nemean lion. It was an impressive shrine for any gladiator looking to bolster his courage through divine inspiration.

The practice field held a seething mass of more than one hundred gladiators and venatores. Some fought one-on-one with wooden swords, others swung heavy swords against wooden posts and straw mannequins. Overseeing each area were the doctores, the personal trainers who specialized in the various fighting styles. Quintus could also see a number of armed guards pacing the shaded hallways under the portico. Slaves, kitchen staff, and armorers scurried past, attending to their own agenda. There seemed to be as many support personnel in the school as there were fighters.

The three visitors and their horses were left standing in the entranceway, ignored by the workers and fighters alike. From the expression on their faces and their twitchy eyes, Quintus could tell that the two small-time hoods were intimidated by the harsh, muscular men on the training field. They kept their mouths shut until an older bald man approached. His stocky build complemented the hard face, which surrounded a nose that had obviously been broken on many occasions and not once set correctly. He wore multiple scars on his arms and legs proudly, like battle decorations.

"I haven't got all day, ladies. What do you want?"

The two bandits looked at each other and dismounted.

"Are you Titus Cassius Petra, the lanista?"

"No . . . I'm Messalina the wood nymph," the man said in a gravelly voice. "Of course I'm Petra. What do you two assholes want?"

"We have a new recruit for you." The large bandit tried to sound equally tough, but it came across as a paltry act compared to the battle-hardened lanista.

Quintus watched the lanista lean to the side and look around the burly thug to study him atop Ceres. To his dismay, the lanista started to laugh.

"Why are you wasting my time?" The lanista turned to walk away, calling for the guards to remove the intruders. All three saw their hopes fading rapidly.

The weasel spoke up. "Wait, Petra!" A number of servants and fighters in the training area stopped to see who had been so disrespectful to their lanista. The weasel went on talking. "You have not seen this kid fight. Look at what he did to my arm!" He held up his left forearm, revealing a long cut held together with crude stitches he had sewn into his own skin, using his partner's long greasy hair as suture material. "His blade was a blur. I didn't even see him strike."

The lanista turned and walked back to the visitors. He stepped directly in front of the man who had just spoken. The flattened tip of his crooked nose met the pointed tip of the weasel's and his small black eyes bored holes in the man's skull.

"Within this school I am 'Dominus,' the lord and master. By Jupiter's holy ass, if you ever call me by my personal name again, I'll slit your throat. Do you understand me?"

Quintus couldn't help but grin. The weasel seemed petrified. He could not move his lips to answer.

"I'm sorry, Dominus. He meant no disrespect," interrupted the larger bandit. "We are unfamiliar with the customs of the familia gladiatoria."

The lanista stepped back and the weasel began to breathe again. Petra looked down at the man's forearm then up at Quintus.

"Did you do this, boy?"

"Yes, sir. They tried to steal my horse."

"So, you rob the boy then complain that he cut you. Is that it?"

The larger man answered. "No, Dominus. He's a runaway slave we captured. He has no owner's markings so we don't know where to return him. But my comrade is right. He has the speed of Mercury and the fighting spirit of Hercules. We felt he would be perfect for you."

The lanista looked again at Quintus.

"How old are you, boy?"

"Eighteen." Quintus figured he could easily pass for two years older than his actual age. He was concerned that he would be rejected outright at sixteen.

"I doubt it. He's too young for us." Once again Petra turned and began walking away. "Go peddle him in the slave market."

Quintus saw his dream being shattered before his eyes. He was not about to let these two idiot bandits ruin the plan he had set for himself. It was time to take control of his life again. He jumped from the back of the horse and ran to a nearby stand of wooden weapons. He grabbed one of the wooden practice swords and spun toward the lanista.

"Dominus! Do not send me away! I'll prove my worth right now. Pit me against any fighter on this field."

Petra stopped walking and looked at Quintus. His hard face showed surprise at the boy's reaction.

"Most slaves would be overjoyed to hear their sentence to a gladiator school was commuted," the lanista said. "It sounds like you *want* to be here. Are you not a runaway slave being sold against your will?"

"No, Dominus. I'm an orphan who seeks a new life as a gladiator. I was already on my way to your school when I was snatched up by these two."

Petra raised a gray eyebrow. He glanced behind him toward one of the doctores who had been training three men to fight as thraex. The instruction had ceased and all eyes were now on the episode at the front gate. The lanista nodded toward the Thracians. The doctore pushed the larger of the three trainees forward.

"Alright, junior," the trainer said to Quintus, "let's see what you can do against Flavius here."

Quintus tightened his grip on the rudis, the wooden practice sword he held in his right hand. Flavius dropped his small shield and helmet in the dirt and crouched into a defensive position, his curved wooden sica held securely. In his overeager impatience, Quintus charged the man before considering a strategy. The fighter took a step to the left, met Quintus's single thrust with an easy parry, then whacked the boy across his bottom with the flat side of his sword as he rushed past. The stroke sent Quintus sprawling into the dirt at the feet of the other Thracians. Laughter erupted from the training field. The hot streak of pain that burned across Quintus's buttocks was matched by the intense heat of embarrassment that flushed across his face. He sat there for a minute with the laughter ringing in his ears. Suddenly his father's voice came upon him as if his ghost stood just a meter away. *Never let an opponent see you upset, either from fear or emotion. It will give him the advantage.*

The lanista shook his head. "I hope you can do better than that, kid. Or else you're really wasting my time."

Quintus stood, studying his opponent for the first time. The man pranced about in a circle with a wide grin as the other fighters goaded him to give Quintus a good beating. He was a big man. Judging from the scars on his body, he had seen a few fights in the arena. Quintus knew the only way he could best the man was with speed. He approached cautiously this time. The Thracian's grin turned to an evil smile that told Quintus if he connected with another blow, it would inflict even more pain than was currently searing across the cheeks of his ass.

The rudis in Quintus's hand began to swing from side to side and in an instant he was face-to-face with the fighter, trading blows. The speed of the two wooden blades created a brownish blur. Without shields, the wooden swords were working as both offensive and defensive weapons. The fighters stood toe-to-toe, countering each other's attack thrusts with swift blocking maneuvers. The Thracian's blows became more fierce, but Quintus refused to surrender even a few centimeters of ground. He increased the power of his own thrusts and was startled to see his opponent take a half-step back. The subtle abdication gave Quintus the confidence he needed. He launched an assault of thrusts and ripostes that backed his opponent up to the shield and helmet that still lay on the ground where he had dropped them. Quintus made a quick lunge to the chest, sending his rival tumbling backward over the helmet and flat onto his back in the dirt. In a second, Quintus was on him with the blunt tip of his rudis pointed squarely at his opponent's throat. Trainers and trainees let out a loud cheer and applauded the boy for his impressive display.

The shock on the Thracian's face turned to a sneer. "Lucky move, kid," he whispered hoarsely. "If they match us again, you'll be sorry."

Quintus reached for the Thracian's hand to help him up. The embarrassed fighter smacked the boy's arm away and pulled himself up, prompting a new round of laughter among the fighters.

"Not bad, kid," said the lanista. He turned to the two bandits. "Alright, I'll take him. I'll give you one hundred sesterces."

Quintus's heart leaped in his chest.

The bandits looked at each other. The offer was more money than they could hope to steal from wayward travelers for the next month. But the weasel winked at the bigger thief and addressed the lanista.

"After a display like that, you insult us with an offer of a hundred sesterces?"

Petra approached the weasel again.

"Look, you fucking idiot, do you think I'm as stupid as you two are? You come in here with a kid you've obviously kidnapped, and then you think you're going to rob me like you tried to rob him? I'll tell you what . . . I've reconsidered my offer. For the one hundred sesterces, I'll now also take the horse."

The bigger thief jumped in before the deal got any worse.

"Fine, sir. The horse and the boy for one hundred sesterces." He then smacked the weasel hard on the back of the head. "He's right. You're a fucking idiot."

Petra called to the thraex trainer. "Julianus, collect one hundred sesterces from the accountant and bring it here. The rest of you ladies get back to work. Show's over."

Quintus's ears perked at the trainer's name. Julianus! Quintus had heard his name many times. He was a great Thracian fighter who had been awarded a laurel wreath and his freedom by Claudius at the amphitheater in Rome. This explained the high caliber of gladiators who had fought in Aquae Sulis two days ago.

Petra scanned the field. "Lindani!" he called out. A young black man with finely braided hair hanging to his shoulders dropped his hunting spear and jogged to Petra's side.

"Yes, Dominus?"

"Lindani, take our new playmate here to a cell in the recruits' quarters and get him settled."

"Yes, Dominus. And his duties?"

The old lanista looked Quintus up and down. "Bring him to the kitchens. We're short handed there right now. If he proves his worth, we'll get him out on the training field assisting the doctores in a few weeks."

"Yes, Dominus," said Lindani.

"What's your name, boy?" Petra asked before he was led away.

"I am Quintus Honorius Romanus."

"Oh, I see," Petra said in a mocking voice. "Well, here you're just 'Quintus.' Where did you learn to fight like that?"

"The basic attack positions were taught to me by my personal bodyguard, Aulus Libo." Quintus spun the rudis in his hand, mimicking Aulus's flashy move, then replaced it in the rack. He thought he detected a flash of recognition in the lanista's dark eyes. "The cunning was learned from attending every gladiator contest in Rome for three years before I came to Britannia."

Petra thought for a moment. "Personal bodyguard, huh? More likely from the other street urchins. Either way, you're in for a rude awakening here."

Lindani took Quintus by the arm and led him toward the barracks under the east portico. Quintus could feel the lanista's eyes still on him. He stopped and turned around. He saw that Julianus had returned with the money for the thieves.

"This is a smart thing you're doing, Dominus. That is money well spent. Someday I'll be the greatest gladiator in the Empire." Quintus had such conviction in his statement that the group stared at him for a moment.

"Yeah well, let's see if you can get past serving lunch first, eh, Hercules?" the lanista replied. He turned back to the two thieves. "Are you two assholes still here? Take your money and get out of my ludus. Now." The armed guards stepped forward to underscore Petra's order. The thieves were on their horses and out the gates within seconds, leaving Ceres behind.

Quintus felt a tug on his arm and he resumed his trip to the barracks. The Doric columns slid past as he and Lindani walked under the shade of the portico roof. The sounds of the training field filled the open hallway and sent a tingle down Quintus's spine.

"The new recruits' quarters are poor accommodations compared to the veterans, but it is shelter over your head." Quintus had a hard time understanding Lindani. In his Rome villa they had owned two slaves from Nubia, but Lindani's heavy accent was different.

"You're the one who fought the three boars the other day in Aquae Sulis,"

Quintas said. Lindani seemed surprised that he had seen the games. "That was an amazing display of artistry with a bow. How long have you been a venator?"

"I have hunted in Ethiopia since I was six. I have been in the service of Dominus Cassius Petra for eight months."

"The crowd loved you. That must be a wonderful feeling, to be adored by so many."

Lindani smiled. Quintus had forgotten how white his teeth appeared against his jet black skin. "It *is* a wonderful feeling. But the bag of coin is more wonderful, no? I will use it to buy my freedom someday."

The disparity struck Quintus immediately. Here he was, fighting to get into the school, and here was Lindani, fighting to get out.

"But don't you enjoy the challenge? Don't you enjoy the roar of the crowd?"

"Yes. But I enjoy life more. You are forgetting that at any minute your life can end in the sand. I had but a single arrow left against the boars. Had I missed the shot, they would have killed me for sure." Quintus looked across at his companion. Lindani grinned. "Good thing I never miss, eh?"

Quintus could feel Lindani studying him as they walked. "So you want to be a gladiator?" the venator finally asked. "Most who come do not want to be here."

"I know. But this is a life I've always dreamed about. I'll be the best in the Empire someday."

"That is a big task you set for yourself. I think first you should be concerned with keeping the rats out of your cell."

They arrived at the space that Quintus would now call home.

"You will take this cell," Lindani said. He pulled open a heavy wooden door revealing a small, dank cubicle about three meters square. The stench of urine and feces struck Quintus like heat from an oven. Other than a dirty straw mat on the floor, the room was bare. The reddish-brown walls were plastered smooth, except for where the surface was lacerated by the graffiti of previous residents. Amid the crude drawings and lewd phrases, an empty alcove was centered on one of the walls. A small grated opening in the upper part of the door let in the only natural light.

"As you move up in ranking, the cells get better," Lindani said after a few seconds. Quintus realized the disappointment must have been evident on his face. "This one belonged to one of the fighters killed at the games you saw in Aquae Sulis. Unfortunately many of the new recruits, especially the war prisoners, use their cell also as their latrine. I am sure you would rather use the real latrine, which is down that corridor."

This was far from the accommodations Quintus had anticipated for the heroes of the arena. But he saw the stark logic of it. The meager cells were a powerful incentive for novices to win bouts and improve their status in the ludus. He also did not want to make the same mistake he had made at the Viator villa. He was not about to earn a permanent reputation as a chronic complainer. His days as "Grumbles" were as far behind him as the cleaning of horse stables.

"This will be fine. What's that alcove for?"

"Many fighters and hunters bring their own personal icon to look over them during their time here. If you have one, place it there and it will always be near."

Quintus had the perfect occupant for the space. "Well, at least I'm in the school. I'll prove my abilities and be into the veterans' quarters in no time."

Lindani smiled at Quintus's optimism. "The dominus must already like what he sees. He has assigned you to the kitchen. Most of the new recruits start with latrine duty."

Quintus took the small bag from under his belt and tossed it onto the smelly straw mat, laying claim to the fetid cubicle. "Alright. I'm home. Which way to the kitchen?"

Lindani grinned again. "Come this way."

Quintus was impressed with Lindani. He guessed him to be only a few years older than he, with a sense of self confidence that rivaled his own. The venator was quiet and unassuming, yet always had a smile on his face.

He led Quintus across the practice field, passing directly in front of the statue of Hercules. Quintus studied the marble likeness as he passed. The detail in the god's face and the impressive workmanship in the Nemean lion pelt rivaled some of the finest statuary in Rome. Curiously, he noticed the marble was worn smooth across the right hand where it grasped the gladius.

A sudden roar from an attacking retiarius on the practice field caught his attention. The man had already ensnared a secutor in his net and was moving in with the blunted spear that substituted for his sharp trident during practice sessions. He caught his opponent square in the chest, knocking him to the floor and sending his large orange shield sliding across the dirt. A doctore rushed in to grab the retiarius's arm before he inflicted any further damage.

"Are the men treated fairly here, Lindani?"

"Well, they do not spare the whip or the rod with those who cause trouble. But those who work hard and learn are treated fairly. Remember, the dominus has a big investment here. He has to keep his fighters in good working order. He treats the veterans who have proven their ability and loyalty especially well."

The secutor was slow in getting up and two attendants responded immediately, helping him to his feet and inspecting the bruise that was beginning to grow on his chest. Quintus heard one of the fighters seated on the sidelines shouting insults at the injured man, the comments too harsh to be considered good-natured. The seated fighter had a white band tied around his upper chest. The three small bloodstains on the bandage at his shoulder told Quintus exactly who the man was.

"That's the secutor who was pinned to the ground with a trident in Aquae Sulis the other day. How is he up and about so quickly?"

"The dominus has some very good physicians. Their potions work magic. They manage to get the fighters back in the arena quickly. And his unctores, the masseuses, tone our bodies well. The food is also good. There is much barley and meat to bulk up the fighters."

"Do the men get along or is there competition among the fighters?"

Lindani thought for a minute before answering. "It is neither. You learn quickly here not to make close friends, for one day you may face that friend in combat in the arena. Yet there is also a bond among us like I have never seen before. We are all part of a special group. One day we are scorned and the next we are worshipped. That breeds a brotherhood like no place else in the Empire."

This was precisely the soul of the familia gladiatoria that Quintus wanted so desperately to know.

"Of course, the war prisoners still hate everyone here," Lindani continued. "And criminals are still criminals. So it is far from a happy little family."

Quintus had to smile at Lindani's nonchalance about life in the ludus. They entered the mess hall and walked down the central row between the long tables and into the busy kitchen.

"Lindani, have you finally brought me some decent help?" asked the overworked head cook. He and an assistant were mixing a large batch of cereal gruel. The old assistant was limited in his usefulness, having only one good arm. The other had no hand attached.

"Yes, sir. This is Quintus. The dominus says he is yours, at least for a while."

"Excellent. Quintus, you can start by cleaning out those pots. Then help us mix another batch of miselania for lunch."

"No problem. Is the well out back?" Quintus asked as he grabbed two of the large pots and headed at a trot for the doorway.

"Out the side door and around the corner," the cook answered.

As Quintus approached the door, he overhead the cook speaking to Lindani. "It's about time you brought me someone helpful, unlike this one-armed sloth." The sentence was punctuated with a crack as the cook smacked his old assistant in the head with a large wooden spoon.

"Yes," Lindani replied. "This is a good one. I can feel it."

The call for lock-down came shortly after sunset. The sound of heavy bolts being thrown echoed through the barracks as the prisoners-of-war and criminals were locked into their dingy cells. Lindani returned to the kitchen to escort Quintus back to the barracks. His entire first day had been spent learning his duties in the kitchen and cleaning the mess hall. While the work was less than challenging, his spirit soared.

"You will not be locked in your cell since you are a volunteer," Lindani explained as they crossed the dark practice field. "The lanista feels if you asked to be here, you are not going to try to escape. The best veterans are also allowed their freedom, but are expected to be in their cells by lock-down, unless they are being rented for the night."

"Your fighters are rented at night? What for?"

"All lanistae add to their income by renting their most popular fighters to rich women and couples at night. It is the best fantasy, eh? A long night of sex with a victorious gladiator. The fighters can make as much money for a night with a wealthy couple as they can for an arena bout. Same for the lanista."

Quintus had often heard lanistae referred to as "pimps," but he never realized the slander was literal. In his naïve, sheltered youth he had never considered the gladiators being used for anything but arena games. These night games were an added bonus, both for the fighters and the lanista.

Curiosity got the best of Quintus. "How about you? You get rented out a lot?"

Lindani's cackle of a laugh rose into the night sky. "Ah, Lindani never kiss and tell. But let us say that a skinny hunter is not as popular as a well-built gladiator."

They arrived at the new recruits' barracks and Lindani pulled open the door to Quintus's cell. Once again the nauseating stench hit them, but Quintus refused to acknowledge it.

"Try to breath through your mouth for a few nights until the smell disappears."

"I'll be fine. I'll see you in the morning. And thanks for breaking me in today."

Lindani smiled. "You will do well here. You have the right spirit."

The hunter shut the door and the echo of his light footsteps faded quickly to silence in the small cubicle. A few sparse rays of torchlight squeezed through the grated window in the door. Although no bolt was thrown, Quintus was suddenly overwhelmed by a feeling of gloom and claustrophobia. He closed his eyes for a few minutes and fought off the panic. This meager, filthy cell was certainly not what he had envisioned. Had he made the right decision in coming here? He pushed the thought from his mind. There was no second-guessing. He *had* made the right decision.

He laid back on the thin dirty mat which made his straw bed in the Viator villa seem like a luxury berth. He stared at the far wall. The dim torchlight from the hall illuminated the empty alcove. Quintus knew what would settle his nerves. He reached for his bag and withdrew the only item it still sheltered. He sat up and placed the tiny terra-cotta ship captain on the base of the alcove. The opening had been designed for a much bigger statue. But this tiny relic would be his sacred icon. This would be the image that would give him the strength to follow his dream.

But would it help keep him alive on the day he stepped into the arena?

XI

November AD 64

LEARNING THE LAYOUT and training operation kept Quintus enthusiastic and occupied for his first month at the ludus. He discovered early on that the few men who were at the school voluntarily, like himself, were afforded much more freedom and respect than the prisoners and condemned men who were pressed into fighting against their will.

By the second month he was volunteering for odd jobs in between preparing and serving meals for the fighters. His plan to aggressively seek ways to help out on the training ground was paying off. He became well liked by the staff for his willingness to take on any task, no matter how menial. Both the staff and the veteran fighters were also impressed with his voluntary participation in the grueling early morning exercises and strength workout.

By his ninth week he was spending his afternoons at the armory, assisting with the maintenance of the practice weapons while the armorers prepared for an upcoming bout in Glevum. He admired the extensive collection of metal weapons used in the games, which were never allowed to leave the walls of the armory except under escort by the armed guards. The stories of the Capua uprising led by Spartacus 137 years earlier lingered in the minds of lanistae throughout the Empire.

Now, after three months of menial work, Quintus was beginning to wonder if things were ever going to change. Was life at the gladiator school going to be any different than life as a villa slave? The servile labor was growing tiring. At what point would gladiator training begin? "Be patient, Quintus," Lindani would often say. "Your time will come. Do not be so eager to learn how to die."

Over the months, Quintus had grown close to Lindani. There was something about the young man he liked. Perhaps it was his easygoing attitude, or his friendly nature, or his gleaming smile. Since Lindani was a venator and Quintus would, hopefully, someday train as a gladiator, they never gave much thought to the unwritten rule of no friendships within the walls of the ludus. There was no chance they would ever face each other in the arena.

Quintus's 105th day at the school began like all the others: up early for the workout, assist with breakfast and cleanup, then onto the training field to help out wherever he could. On this morning he wandered to where three thraex were training against a murmillo. Outfitted and armed in the style of the fierce warriors from Thrace, the Roman province south of the Danube, the three fighters carried small, square parmula shields and curved, wooden sica swords. Their lightness and swiftness were countered by the murmillo's large scutum shield.

"Your parries need work, Flavius," yelled Julianus, the head trainer who also worked as the Thracian doctore. "That's why even Quintus here was able to knock you on your ass his first day." Quintus noted that Julianus often used the embarrassing beating to provoke some of his lazier gladiators to work harder. The more Quintus watched Julianus drill the men, the more he realized just how good a trainer he was.

Quintus put Julianus's age in his late thirties, although his tall frame was as solidly built as any of the younger fighters. His dark olive skin reflected many years of working on the open-air training field. His face was rugged, yet handsome, with an aquiline Roman nose and a thick crop of black hair that became curly as it dampened with sweat. The squint that seemed permanently etched on the right side of his face gave his fighters the impression they were always being scrutinized, even off the training field.

"Now again," Julianus yelled. "Be on guard . . . Attack!"

Flavius approached his sparring partner and their wooden swords went to work. A cloud of dust erupted around their bare feet as they shuffled and repositioned themselves to gain the advantage. Quintus was surprised to see the murmillo training without his helmet, although he understood why. The fighters often complained that training for hours in the confining head armor took its toll.

"Keep your parmula raised. What's the matter with you?" yelled Julianus. "Watch the press. Watch the press!"

It was too late. The murmillo pushed Flavius's sica aside and lunged toward his chest. In a delayed attempt to block the thrust, Flavius swung his parmula high in front of him. The unconventional move caught the murmillo square in the face. Without the protection of his helmet's visor, the cartilage in his nose snapped against the metal shield, sending a torrent of blood down his chin.

"Hold!" yelled Julianus. "Well, perhaps now you understand why our armorer spends time making helmets with visors. Physician!" he yelled across the practice field. Two medical attendants sprinted across the field and helped the injured fighter to the infirmary. This left the three Thracians with no sparring partner. Quintus saw an opportunity.

"Doctore! Allow me to help. I'd be honored to spar with these fine men, at least until their training partner returns."

"You've been itching for an opportunity like this, haven't you?" said Julianus. Quintus answered with only a smile. "Fine. Flavius, help him with his manica and fascia. And this time helmets will be worn."

The white quilted manica padding was strapped to his right arm and the twin fascia pads were strapped to his legs. Quintus was comfortable with the padding and the gladius, but he had never worn a murmillo's helmet and had never used the large scutum shield. The helmet was placed on his head and the chin strap secured. The claustrophobic feeling was immediate. Visibility through the two grated eyeholes was slightly better than he had anticipated, but there were no other openings in the helmet for ventilation or hearing. He became acutely aware of the echo of his own breathing.

Julianus handed him the scutum. He was familiar with its weight, having helped move the heavy shields around the field on many occasions. He was simply not sure how long he could do battle with this mass of wood, leather, and metal in his left hand. Quintus practiced some moves at the edge of the sparring area.

"Flavius, you've already had your ass kicked once by this young man. Masala, let's see what you can do here. Gladiators in position."

They both stepped forward and faced each other. Masala was larger than Flavius, and Quintus suddenly wondered if this was such a good idea. Quintus extended the bottom of the scutum out in front of him to protect his forward thigh, just as he had observed so many fighters doing over the past weeks. He held his gladius close to the right side of his shield, the blunted tip aimed directly at his opponent's head. Julianus gave the first signal.

"Be on guard . . . "

The fighters took a few tentative steps toward each other. Quintus figured he should just go for it. What was the worst that could happen? He'd get knocked around a bit. But he would be gaining experience. It had taken three months, but this was what he was here for.

" . . . Attack!"

Quintus came out fighting hard and immediately backed his opponent up three steps. He tried to fight as though the new foreign objects on his body did not exist. The helmet was easier to forget than the shield. He quickly realized that he would need to work on building upper body strength. The thraex fought back with determination and began to hold his ground. Quintus made an effective feint and advanced again with a series of powerful blows.

"Hold!" the trainer yelled. Both fighters immediately disengaged. Julianus looked at Quintus. "You need to slow down there, Hercules. You'll be dead tired in no time at that pace. Besides, I'm here to train these Thracians, not you. Work as a good sparring partner."

"Yes, sir. Sorry."

"Don't apologize. That was good fighting, especially for someone who's never fought as a murmillo before. Just do as I say. Now . . . Be on guard . . . Attack!"

Quintus concentrated on mixing up his attacks and throwing as much variety as he could against the Thracian. He knew that his form was not perfect and his technique was often sloppy, but he tried to make up for it with sheer determination. The periodic stand-downs called by Julianus to discuss strategy and form with the thraex gave Quintus time to catch his breath. After twenty minutes, the trainer swapped Thracians and brought the third man in against Quintus. They battled on and off for another fifteen minutes, but it became obvious that fatigue was draining the inexperienced sparring partner.

The large scutum was taking its toll on the muscles in his left arm.

The timing of the injured murmillo's return could not have been better. Julianus signaled his arrival with a loud laugh. The man made a peculiar sight, with a large white pad held across his nose by strips of linen wrapped around his head. Two smaller rolled linen strips protruded from his nostrils like misplaced fangs.

"You look like someone jammed a couple of flutes up your nose," laughed the unsympathetic trainer. "Put your helmet on and let's go. Quintus, give the flute man back his gear."

Quintus was exhilarated at having completed his first real training session. Although exhausted, he would have continued fighting until the sun went down if asked.

"Nice job, Quintus. Come see me later this afternoon."

Quintus wasn't sure if he heard Julianus correctly. See him? The head trainer? Could this be the break he'd been waiting for? It was going to be a long afternoon.

The venatores were lined up against the rear wall of the ludus. Quintus spotted Lindani right away. The back gates were opened and, flanked by two guards, the hunters filed out to the sprawling venator training field behind the school. Quintus joined them.

"I had my first training today."

Lindani seemed surprised. "I thought you were still mixing cereal and barley gruel in the kitchens."

"I am, but Julianus needed a sparring partner for the Thracians. I was in the right place at the right time. I did well, too, except I can barely lift my arm after swinging that damn scutum around for an eternity."

"Now you see why I prefer the bow and the hunting spear."

"Shut your mouths back there!" The voice came from the head venator trainer, a short, ill-tempered man despised by the hunters. "You think this is a social visit with the local whores? Get to work." The grizzled trainer turned to begin work with the spear hunters.

"Yes, Doctore." Lindani rolled his eyes at Quintus and prepared to fire first at the sagittarii range.

Quintus enjoyed watching the four assistants run this ingenious contraption. A set of ten wooden animal targets were attached to leather hinges on a series of timbers thirty meters downrange. The targets were made to pop up with ropes activated by the assistants. An eleventh wooden cutout of a full-size stag was built with wooden wheels that ran in two deep ruts on a lower timber. Using a different set of ropes, it could be pulled across the firing alley in front of the other animals. The sequence of events was known only to the assistants.

Quintus stepped back as Lindani readied himself. The young venator closed his eyes and took a deep breath. He slowly pulled an arrow from his quiver and set it in place against the bowstring. His eyes opened and he gave a quick nod.

The workers began pulling the ropes in their assigned sequence and Lindani began firing arrows. He reloaded a bow faster than any sagittarius Quintus had ever seen. As if he could sense the sequence, the arrows were in the air almost before each silhouette popped up. The stag was sent rolling across the firing alley and two arrows were in its head before it reached the opposite side. The remaining three targets were dispatched and the exercise was over in less than twenty seconds. Not a single arrow missed, each placed dead center in an animal's ribs.

"Well done, Lindani! That was amazing," Quintus said.

"They are just wood, no? It is the real animals that present the challenge." Something on top of one of the timbers seemed to catch Lindani's eye. "Ah, like this one," he said as he nocked a bonus arrow.

Quintus saw nothing until the arrow pinned a small field mouse to the wooden silhouette of an antelope. But the person who had the best view of the rodent's death throes was the middle-aged assistant who had entered the target area to retrieve the arrows. The mouse hung less than a meter from his head. He turned to look uprange at Lindani, his face contorted in a fit of rage.

"Are you crazy? You stupid son of a bitch! You almost killed me!" Before the words left his mouth he was charging up the firing alley, his face turning a deeper shade of crimson with each long step.

"Settle down," said Lindani with a wide grin. "It was not even close to you."

The small group of archers let out a chorus of yells and whistles as Lindani hopped and jumped with the grace of a gazelle, avoiding the worker's frantic punches. The laughter of the group rose louder than was prudent on a ludus training ground. In an instant, the venator trainer was in their midst. He raised his arm and Quintus saw a short black whip, each of the nine splayed leather strips tipped with a tiny metal ball. He brought it down hard across Lindani's back, knocking him to the ground. Again and again the metal slugs split the skin of the African's bare back. The beating continued until it was painfully obvious that the punishment far outweighed the crime. Quintus stepped forward to protest. Lindani's head snapped up, throwing his long braids back. The look on his face spoke clearly to Quintus: *Do not interfere. Keep your mouth shut.* But Quintus had to say something. He could not bear to see his friend beaten any longer.

"Doctore, please! He's had enough for—"

Before he finished the sentence, Quintus felt the lash of the whip across his face. The sting was so severe he spun and fell to his knees without realizing he was down. His jaw began to swell and blood welled in his mouth. Behind him he could hear more lashes raining down on Lindani's back. Finally the slap of leather against skin ended. Quintus tensed, fearing he would be next.

"Now, would anyone else like to have fun out here on my training ground?" growled the trainer. The group stood silent.

Quintus felt a hand grab the back of his tunic and he was yanked to his feet. The sadistic doctore looked hard into Quintus's swollen face.

"How about you, boy? Did you have something to say to me?" The splayed leather strips of the whip were shoved inches from his nose. He could see bits of Lindani's black skin and red blood stuck to the metal slugs. "Well?"

Quintus stared into the madman's eyes for a moment, a combination of fear and rage seething inside him. But he knew if he said another word he'd be beaten worse than Lindani. He broke his stare and looked at the ground. "No, Doctore. Nothing."

"Fine." He shoved Quintus backward. "Then get the fuck off my training field before I use your ass as an archer's target."

"Yes, Doctore."

"The rest of you get back to work. Now!"

Quintus glanced at Lindani who remained facedown on the ground, breathing heavily, bloody welts rising on his back. Quintus slithered away, spitting blood and rubbing his swollen jaw. He had seen men beaten at the school before. Almost every day. But they were the prisoners and the condemned men who did not want to fight. They were not his peaceful, unassuming friend. Perhaps if he had not been there for Lindani to impress, this never would have happened. The thought weighed heavily on him.

By midafternoon, the training circles began to break up and the fighters commenced their afternoon strength training. Quintus returned to the Thracian cluster as Julianus was dismissing his fighters for the day.

"What in Hades happened to you?"

The bleeding in Quintus's mouth had stopped, but the left side of his face was still bruised and swollen. "I made a mistake on the venator field. It's nothing."

"Well then, grab a sica. Let me see you go through the numbers."

Quintus had toyed with the curved sword and was familiar with the difference in its balance compared to the gladius. He assumed a defensive stance and stepped through the basic attack positions and moves that were taught to every new swordsman. Aulus had drilled Quintus on them many times in the garden of his villa peristyle in Rome.

"Well, you have the basics, although some of your positions are a bit sloppy. Here, suit up in the thraex armor and let's spar a bit."

Julianus tossed him the white arm and leg pads, along with a small square shield and a large helmet. Quintus was much more comfortable with the lighter parmula.

Julianus grabbed a gladius and scutum. He did not bother donning the pads or a helmet.

"You don't heed your own advice, Doctore? I doubt the physician wants to set two broken noses in one day." Quintus felt more relaxed and freer to speak, being alone with the trainer. He sensed Julianus liked him.

"Don't you worry about me. Be on guard . . . Attack!"

Quintus steadied himself and did not overreact to the command. He approached slowly, then swung his sica. He saw right away that Julianus was a much more able opponent than the three trainees. Each lunge, thrust, and cut was perfectly parried by the trainer.

"Keep that parmula up. Or do you want to give me the opportunity to do *this?*" On his final word, Julianus's sword streaked in and slapped Quintus hard on the shoulder. In an arena battle, it would have been a debilitating blow. Quintus was stunned at the older man's speed.

"Come on now, stay focused. Let's see how well you can parry with both sica and parmula."

The trainer lunged forward and began an aggressive advance. Quintus could not hold his line and began to retreat, delivering a few blows when the opportunity arose. On his sixth step backward, he stumbled. It was not a fall but it was enough of a fault to wind up with his opponent's gladius against his ribcage. Another arena death blow. Quintus let out a groan of frustration.

"Calm down, Quintus. Rule number one: Never let your opponent see he's shaken you."

The words came like a long-lost friend to Quintus and he lowered his sword.

"What's wrong? Be on guard."

"I'm sorry. It's just that I've heard those words before. Both from my father and from my friend, Aulus."

"It's good advice. You should heed it. Now be on guard."

They worked for another half hour, focusing first on defensive positions then on attack moves. Julianus stopped periodically, as he had with the Thracian gladiators, to adjust Quintus's sword position or to demonstrate a more effective technique. The time passed quickly.

"Shouldn't you be helping to cook the goat and mutton now?" Cassius Petra, the lanista, stood a few paces away, hands on his hips and a scowl across his aged face. Quintus glanced around and saw they were alone on the practice field, which meant there would soon be hundreds of fighters and staff workers descending on the mess hall.

"I'm sorry, Dominus. I lost track of the time." Quintus ripped the pads and helmet from his body and ran for the kitchen. The cook's bellow could be heard across the practice field when he finally laid eyes on his wayward assistant.

. . .

Cassius Petra watched his new young recruit sprint across the training ground.

"This kid is damn good, Dominus," Julianus said. "He fights better than men who have been here for a year."

"I agree," Petra answered without taking his eyes from Quintus. "That's why I bought him. But he's young. He has no strength."

"Is there anything stronger than the heart of a volunteer? Remember, he's here because he wants to be here."

The lanista studied the equipment strewn about the dirt for a moment. "So you think he's ready then?"

"I do." The reply came without the slightest hesitation. "He's a natural. With the right coaching, I feel he'll develop into one of our best fighters."

The lanista looked at the trainer. Julianus was his senior doctore. In his prime, he was one of the greatest Thracian fighters in any Roman arena. Petra knew he would trust this man with his life. Was there any reason he shouldn't trust his judgment on this issue?

"Fine. But let's get Glevum behind us first. Don't tell him anything until after the games next week."

"Very good, Dominus."

"And *you* tell the cook we're cutting back on his kitchen help again. That crazy old toad will take a butcher knife to me if I tell him. Have a gladius handy when you break the news."

Julianus smiled. "Yes, Dominus. Leave it to me."

It was dark when Quintus and the old one-handed kitchen assistant carried the dinner pots to the well. The torch flame cast dancing rays on the large iron vessels as they scrubbed them. In the silence, Quintus could not take his mind off the sight of Lindani lying on the training field.

"I heard your friend took a beating this afternoon," said the old man, as if reading Quintus's mind.

"Yes he did, and I'm still wondering if it was my fault." The welt on Quintus's jaw stung as he spoke, but he knew it was a minor ache compared to what Lindani must be feeling.

The old man looked over the rim of a large black kettle as he spoke. "From what I heard, it seems he decided to have some fun on the training ground. The doctore who trains the venatores is not one for jokes."

"I know. But if I hadn't been there, he wouldn't have been showing off. Now he lies in his cell bleeding."

The old man looked past Quintus. "Actually, he seems to be getting some fresh air."

Quintus turned and saw the unmistakable silhouette of Lindani approaching along the back wall of the kitchen, the gleam of his white teeth showing in the firelight before his dark body. Quintus dropped the pot and jumped up to inspect his friend's tattered back.

"How are you feeling?"

"The physician worked an ointment into the worst of the cuts. His poultice of ground comfrey leaves and cabbage works magic. I will live to fight more beasts. But you, my friend, must learn to stay out of such matters. I hope you learned never to question the action of a doctore again. You were lucky to get away with only a single blow."

Quintus returned to his crusty cooking pot. "And if it was me getting beaten like that, tell me you wouldn't have said something. " Lindani's silence helped Quintus make his point.

"I saw you getting a private fighting lesson this afternoon," the African finally said.

Quintus wondered how Lindani had recognized him under the Thracian helmet, then realized he was the only person on the field wearing an olive tunic rather than the traditional subligaculum loincloth.

"I didn't do as well against Julianus as I did against the trainees this afternoon. But I learned so much from him. He's an excellent trainer."

"His thraex fighters always do very well in the arena," said the old man. "He is one of the dominus's most trusted associates."

"So you are really going through with this?" asked Lindani.

"Through with what?"

"Through with this crazy idea of becoming a gladiator."

"Don't you start, too." Then Quintus looked at the old man. "Did you put him up to this?"

The old man shook his head. "No. But you know damn well I agree with him." He pushed the stump of his left arm at Quintus. "This could be your arm in a few months, boy. I was sentenced to become a gladiator for robbing a caravan many years ago. Once I got here, I too wanted the glory and adulation of the crowd. I too wanted to be a hero. I saw a great life here. But after just three fights, *this* is what I got. My net hand sliced cleanly from my body by a secutor. The crowd cheered. And because I fought well, they spared my life. But you know what? Within a moment, they had forgotten my name. They had forgotten all about me. I was just another bleeding body dragged from the sand. Now I live my final days washing pots and pans with my one hand. *That* is the reality of a gladiator's life—at least those who are spared from death." The old man returned to struggling with the pot. "But you don't want to listen. You're a pigheaded fool."

"And what of fighters like Julianus?" Quintus countered. "He had a long and glorious career in the arena. People adored him and he made an enormous amount of money. He was a favorite of the Emperor Claudius. He loved the arena so much he has returned to train others to win there."

The old man looked across the well at Quintus. "Yes, I can't deny that some have had success in the arena. But for every one whose name becomes enshrined, there are thousands each year who die in the sand or are left maimed like me and live their final years in poverty."

Quintus stared at the old man for a moment. "Then I will be that one in a thousand." His voice lacked any sense of doubt. There was no other outcome to his fate in the arena. There was nothing to worry about.

The old man looked at Lindani.

The African shrugged and smiled. "The man has a calling in his soul. Who are we to argue?"

The pots were ready for cooking once again, and Quintus helped the old man take them back to the kitchen. He returned to Lindani, and together they sat beneath one of the tall larch trees that lined the side wall. The crisp air of the autumn night provided a clear view of the heavens beyond the bare tree limbs.

"That really was an amazing shot today with that mouse," said Quintus. "I know that bastard doctore didn't teach you to shoot like that. Who taught you to hunt?"

"The elders of Axum."

"Is that your tribe? Where were you born?"

"In a small village near the Kingdom of Axum in Ethiopia, south of the land you call Nubia."

"You speak Latin well," Quintus said. "How does someone from Ethiopia come to learn the language of the Empire?"

"From the legionaries in Egypt and North Africa. Then, the dominus had one of the ludus slaves teach me to read and write."

"Does your name mean something in . . . What language did you speak?"

"Ge'ez. Yes, in Ge'ez 'Lindani' means 'he who is patient.'" The Ethiopian smiled. "It is not a name that would suit you well."

Quintus laughed. "Alright, so I push a bit to get where I want to be." He broke his gaze from the constellations and looked at Lindani. "This obviously isn't where you want to be. So what brought you here?"

"That, my friend, is a long story."

XII

November AD 64

THE DEEP BLUE of the cloudless sky presented a perfect contrast to the golden earth tones of the African plain. The warm breeze blew a succession of rolling waves though the tall grass that hid Lindani. He crouched motionless on the ground, all his senses perfectly tuned to his surroundings. He had been in the same position for more than four hours. As he waited, he contemplated his name: "He who is patient." He smiled to himself. Patience was more than a virtue on the African plain; it was the difference between death and survival.

He carefully scanned the rolling hills around him, using his ears and nose as well as his eyes. He thought back to his training by the elders. When he was only six, they would cover his eyes or plug his ears to sharpen his other senses. By eight he was able to detect the footsteps of a tiny dik-dik antelope from fifty meters away. But this was only part of what made him the best animal tracker and hunter in all of Ethiopia. Most of his abilities came on another level. Lindani knew it derived from the gods. He had developed an innate ability to know the beasts, to mimic them, to anticipate their moves, to think like them. The Axum chief had recognized the power when he was still young. Only once every hundred years did a boy exhibit the gift. Lindani was the chosen one. It did not take long for the Legend of Lindani to travel throughout Ethiopia and Nubia.

As the years passed, tales of this famed hunter reached the garrison of legionaries stationed in Egypt. Lindani's elephant hunts were always successful, and on one of his trips up the Korosko Road and the Nile to deliver ivory to Egypt, he was recruited by the Romans. They sent him west to Carthage on the North African coast. Besides keeping the peace in the southern Empire, it was the job of the Third Augusta Legion at Carthage to obtain beasts for the games of Rome. Frequent expeditions were mounted to keep the flow of exotic species streaming north from the African plains and rivers to the arenas of the Empire. The legionaries considered a hunter of Lindani's caliber an asset to the Empire. He was sought out and pressed into service, helping to gather beasts for the arena.

This was Lindani's third time leading a hunting party for the Romans. The spot he chose was downwind from an animal trail that led to a popular watering hole. Where the trail wound through a copse of trees, he had directed the installation of a well-camouflaged corral. Once the animals passed his spot, they would be chased into the trap. Lindani slowly reached down and felt for his hunting spear. He sensed the prey was near.

There was a rustling behind him. It took all his willpower to turn slowly rather than snap his head around. But he already knew the source of the noises. His gaze rested upon the two Roman soldiers in their dark red tunics seated a few meters behind him. They had been fidgeting all afternoon. He patiently motioned for quiet again. It was the fifth time in the past hour.

"How much longer do we have to sit here?" asked the optio from III Augusta. "My father didn't arrange for me to join the legions to bake in this African sun all day."

The young officer's voice was whispered, but to Lindani it might as well have been shouted from the hillside. He replied only with hand signals. *Sit tight. Remain quiet.*

"This is bullshit," said the younger, more fidgety, of the two soldiers.

Lindani's eyes grew wide, not because of their flagrant breach of hunting protocol, but because of a scent he suddenly detected in the breeze, which caressed his face.

"What's wrong with him?" whispered the optio.

Lindani slowly held up his hand and gave a terse shake of his head. His hand gestures reiterated the plan of circling behind their prey and driving it into the corral.

"Yes, yes we know, you fucking savage." The optio's voice was louder this time. "All we need is a fucking animal."

The fidgeting legionary readjusted to a kneeling position. "This is nuts. My legs are killing me." He stood up to stretch, his head clearing the crest of the tall grass. "There's nothing on this damn trail."

The roar of the large male lion standing just ten meters in front of him told him otherwise. The bare heads of the three lionesses standing behind the male drove home the legionary's peril. All four stood staring into his widening eyes.

Lindani's voice was low and calm as he continued to lay concealed in the brush. "Do not move. Remain absolutely still." He knew the hunters had just become the hunted.

The Roman's knees began to shake. The three females suddenly bolted. The quick movement made him whimper out loud. The male seemed to sense his fear and roared again, the sun glistening off its four lengthy canine teeth. The ferocious display was too much for the soldier. He turned and ran.

"Do not run!" Lindani yelled.

From where Lindani and the optio lay in the grass, the pounding of the lion's paws sounded as if it was coming right over the top of them. The optio began to shake violently, then he too jumped up to run. But he did not have a chance. As the lion charged through the tall grass, the new target of opportunity rose directly in front of it. The lion leaped and was on top of the young officer in a second, its fangs sinking deep into his bare neck. The optio's scream forced Lindani to his feet. He charged forward, the tip of his hunting spear parting the grass as he flew toward the lion.

"What's going on up there?" The voice was distant in Lindani's ears, as each running step brought him quickly toward the lion's hunched flank. It took him a moment to realize the screams and commotion had been heard by the centurion and soldiers stationed in the trees near the corral net. They would be charging up the hill at any moment.

Lindani's momentum drove the spear deep into the lion's side. The animal released its victim and spun to face the new threat. The sudden move jerked the spear from Lindani's hands, the long handle wobbling as it protruded from the cat's flank. With the optio's blood dripping from its giant fangs, the lion growled in the African's face. Lindani remained motionless, staring into the animal's angry yellow eyes. The Roman officer's moan caught the cat's attention and it plunged its teeth back into his neck. Lindani dove for the spear handle and wrenched it from the lion's body. The lion shook violently, then dropped the young officer and joined its mates, running back across the plain. As the optio's body hit the ground, Lindani watched the head roll free of the torso.

The heavy sound of footsteps coming up behind made him spin, spear at the ready. The fidgeting legionary was there. He had returned from his cowardly flight across the grass. Lindani watched his eyes dart nervously from the dead optio to the centurion running up the hill from the corral.

"I could have used your help," Lindani said.

The soldier continued to stare at the head of his optio, whose lifeless eyes still reflected the shock of what had happened.

"Your comrade would still be alive if you had not run."

The words seemed to register and the soldier studied Lindani for a moment. He suddenly snatched the weapon from the African's hands and slowly raised the bloody spear point.

"Over here! I need help!" he shouted.

The sounds of the ten running legionaries drifted up the hill.

"What are you doing?" Lindani asked.

The soldier ignored him. He called again to the troops. Lindani knew something terrible was going to come of this scene.

"What happened here?" yelled the centurion as he approached.

The soldier answered first. "Our great hunter here jumped up too soon. The lions were right in front of us and one of them jumped the optio. Our African friend panicked and did nothing, so I grabbed his spear and fought the beast off. But it was too late for Servius."

The centurion diverted his gaze from the severed head of his best deputy. He moved menacingly toward Lindani.

"You were hired to protect my men from these beasts, not get them killed."

"I did not get this man killed. The truth is much different from what you just heard."

The centurion moved closer to Lindani. "Are you calling my man a liar?

Do you expect me to take the word of an African savage over that of my own legionary?"

Lindani knew it was useless to argue.

"The last image I saw as a free man was the leering face of that young legionary whose impatience got his optio killed."

Quintus sat in rapt attention as Lindani finished his story. He was feeling the warm African sun in his mind and had not noticed how much colder the night air had become.

"So how did you end up here in Britannia?"

"I was sold at a slave market in North Africa as a venator. Dominus Petra also has a gladiator school near Carthage. The doctores from that troupe told Petra about me, and he had me shipped here to Britannia. Apparently there is a lack of good venatores in the north. I already knew the animals well, so I had only to learn the ways of the familia gladiatoria and I was in the arenas."

Quintus was struck by the parallels of their two stories.

"I, too, was betrayed into slavery by a devil looking to save his own skin." It was now Lindani's turn to listen as Quintus told his tale of sea storms, deception, slavery, and epiphany.

Lindani sat quietly for a while after Quintus had finished. "It seems we have much in common, you and I. There is great mystery in the ways of the gods. Perhaps we are a part of some larger plan."

The conversation was interrupted by the call for lock-down in the barracks. The two young men walked together in silence across the practice field. As they reached the portico, Quintus touched his friend's shoulder, careful not to contact the inflamed welts on his back.

"Hope your back feels better tomorrow."

Lindani smiled. "Not to worry. Everything is for a reason. If not for my beating today, maybe I would not hear your story, eh? Now I know there is another here like me. We understand each other."

Quintus watched the Ethiopian bounce down the corridor toward the venator cells. He wondered if Lindani ever saw a negative side to anything that happened to him.

• • •

During the next few days, Quintus spent every available minute observing the training sessions taught by Julianus. Even after his single one-on-one lesson with the doctore, he was able to recognize the mistakes being made by the trainees before Julianus stopped the sparring for instruction. He watched each day's session with a new intensity, but was becoming disappointed that Julianus allowed him no further personal training time. Quintus felt it was time to speak up. He approached Julianus one morning after breakfast.

"Doctore, have you spoken with the dominus about my fight training? When may I move from the kitchens into gladiator training?"

"The time's not yet right, Quintus. Be patient."

Here was another lesson in patience, Quintus thought. He was growing restless with these lessons in patience. What he sought were lessons in combat.

That afternoon the fighters were called to a meeting on the north end of the field in front of the statue of Hercules. Quintus had not seen a ludus assembly before. He stood to the side to observe. Petra mounted a small platform to address his familia. He was flanked by his staff of doctores and the few administrators who manned the operations office.

"Tomorrow we fight in Glevum," he began, his deep scratchy voice easily carrying across the field. "The magistrate is giving games to celebrate his fifth year of reelection to the post. It seems that as long as his income exceeds his bribes, the man will continue to be reelected." Quintus smiled to himself. It was interesting to see that the financial influence of elections was as flagrant in the provinces as in Rome itself. "I want good games, ladies. This is our home crowd and this magistrate is my best client. I will personally deal with any slackers tomorrow. Assuming you don't get your balls chopped off in the arena, I will cut them off and serve them to you for dinner upon our return. Do I make myself clear?"

A chorus of "Yes, Dominus!" erupted from the crowd, loud enough to make Quintus jump.

"Fine. Most of you know your rankings. You new maggots will only be fighting other new maggots. Fight well if you wish to move from your scum ranking of tirones to the glory of the highest ranking primus palus. Do you want out of your tiny shithole of a cell?"

"Yes, Dominus!" The chorus came from the green recruits, including Quintus.

"And do you want to be treated with more respect in my ludus?"

"Yes, Dominus!"

"Then it's very simple, ladies . . . Win."

Petra stepped from the platform and walked toward his office, leaving the final organization to his staff. Quintus was more impressed with Petra each time he saw him. There was a steadfast toughness about the old man, but also a strong sense of fairness. He ran his ludus by a simple rule: Do well and you will be treated well; do poorly and you will be treated poorly.

After some final instructions by Julianus, the men were dismissed. Quintus saw that rather than leave en masse, the men were lining up in front of the large statue. As they filed past, each touched the marble hand of Hercules where he held the gladius. Quintus realized now why that part of the statue had been worn flat. This was a tradition of good luck, a way of asking the patron god of gladiators to watch over each fighter in the next day's games. Many of the Roman fighters stopped to voice a brief prayer. The Germanic and Celtic prisoners of war who did not recognize the god as their own ran their hands quickly across the stone sword hilt and moved on.

"Quintus, come here." He recognized Julianus's voice. He sidestepped the stragglers while running to the platform.

"Yes, Doctore?"

"Quintus, I want you to carry the Thracian weaponry into the arena tomorrow. See the armorer for your instructions in the morning. Now help with setting up for the banquet." Julianus was pulled aside by one of the other trainers before Quintus could respond.

"Yes, sir," he mumbled to himself. The realization grew as he jogged toward the mess hall door. Tomorrow he would take his first steps on the floor of an arena. While it was true that the carrying of weapons in the parade was the job of a slave or an assistant, it was still considered an honor to be a part of the pompa.

A group of slaves was already moving the long dining tables outside onto the training field when Quintus arrived. It was interesting for him to see the backstage preparation of a special ritual in which he had participated as a spectator many times. The traditional games banquet was a unique opportunity for the public to walk among the gladiators and hunters while they ate what might be their final meal. With a small army of slaves, assistants, and new recruits laboring through the late afternoon, it took almost three hours to ready the feast.

As darkness fell, Quintus began lighting the dozens of tall torches that had been set in a wide circle around the banquet tables. Suddenly Lindani was there beside him in a scarlet robe.

"So you will be in the arena tomorrow, yet not risking death. That is a good situation," said the African.

Quintus smiled. "Hey, it's only carrying weapons, but it's a start. It beats cleaning horseshit out of stables."

"There is not much that does not beat cleaning horseshit out of stables, no?" Quintus laughed at Lindani's bizarre accent. "You had better go and cook my peacock tongues before you are in more trouble, eh?" Lindani said smiling.

"Yeah, the day you'll get peacock tongues is the day you're brought to Rome to fondle Nero's balls while he throws you scraps."

The two laughed together as the wooden gate was swung open and more than two hundred spectators made their way onto the school grounds. The junior fighters were already seated at some of the tables but the veterans, the crowd pleasers, timed their arrival to solicit the most applause. Some of the loudest cheering was in response to Lindani's entrance into the dramatically lit circle.

Quintus smiled as Lindani took a long theatrical bow, milking the adulation for a few moments. He was an impressive sight in his traditional native robe and beaded headband. But he shattered all sense of poised distinction when he looked slyly at Quintus and winked. It seemed Lindani could never take anything too seriously.

As he had done years ago with his father at these banquets, Quintus began trying to predict which of the fighters would be dead by this time tomorrow. But now this macabre fascination was different. Now he personally knew many of the fighters and hunters who sat at these tables. Suddenly it was like predicting death within his own family. Would it be Flavius, the Thracian he bested his first day here? Or perhaps one of the other thraex trainees with whom he had worked every day. His eyes continued to scan the tables until they fell on Lindani. Perhaps it would be Lindani. The thought made Quintus realize the wisdom of discouraging close friendships within the ludus walls. Anguish would come not only from the death of a friend at your own hand. The anguish would come simply from the death of a friend. Your companion, your confidant, your friend would still lie dead in the sand. He watched Lindani eat and the question would not leave his mind. Would this be his best friend's last meal?

XIII

November AD 64

T HE COOL MORNING AIR was thick with tension in the dark tunnel. Condensation dripped from the stone walls, making it even more
uncomfortable. Quintus could hear some of the men praying, while
others stood silently in line waiting for the arena doors to open. He glanced at
the men around him and wondered how many of the fatal predictions he had
made to himself the night before would prove accurate. He looked forward
and saw the only smiling face in the crowd watching him. Lindani winked
one of his blazing eyes and Quintus returned a tentative smile. He was nervous, not for himself, but for these other men who were about to do battle. He
fidgeted as the metal swords and Thracian helmet lying across his forearms
seemed to get heavier.

Lindani's form suddenly became a silhouette against a white light so
brilliant it caused Quintus to squint. A blare of trumpets accompanied the
opening of the oak doors and the line began to move forward slowly. It took
a minute for Quintus's eyes to adjust to the bright daylight. He could barely
make out the cheering mob of spectators that filled the stands through the
arched opening ahead of him. As he stepped through the entranceway, he felt
the cold wet stone under his bare feet turn to warm soft sand. The sensation
made him pause, causing the fighter behind to give him a firm shove. For the
first time, Quintus stood upon the sand of the arena.

His senses overloaded. The combination of crowd noise and brass trumpets
was deafening. The Glevum arena was bigger than the amphitheater at Aquae
Sulis, holding perhaps fifteen thousand spectators. The roar of the capacity
crowd sounded much different from the floor of the arena than from the seats.
Here, every bellowing mouth in the circular amphitheater was facing the

participants, creating a wall of sound like nothing he had ever heard.

After marching a quarter of the way around the arena, Quintus began to relax and enjoy the spectacle. He studied the cheering faces—mostly older in the front, gradually growing younger as the symmetrical tiers filed back toward the towering top rows. Adulation came from every level: the government, the patricians, the merchants, the military, and the rabble at the top. Many of the women screamed louder than the men. Some exposed themselves by lowering their tops or raising their stolas, enticing the veteran fighters with the rewards to be enjoyed on nights to come if they survived today's events.

As the procession reached the halfway mark, a feeling swept over Quintus, one he had never experienced before. These fifteen thousand people were cheering for his team, his familia. His pride rose to the point of tears, which he hoped could not be detected by the audience in the front rows. While he knew he only carried weapons and armor for today's games, he had never been prouder to be a part of anything than he was at that very moment. He knew that very soon this crowd would be cheering only for him.

Once the pompa ended, the games began promptly. For the first time, Quintus viewed the action from ground level, standing behind the grating that was lowered across the mouth of the entrance tunnel. Between bouts he assisted the doctores with prepping each hunter and fighter for combat.

As usual, Lindani opened the games, doing well against three more wild boars. He employed both hunting spear and bow to slay the animals one at a time. The final arrow was sent into the last boar while Lindani's head was deliberately turned in the opposite direction. Without even sighting his target, his shaft pierced dead-center into the animal's left flank. The boar dropped neatly alongside his two predecessors, creating a perfect line of three dead hogs in the center of the arena. Once again, Lindani proved to be a crowd favorite.

Five hunts were followed by seventeen gladiator bouts, a few with multiple participants. Julianus was kept busy refereeing most of the matches. From his vantage point in the entrance tunnel, Quintus was surprised to hear all the coaching the seasoned trainer provided the fighters during their bouts. It was one of the many fine points of the games impossible to experience from the cavea seats. In one contest, Julianus was forced to use his whipping rod on a new prisoner who refused to fight. It was a minor blemish on an otherwise fine day of games provided by the Familia Gladiatoria Petra.

As night fell, the troupe was in their transport carts headed back to the ludus on the outskirts of town. They had lost only five fighters and one inexperienced venator during the day's events. One of the fighters not making the return trip was Tyranus, a veteran murmillo of primus palus ranking. His defeat by a younger fighter was a surprise to everyone and his lack of enthusiasm in the arena that day resulted in an angry crowd calling for his blood. Quintus knew that Cassius Petra was equally angry. Although he was compensated for the loss by the magistrate, this was one less veteran fighter he would be able to charge good money for on future rosters. Such prospects always put lanistae in a bad mood.

As soon as the equipment carts were unloaded at the ludus armory, Quintus went in search of the lanista. His heart pounded with enthusiasm as he scoured the grounds. He found him huddled with Julianus on a bench behind the statue of Hercules. Based on Petra's irritated look, Quintus assumed they were discussing the loss of Tyranus. Julianus looked up at his approach. Quintus thought he detected a warning in the eyes of the trainer and realized at the last minute this was the wrong time to approach the temperamental lanista. But before he could leave, Petra turned and saw him.

"What do you want?" The tone was unmistakable. It was bad timing, but Quintus felt trapped into speaking up.

"I'm sorry to interrupt, Dominus. I just wanted a word with you about my future here."

"Why? The blood too much for you your first day down on the sand? You want out?"

"No, Dominus. Quite the opposite. I want to know when I may take the oath and begin my formal training."

Petra looked at Julianus. It was impossible for Quintus to read what either was thinking. There was an awkward silence. Quintus continued.

"On the sand today I realized I'm ready to dedicate my life to this challenge. And I know it's a difficult one. I know we returned tonight without six members of our troupe who died on the sand today. But I'll be a better fighter than they were. I know it. I can feel it."

There was more silence. Quintus felt perhaps it was better to stop speaking; let them consider his request in quiet. After what seemed an eternity, Petra spoke. He began with a curt shake of his head.

"No. You're not ready yet." Petra turned his back on Quintus and resumed his discussion with Julianus.

Quintus was stunned. All his hopes, plans, and dreams were shattered with one curt remark. He couldn't accept it.

"But, Dominus, I *am* ready," he boldly interrupted. "I'm ready to touch the hand of Hercules. I'm ready to fight for the crowd. I'm ready to put on a good show . . . "

"And are you ready to die?" Petra's anger reached the boiling point. He was on his feet and in Quintus's face. "Are you, boy? You're ready for all the glory, but *are you ready to die?*"

Quintus stood firm with the lanista's crooked nose against his own. As if sparring with a gladius in hand, he refused to surrender a centimeter of ground. Instead he looked up at the statue.

"If Hercules deems it so, then yes, I'm ready to die."

"Then *that* is why you will not fight. I don't want somebody who is ready to die. I want somebody who is ready to kill." Quintus realized he had given the wrong answer. "Can you do that, Quintus? Can you kill? Are you ready to look into another man's eyes and kill him? I don't know what your background is, and I don't really care. I can tell you were never a soldier, or a thief, or a murderer. You're far too smart for that. But I can also tell you've never killed before. Are you ready for that?"

The menacing tone of the lanista's voice put Quintus on edge. After the last mistake, he was unsure how to respond. He again looked up toward the statue hovering over Petra, as if imploring the god for the right answer. Petra angrily grabbed him by the jaw and forced him to look straight into his black eyes.

"Damn the gods! Forget that fucking statue and look at me!" Quintus was shocked at the lanista's sudden blasphemy. "These other men have no choice. They were all sentenced to be here or bought at slave markets. But you *do* have a choice. You volunteered to be here. And I'm giving you this one chance to walk out of here a free man, my one hundred sesterces be damned.

But if you decide to stay, I want you to look me in the eye and tell me that you are ready to kill a man in cold blood."

The candor of the words hit Quintus like a blow to the stomach. He could not respond. Petra released the firm grip on his face and turned to leave. "You sleep on that and come see me tomorrow. Then tell me if you're ready for the arena."

Julianus sat looking at Quintus for a moment, then rose and followed Petra. Quintus stood at the base of the statue, not knowing what to do, the lanista's words echoing in his ears. After a few moments he walked alone to his cell and shut the heavy door behind him.

For much of that night, Quintus lay awake on his straw mat. The torchlight filtering through his small window seemed to highlight a line of graffiti on the far wall. Quintus had read it countless times but never really understood it until that night. *"Ut quis quem vicerit occidat."* "Kill the vanquished whoever he may be." A single hesitation could cost him his life. This was not just sparring with blunt wooden weapons. This was life and death, and as Tyranus had learned that day, it is easy to die with one wrong move or a moment's hesitation. How many times had Quintus been hit with the wooden swords? What if they were sharpened metal? And what if *he* had the advantage? Could he do it? Could he kill, in cold blood, a vanquished opponent kneeling before him begging for mercy? It was no longer about the roar of the crowd. It was now about the taking of human life. That was the cold, hard reality of it all. And that was the part of becoming a gladiator he had yet to acknowledge.

The sun was a dull orange disk, still low behind the larch trees, as it filtered through the dawn fog. Quintus sat in the morning chill, his back propped against the wall beside the lanista's door. At the sound of the latch moving against the doorframe, he was on his feet. The coarse wood of the door gave way to the equally coarse face of the lanista. Quintus saw no hint of surprise as he stared into his bloodshot eyes for a moment.

"I can do this, Dominus. I'm ready." Quintus had practiced saying the words for an hour. He wanted no hint of naïve enthusiasm and no pretension, just a serious, even tone to his voice.

Petra nodded slowly. "Meet me at the statue when the sun clears the trees," he said as he walked away.

The words washed over Quintus like a bucket of cold spring water. He ran to the latrine, which he should have done an hour earlier but he had been afraid of missing Petra. He arrived back on the field as the first rays of sun lit the white marble face of Hercules. He stood alone at the base of the statue, enveloped in the thin fog that still lay upon the practice field. He heard the sound of feet approaching and, like two ghostly silhouettes, Petra and Julianus appeared. They approached with a stiff military bearing and positioned themselves at the base of the statue, facing Quintus. Julianus spoke first.

"Quintus Honorius Romanus. Are you ready to take the Gladiatorial Oath?"

The Gladiatorial Oath. The words caused a lump to form in Quintus's throat.

"I am."

Petra stepped forward. "Then repeat after me. 'I undertake . . .'"

There was no need to lead Quintus in the oath. He had already recited the words a hundred times to himself.

"'I undertake to be burnt by fire, to be bound in chains, to be beaten by rods, and to die by the sword.'"

Quintus saw a slight smile crease the face of the old lanista. Petra pulled a small bag from the fold of his cloak. "Even though I paid those two assholes a hundred sesterces for you, I'm considering you a volunteer. As such, you're entitled to the standard volunteer bonus of fifteen hundred sesterces." He handed the sack of coins to Quintus. "Don't spend it all on one whore." With that, Petra turned and headed toward the mess hall.

Quintus looked at Julianus. "I meant what I said about being the best some day. You'll not regret this."

"I know. We had already decided last week to start your training after the Glevum games. That episode last night was the dominus's way of being sure your commitment is complete."

Quintus smiled. "It's what I want."

Julianus slapped him on the shoulder. "Good. Get something to eat. You have a long day ahead of you."

The trainer walked away and Quintus was left alone at the base of the statue. After a moment he took a step forward, raised his arm, and touched the smooth hand of Hercules.

"So, what you seek is granted." The voice came from behind and Quintus turned to see Lindani emerge from the haze.

"Did you think I'd settle for anything less?" he said with a grin.

Even in the fog, Lindani's white teeth gleamed as he smiled. "No. Nothing less."

Quintus helped the cook and his one-handed assistant serve breakfast that morning, even though he had been officially promoted beyond that task. It was his way of saying good-bye to both the workers and the first stage of his life at the ludus.

Within two hours of taking the oath, Quintus was on the training field in a bright yellow subligaculum loincloth. He had made a small personal ceremony of discarding his olive slave tunic by rolling it into a tight bundle and holding it up to a hallway torch. He placed the burning fabric reverently on the floor of his cell under the alcove, where he and his terra-cotta ship captain watched it turn to a pile of black ash.

As part of his private ceremony he had made a vow. He had already told Petra and Julianus that he would be the best. Now he told himself. It was more than a matter of pride. A mere mediocre fighter, even if he won many of his bouts, always stood the chance of being sold or traded to another ludus. But the top fighters, the best of the best, were able to make their lanista a great deal of money. The chances of them being sold were slim. This was the status he would now achieve. He had already lost one family. He was not about to allow himself to lose another.

He was issued the yellow subligaculum by the supply office. It had taken him a good half hour to learn the technique of folding the cloth into the large triangle which was tied around the waist, pulled between the legs, and tucked tightly under the knot at the front. He wore the standard-issue uniform with pride as he stepped onto the training field, although no one other than Lindani had taken notice of his new wardrobe.

In spite of Quintus's natural talent, Julianus started him like all the green tiro fighters. He coached him through the numbers, correcting each foot placement and sword position. He sent Quintus to work against the palus, a two-meter high wooden post planted in a corner of the training field. An assistant doctore handed him a heavy metal sword and began stepping him through the palus routine. Quintus was more interested in the weighty sword than in learning to fight a wooden pole. He noticed that the edges and tip of the sword were filed blunt, a safety measure for both fighter and staff.

"Why is it so heavy?" he asked the assistant trainer. "I would never use anything this heavy in the arena."

"It builds up your arm strength. Work with that for a while then pick up a standard gladius or sica. It'll seem like a feather in your hand."

Quintus was glad to hear it. He had decided that his primary concentration should be on building upper body strength, the weakness he had recognized in his two earlier training bouts. He went to work on the palus, sending pieces of wood splintering off with each blow. The assistant trainer stepped in periodically to correct a move or strike position. Even in the cool November air, Quintus quickly worked up an intense sweat, but after a few hours he became bored working against the inanimate object.

"It's important you know these moves well before you begin sparring," the assistant warned.

"I know them. After lunch I'll return to Julianus's session."

The assistant trainer shrugged and moved on to another green recruit.

Quintus gulped down his lunch in minutes and was back on the training field before the rest of the trainees. He worked alone near Julianus's training area, eyes closed tightly and metal sword swinging slowly through the basic number positions against an imaginary palus.

"Back so soon?" Quintus opened his eyes to see Julianus standing next to him.

"Working against a wooden pole is not much of a challenge," Quintus said as he continued to step through the numbers.

"That's true. But it's an important part of the training. If your strikes and thrusts are not executed properly, the attacks are easily parried by an experienced fighter. Plus it helps build endurance. But if you feel you're ready to spar, let's get to it." Quintus knew that Julianus was the type of trainer who allowed his students just enough rope to hang themselves. His technique was to let the tiros make their own painful mistakes, then they'd learn to do things his way. Quintus was determined not to let that happen to him.

As the Thracian trainees returned from lunch, Julianus paired them up against some of the murmillo trainees for the afternoon sparring matches. Quintus watched each bout intently, absorbing every word uttered by Julianus. After a few hours, it was his turn to fight.

"Alright Hercules, let's see how much you learned fighting against that wooden pole."

Rather than pit Quintus against another trainee, Julianus himself strapped on the murmillo armor. As he worked, he described the style to Quintus and the other tiros.

"The murmillo was originally called the Samnite. There is a proud heritage there. After Samnium's defeat by Rome, the captured weapons and armor were used to equip the very first gladiators. So let's see if I can maneuver this big scutum shield against the speed of Quintus the thraex here."

They faced off in the crouched defensive position and Julianus gave the order.

"Be on guard . . . Attack."

Quintus came out swinging in a controlled, calculated opening assault. The wooden sica in his hand did feel as light as a feather after working with the heavy metal sword all morning.

"Concentrate on the basics," Julianus coached as they fought. "Nothing fancy right now."

Quintus advanced with a direct thrust. Julianus easily parried the wooden blade.

"Tip's too low. Get it up."

Quintus advanced again. Again Julianus parried.

"Come in over the scutum. Try it again."

For twenty minutes the two advanced and retreated, yet at no time did Quintus come close to touching Julianus with his blade. The trainer called "Hold" and Quintus was quick to remove his helmet in frustration.

"I countered every one of your attacks," Julianus pointed out. "They're good moves, but they need work. Now do you understand the purpose of working at the palus?"

Quintus nodded as he wiped the sweat from his brow with his forearm.

"That's it for today. I want everyone on their workouts. Quintus, let's get a routine set up for you."

The two worked out together for another hour, with Julianus setting up a challenging regimen for his newest fighter, designed to build his strength, endurance, and flexibility. The routine included leg lifts while holding two pails of water, the tossing of a heavy leather bag loaded with soil, and wrestling with his fellow tiros. Having gotten little sleep the night before, Quintus was tiring easily after his first full day of training. Julianus pulled him aside before dismissing the rest of the troupe.

"Go to the unctores' room. Let them massage some of the aches out of those muscles before the rest of the troupe gets down there."

Quintus welcomed the few minutes of total relaxation. While he had assisted in the massage rooms in the first weeks, he had never had the masseuses work their magic on him. Kitchen help was not entitled to such luxuries. Now as he laid on his table receiving what would become his daily rubdown, he thought about the fact that his days of replenishing the oils, cleaning the strigilis used to scrape the skin, and gathering the scrapings and used oils were over. The slaps on his back and shoulders, the kneading of the tense muscles, the smell of the scented oils made him feel he was lying in the midst of paradise on the Elysian Fields. From his table, he watched as a slave gathered the refuse. Hard as it was to believe, this slave was actually producing income for the lanista. The bits of scraped skin and the greasy, used oil he was gathering were bottled and sold as a restorative lotion to aging patrician women. The handsome profits were split between the lanista and the unctores. Quintus smiled as the oil scraped from his own skin was poured from the oil pan into a small bottle. He had not even experienced his first arena battle, yet here were his scrapings being sold to the public. Such was the mystique of the gladiator.

Quintus felt refreshed and rejuvenated as he sat with the rest of the troupe for dinner. It was the first time he had been allowed to join the masses for a meal since he had arrived at the ludus.

"So, for a change you eat with the rest of us," Lindani said, seated next to him.

"Now I can eat in peace instead of serving your skinny ass all the peacock tongues you can eat."

Lindani laughed. "I do not remember ever getting peacock tongues from you. They came from Nero as I fondled his little stones."

Thunder rolled in the distance as the two friends enjoyed their first meal together.

The rains came heavy that night, sending sheets of water across the muddy practice field. The sound of the raindrops against the roof and walls always had a strangely comforting effect on Cassius Petra. But as he laid in bed this night he continued to hear another sound mixed with the rainfall and thunder. It was a familiar rhythmic pounding, yet thoroughly out of place in the middle of the night. His curiosity at last overpowered his weariness, and he rose from his comfortable bed to open the door.

He found Julianus leaning against one of the columns in front of his quarters, dry under the portico roof that protected him from the storm. His back was to Petra as he gazed out into the rain.

"What the fuck are you doing? And what's all that banging?"

Julianus glanced over his shoulder, then turned back to the flooded practice field. "Take a look."

Petra stepped out the door and walked across the cold stone passageway to join Julianus at the column. In the distance he could make out a figure wielding one of the heavy metal practice swords against the palus in the midst of the downpour.

"Quintus."

Julianus nodded. "The kid's got grit. Today I told him he needed more work at the palus. I guess he couldn't wait until tomorrow."

Petra shook his head. "I've never seen anyone quite like this kid. He's the youngest I've ever taken into one of my schools, you know."

"He's the youngest I've ever trained. But he's like a sponge. He absorbs every word, every nuance of combat. It's like he's been training for years."

Petra stared into the rainstorm. "He has." He turned and walked back toward his quarters. "Get that stupid kid out of the rain and send him to his cell."

As he reached the door, Petra turned to watch Quintus take a few more controlled swings at the palus before Julianus reached him and ordered him back to his cell.

"You did good, Aulus," he mumbled to himself. Then he shut the door and went back to bed.

XIV

May AD 65

QUINTUS SPENT THE FOLLOWING months focused on two objectives: increasing his strength and improving his swordsmanship. Besides the instruction given him by Julianus and the other doctores at the ludus, he sought new sources for guidance. His freedom as a volunteer and the bonus money he was awarded gave him the opportunity to explore the nearby town of Glevum.

He rode Ceres into town and spent time at the local baths, talking about health and fitness with the personal trainers and unctores who serviced the wealthy citizens. Much of what he heard mirrored his training at the ludus, but every once in a while, he would glean some new morsel of information, increasing his insatiable thirst for knowledge.

He began to put the fresh advice into practice at the school. He developed his own system of strength training, modifying a cart yoke to hold an adjustable amount of weight, usually heavy rocks, which he pumped up and down or laid across his shoulders as he executed a series of squats. He built a low bench to allow himself a wider range of movement while lifting the weights. He got some of the guards to use their sharp weapons to clear off a thick horizontal branch on one of the larch trees. Each day he used it to pull himself up thirty times. He lifted buckets of soil and rocks, learning to curl his arms and wrists toward his chest for maximum effect. He even sought out the assistant venator trainer who had built the ingenious moving target contraption to develop a counter-lever system that allowed him to lift a bucket of heavy rocks by pushing a wooden beam with his legs.

His fellow fighters, especially the conservative veterans, ridiculed his novel devices. But after just a few months the results began to show on Quintus.

His shoulders became broader and his upper arms and legs almost doubled in circumference. The physician and unctores in the ludus massage rooms were amazed. They recommended to Petra that Quintus's devices and regimen be used by all the fighters.

Quintus had already offered the use of his apparatus to anyone who wanted to work with them, but few took advantage of the offer. He pressed Lindani especially hard, but the lanky African refused. It was speed and agility, rather than brawn and raw strength, that provided him with his arena victories. He did join Quintus on his morning runs, which had increased from a few laps around the practice field to mini-marathons through the surrounding hills.

As they returned from their ramble one spring morning, Petra assigned Quintus to the secutors.

"I was wondering when he'd get around to trying me out as a chaser," Quintus said as he walked with Lindani toward his new group. "I'm not going to like this style. There's no vision from the helmet and lugging that heavy shield while you're chasing down a retiarius doesn't look easy."

"Who ever said the life of an arena fighter was easy?" Lindani said with his broad smile.

"I like fighting as a thraex. And working with the net and trident as a retiarius was a challenge. But he had me fighting as a murmillo last week. Those damn scutums are just too much to deal with."

"The dominus sees promise in you. He wants to be sure you are in the right position to make him good money, eh?"

A stern call from the secutor doctore interrupted them. "What the fuck is this, a social banquet? Quintus, get your ass over here and get ready."

Quintus donned the leg and arm pads and secured his helmet. As he predicted, the two tiny eyeholes, just 35 millimeters across, severely limited his vision. He hefted the large shield, a full meter-and-a-half in height, and took his position opposite a nimble retiarius.

The doctore ran Quintus and three other tiros through a set of drills designed to ward off the toss of a retiarius's net. As their opponents tossed the retes, they practiced side jumps, quick retreats, and the preferred method of crouching while raising and slanting the large shields, causing the net to slide harmlessly over their heads. Quintus was glad his upper body strength had improved. A few months ago, the constant raising and lowering of the heavy shield would have drained his strength quickly. Now, hours into the exercise, his stamina was holding firm.

After the lunch break, they worked on parries against the trident, a quite different technique than parries against the sword. Quintus had apparently caught the eye of the trainer.

"Alright, enough drilling. It's time to spar. Quintus stand ready. Gracchus stand ready."

Quintus stood face to face with the nimble retiarius. Gracchus had survived his first two arena battles and performed reasonably well, although Quintus knew he was quick to retreat when the action became hot. Today he seemed more confident, being paired against a novice like Quintus.

"Be on guard," called the doctore. "Watch that rete, Quintus. Attack!"

The net began swinging at Gracchus's side and was soon raised over his head. Quintus tried his best to keep his eyes on both the net and the blunted points on the wooden trident. The tiny eyeholes of his helmet created an annoying black edge around Quintus's field of vision. But he was still able to see Gracchus's left arm muscles tense and he knew a toss was coming. As the rete flew forward, Quintus was already crouched with his shield raised.

"Good!" shouted the trainer. "Nice anticipation. Now counter."

Before Gracchus could recover the net with the retrieval cord that was tied to his wrist, Quintus lunged forward, his rudis a blur in the air. The retiarius parried the attack with his trident pole, then began a running retreat as he gathered his net for another throw. This was the part of fighting a retiarius Quintus hated. He drew a breath and took off after his opponent, lugging the large scutum as he ran. The agile retiarius, unhampered by heavy armor, easily outmaneuvered Quintus and was soon in position to attack again. He swung the net low and caught Quintus hard around the ankles as he charged. Quintus realized his mistake before he hit the ground, but it was too late. The short match ended with the wooden trident at his neck. He punched the ground in anger over his own stupidity.

"You're dead," yelled the doctore. "Now on your feet and try it again. And don't rush it this time. Wait until the time is right to make your move."

Quintus stood and faced the retiarius again. The smirk on Gracchus's face got Quintus's blood boiling. He was not about to let this man best him a second time.

"Attack!"

Quintus lunged first, causing Gracchus to jump back. But his trident thrust upward, barely missing Quintus's shoulder.

"Watch it. Don't get careless," came the trainer's voice.

The two circled and feinted attacks. The net sang as it was swung through the air faster and faster. Quintus forced his opponent's hand by charging. The rete flew. Quintus's heavy shield sprang up. Again the net slid off the scutum and dropped harmlessly behind him.

"Good! You learn quick," yelled the trainer.

In a flash, Quintus was upright and in pursuit of the retreating retiarius. Again the heavy shield and limited vision hindered the chase. Gracchus weaved from side to side as he ran, frustrating Quintus's ability to gain an advantage. The retiarius gathered his net, planted his foot on a sharp turn, and swung the weighted ends of the rete at Quintus's head. The lead weights glanced off his faceplate and Quintus was momentarily thankful for the smooth design of the secutor's helmet. He lunged again from behind the shield and caught Gracchus across the forearm with his rudis. In the arena, it might have been a debilitating blow. But just as Quintus felt he had finally gained the upper hand, Gracchus took off running again. Quintus cursed out loud and resumed the chase. They zigzagged through the dirt of the practice field, and again the heavy shield slowed Quintus down. His breathing was becoming labored and his head was spinning from a combination of the afternoon heat and total frustration. Gracchus must have sensed the situation, for he stopped short and resumed his attack. Quintus had the presence of mind to hurdle the low swing of the net this time, but he took another hard whack from the rete weights across his facemask. As he thrust forward with his rudis, the retiarius once again resumed his running retreat. Quintus hollered in frustration. He threw his large shield to the ground and took off in pursuit. Now he felt more in control, more equal to Gracchus's agility.

"Not a smart move, Quintus," Julianus yelled as he joined the secutor doctore on the sidelines. He had been watching the bout from a distance and moved in closer to witness the conclusion.

Gracchus spun on a tight turn and faced Quintus, a weapon readied in each hand. Quintus suddenly felt naked with only his short sword. In a second, the net was loose and flying toward him. His natural reaction was to duck, but without the protection of his shield, the rete formed a perfect dome over him as the weights hit the dirt. He struggled to free himself from the trap until he felt the rounded points of the wooden trident against his chest.

"Fuck!" Quintus yelled through the open squares of the net hanging over him like a wet blanket. "I'm not a secutor, Doctore. I can't just chase people around the arena. Fuck this!"

Julianus looked at the secutor trainer and shook his head. They released Quintus from the net and removed his helmet. As Quintus looked up, Julianus was right in his face, anger evident in his eyes.

"Let me tell you something. You need to channel that temper of yours against your opponent rather than against yourself. Otherwise it's not your opponent who's going to kill you in the arena. You're going to kill yourself."

Quintus wiped the sweat from his eyes and spat on the ground. But Julianus's last five words rang in his ears. That single statement, short and to the heart of the matter, struck a chord in Quintus. There was no question the head doctore was correct. He needed to channel his fire.

"The kid's doing well," Julianus said as he ripped another hunk of meat from the chicken leg in his hand.

Petra looked up over the lip of his soup bowl as he slurped the remnants of his vegetable broth. His head trainer sat across the small table from him in his quarters, where the two ate in private when there was business to discuss. He was anxious to hear an update on Quintus, but allowed Julianus to swallow before prompting him for more information.

"I was afraid his new bulk would affect his agility and slow his reaction time," said the lanista.

"Me, too," Julianus answered. "But I've seen a steady improvement in his swordsmanship and fighting technique. He's not much of a secutor or murmillo, but he can handle just about anything else."

Petra nodded in agreement. "His dedication is fierce. If I had fifty more like him I'd take on the Imperial school in Rome."

"Some of the other fighters are starting to take up his exercise methods. We may not have the best swordsmen in the Empire, but they'll be the biggest, meanest looking bastards in the arena."

Petra grunted a short laugh and pulled another roasted chicken off the pile on the serving tray. "Well, we'll find out soon enough. I got word today that the old magistrate at Aquae Sulis finally met the ferryman. He's dead."

"Don't tell me. How old was that cheap son of a bitch, about a hundred?"

"At least. Anyway, they'll be electing a new magistrate there soon. He'll probably call for games in a month or so to flex some muscle."

Petra stared at Julianus until the trainer looked up at him over his chicken leg. The squint in Julianus's right eye became more pronounced as he picked up on the lanista's thought. "And you want to know if the kid's ready yet . . . "

"I don't want to blow it, Juli. This kid's too valuable to us. I'm counting on him to provide us with a wealthy retirement someday. Is it too early to put him on the sand?"

Julianus ripped another piece of poultry off the bone with his teeth, then spoke in between swallows. "Well, if we don't, we'll never hear the end of it from him. This kid has the patience of a gnat."

"I don't care what *he* wants." Petra rarely had to raise his voice to his trusted assistant, but this was a different matter. He had a valuable asset to protect. As he looked across the table, he saw Julianus staring at him through narrow slits. Did the trainer sense there was something more? Julianus scratched idly at his hooked nose, leaving it shiny with chicken grease. Finally the awkward silence was broken.

"I'm just saying that his morale is incredible right now," Julianus continued. "With a volunteer, that fighting spirit is more valuable than training. I can train his mind and body, but I can't train his spirit."

Petra quietly considered the thought. They continued eating in silence for a few minutes. The lanista poured another cup of wine and took a long drink.

"Who would you put him up against?" he finally asked.

Julianus thought for a while. Even though the selection of opponents was not supposed to happen until a random drawing on the day of the games, all schools had ways of being certain that select fighters were paired.

"That's tougher than it seems. He's far too good to put against another green tiro. He'd be done with him in a few seconds and the crowd would feel cheated. Even if we told him to stretch it out, the mismatch would be obvious. On the other hand, he lacks any arena experience. So pitting him against a veteran is risky. If he chokes in front of the crowd, he's had it."

As he listened to the options, one point became obvious to Petra. "I'll tell you this. Find someone he won't mind killing."

Julianus stopped eating and looked at Petra.

"It's the one thing Quintus has never done," Petra continued. "He has never killed. He needs a *reason* to kill his first opponent."

After a moment, a smile crossed Julianus's face. "I know just the man."

Back to fighting as a thraex, Quintus had just completed an impressive assault against a veteran murmillo when a "Hold" was called across the entire practice field. He noticed that the small platform had been set up in front of the statue. That could mean only one thing. Games were being called. His heart pounded. The hunters and fighters gathered as Petra took the podium. This time, Quintus remained in the center of the crowd rather than moving to the perimeter. He was now an active part of this familia.

"It seems the old magistrate of Aquae Sulis is dead, may the gods watch over his soul."

The mention of the town's name sent a shiver down Quintus's spine.

"A new magistrate has been elected, and he's called for games to honor the occasion."

Excitement mixed with dread in Quintus's mind. Of all the arenas in Britannia why would his first fight have to be at Aquae Sulis? What of the Viators? Surely they would be there to honor the new magistrate. If Quintus was recognized there could be serious trouble. Not only was he a runaway slave, but a horse thief as well. He would need to keep his helmet on at all times, even during the pompa.

"Apparently this politician has some decent money," Petra continued. "He's hiring double the usual number of fighters from me and wants bigger beasts for the hunts. We will give this man a good show, right, ladies?"

A loud chorus of "Yes, Dominus!" rolled across the practice field.

"There's a good chance this man will become my new favorite client. So we will give him a *very* good show, right, ladies?"

"Yes, Dominus!"

"Must I remind you how slackers will be treated upon return to our ludus?"

"No, Dominus!"

"Alright then. We leave tomorrow."

Petra was replaced on the platform by Julianus, who began reading the roster of ninety fighters and hunters who would be traveling to Aquac Sulis.

"Valentinus . . . Didius . . . Memnon . . . "

Quintus's heart pounded faster as each name was read.

" . . . Roscius . . . Lindani . . . Flama . . . "

Why was he not being called?

" . . . Balbus . . . Castus . . . Quintus . . . "

The sound of his name was like a songbird's melody in his ears. Every bone in his body, every newly developed muscle in his solid frame was ready for this. And his confidence soared knowing that Petra and Julianus felt he was ready, too.

Before Julianus finished reciting all the names, a queue had formed in front of the statue. At the head of the line, Quintus said a short prayer and touched the worn marble hand of Hercules. Within two days he would know if the god's grace would help keep him alive.

XV

May AD 65

THE HOLDING CELLS under the Aquae Sulis arena were smaller than the ones in Glevum, but the warm May weather made them seem less dank and depressing. From his bench in a cramped cell, Quintus noticed that the troupe's guards had swelled in rank, he assumed to insure against prisoner escapes. Julianus entered the common area just outside the cell doors and began pairing the fighters based on the lottery that had just been held with the game organizers. A few last minute name swaps had assured the specific pairings he and Petra desired. The names were a murmur to Quintus, who was beginning to get a queasy feeling in his stomach. He fought back the nausea. He was determined not to succumb to something so foolish as "first-fight jitters."

"Quintus . . . " Julianus's voice suddenly became clear in his ears. " . . . will fight Memnon." Quintus knew the name. He scanned his cell but none of the faces matched. He surveyed the cells across the hall until his eyes locked with those of the heavy-set murmillo he recognized as Memnon. He had trained a few times with the man and recalled that he did not like him; nobody liked him. He was an unpolished brute of a fighter who enjoyed getting in an extra lunge after a "Hold" was called. Just last week the guards had to be called onto the practice field to break up a fight started by one of his late ripostes.

No, Quintus did not like him. But was he ready to kill him? The thought brought a new bout of nausea, which he dared not reveal. Instead, he thought about that critical night in November when Petra had challenged him. After long hours of soul searching in his ludus cell, he had finally rationalized the concept of taking another life in the arena. The majority of these men were either condemned to the ludus for committing some heinous crime or were prisoners of war. A few others, like himself, were volunteers. If he faced a condemned man, he would simply be exacting the justice sentenced on the man under the laws of the Empire. If he faced a war prisoner, he would be punishing his opponent for taking up arms against the Empire. And if he faced another volunteer like himself, the opponent knew the risks of glory and chose to face combat willingly. In any of the three cases, the killing would be justified to Quintus. Once he had etched that answer into his heart, he had responded to Petra with his simple declaration: "I'm ready."

But now the day had come when he had to put that justification into practice. He looked again through the bars across the hallway and studied Memnon. His opponent had not relinquished his visual hold on Quintus. His mouth seemed frozen in a perpetual sneer. From the evil in the man's eyes, Quintus realized he would need to shake any doubt from his mind, or not live to see another sunrise.

"Nothing to worry about," Lindani said, seated next to him on the bench. The African's quiet voice had a soothing effect on Quintus's nerves. "He has two wins only because he scared his opponents. The man is all bluff and no brains. Keep your head and it is an easy victory for you."

"Gladiators, on your feet." The order came from Julianus. "Queue up for the pompa." The sudden command caused Quintus to panic, not over the fight he would encounter but because he had forgotten to keep his helmet nearby. Should the Viators be in the cavea, he had to shield his identity or risk having the legionaries waiting to arrest him the moment he stepped out of the ring. The fighters were hustled from the cells and led up the long tunnel to the arena. As he walked toward the portal, Quintus looked frantically for the slaves and assistants carrying the armor. Suddenly there was a hand on his shoulder.

"Settle down, Quintus. What's wrong?" It was Julianus.

"Nothing, I'm fine. I just need my helmet."

Julianus's permanent squint became more pronounced. "Why do you want it for the pompa?"

Quintus looked Julianus directly in the eye. "Trust me, doctore. I need my helmet." As he hoped, the serious tone of his statement told Julianus to find his helmet. The queue crept closer to the doorway. Julianus called for the thraex armor bearer. The trumpets blared just outside the door. A young slave ran up the passageway, swords and helmet clinking loudly in his arms as he ran. Daylight streamed in as the door was pulled open. Quintus grabbed the golden helmet from the slave's arms and jammed it on his head. A second later he stepped through the portal onto the warm sand, his tall black-and-white horsehair plume brushing the crossbeam of the doorframe.

The cheering was muffled somewhat by the headgear but still impressive. Quintus took a few deep breaths and tried to relax behind his visor. As he began his walk, he studied the mob through the helmet's circular grating. For the first time, the crowd was cheering for *him*. He noticed two middle-aged noblewomen in the front row who seemed to be discussing his physique as he passed. One waved and squeezed her friend's right breast for him. He was disappointed that the visor blocked his appreciative smile.

"I think they wish to meet you after the games, no?" said Lindani as he followed behind Quintus, his golden yellow tribal robe flowing in the warm morning breeze.

"There's two. I'll share," he yelled over his shoulder.

He kept a watchful eye for the Viator family as he walked, focusing on the first few rows. He noticed a larger number of Celtic and Briton tribal chieftains in the lower seats than the last time he had surveyed the Aquae Sulis crowd from his tree perch. The oak tree! He looked up beyond the top tier of the arena and there was his viewing platform from last year. He studied the branches for a moment and could clearly make out the form of Decimus, his young treemate. He whispered a private hello, wondering how the boy would react if he knew he was one of the gladiators marching before him today.

As he relaxed and soaked in the adulation, he began to respond to the crowd's cheers with an occasional wave. When he looked up after a short bow, Julianus was next to him.

"This is what you've been waiting for, Quintus. Drink it in. It'll go to your head like wine."

"It already has," Quintus said through the visor holes. "And I'm loving it."

After a few more steps the pompa approached the covered podium seats. Quintus continued to scour the front rows for any sign of the Viators. He thought it odd that they would miss the first games of the new magistrate.

"Line up and bow to the magistrate and his sponsors," Julianus prompted.

The hunters and fighters assembled directly in front of the prime seats and prepared to offer homage to the officials. Quintus gave up trying to find the family and directed his attention to the podium. What he saw stunned him beyond words. There in the sponsor's seats sat Sextus Viator and his wife, Julia Melita. Between them, in the ornate magistrate's chair, sat Lucius.

As the fighters continued filing into line, Quintus heard one of the veteran murmillos speaking with Julianus.

"By the gods . . . They went from a crippled old prune to a snot-nosed teenager."

"He's supposed to be some kind of business genius," Julianus answered, keeping his voice low. "Even the representatives the dominus dealt with say he's a vulture. That's his uncle and aunt. They're worth millions, which I'm sure had something to do with his election."

Quintus was too shocked to speak. Julianus gave the order to bow, but Quintus stood transfixed until the trainer's hand connected with the backside of his helmet and jolted him out of his stupor. Julianus stepped up alongside him.

"Pay attention, Quintus. Don't be disrespectful to the man who pays our wages."

Sextus stood and waved the crowd to silence.

"Gentlemen and ladies, citizens of Rome, and our fine guests . . . We welcome you to the first games in a new era for Aquae Sulis." He paused for the anticipated applause, which came with enthusiasm.

Quintus could not take his eyes from Lucius. He had grown dramatically in the past year, not only in stature but in disposition. His bearing and mannerisms radiated a mature sense of self-importance. His curly brown hair was now neatly trimmed in the short style favored by upper-class citizens. The prominent brow over his deep-set brown eyes and wide nose gave him a serious, determined look. Quintus had to admit that, despite his young age of eighteen, he made an imposing figure seated in his white toga. Julia sat to his right, stunningly beautiful in her low-cut white stola, her hair much longer than Quintus remembered. Only his uncle looked the worse for their year apart, having added another fifteen or twenty pounds to his already ample frame.

"As most of you know," Sextus continued, "I have been asked on many occasions to run for office in our fine town." The roar of the crowd verified his standing with the patrician class. Quintus had not realized the extent of his uncle's popularity in the region. "But, unfortunately, my years are too advanced to grant me the energy needed for such a task." A few good-natured jeers arose from the crowd, which Sextus acknowledged with a smile. "However, I have no doubt that the new magistrate I have sponsored will guide the peaceful development of our beautiful town of Aquae Sulis into a jewel of the Roman Empire. I am most honored and proud to present to you my nephew . . . and the new magistrate of Aquae Sulis . . . Quintus Honorius Romanus!"

The crowd jumped to its feet cheering the new local leader. On the sand, Quintus could feel the eyes of Julianus and Lindani upon him even through the bronze helmet. He was sure that Petra was nearby with an equally puzzled gaze aimed in his direction.

"Is that magistrate's name just an amazing coincidence or do you have a good explanation for this?" Julianus asked in a low voice. "And does it have anything to do with you hiding under that helmet?"

Quintus turned and looked through the grating of his visor at Julianus. "It's a long story. I'll explain after the games."

"You'd better not die before I find out what's going on here."

"That's not going to happen." Quintus paused. "But if it does, see Lindani. He knows the story."

Quintus's mind raced as the pompa marched back to the entrance tunnel. The relaxed state he had attained under the cheers of the crowd was a distant memory, replaced by the nausea of extreme nervousness. This was an unexpected distraction he could do without on the day of his first arena battle.

"I'm not happy with this barbarian seated behind me," Lucius whispered to Julia from his ornate seat of honor. He watched her glance at the large man with his flowing brown hair and mustache to be sure he hadn't heard the comment. Lucius did not care if he did.

"We've gone over this," she whispered back through clenched teeth. "He's the chieftain of the largest Briton clan in the region. If you want to make a name for yourself in this province you need to pacify the local tribes. Yes, they're barbarians. But at least they're *our* barbarians."

"Well, I hope this open-arms policy of yours works. Really, Julia, sometimes you meddle more than Agrippina."

Lucius knew the comment would cut deep with Julia. Her admiration for Nero's intrusive mother was well known at the villa. He saw her glance at Sextus and when she saw her husband deep in discussion with business associates, she pulled her chair closer to Lucius.

"Let's not forget who put you here." Her voice was quiet but her words were fierce. "You know damned well it wasn't Sextus. The man is happy selling togas. If it wasn't for me, you wouldn't be sitting at the center of this podium. Do you know how many strings I had to pull to put someone of your age into the magistrate's office?"

Lucius could offer no argument. He knew every word was true, but the thought of this woman having so much control over his destiny was unsettling. This was a position he knew he could have attained on his own, but her impatience had accelerated his plans. He gave a curt nod. But Julia wasn't finished.

"And how dare you speak of our Emperor's late mother in such a tone. Agrippina should be a goddess. Without her guidance, Nero would be nothing. He *is* nothing now that she's gone. She orchestrated his rise to power and the ungrateful bastard had her killed. She's a martyr. There's not a woman in the Empire who shouldn't worship at her feet . . . "

"Alright, alright," Lucius interrupted. "Enough about the wonders of Agrippina. Let's not get carried away with the intrigue of politics only a few weeks into my term."

The patronizing look she gave him aggravated him all the more. For all her obvious charms, the woman could be frustratingly obstinate. But before the discussion could become any more heated, it was cut short by the trumpets heralding the hunts.

"So that is the scum who stole your soul?" Lindani asked as he and Quintus watched Lucius through the tunnel gate. Quintus's former slave was deep in discussion with Julia on the podium.

"He stole my name, but not my soul."

"I am not so sure about that. That could be you seated there in the magistrate's chair instead of standing here in this tunnel of death."

"And why is that?" asked a third voice in the tunnel. They turned to find Julianus standing behind them.

Quintus took his helmet off and slid to a sitting position against the tunnel wall. "Go ahead, tell him," he said to Lindani.

As two venatores stalked a large buck in the arena, Lindani related the highlights of Quintus's story to Julianus. The trainer listened without interruption. When the story was over, he looked at Quintus.

"Is all of that true?"

"Yes, sir. Except he left out the part where I stole their horse."

Julianus looked at him for a minute before he spoke. "Then don't give the bastard the satisfaction of dying for him today." As the words left his lips, the large deer was slammed up against the gate next to them, the bloody tip of a hunting spear protruding from the side of the animal and through the grating. The stag kicked violently then fell dead at their feet.

Lindani smiled. "Yes. You do not want to look like *that* before your aunt and uncle."

"May Hercules watch over you both today," Julianus said as he moved down the tunnel, attending to a hundred details before the gladiator bouts began.

"Why aren't you in the arena yet?" Quintus asked Lindani.

"They have saved me for the final hunt today. The dominus does not want his show to become too predictable." They watched as the stag was dragged from the arena with two hooks. "Today will be difficult."

Quintus was surprised at Lindani's comment. He had never seen him show concern before a venatio. "Why is it any more difficult than your others?"

"Your friend in the magistrate's seat wants an exhibition of drama to conclude the hunts this morning. He has ordered me pitted against three bears."

"At the same time? That's suicide!"

"Dominus Petra complained also. They agreed to have each bear released after a count to one hundred, whether the one in the arena has been killed yet or not. But I only get three arrows, one for each bear." The hunter looked at Quintus. "It should be interesting, no?"

Quintus looked down into Lindani's quiver. Only three feathered shafts were visible. "This is crazy. What happens if you miss?"

Lindani's teeth showed brightly. "You know I never miss." Quintus wasn't convinced. "But if an arrow does not take one down, I have this." Lindani reached up and tapped the pole of his hunting spear which protruded from a pouch in the quiver strap hung over his shoulder. Beneath the smile, Quintus could see the concern in his friend's eyes.

"You'll kick their ass like you always do," Quintus responded. He tried to appear cavalier but was afraid his concern showed.

"We shall see."

They watched through the iron grating as the hunts progressed through the morning. Venatores worked solo and in teams to dispatch three stags, five boars, ten deer, one lion, and three bulls. A dodger lightened up the crowd by continuously vaulting a giant auroch with his long pole, until the beast charged a bit quicker on one pass, snapping the pole and bringing the dodger down on one of its long horns. The bearded buffalo pranced around the arena with his trophy impaled on his horn, writhing in agony. It took five handlers to rope the animal, salvage the dodger's mangled body, and return the beast to its cage to fight another day.

All too quickly the trumpets blew and the iron gate in front of them began to rise. Across the arena, attendants were busily raking the sand over a puddle of entrails left by the dodger.

"Alright Lindani, you're up," said the arena manager in the tunnel after checking his schedule.

"I'd rather fight a rival on two legs than four," Quintus said. "At least they're predictable."

"Ah, it is not the number of legs that concerns me," answered Lindani. "It is the number of teeth in their mouth, eh?"

Quintus smiled. "Just don't get close enough to count them. Good luck, my friend."

As his name was announced by the herald, Lindani raised his bow and walked out of the tunnel onto the sand. He had stripped off his golden yellow robe and wore only a matching yellow loincloth and a beaded choker. A tremendous roar from the crowd echoed down the tunnel. Quintus stayed close to the gate to keep an eye on Lindani's battle, while he contemplated his own. The bolt was drawn back on the wooden door to the left of the tunnel opening. A large black animal darted past the gate and charged across the sand. He hoped Lindani was ready.

The African hunter's eyes were locked on the charging black bear from the instant the door flew open. The blood streaks down its side told him the beast had been driven sufficiently mad by the animal handlers backstage. The bear would now take its revenge on the only human in its path.

Lindani nocked his first arrow. He aligned the shaft with the bear's forehead but did not fire. He allowed the animal to continue its charge, partly for theatrical tension and partly to be sure his target was close enough to allow the arrow tip to penetrate the thick skull. The bear closed the distance from thirty meters to ten meters quickly, its bulk propelled through the sand by blind fury. Finally Lindani released the arrow. It found its mark directly between the animal's eyes. But the bear kept coming, the arrow shaft bouncing in its bobbing head as it ran. Lindani was alarmed. The arrow tip did not pierce the skull and imbed in the brain. In spite of the danger, he continued to radiate nothing but confidence, both for the sake of the audience and the attacking animal. With an almost inhuman burst of speed, the hunter sprinted to the right a few steps then abruptly changed directions and charged the bear. He already had a second arrow nocked and let it fly as he passed the snarling animal. It hit just behind the front left leg and buried deep enough to puncture the beast's hyperactive heart. The bear plowed a furrow in the sand as it dropped in midstride.

The crowd reacted with a resounding cheer but Lindani was too busy to notice. He considered his plight of having just one arrow left for two more bears. His spear was available but he preferred to extinguish these fierce creatures from a distance rather than at the end of a two-meter stick. The game organizers said only that he could work with three arrows. They never said he couldn't reuse the arrows. He ran to the carcass but before he could retrieve either missile, the crowd's roar mingled with the roar of another black bear, telling him his second foe was in the arena.

He watched the animal run across the sand, not at him but toward the wall to his left. The bear's eyes were on him, but he apparently favored a less direct approach than his predecessor. This suited Lindani. He nocked the last arrow from his quiver and took aim. The instant the twang of the string reverberated from the bow, the bear expelled a burst of speed it had held in reserve. The unexpected change in velocity caused the arrow to hit a few inches behind the intended impact spot, wounding the bear but not dropping it.

Another earsplitting roar from the crowd warned Lindani that something else was up. Keeping his eyes on the wounded beast, he reached down and tried to wrench the arrow from the head of the first bear. The metal tip was buried deep enough in the skull to prevent an easy extraction. He flicked his eyes to the right. The third bear was charging him from the open wooden door. He would need to discuss the simple concept of counting to one hundred with the animal handler.

He reached over his right shoulder and drew the hunting spear from its sheath, slipping the bow over his left shoulder. The wounded bear continued to run along the wall, as if debating the right time for its assault. The motion drew Lindani's attention farther and farther from the third bear, already halfway across the arena. The thought crossed his mind that the animals were coordinating their attack to split his attention far right and far left. No. Perhaps craftier opponents like lions or wolves would work together, but not two burly German black bears. They were not that smart. But the fact remained, in order to keep watch on the wounded bear he had to virtually turn his back on the other one. Lindani put all his senses to work. He *felt* the charging beast rather than seeing it. The tip of his hunting spear and his eyes followed the wounded bear while it circled, as the vibrations in the sand told him the distance of the third charging bear. The roar of the crowd grew with every meter the beast closed on its victim. Calls of "Behind you!" and "Watch out!" rang from the front seats clear enough for Lindani to judge their intensity. Those cries helped him as much as the vibrations that were growing in the soles of his feet. He sensed the excitement in their voices. He felt the ground moving. Death was drawing closer. Closer still. Another moment. *Now!*

He dropped to the ground and rolled sideways, planting the base of the spear into the soft sand and swinging the point over him to face the charging animal. The momentum of the running bear brought it directly into the sharp iron tip. As spear pierced flesh, Lindani pivoted the weapon upwards impaling the bear on the hunting spear. He laid on his back in the sand looking up at the enraged animal hovering precariously over him. Swiping claws missed Lindani's face by centimeters. Blood ran down the spear shaft from the animal's underbelly, covering Lindani's black arms in red ooze. He held tightly to the pike, keeping it upright until the iron tip did its damage, puncturing every organ it could find as the bear's own weight pulled it farther onto the spear. The beast snarled down at him from its deadly perch. Finally the struggling ceased and Lindani watched the life-spirit abandon the bear's eyes.

The crowd was in a frenzy. With Lindani's last arrow still protruding from its side, the bear along the wall finally charged. Lindani felt the vibrations of the seven-hundred-pound animal as they coursed through his back. He tilted his head back in the sand to see the grotesque vision of an upside-down black bear racing toward him, fangs bared and dripping with a pink mixture of saliva and blood. The problem was, Lindani was out of weapons. He had to stall for time. He pulled back on the spear shaft. The dead bear hovering above him teetered over his head and fell between him and the new threat. The charging bear collided with the carcass of its companion, infuriating the animal. In frustration, it ripped a furry hunk of meat from the flank of the dead bear.

The distraction gave Lindani the extra second he sought. He was on his feet and sprinting toward the body of the first bear before the wounded animal knew he was gone. He needed to cover only a few steps but it seemed like a kilometer. The wounded animal spat the meat from its mouth and charged after the hunter. Lindani petitioned every god he could think of, praying the arrow in the side of the dead bear would be easier to wrench free than the one in its head. He would have only one opportunity and it had better work. He slipped the bow from his shoulder as he ran. The bear's hot breath was on his back as he dove. He flew over the body, grasping the white shaft of the arrow as he passed. It pulled free. Tucking his head under, he somersaulted into the sand. His momentum carried him forward to a standing position, the bloody arrow already nocked in the bowstring. His head snapped around as the charging bear raised up on its hind legs. The hunter stared directly into the teeth coming at his face. He fired the arrow with all the power he could muster. It struck the bear in the throat and passed completely through its trachea, severing its air supply. But the wound was not enough to stop the charge and the beast enveloped Lindani.

XVI

May AD 65

L UCIUS SAT FORWARD in his chair, for once caught up in the excitement of the games. An unusually sympathetic scream came from the crowd. He could see only the black fur twitching and jerking on top of the hunter. And then it was over. There was no more motion from the bloody pile on the sand. An eerie hush came over the crowd. Soon there was only the sound of the birds nesting in the large oak tree.

Lucius looked at Julia. "So will it cost us extra since the lanista now lost his best hunter?"

Julia shrugged nonchalantly. "We'll see what we can negotiate with . . . "

She was interrupted by a gasp from the crowd. The bear's paw moved. Then its head lifted a few centimeters off the ground. A murmur grew across the cavea as the bear appeared to be getting up. Its right leg raised and it rolled to the left, flopping heavily on its back. Lucius watched in amazement as the hunter sat up, like an evil spirit rising from the dead. He struggled to his feet in the center of the hushed arena, the black bear dead at his side. He slowly raised his arms and punched toward the sky, a victory cry rising from his throat. His shout was quickly drowned by the deafening roar that erupted from the seats. The Celtic chieftain behind Lucius, who had tangled with bears often near his remote settlement, whooped the loudest.

Lucius once again felt Julia's presence close by his ear. "The whole crowd adores this hunter," she whispered. "You should toss him a few extra gold coins."

Lucius glanced at her, then stood and waved the hunter over. The spent venator staggered to the foot of the podium, still struggling to catch the wind that had been driven from his lungs by the weight of the bear. His slender body was covered in blood, most pumped from the neck wound of the bear, some from a wide cut over his left eyebrow. He raised his head slowly and gazed toward the podium. His eyes were iridescent orbs peering from the mask of red gore that covered his face. A chill ran down Lucius's spine as their eyes met. He swallowed hard before he spoke.

"You have hunted well, venator," he announced loudly so all could hear. "Here is a token of my appreciation for your hard work. May the gods be with you on your future hunts."

He tossed five gold pieces into the arena and they landed at the hunter's feet. But the hunter never looked down. He held his stare on Lucius. The crowd resumed its enthusiastic cheering, but the man in the arena did not move to acknowledge their praise. Lucius dropped back into his seat, but the hunter never blinked. Lucius quickly became uncomfortable with the man's mysterious eyes locked upon him so intently.

"Why does he stare so?" he asked Julia.

"I don't know. Maybe it's some sort of African tradition not to avert your eyes from a superior."

Lucius began to feel that the hunter was somehow looking beyond his face, that he was staring into his soul. He tried to turn away but the venator's gaze was almost hypnotic. With effort, he broke the spell and brusquely waved the hunter away. He signaled for the trumpets to announce the midday break. As they sounded, the venator finally bent over and picked up the coins. From the corner of his eye, Lucius saw the man give him another look before he walked to the tunnel.

An uneasy Lucius leaned toward Julia. "An unappreciative lout, isn't he?"

But Julia was deep in discussion with the Celtic chief seated beside her and did not respond.

From the tunnel entrance, Quintus watched Lindani at the foot of the podium. The young Roman was able to breathe again after seeing the bear collapse on Lindani. The horrible thought of returning to the ludus without his close friend was now a distant memory. He glanced up at Lucius as the spineless bastard dropped back into his seat. He knew Lucius well and he sensed an uneasiness in him as he dealt with the victorious hunter before him in the sand.

Finally, Lindani retrieved his reward and walked toward the tunnel entrance. Quintus was shocked at the amount of blood that covered his friend.

"You had me nervous there for a minute," Quintus said as he placed Lindani's arm over his own shoulder to help him back to the cells.

"Not as nervous as I just made your friend," Lindani replied with a smile. "It is funny how jittery Roman politicians become at the cold stare of a foreigner. Especially one covered in the blood of his foe."

The short lunch break ended with the afternoon pompa. The glittering gold of the earlier ceremonial armor was replaced by the silver, copper, and brass of the fighting armor. Quintus again remained hidden behind the visor of his thraex helmet.

The trumpets heralded the first of the combats to begin. Quintus was third on the roster so he remained near the gate. The first bout was far from impressive. A tiro retiarius was matched with an equally green secutor. While it was common for the retiarius to flee after a poor cast of his net, this one refused to fight at all after his first toss. Julianus, working as referee, used his whipping rod to convince the fleeing retiarius to make a stand. Once caught by the secutor, the crowd was quick to turn their thumbs to be sure they never had to suffer through his cowardice again.

Quintus kept a close eye on the podium. Lucius hardly glanced at the mob before hastily condemning the man to death. He obviously had hardened himself to the sight of blood.

"Fight well and you needn't worry about that becoming your fate." Quintus recognized the gravelly voice of the lanista before he turned his head.

"Don't worry, Dominus. I'll fight."

"You damn well better," Petra said. "Just remember what you've been taught. Not just by me and Julianus . . . but by Aulus, too."

The name came as a shock to Quintus. "You know of Aulus?"

"You mentioned him on your first day at the school. I saw you spin the rudis before you laid it back in the rack. That was Aulus's move." Petra looked toward the arena where the second battle was getting under way. "I knew Aulus Libo from my days in the arena. The two of us were at the Ludus Magnus in Rome together. We fought often. Mostly in sparring matches, but once or twice in the arena. We were good friends, in spite of the code. That's why . . . "

Petra suddenly stopped speaking. His eyes seemed to glaze over as he stared into the arena.

Quintus leaned forward to see what was wrong. After a moment, he touched Petra's shoulder.

"Dominus? 'That's why' what?"

Through the holes of the helmet visor, Quintus saw the lanista's solemn face look at him.

"That's why it hurt so much when I delivered the wound that ended his days in the arena."

Quintus was stunned. He lowered his head without a word. Petra looked back into the arena before he spoke again. "I assure you the scar inside me is as deep and lasting as the scar across his right shoulder."

Quintus thought for a moment then looked at his lanista. "Then I guess, in a way, you've been training me all my life for this moment. The cut of your gladius sent my bodyguard and trainer to me. If it wasn't for your blow, Aulus would never have been a part of my life."

Petra nodded quietly. "I'd often wondered what became of Aulus. I'm glad he was sold into a good home. Is he well?"

Quintus wasn't sure if he wanted to awaken these dreadful memories before his first arena bout. But he owed it to Petra to answer the question.

"I'm afraid not, Dominus. He's gone. He was lost in the same storm that killed my parents. He died saving my life in the water."

Petra took a deep breath and became quiet. Quintus could read his thoughts: Yet another comrade from his generation was gone. There were probably not many left. Quintus was happy to let it drop. He was about to step into the arena and was not in the right frame of mind to have this discussion. There were already too many distractions this day. But Petra seemed intent on keeping his attention off his upcoming fight.

"So I take it that *you're* the real Quintus Honorius Romanus, not that teen-aged ass sitting on the podium."

"You saw the introduction by my uncle?"

"Yes. And Julianus filled me in on the rest of the story."

Quintus looked at the lanista. "So are you going to turn me in as a runaway and a horse thief when I step out of the arena?"

Petra's crooked teeth showed as he smiled a rare smile. "And lose the kid who's going to make me rich? You must be madder than a latrine rat. Now get ready, you're up next." The lanista turned and ambled back down the tunnel. His final statement echoed off the stone walls as he walked. "Why not win this battle for Aulus?"

The words gave Quintus a focus for his bout. But as his time drew near, his nerves were on edge. Petra's space at the gate was taken by another body. Quintus glanced to the side and saw the brutish face of Memnon, his arena opponent, glaring back at him, the evil sneer still trying to work its psychological damage. Quintus was losing patience with the waiting and with Memnon's mental provocation. He leaned forward and offered some mockery of his own.

"Fight hard out there, Memnon. Then you'll be spared when I knock you down and have my sica at your throat."

The grin on his opponent's face was replaced by a scowl. Quintus was pleased his comment had an effect on the brute. But rather than acknowledge the taunt, Memnon let out a sudden coarse grunt directly into Quintus's visor. The reply was so bizarre and unexpected it startled Quintus, which prompted a drawn-out theatrical laugh from Memnon. Most in the tunnel paid no heed, but the patronizing sound bothered Quintus just the same. This man would soon pay. Quintus was distracted by the young slave crouched below him, checking the security of his leg guards and the leather straps holding the mail secure to his fighting arm. A loud roar from the crowd signaled the end of the second match.

"You two. By the gate. You're up next," the coordinator yelled.

The months of practice and preparation, the cuts and bruises, the strength training and the soul searching all came down to this moment. Quintus checked the security of his helmet, the tall plume of his ceremonial helmet now replaced with the traditional metal griffin that signified the Thracian fighter. Memnon secured his helmet, similar in appearance to Quintus's but sporting an angled crest flanked by twin red feathers.

The gate began to rise but before either fighter stepped forward, the lifeless body of the defeated hoplomachus from the second bout passed them, carried by two bulky attendants. The first two contests had both ended in death. Quintus's knees began to shake, but he kept his legs spread so the tops of his metal greaves did not rattle together.

The trumpets blew, the herald made his announcement, and Julianus signaled the next two gladiators into the arena. Side by side, Quintus and Memnon stepped from the dark tunnel into the sunshine. As he walked toward the center of the arena, the scene became surreal to Quintus. Everything moved in slow motion. The arena was suddenly enormously wide and he felt as if it took forever to reach the middle of the circle. The crowd noise was strangely distant.

"Quintus! Pay attention." The stern voice came from Julianus. The trainer could tell from Quintus's trancelike movements that he was distracted and nervous. Julianus whacked the side of his helmet with the rod. The crash reverberated in Quintus's ears and snapped him from the lethargic state. His senses sharpened and he focused his attention on the task at hand.

"You alright?" Julianus asked.

Quintus nodded.

"Then take your positions."

Memnon moved his large scutum into position at the front of his body. Quintus tightened his grip on his small parmula. The tiny shield suddenly seemed terribly inadequate. He wondered if these were to be the final moments of his life.

"Be on guard . . . Attack!"

Before the final word left Julianus's lips, Memnon was already charging at Quintus. He unleashed a violent assault of cuts and thrusts, none with grace or clarity but dangerous all the same. Quintus was immediately forced to give ground. His bare feet stepped backward through the sand until his left foot dug into a shallow furrow, collapsing his leg from under him. As he felt himself going down, he pushed hard with his right leg, creating enough momentum to roll backward and come up on his feet. But Memnon was on him again, beating against his small square shield with maximum force and driving him once again onto his back in the sand. The brute attempted a debilitating thrust to his chest, but Quintus rolled sideways and avoided the iron blade. The few seconds it took Memnon to recover gave Quintus enough time to gain his feet once again.

The crowd sensed another poor fight and immediately began taunting the fighters with howls and catcalls. This was not how Quintus had pictured his first arena bout. But the sight of Lucius and the Viators on the podium had confounded him. Nothing seemed right after that. And he was now in an ironic, deadly position. If he fell at the point of Memnon's gladius, the final judgment of life or death would be decided by the person he despised most in all the Empire. His life would literally be in Lucius's hands, or more precisely, in the thumb of Lucius's hand. Quintus's own slave would decide whether he lived or died. The thought was too absurd to comprehend. But it brought reality into focus, even clearer than the whack on the head he had received from Julianus. *Don't give the bastard the satisfaction of dying for him today.* The trainer's words rang in Quintus's ears. It was time to make a stand. It was time to fight.

Quintus took a deep breath as Memnon recovered and approached again. In a flash of shining metal, Quintus's sica engaged Memnon's gladius with blinding fury. The brute lost ground, his defiant attitude melting with each backward step he took. The crowd suddenly gained interest and the taunts turned to cheers. Julianus, too, shouted encouragement to his pupil. Quintus's attack was relentless, hammering a series of powerful blows from right, left, up, and down. Memnon's self-preservation instinct matched each lunge with an effective parry. For almost five minutes, the two gladiators pounded away at each other. Sweat glistened on Quintus's broad chest and back, washing away the sand from his two falls. He saw an opportunity and made a running charge at Memnon, scoring a hit on his left arm just above his shield. The charge spun the fighters around and Quintus now faced the podium. The sight of Lucius seated in the magistrate's seat provided more fuel for his fire. There was simply no way that Quintus was going to die to honor that bastard. In that instant, he knew he had won his first arena bout. Bringing it to a physical conclusion was just a formality. He reprised his attack at full force, his sica a blur of iron.

Quintus sensed that Memnon's shield arm was weakening. He worked on the shield, beating at the top of it and across the silver boss that protruded from the center. Almost imperceptibly, he saw it slip to one side. The blood flowing from the deep cut on Memnon's arm had reached his hand. Quintus knew his enemy could no longer grip the heavy shield with the handle covered in the slippery liquid. He hit the shield again and again until finally the scutum dropped to the sand. Calls of *"Hoc habet!"*—"He's had it!"—rang from the front rows. Without his scutum, a murmillo could not survive long. Against Quintus's tremendous strength and everlasting endurance, Memnon's end came quickly. One last press from Quintus knocked the gladius aside and dropped Memnon to his knees, the tip of Quintus's blade at his throat.

Quintus glared at the downed fighter, who quickly raised his first finger in the traditional appeal for mercy. Julianus stepped forward and grabbed Quintus's arm, a symbolic gesture to hold off the deathblow until the fate of the vanquished was established.

Quintus panted through clenched teeth as he stared down at Memnon. "I warned you to fight well, so you would be saved in this situation. But you found it funny. You thought it more important to humiliate me. Well, let's see if the crowd felt you fought well enough to live. Do you deserve a missio, Memnon?"

Quintus looked up at the crowd, their cheering and applause echoing in his metal helmet. He saw thousands of white handkerchiefs fluttering like an immense flock of doves across the cavea. The mob wanted mercy.

"Disregard the crowd," said Julianus. "This is the magistrate's games and whatever he says goes."

All eyes were now on Lucius. The young magistrate did not yet have his arm raised. Quintus knew him well enough to know what was running through his mind. He was considering demonstrating his new authority by sentencing this man to death against the will of the crowd. He raised his arm and basked in the power he now held over men's lives. A depraved smile crossed his face. Quintus prepared mentally to execute his first victim. Before Lucius's thumb turned, Julia suddenly leaned forward and whispered in his ear. It appeared to Quintus that she knew Lucius as well as he did. The smile disappeared as Lucius reached into his sleeve and withdrew a white handkerchief. He waved it abruptly across his chest and dropped dejectedly into his seat. The crowd erupted in applause.

"Missio!" Julianus announced loudly. He pushed Quintus's sica aside and helped the bleeding, defeated fighter to his feet. "A good fight, Memnon. But I think you underestimated your opponent."

Julianus looked at Quintus. The young Roman wondered if the trainer could detect his relief through the visor grating. "Excellent work, Quintus. Your first fight and your first victory. And it seems you've won the crowd."

Quintus raised his weapon in victory and the clamor became deafening. It was the moment for which he had waited so long.

"Don't forget to visit your friend's podium if you want to collect your winnings," Julianus said quietly as he gathered up the discarded weapons. He led Memnon back to the tunnel, leaving Quintus alone on the sand to bathe in the glory that came from triumph in the arena.

Quintus approached the podium, involuntarily touching his visor to be sure his face was well concealed. He could see his uncle cheering enthusiastically. Without a word, Lucius lifted a palm frond and a small bag of coins from the nearby table and tossed them onto the sand. His disappointment at not ordering another execution was still evident. Quintus retrieved the rewards, offered a terse salute, and walked quickly toward the tunnel before anyone on the podium had the opportunity to speak to him.

Lucius watched the fighter gather his winnings and hurry toward the tunnel. He felt Julia's presence once again beside his face.

"You could have at least said something to the man," she said quietly into his ear.

He was growing tired of the relentless directions as to how he should act on the podium. "Like what? What do you say to this rubbish?"

Julia sighed heavily. "Really Quintus, you need to become more refined at the games. You could have made a comment about him having the same name as you—or did you not even hear the herald or read the program? See . . . 'Quintus.'" She pointed out the name on the listing, but Lucius did not bother to read it.

"Wonderful. What does it matter? These men are all scum. We both know they've only been hired today to further my career. Is it important I know their names?"

"There's protocol at the games."

"Well, perhaps if he fights for me again someday I shall remember to engage him in conversation."

Julia leaned back in her chair without responding. Lucius glanced over his shoulder and found her staring at him with a look that could pierce mail. He gave her a wink then turned back to the arena. If she was going to try to manipulate him, he thought, she had better become more adept at it.

Beneath a waning moon, the transport carts lined up beside the arena. The last of the equipment was being loaded by torchlight under the watchful eyes of two armed guards. Julianus gave the order for all gladiators and venatores to climb into their wagons. Quintus made his way to the cart in which he had ridden that morning. The return trip to the ludus would be much less stressful than the trip to the arena. He grabbed the support pole to pull himself up into the hay on the cartbed when he felt a hand on his back.

"This is the wrong cart," Julianus said. "You should try that one over there. The ride will be much better."

Quintus looked at the next cart and saw it already contained a number of the veteran fighters, including Memnon, who sported a bloodstained cloth tied around his upper left arm. His tired, glazed eyes stared at Quintus.

"That's okay," Quintus replied. "I like this one." He reached again for the pole, but Julianus grabbed his arm.

"No, I'm afraid I have to insist you ride in the other cart. Trust me."

Quintus made his way uneasily to the next cart. The veterans all watched his approach. Quintus was sure there would be a revenge fight before the caravan reached the ludus in the morning.

"Come on up. There's plenty of room," Memnon said. His evil grin had returned. Quintus pulled himself up, and the ox teams were prodded forward.

The first few minutes on the road passed in silence, except for the sound of the ox hooves and wooden wheels on the paving stones. Quintus relaxed and settled back in the hay for the long trip home to Glevum. Memnon soon broke the silence.

"So our little tiro is an arena veteran now. How's it feel, Quintus?"

Quintus couldn't believe Julianus had thrown him to the wolves like this.

He tried to walk the fine line of standing up to these hard men without provoking them.

"You were in the same position not too long ago, Memnon. Don't you remember?" He knew he should have let it end there, but felt the need to go on. "Or did I knock your memory loose today?"

A chorus of "Ooohhhs" came from the five other seasoned fighters in the cart and all eyes turned to Memnon. The evil grin wavered for an instant, then returned. He sat forward to get closer to Quintus.

"You know what we do to tiro fighters who score a victory against a veteran on their first match?" Quintus swallowed hard as Memnon and the others leaned even closer. "We do *this!*"

Quintus felt a hand reach under his subligaculum and grope his testicles. Fearing the worst, he grabbed the offending arm. After a tense second, he realized that the arm was too thin and frail to belong to any of the fighters. He looked down as a beautiful female form emerged from under the hay, her right arm half-shrouded under his green loincloth. The cartbed erupted in loud laughter and Quintus realized he had been had. With a smile, the girl gently released her hold on his scrotum, worked his loincloth loose, and began slowly stroking his shaft, just enough to break the ice and get him interested.

"Dionysia here is our biggest fan," Memnon yelled through the howls of laughter. "Tonight, she wants to welcome you to the familia. And take my word for it, this girl can suck the tiles off a mosaic floor."

Her hand pumped faster as she became energized by the shouts of the fighters, who brushed the hay from her naked body. The moonlight provided just enough illumination to see the dozen hands groping her sensuous curves. Quintus was astonished that such a beautiful woman would be spending the next few hours servicing each of the grizzled fighters in the cart. With a squeal of delight she buried her head under his loincloth and went to work with her tongue.

"Welcome to the troupe, Quintus," Memnon said as he sat back to wait his turn. The sounds of laughter and rigorous sex danced across the river Avon as the caravan wound its way back to Glevum.

XVII

May AD 65

Q UINTUS AROSE RESTED and relaxed. He would have liked to watch the sunrise, to thank Hercules for allowing him to witness another daybreak. But after a full night of traveling in the uncomfortable carts, few of the fighters ventured out of their cells before noon, including Quintus. Petra declared a day of rest for all those who fought in the games—at least all those who fought *well*. Three gladiators who presented a marginal performance in the eyes of Petra and Julianus, yet were miraculously spared by Lucius and the crowd, were forced to rise at the regular time, endure ten lashes from the metal-tipped whip, and spend the day running countless laps around the practice field until they dropped from exhaustion.

After lunch, Quintus was back on the field alone, working vigorously against the palus. He had not thought of Lucius for many months, but now he could not push the image of his rival, seated on the arena's podium, from his mind. He pictured Lucius's face on the palus, which added a surge of power to his sword arm.

"Are you releasing your frustrations on the poor wooden pole?" asked Lindani, as if reading Quintus's mind.

Quintus kept working as he answered. "I just can't get that bastard out of my head. I can't believe he's a magistrate."

"What does it matter? You allow too much poison into your mind. Concentrate on winning your next bout. That is how you must think now, from arena to arena. Do not let one win go to your head. Although, I will say that I have heard many good things about your first fight."

"Sorry you missed it. How's your head?"

"It is fine. And I did not miss your show. When I heard your name announced, I pushed the physician away so I could watch from the tunnel. It was
a slow start, but you did well."

The conversation was interrupted by a commotion at the front gate. Guards
escorted fifteen prisoners from the rebellious Germanian frontier into the
ludus. The barbarians' long matted hair, beards, and mustaches, along with
their woolen leggings and bear-fur capes, set them apart from the Roman and
Briton prisoners. The heavy chains linking their neck shackles rattled as they
were marched across the practice field to the barracks. Quintus continued
with his swordwork at the palus, until he heard gruff laughter coming from
the parade of new prisoners. One called out with a heavy accent that made the
words difficult to understand, but the meaning was unmistakable.

"Hey, gladiator! You fight well against a piece of wood. Soon you face me.
I strike back harder than the wood pole." The prisoners erupted in another fit
of laughter.

Quintus studied the bearded barbarian who taunted him. After a few seconds, he casually tossed his gladius in the air, snatched the weapon by its
blade, and tossed it at the line of prisoners. The sword point found its mark
in the dirt at the feet of the loudmouthed German, and the gladius wobbled
from side to side between his legs. Stunned rage grew on the prisoner's face.
He leaped out of line and attempted to charge Quintus, but the neck shackles
allowed him only a few steps. The guards responded quickly with whips and
spears, prodding the enraged German back into line.

Quintus laughed loudly. "Looking forward to meeting you later, handsome." He punctuated his response with a wink.

"It is good that you are quick to make friends," Lindani said with a laugh.

As he did with many of the Teutonic barbarians, Petra ordered more than
half of the new prisoners to begin training as hoplomachii and murmillones,
although they often fought in their native garb rather than the traditional
subligaculum. And, as a thraex, it was not long before Quintus was face-to-
face with the testy German on the practice field. Quintus's swift, elegant style
easily bested the German's lumbering fighting technique, frustrating the barbarian and amusing Quintus to no end. But the bulky German fought dirty

and caused more than his share of bloody noses and bruises on his opponents, Quintus included.

The new faces were only a minor distraction to the determination Quintus put into his training. He continued to work out in the mornings and late afternoons with his muscle-building equipment. Each month added a few more centimeters to the solid mass of his chest, neck, arms, and legs. The unctores continued to fawn over Quintus's physique, imploring more and more of the fighters to take up his regimen. While most of the men spent their occasional afternoons of free time rolling the bones and gambling away their arena winnings, Quintus continued to ride Ceres into Glevum to meet with the trainers and unctores at the bath complex. Yet as spring turned to summer, his education there eventually subsided. It seemed he had finally absorbed all the knowledge the trainers had to offer. But that changed dramatically one late afternoon in June.

After a refreshing plunge in the cold frigidarium pool, Quintus slipped his tunic on and headed toward the exit. A flash of yellow caught his attention as he passed the portal to the palaestra—the open-air yard used for exercise and wrestling. He stopped in the hallway and took a few steps back. What he saw through the doorway would change his life forever.

Alone in the center of the courtyard, surrounded by flowering vines and tall green shrubs, an elderly gentleman was in the midst of a slow and beautiful ritual. In his hand was a curved sword, longer than the sica Quintus wielded in the arena and with an extended hilt designed for a two-fisted grip. The man's face was like none Quintus had seen before, at once gentle and serene yet emanating some vibrant hidden power. His eyes appeared to be closed, but were so narrow and slanted at the ends it was hard to tell for certain. A narrow beard of pure white fell from his wrinkled chin and sat atop the yellow robe, which overlapped in the front and was tied at the waist with a brown and gold sash. The old man moved with the grace of a young dancer. His slow, deliberate movements were occasionally punctuated with bursts of speed and energy that contradicted his age and small stature. The orange light of the late-afternoon sun flashed on the polished sword blade that slowly circled the man's bald head, then suddenly slashed out before him. Quintus stood frozen in fascination as the man did battle with his imaginary foe. The scene was quite simply one of the most surreal and beautiful things he had ever witnessed.

"Master Sheng is something, isn't he?" Quintus recognized the voice of the bathhouse manager next to him, but never took his eyes from the old man in the palaestra.

"Where is he from?" Quintus asked.

"The Far East. He showed up here a few days ago. Speaks fairly good Latin, actually. He says 'travel is knowledge,' so he's been wandering the Empire for a few years now."

"What is this ritual?"

"He calls it *wushu*. He says it means 'the art of fighting.' Something about connecting the mind and body with some internal force. I don't know, it's beyond me. I'll tell you one thing, though . . . The man knows his medicine. He's shown us some very unusual healing practices from the East. He carries a small rack of tiny bronze needles that he sticks in the body to help with pain. Everyone who's tried it says it works. He's very much in demand here now with my older clients."

"I want to meet him," Quintus said without hesitation.

"Sure, but let him finish his exercise. He gets into a . . . a . . . trance, I guess you'd call it."

Quintus and the manager stood watching for a few more moments. Quintus could have watched all night long. The man finally came to rest with his sword upright, both hands grasping the long hilt and the back of the blade resting near his forehead. He opened his eyes and smiled at Quintus.

"You are a warrior who appreciates the martial arts," the old man said in a strong voice with an unusual accent. Quintus was not sure if it was a question or a statement.

"If this *wushu* is a 'martial art,' then you're correct," Quintus said. "I never knew battle could be so beautiful."

"Ahh. Are not the deadliest vipers also the most beautiful?" the man said with a smile. "What you call 'beauty' is merely discipline and focus." The man looked Quintus over with eyes that were full of life and vitality. "You are a fighter. Do you fight with discipline and focus?"

"I'm well-trained, if that's what you mean," Quintus answered.

"Your body is obviously well-trained. But do you control your *chi*, your internal energy?"

Quintus looked at the bathhouse manager, who smiled and shrugged. "Don't look at me. Like I said, he's beyond me."

The Easterner smiled at Quintus. "What is your name, fighter?"

"I am Quintus Honorius Romanus."

"Come sit with me, Quintus Honorius Romanus. We have much to discuss." The Easterner led Quintus to a bench at the side of the exercise yard and the bath manager went about his duties.

"I'm an arena fighter, a gladiator," Quintus said. "May I?" He pointed toward the long curved sword, and the old man handed it to him with a nod.

"I have seen these fights," Sheng said as he stroked his beard. "I do not understand the attraction. But I have learned never to pass judgment on another's culture."

Quintus swung the sword as he sat, marveling at the weight and balance. "I love every part of the arena," he said. "I love training to fight and I love fighting. There is no truer test of a man's power, both physically and mentally."

The old man smiled. "Ah, so they have trained your mind as well. That also is the first step of *wushu*. The trainee must practice again and again with the correct intent. Then you become part of the movements and they become part of you. When the intent is right, the *chi* is strong."

Quintus handed the sword back to Sheng, who laid it on the bench beside him. "What is this *chi*?" Quintus asked. "Is it something that could help me in the arena?"

"It helps you already. You need only harness it and control it like a horse. To do this you must learn the ways of *Taiji*. This, too, is part of *wushu*. Every movement has a purpose. By understanding this, then the body is connected to the mind."

Quintus could not take his eyes off Sheng. Although he did not understand much of what the old man meant, he felt an instant connection with him and his philosophy. Somehow, he sensed this was the next step in his own quest for knowledge.

"What is your goal, Quintus?" the man suddenly asked, as if reading Quintus's mind.

"I want to be the best," Quintus said, his head rising with pride.

Sheng nodded slowly. "Then you must walk the path of enlightenment." He stood up. "Come. Stand next to me and follow my motions."

Quintus reached for the sword.

"No," Sheng said. "Leave the weapon."

"But I fight with a sword. Shouldn't I train with one?" Quintus asked as he stood.

"The weapon is but an extension of the hand, nothing more. Master the movements of your body and the sword will follow."

Quintus moved next to the man and tried to copy the slow, rhythmic motions of his arms, legs, and torso. Sheng talked him through the steps with a voice as hypnotic and relaxing as the movements.

"In motion you must feel peace. Be as if you are standing in a pool of water, moving so slowly as not to create a wave. You must seek stillness in motion. And when standing still, you must feel your body expanding and contracting, creating energy. This is motion in stillness. This is the yin and yang."

In mimicking the movements, Quintus realized just how in control the old man truly was. For while Quintus's legs and arms shook and faltered, Sheng's showed nothing but fluid motion.

"The *chi* is your energy and the mind moves the *chi*," he continued. "Think about which body part you are going to move next and place your intention there. This creates a path for the *chi* to follow. You must learn to visualize the flow of *chi* through your body rather than the physical movements."

Once Quintus learned the repetition of the moves, he closed his eyes to focus his self-awareness.

"Each position has an offensive or defensive function," Sheng explained. "You must learn the movements and allow the *chi* to take you there."

"My movements in the arena are dictated by my opponent," Quintus said quietly as he worked. "I exploit his weaknesses and counter his aggression."

"You must become one with your opponent, Quintus. You must think as he thinks. Only then will you know his intention."

The words had such a familiar ring to them they caused Quintus to pause in his routine and look at Sheng. "That's exactly the philosophy of my Ethiopian friend, Lindani, who fights the beasts. He knows the animals. He understands how they think."

Sheng continued his fluid dancelike movements with closed eyes. "I have learned that the teachings are there in many cultures. The bird and the butterfly are different, yet they both take wing and fly."

At that moment, Quintus knew these teachings would take him to another level. He opened his mind to engage a much different type of learning. Julianus and Petra would train his body and mind, but this man would train his warrior spirit.

Petra was up earlier than usual. He especially enjoyed the crisp air of August mornings. He leaned against the pillar in front of his door watching Quintus work alone on the practice field. The new graceful sword exercise the young Roman had developed fascinated him. He heard Julianus's door open behind him.

"That's quite a routine he's worked out," Petra said without turning around.

"I've seen a dramatic improvement in his reflexes and reaction time," Julianus said as he joined his boss at the pillar. "Since he started these peculiar exercises, he is much more aware of his opponents' intentions. The other day he seemed to parry even before the thrusts were thrown."

Petra watched the young Roman work. "He's developing an interesting style. I don't think I've ever seen anyone move as quickly as he does, especially considering his size. I'm glad I don't have to face him on the sand. But perhaps our loudmouthed German friend would like to."

"For the Londinium games? Are they set?" Julianus asked.

"I just got word last night. They want us there in two weeks. See to it that those two face each other. The German's a brute, but it'll be the type of fight people will remember. Personal grudge matches always make good arena bouts."

Quintus looked down into the brownish waters of the Tamesis River as his oxcart rumbled across the long wooden bridge leading to the Londinium wall.

The troupe had arrived a few days early in order to rest from the three-day journey and to take part in the pre-games banquet. Past the wharves and warehouses that stretched for two kilometers along the riverfront, Londinium lay spread across two hills. At the summit of the eastern hill sat a noble town forum, while the western hill was crowned with a huge oval amphitheater. Quintus studied the structure through the wooden bars of his cart bed. There were no fatalistic thoughts in his mind this time. He simply wondered how his second arena bout would end.

The game preparations and banquet passed quickly. Quintus found himself anxious to get back into the arena. Now more comfortable in the surroundings, he was curious to see what he had missed the first time due to tense nerves and distractions.

The pompa was more festive than at Aquae Sulis, enlivened by a full orchestra, a rarity in the provinces. The simple melodies, played on a stringed cithara, panpipes, flutes, cymbals, and a water organ, filled the cavea. The mob was the usual Britannia mix of local politicians, provincial Roman citizens, Briton and Celtic natives, homesick soldiers, and the rabble in the top tiers common to all amphitheaters. The cavea also held a number of ship hands from around the Empire who were lucky enough to be in port on the day of the games. Quintus noticed that the crowd seemed more rowdy than most.

"The people of Londinium love their games," Lindani said as he stretched his muscles in the entrance tunnel after the parade. "And word spreads quickly from this port. Make a name for yourself here and you will soon be known throughout the Empire."

Quintus smiled at him. "I guess that explains why everybody seems to know your skinny ass whenever you prance into the arena."

"What can I say? I think it is the exotic skin color the women here like, eh?"

"No bears today, I hope."

"Only your friend, Lucius, is crazy enough to come up with that idea. Today I will drop ten eland." Quintus wrinkled his forehead at the animal's odd name. "They are large antelope from the plains of Africa," Lindani explained.

"Well, I'd still rather face an opponent on two legs than four."

"And I tell you, it is not the number of legs, but the number of teeth that is of concern. The eland have large horns but very few teeth. They are of no concern."

Quintus was more relaxed for his second bout, an attitude that apparently did not escape Lindani. "So you fight our German friend today, eh?"

Quintus raised an eyebrow. "Amazing how that worked out, isn't it?"

"You will do well. You think with your head. He thinks with his fists."

A fanfare drifted from the orchestra section, and the herald announced Lindani's name. The biggest cheer of the morning rolled across the arena.

"See what I mean. They know your skinny ass everywhere," Quintus said with a smile.

"The women of Londinium await." With that, Lindani was in the sunshine, his bow and multiple hunting spears raised above his head. Quintus could hear the women seated near the tunnel entrance screaming Lindani's name.

"I give you a forest this time, Lindani!" yelled the games editor, the local proconsul, from his canopied podium seat. Lindani bowed and scanned the podium. Next to the regional governor sat his wife and two teenaged children. Lindani knew that this proconsul was one of his biggest fans, so he pandered more to the podium in Londinium than in any other province. It also meant a more substantial bag of coins at the end of the hunt.

"I think you will also recognize your quarry from the plains of Ethiopia," the proconsul added.

"Thank you, sir! I feel I am back home in Axum," Lindani lied, yelling above the substantial crowd noise.

Tall fir and ash trees in camouflaged containers had been distributed throughout the arena to simulate a hardwood forest. The trees were both a help and hindrance to the venator, providing protection for man and animal alike. Lindani used the branches from one of the ash trees to hang his bow and flowing red robe.

As he completed his theatrical bows, the orchestra played a short fanfare and a heavy wooden door along the arena wall jerked open. Into the arena sprinted ten large eland, their spiral horns glistening with gold dust, added by the arena manager as an artistic touch. Lindani carefully studied their movements for a second, reacquainting himself with the largest and most powerful member of the antelope family. Like a lion selecting his particular prey from a herd, Lindani chose the first eland to die. He ran it down, whooping and yelling a strange medley of guttural sounds, until he was in position. A hunting spear sprang from his right hand and the buck dropped. The next four went down in similar fashion, inciting the crowd further as each antelope's nose plowed into the sand. Numbers six and seven were dropped together as his final spear passed through one neck and drove solidly into the other. Dispatching two beasts with a single weapon had become the African's trademark move and the crowd responded with wild applause. With two arrows already drawn from his quiver, he unhooked the bow from the tree branch and nocked both missiles on the bowstring. The three remaining eland were now panicked, darting wildly among the trees as they leaped over the dead bodies of their brethren. Lindani used his best animal mimicry to challenge one of the proud bucks and successfully got it to charge him, golden horns lowered for attack. He lifted his bow horizontal to the floor, took aim, and fired his double load. Both arrows penetrated the eland's skull, one under the left horn and one under the right.

"Now you have an extra set of horns to visit your gods, no?" he yelled. The first few rows heard him over the din and responded with loud laughter and applause.

He ran to the tree that held his scarlet tribal robe and swung up into the branches like a primate, grabbing the robe as he went. He straddled a high branch and began firing a series of arrows into the ground, carefully herding buck number nine into position. As the confused eland crossed under Lindani's tree branch, the hunter tossed down his robe, catching the bright material on the tips of the horns and covering the antelope's head. The eland tossed and bucked wildly under the covering, much to the delight of the audience. Lindani released it from its torment with another well-placed arrow to the back of the head.

The peculiar sight of the red cloth flopping from the head of the manic antelope sent the last eland into a furious delirium. As Lindani dropped from the tree, the animal bolted away at top speed. To every spectator, including Lindani, it looked as though the antelope would simply run full force into the high stone wall. At the speed it traveled, there was no way to avoid the collision. But the eland was apparently not yet ready to die. In one astounding leap, the buck vaulted the wall and landed in the midst of the politicians and dignitaries seated in the front row. Chaos erupted. Well-to-do spectators trampled each other to get out of the raging animal's path.

For the first time in his career, Lindani did not know what to do. He had never seen an animal leap the four-meter wall, although he had heard stories of it happening in the provincial arenas. He watched as the large buck regained its feet and charged along the first row, its menacing spiral horns striking at anyone in its path. Many of the spectators jumped into the arena to escape the charge. Blood from those who did not move quickly enough began to stain the gold dust on the horns. Lindani looked ahead of the charging eland. The podium lay directly in the animal's path. He saw the look on the governor's face change from howling laughter to dread as he watched the beast rapidly close the distance to his family. His children screamed as they were knocked from their chairs in the crush of people. The proconsul looked to Lindani, pleading for him to do something. The hunter drew back his bow and sighted down the arrow's shaft. Each time he was about to release, the enraged beast crossed behind a tree or a spectator leaped up and blocked his line of sight. Lindani stayed calm and continued to follow the animal with the metal arrow tip as the eland ravaged the circuit of the cavea. Legionaries ran toward the podium to offer the governor protection, but their speed could not match the charging buck. The governor's daughter screamed. His wife shielded their son. At last, Lindani's field of vision cleared as the eland emerged from behind one of the tall ash trees. He released. The arrow barely cleared the thick tree trunk. It imbedded in the right side of the giant antelope just behind the shoulder blade. Its heart pierced, the eland toppled forward. The red and gold horns grabbed the wooden bench seats causing the buck to somersault and land flat on its back less than a meter from the governor's screaming daughter.

For a moment there was stunned silence. Then the heavy arena door once again flew open with a loud crash. The crowd of spectators who now found themselves on the wrong side of the arena wall panicked, fully expecting another group of wild beasts to sprint into the arena. But this time, a Roman legionary in full armor passed through the portal at a dead run toward Lindani.

The soldier dodged the spectators, who ran in all directions, seeking a path back off the killing floor of the arena.

"Lindani! Watch out!"

The hunter heard Quintus's warning just as the first lash of a whip landed across his back. He dropped to his knees, knowing better than to fight back against a soldier of Rome. Across the chaos of the arena, he could see Julianus in the tunnel next to Quintus, yelling for the gate to be raised. As the grating began to lift, the trainer dropped to the floor, rolled through the narrow opening and sprinted across the sand. He grabbed the soldier's arm as it was swinging down for the fifth time, but before he could protest the punishment, the governor called out.

"Legionary, put that whip away! That man has saved my life."

"But, sir, he reacted too slowly."

"Nonsense!" yelled the governor as he helped his family back into their seats. "If he could have gotten a clear shot, he would have taken it sooner. He did not plan for this . . . this . . . mythical flying antelope to launch itself into the audience."

Nervous laughter came from those seated around the podium. From his kneeling position in the sand, Lindani watched the savvy politician struggle to lighten the mood. The governor was smart enough to realize disastrous games did not make good politics.

"Have the attendants drag all this fresh meat to the east wall of the amphitheater and set up a cooking fire," the governor yelled. He then addressed the entire crowd with a louder voice. "We shall all take our revenge on the beasts by feasting on their carcasses after the games!" A roar of approval went up across the arena. He then pointed to the dead eland at his feet. "And since this one has delivered himself to me personally, save him for those of us on the podium." The governor's family and friends let out a loud cheer as the attendants dragged the bucks away, along with the wounded spectators. Those audience members in the sand exited through the tunnels and made their way back to their seats.

Lindani looked up to see the legionary pull his wrist free of Julianus's grasp and walk toward the tunnel. The trainer helped Lindani to his feet.

"Lindani!" the proconsul called. "I'm sorry for the overreaction of my guard.

Sometimes they take their role a bit too seriously. Here is a gift for saving my family." A hefty bag of gold landed at his feet.

"Thank you, sir," Lindani replied as he retrieved the bag from the sand. Its considerable weight helped lift his spirits and deaden the pain searing through his back. A clamorous cheer—mixed with a chant of "Lindani! Lindani!"—rose from the crowd as Julianus assisted him from the arena.

"Unbelievable," Quintus said in the tunnel entrance. "You kill half the damn spectators and they cheer you anyway. I don't know what it is about you Ethiopian hunters."

Lindani smiled and jingled his bag of coins as he made his way to the physician's ward at the end of the tunnel. "For this much gold, I'd let them beat me after every performance."

The march of the gladiators began after the midday break. The parade was distinctly more impressive accompanied by the full orchestra, rather than the usual trumpet fanfare, and led by the governor's lictors in their scarlet tunics, carrying their bundled axes. Quintus drank in the cheers and studied the crowd as he went. With the bulky helmet off, his handsome face brought even more calls from the women than his broad chest alone. This was why he had entered the craft. The fame. The accolades. And, if he survived, the money. He was only beginning to build his reputation, but he knew soon they would recognize him and cheer his name on sight.

The procession filed back into the tunnel and he sat on the long bench near the back wall, awaiting his bout. He was scheduled toward the middle of the program, a better slot than last time. The German seated himself across the tunnel and attempted a psychological war similar to Memnon's. Quintus was having none of it. He struck up conversations with some of the veterans and the others who were not nervously praying. After two hours, he and the German were called to the head of the tunnel.

"Now you will regret tossing the gladius at me on my first day," the German taunted through the oval visor of his murmillo helmet as they reached the gate.

Quintus casually secured his griffin-crested helmet. "The only thing I regret is not aiming a meter higher and lobbing off that tiny barbarian prick of yours." Before the German could react the gate rose, and the herald bellowed their introductions.

"From the German border, a bull of a Teutonic fighter making his first showing in the arena today. I give you . . . Aylmar!" The German remained in the tunnel looking at Quintus for a brief moment. He then stepped into the arena to a mixture of cheers and boos, acknowledging the latter with hand gestures that everyone assumed were insults in some Germanic culture. This, combined with the bizarre sight of his baggy woolen breeches, had the audience laughing as the herald continued.

"From the city of Rome, a talented new fighter with an impressive win on his record. I give you . . . Quintus!" The young Roman stepped into the sand with his arms spread wide. He could see Julianus watching him carefully from his refereeing position near the arena center, scrutinizing him for any sign of the nervous stupor he had been in before his first battle. Quintus decided to let him and the crowd know he was ready for this fight. He struck a pose, sica poised forward beside his helmet and parmula extended in front of him. He slid forward and worked his weapon through a swift, beautiful *wushu* exercise that ended in another dramatic pose. A deafening roar erupted, inciting Quintus and irritating his opponent.

"You ready now, Hercules?" Julianus asked with a smile.

"Let's do this," Quintus replied.

"Then take your positions." Julianus leaned toward Quintus as the fighters assumed their opening stance. "Be careful. Don't get too cocky," he whispered.

"Be on guard . . . Attack!"

A piercing yell came from the German fighter as he lunged forward with his gladius. Quintus stepped to the side and easily parried the blow, then passed Aylmar, slicing at his back. The move was so fast, most of the spectators did not realize Quintus's sica had connected with flesh until a stripe of blood suddenly appeared across his opponent's shoulder blades. The crowd responded with a sound of awe rather than a cheer.

Quintus could sense the German's shock behind his visor. Again the brutish barbarian charged, this time unleashing a more calculated series of blows and thrusts, ending with a strike Quintus had never encountered before. Aylmar walloped the side of Quintus's helmet hard with the gladius, the earsplitting clang momentarily stunning the young Roman. Immediately there was an outcry of boos from the audience. Julianus never encouraged head blows and he lashed out with the rod as a warning. But the German, in his fury, apparently never felt the sting. Quintus retaliated with an advance that forced Aylmar into a quick retreat. After six or seven steps the German stopped. He held his ground, pounding away at Quintus's small parmula. Quintus saw a brief opening and flicked the tip of his sica. Aylmar stepped back, looking down at the blood seeping from a deep wound across his chest.

The muscles tightened in the German's arms and neck. Unexpectedly, he raised his sword hand to his own helmet. Quintus paused, puzzled as to what the barbarian was going to do next.

"Watch him, Quintus," Julianus warned.

The German's fingertips wrapped around the brim above his visor. In a flash he ripped the helmet from his head, his long brown hair falling to his shoulders. His engorged face, a portrait of pure hatred, matched the violet-red of his breeches. With a howl he flung the helmet at Julianus, then went after Quintus like a wild animal. Quintus thrust hard to keep the madman at bay, but the German used his heavy scutum to plow into Quintus's chest, knocking them both to the ground. The bout had become a wrestling match.

Quintus tried desperately to break free. It was an attack he had never trained for. He had to use gut instinct. He rolled right and left to try separating from the brute. Still Aylmar's face was locked against his visor, his rancid breath streaming through the air holes. Quintus managed to pull his sword arm free of the tangle, but his assailant was too close to strike. He swung hard with the hilt of the sword, catching the German across the face. Blood spewed from his broken nose. Before Quintus could draw back his arm for a second blow, the barbarian sunk his rotting black teeth into the flesh of Quintus's forearm. The young Roman let out a cry that rose above the frenzied mob. He smashed at the back of the German's head with his parmula until he was able to wrench his arm free. As it came away, he could see a hunk of his own bloody flesh dangling from the barbarian's mouth.

The sight pushed Quintus to the breaking point. He shook one leg loose from under the weight of his attacker. His knee drove up hard against the

German's groin. The pain seemed tempered by adrenaline, but it distracted Aylmar enough for Quintus to roll free. Blood streamed down his arm from a sizeable hole, making it difficult to hold his sica. But Quintus had had enough of this barbarian. As the German sprang to his feet, Quintus attacked with a fury that Julianus, and the spectators, had never seen before. His sica was virtually invisible to the eye. The barbarian was forced to give ground. Unable to tell where the blows were coming from, Aylmar tried to hide his enormous body behind the scutum. Attempts to parry with his gladius were useless. Quintus's sica found every square centimeter of exposed flesh. Bloody bits of muscle and tissue flew from the German's arms and legs. Quintus never relented, at one point spinning his body in a circle to gain more momentum in his sword arm. It was a move the trainers had seen Quintus execute during his exercise routine, but no one had ever seen him unleash it on an opponent.

The German finally began to weaken under the tremendous onslaught. After a full two minutes of battering, his scutum slid a few centimeters to the right. Quintus exploited the minor mistake to full effect, slicing the German across the left side of his abdomen, opening a gash wide enough for his entrails to protrude. Aylmar fell backward and grabbed his side, holding his guts from spilling into the sand. Quintus was over him in a second with his sica pressed against his chest. The rage in Quintus's eyes told Julianus he might not wait for a decision from the proconsul before pronouncing the death sentence himself.

The trainer grabbed the hilt of the sword. "Wait for it, Quintus. Don't ruin this now."

Defiantly, the German refused to raise his finger to plead for mercy from the crowd. Quintus knew he would never get it anyway after the flagrant violations of arena protocol. Cries of *"Jugula!"*—"Cut his throat!"—poured from the crowd.

"Hold for the editor," Julianus warned.

Quintus's chest heaved as he gulped air, awaiting the inevitable decision. He looked down at the German, who stared defiantly into his face.

"I thought I'd have a hard time with my first kill," Quintus said between clenched teeth. "But this is going to be a pleasure." He looked up toward the podium and saw the governor's thumb already turned down.

Julianus released his grip on the sica. "Assume the position!" he ordered, but the German ignored him. He was not going to cooperate in his own honorable death the way he had been taught at the ludus. Julianus grabbed him by his chest strap and flipped him to a kneeling position.

"Now grab his leg like you were taught! Die like a man!" he screamed at him. Aylmar stared at them for a second, then spit a mixture of blood and saliva at their feet. Without hesitation, Quintus grabbed the German by his flowing locks, tilted back his head, and sliced his throat.

The amphitheater erupted in a thunderous roar of approval. Quintus dropped the German's lifeless body into the sand and raised his arms in triumph. He untied his chin strap and removed his helmet, allowing the ovation in the cavea to assault his ears directly. The tremendous outpouring of acclaim was for him alone and he reveled in it. Now he had the adulation of thousands all to himself.

He was summoned to the foot of the podium, and the governor waved for quiet from the crowd. "You have fought well, Quintus," the governor said. "I don't think any of us have ever seen Thracian combat executed quite like that before. A most impressive display, especially for only your second bout. I have no doubt your name will soon be known throughout the Empire."

As he finished, he tossed a sizeable bag of gold coins and the traditional victory palm onto the sand. Again the crowd cheered and again they were waved to silence, this time by Quintus.

"With your permission, Proconsul, I would like to make a simple declaration," Quintus called to the podium.

"Go ahead," replied the governor, showing his curiosity as he rubbed his chin.

Quintus cleared his throat, then spoke forcefully enough for every set of ears in the cavea to hear. "Just now, in this arena, Aylmar was not the only one to die. A naïve, innocent tiro also died. If my name is to be known throughout the Empire, let it be the name of the new man who stands before you now. Quintus is dead. From this day on, I will be known as *Taurus*. And I vow to be the greatest fighter in the Empire!"

A thunderous cheer rose like a tidal wave around the arena. The applause was punctuated by a chant that seemed to start at the podium. "Long live

Taurus! Long live Taurus!" He took his final bow and walked to the tunnel. He had to pause as the attendants first dragged the barbarian's mangled body through the portal. He looked up from the bloody path left in the sand to see Petra and Julianus standing at the tunnel entrance, their expressions like those of proud new fathers.

"Not a bad second showing . . . Taurus," the lanista said. "Keep this up and I might have to raise my rates for you."

Quintus smiled. He enjoyed pleasing Petra. "Wouldn't that be a shame?"

"Get to the physician and have that arm taken care of," Julianus said as he readied himself to referee the next bout.

Lindani stepped from behind the trainer, linen bandages wrapped tightly around his torso. "Follow me," he offered. "I just came from there." The African hunter threw his arm over his friend's shoulder as they headed down the tunnel, their upbeat voices echoing off the rough stone walls.

"So . . . it is 'Taurus' now," Lindani said. "I always felt 'Quintus' was not the right name for the greatest fighter in the Empire. I knew you would come to change it someday. Why 'Taurus'?"

"The Amphitheater of Taurus is where my father used to take me for all of Nero's games in Rome. Aulus was always there, too. It seemed right."

"Honoring your father is good judgment. His spirit will bring you strength and courage."

"He and Aulus were both there with me today, Lindani. I felt it."

As they turned the corner and headed down the hall to the physician's room, Quintus was revived with a new breath of life. He was already looking forward to his third match, anxious to put "Taurus" to work.

XVIII

September AD 65

T HE PHYSICIAN USED his sharpest scalpel to cut the flax sutures from Quintus's forearm. The German's bite had left a distinct indentation in his right arm, although the physician's liniment of arnica root and hypericum flowers prevented any infection from the barbarian's revolting mouth. Now, back in the ludus infirmary, Quintus worked his wrist and fingers to be sure the wound did not impair his fighting arm.

"It'll be a little stiff for a while," warned Agricola, the head physician, "but it should be back to normal in a week or so."

"You will be pulling on your rudis again soon, eh?" Lindani said, cackling.

The physician smiled. "I'll bet that 'rudis' of yours will be kept busy from now on. The men tell me you're acquiring quite a following with the ladies."

"Ludus gossip doesn't interest me much," Quintus said casually. After a few more seconds of testing the suture-free muscles of his right arm, he glanced at the physician with an impish grin. "So, what else did they say?"

The physician and Lindani laughed. "Ah, so the unaffected, humble fighter *is* interested in his growing reputation," Agricola said.

"Well, it's good to keep up on one's standing among one's peers," Quintus said with a broad smile.

Before he answered the question, the physician made a show of looking around to be sure they were alone. "Well . . . I overheard Julianus say that they were thinking of jumping your ranking from tiro right to tertius palus, a third-level fighter."

Quintus was stunned. That would mean skipping two lower classes in the meridiani, the mid-level rankings. More practically, it would mean better accommodations in the barracks soon and more money in his winnings purse.

"Be careful, sir," Lindani said to the physician. "Soon the man's head will be too big for his helmet."

Quintus laughed. He watched Lindani's eyes grow wider and a look of inspiration cross his face.

"You know . . . " Lindani continued, obviously formulating some sort of plan in his head as he spoke. "With helmets on their shoulders, every fighter looks the same in the arena. I think what 'Taurus' needs is something to set him apart. His persona must be unique."

"I've seen him fight," Agricola said as he returned his scalpel to the portable medicine chest. "His style is pretty unique."

"No, I speak of something beyond fighting style," Lindani explained. "He must stand alone in a crowd, even during the pompa." He looked at Quintus, his face radiant with excitement. *"Stigmates!"*

Quintus felt his forehead wrinkle. "What?"

The physician smiled. He answered for Lindani. "Stigmates. They're a marking of the skin done with dye."

"Like the Celt warriors with their blue faces?" Quintus asked, still puzzled.

"No," answered Lindani. "These are artistic displays that adorn the body. Our tribal elders and the top warriors in Africa had the markings on their bodies. Once it is done it can never be erased, but when it is done right they are beautiful. They are a window to your soul."

"And what sort of markings do you have in mind?"

"Well, you are now 'Taurus.' You fight like a bull. Why not a bull?"

Quintus was beginning to like the idea, although he still could not picture the end result.

"I've marked some of our ludus slaves with Petra's name," Agricola said. "But I've never seen the markings done as an art. Did you watch it done on your tribal elders?"

"Yes, I helped in the ceremonies. I even created some of the designs. They were pricked into the skin with a sharp needle until blood was drawn. Then the dark mixture was rubbed in. When they healed they became permanent."

"That's the same method I used." The physician went to a set of scrolls he had neatly organized in a wall rack, selected one, and unrolled it. "Here . . . I still have the formula for the dye. One pound of Egyptian pinewood bark, two ounces of corroded bronze, two ounces of gall, and one ounce of vitriol. Mix thoroughly, then soak the powder in two parts water and one part leek juice." He moved to the larger rack that held hundreds of wooden boxes and clay jars of herbs, powders, and tonics. He began lifting containers from the holder. He placed four boxes on the table in front of him and looked at Quintus. "If you want to try it, and you trust Lindani's artistic talents, I still have the ingredients from the last slaves I marked. I can get the leeks from the kitchen staff."

Quintus thought for a minute, then looked at Lindani. "Let's start small and see what it looks like. It's permanent, after all."

Lindani's white teeth showed, and he quickly etched a geometric design into the physician's wax tablet with a stylus.

"He hunts, he runs faster than a gazelle, *and* he's an artist. Are there no limits to this man's talents?" Quintus said with a smile. He looked from the wax tablet to his arm and back again. "Let's do it," he said with a shrug.

The physician seemed happy to accommodate. The artistic project would provide a welcome diversion from sewing up the deep gashes and other bloody injuries that filled his day.

It took two nights to complete the decorative band that wrapped Quintus's well-developed left bicep. The swelling and raw redness, combined with the intense sting of the leek juice, told Quintus he had made a serious mistake. The physician calmed his fears and persuaded him to wait a few days before condemning him and Lindani to eternal damnation for marring the flawless body he had spent almost a year perfecting. Within a week the swelling went down and the relentless itching finally subsided. The black image, similar to the geometric banding found in a mosaic display, took on a dramatic look against his bronze skin. A few of the fighters took notice, but the only opinion Quintus sought was that of Julianus. The response was typical of the cynical trainer.

"If it doesn't make you fight any better, I don't give a rat's ass. But if it gives you some inner strength, then mark up your whole damn arm."

While it did not necessarily produce an inner strength, the marking did make Quintus feel different. As Lindani had predicted, he began to feel "unique." He knew the more elaborate designs his African friend had in mind would help immerse him in the new persona of "Taurus" he was creating for himself. He wanted more.

Within six weeks, Petra called another assembly under the statue. Quintus sat directly in front of the low stage, awaiting word of his next bout. He was more than ready to put Taurus to work. But rather than announce new games, Petra focused on promotions within the ranks.

"Ladies, you will be happy to know that this will be a good-news meeting," the lanista began in his gravelly voice. "I'm glad to see an overall strengthening of this troupe. The Thracians are fighting better than ever. The retiarius fighters are developing a more aggressive style. And more and more of our bouts are ending in missio. When both of my fighters are dismissed standing, that's a sign that the crowds, too, are appreciating the better fights. This is good. I like missio because when you die I have to replace you. I'm sure you like missio because you get to wake up breathing the next morning." The lanista strolled to the far side of the podium, letting his words sink in before continuing. Quintus watched his every move.

"I think a lot of this has to do with the new strength-training programs many of you have started. I know we all laughed at these new horse's-ass contraptions that our wonder boy, Quintus, developed. But, by Jupiter's holy ass, the damn things work!"

Quintus flushed at being singled out. In an odd way, he again felt like the esteemed son he once was, when his father would introduce him with pride to his business associates.

"So what's the message here?" Petra asked rhetorically. "I'll make it clear enough even for you Teutonic barbarian bastards to understand. When you each do well, the entire troupe does well. I can charge more for your services and you will be winning more from the editors in your reward purses. You will also be dipping your dicks into the finest rich women at night." A howl of delight went up from one of the Germans. "Well, not you, Cavell. You'll be fucking goats for the rest of your life." The entire troupe, except for Cavell, broke out in laughter. When it died down, Petra concluded. "Keep up the hard work, ladies. It's beginning to pay off . . . for all of us."

The lanista stepped from the podium and Julianus took over. "The following fighters are promoted in their rankings. Valentinus to primus palus. Roscius to secundus palus. Memnon to quartus palus. And Quintus . . . or rather, Taurus . . . to tertius palus. You will be assigned new cells tonight. That's it. Back to work."

It was a good assembly, thought Quintus. The better and stronger the men got, the more Petra looked upon them with respect. From the voices of the men, Quintus could tell morale was beginning to build. There were still the personal squabbles that were present in every ludus, but on the whole, the camaraderie was growing into pride for the troupe. A few of the veterans congratulated Quintus on his two-level jump in ranking. But what inspired him most was the opportunity to spar with the better seasoned fighters. Now he could hone his skills to perfection.

Quintus slept well that night in his new, bigger cell. His mat was at least twice as thick and comfortable as the first one. A small, barred window allowed fresh air to circulate and afforded a partial view of the green hills and stream beside the venator training field. Beside the wall under the window, he laid out his two victory palms, the older one now brown and dried. Most importantly to Quintus, the new cell contained another small alcove for the fighter's personal icon. His terra-cotta ship captain assumed his place of honor in the niche. Embodying the spirit of his father, his mother, and his friend Aulus, the tiny figurine was a more inspiring and powerful relic than any mere statue of a god could hope to be.

The following morning he was up and running his mini-marathon as usual, his woolen tunic shielding him from the cold morning air. Although there was a lighter spring in Quintus's step, Lindani still easily kept pace with his running partner. Quintus downed a quick breakfast and was on the field early, going through his sword workout.

"What are you so itchy about today?" Julianus asked as he walked to the Thracian training area.

"I'm ready to spar. I want a go at some of the veterans today."

"Oh, I see. You jump up a few ranks and you want to take on the top dogs already."

"Present me a challenge today, sir. I'm ready for anything."

Julianus smiled at the young Roman's enthusiasm. "Alright, well, here comes the second man out and he happens to be a murmillo. How about we start you off against him?"

Quintus turned to see Valentinus, the new primus palus, walking onto the training field. His heart pounded. The man was a veteran of fifteen arena fights, one of the best in the school. This was the challenge he was looking for this day.

Julianus kept the tension mounting for him by spending the first hour reviewing technique and some of the minor mistakes from the previous day's sparring. Quintus's attention was rapt as he sat in the dirt listening, but his knee bounced in anticipation. Beads of perspiration were forming on his forehead by the time Julianus called for the first sparring match.

"Valentinus, suit up. Quintus, suit up."

Quintus sprang up and quickly pulled the heavy tunic over his head, leaving only his yellow subligaculum. Little by little he heard the banging of the wooden swords around him slow down. He was bent over, strapping on his greaves, when he suddenly noticed the extraordinary quiet on the practice field. He looked over his shoulder and was surprised to see thirty pairs of eyes glued to him. But their gaze did not meet his eyes; they looked lower. With a shock it hit him. The stigmates. For weeks he and his two conspirators had worked late into the evening on his markings. He had not planned to reveal the artwork until fully complete, but in his haste to take on the veteran he had forgotten to keep his tunic on. He stood up and turned. An audible gasp came from fighters and trainers alike.

Staring back at them from his chest was the giant face of a Minotaur, rendered in various shades of black ink. The half-man, half-bull image spread from shoulder to shoulder and down to his navel. Curved horns sprang from the beast's forehead above fierce, squinting eyes that stared from Quintus's upper chest. Upon his breastbone sat a broad squat nose, the nostrils linked together with a brass ring. Below the breastbone, two rows of murderous pointed teeth were framed by black lips and streams of hair that conformed to the fighter's tight abdominal muscles.

Quintus turned to see the reaction of the men behind him. More gasps erupted as the fighters were treated to a second image. Across his back, the physician had placed a Gorgon. "To protect you from attacks from the rear," Lindani had said. Serpents radiated from an evil face that stared blankly through two eyes with no pupils. The scales of reptilian skin stretched across the face and onto the backs of the twenty or so tangled snakes that were the Gorgon's hair. A raw redness on two of the snake heads revealed where the markings had still not healed. Some of the more superstitious men averted their eyes, concerned the lifelike image might turn them to stone, as would the real Medusa and her Gorgon sisters.

In the midst of the silence, Quintus looked at Julianus, hoping for words of encouragement. But before the trainer could get his mouth to work, Petra approached. He followed everyone's gaze to Quintus.

"Mars's ass! You look like a fucking mosaic floor!"

The entire troupe erupted in laughter. Quintus felt his face flush with embarrassment and again doubted the wisdom of his decision.

"I'll say this," Petra continued. "It sets this man apart. It tells the audience, 'I am Taurus the Bull, and I am the meanest motherfucker in this arena.' And that's the attitude the mob wants to see." The lanista spun Quintus around to get a better look. "Who did this?"

Quintus hesitated, not wanting to get Lindani or Agricola into trouble.

"I'd like to congratulate them on some fine work," Petra continued.

"It's Lindani's design and Agricola, the physician's, dye."

Petra nodded as he continued to inspect the images. "So now you are Taurus outside as well as in."

"Only in the arena, Dominus. Taurus can be a cruel and vicious man. Outside the arena I remain Quintus."

Petra completed his inspection and studied the young Roman's face. "I like it," he said, then turned and walked away.

"Back to work," yelled Julianus and the sound of the wooden swords once again filled the training ground. Quintus breathed a sigh of relief as he returned to suiting up. A few of the fighters smacked his back and offered a compliment as they resumed their training. He glanced up at Valentinus, who was ready to spar. The veteran fighter gave Quintus a short nod.

"It works," was all he had to say.

Quintus ran through some quick mental preparations, then lined up against Valentinus. At the "Attack" signal the two battled back and forth, each gaining ground over the other before the tide turned again. Julianus shouted advice to both as they sparred, then encouraged Quintus to "stoke it." Quintus reached down deep and exploded with the almost inhuman speed he was coming to perfect. Valentinus was forced to retreat, although he countered many more of Quintus's blows than the lumbering German in Londinium. What Quintus concentrated on now, even more than speed, was anticipation. He had his parmula in a protective position at virtually the same instant Valentinus swung his rudis. He was totally focused on becoming one with his opponent, a new bit of wisdom taught him by Master Sheng at Glevum. Valentinus simply could not find an opening in which to counterattack. As the bout reached a stalemate, Julianus called a "Hold." Both fighters backed off, panting loudly through their visors.

"Not bad," Julianus said with a smile. "I think you both got a pretty good workout. Quintus, you need to pace that speed of yours a little better. Up against a pro like Valentinus, you might wear yourself out before you land the killing blow. Short bursts are better." The trainer looked at the seasoned pro, still huffing and puffing as he stood with drooping shoulders. "Valentinus, find the hole. It's difficult with an opponent who can move faster than a starling, but you have to find the hole in his defense. Alright, take a break. Next two fighters."

Quintus spent the rest of the day replaying the sparring match in his mind. He saw how the principles of the wise Easterner were beginning to come alive within him. He was learning to channel his frustrations and temper against his opponent rather than against himself. He was proud of holding his own against the new primus palus. He knew the bout had a lot of people talking. He just wished he could have landed a single blow on the man's arm or leg.

After his strength training, Quintus began his afternoon *wushu* exercise with a metal palus sword. Although his eyes remained closed, he was acutely aware of every muscle and nerve ending in his body as he visualized the flow of the *chi,* just as Sheng had taught him. When he finally opened his eyes, he noticed Julianus standing by the weapons rack watching him, his right eye almost closed in its eternal squint. Quintus moved closer and replaced the sword in the rack. Julianus sent his assistants to gather up the remaining practice weapons.

"Word is floating through the ludus that there are new games being scheduled," Quintus said in a low voice.

"Are the men that anxious to get into the arena again?" Julianus replied, not committing to an answer.

"There's certainly a renewed energy building here. I think more of the men are beginning to look at the technique as well as pure combat. That's good, right?"

Julianus smiled. "Yes, that's good. It gives the audience what they want and that's always good for the troupe. Remember, the illusion of danger is often better than danger itself." He approved more of the equipment to be locked away, then returned to the conversation. "Yes, new games are being discussed."

"In Aquae Sulis?" Quintus asked quickly.

"No. I don't think you'll be fighting for your old friend, Lucius, again for a while. Apparently there's some political trouble brewing. Something about a legionary raping a chieftain's daughter. Between that and the constant farmland disputes down there, it sounds like there might be a clan uprising soon. That should put the political skills of 'Quintus Honorius Romanus' to the test." Julianus sent a worker away with the last of the equipment. "The next games will be here in Glevum, probably in another month or two."

The last bit of information did not register with Quintus. His mind was still on the news of the Aquae Sulis situation. How would Lucius handle his first big test under fire? Quintus could not help hoping for an unmitigated disaster.

The following morning, Quintus sat once again at the feet of Julianus as he began the day's training. But before the lesson commenced, the ludus gates swung open and an excited young training assistant on horseback galloped to a halt near Julianus. Quintus waved away the dust kicked up in his face by the hooves.

"Briton clansmen . . . hundreds of them!" the assistant yelled, gasping for breath after his hard ride. "All along the road to Aquae Sulis. I saw them from Corinium while I was picking up the supplies. It looks like a revolt!"

Julianus looked at Quintus. "So, we'll see just how savvy our new magistrate really is," he said quietly.

XIX

October AD 65

THE ROMAN COHORT stood nervously under the silver eagle standard of the Second Augusta Legion. The paltry group of five hundred Roman legionaries and a handful of cavalrymen faced fifteen hundred Briton clansmen who lined the banks of the river Avon.

Lucius turned in his saddle and looked down at the double file of inexperienced soldiers behind him. He knew the green cohort was all that stood between the horde and the town walls of Aquae Sulis. The barbarians' blue-painted faces, their hair pulled into wild spikes with limewash, seemed to add to the fear in the pit of the young legionaries' stomachs. Most were fresh conscripts stationed at the resort town as more of a police force than a combat unit. The extent of their anxiety was evident by the shaking hands holding their javelins and the wet streaks of urine running down some of their legs. The tough centurion who sat on the horse next to Lucius was the only Roman warrior in the ranks with any battle experience. He showed no emotion as he watched the clansmen. Finally, he turned to Lucius.

"Remain in place. I'll ride down to speak with their chieftain."

Lucius glared at the centurion. "You can order your men around all you want. But do I need to remind you that I am the magistrate of this town? You have no authority over me."

The centurion's eyes narrowed to thin slits as he spoke through clenched teeth. "This is a military matter. You, sir, are a politician. You have no business even being out here beyond the . . . "

Before the centurion finished his sentence, Lucius kicked at his horse and trotted off toward the line of barbarians. *"Son of a bitch!"* he heard the Roman officer yell. The centurion's horse quickly caught up with Lucius and they rode side by side to the river. The officer's battle medallions and captured Celtic torques clinked against his mail as the white plume of his helmet crest bounced in beat with his horse's canter. Before they reached the clan leader, a spear struck the earth in front of the centurion's black charger, causing him to pull up short.

The Briton chieftain spoke loudly with a harsh accent. "For five years we have lived in peace with the Romans. But now the tribes rally in the name of our late queen, Boudicca, who rose up against you seven years ago, destroying an entire Roman Legion. Once again we shall wage war against the Legions of Britannia unless the vile Roman dog who raped my daughter is handed over to us this day for justice. In addition, our people continue to be removed from their farmlands by your legionaries. These are our farmlands that were guaranteed to us by your own Emperor Claudius. This injustice, too, must cease this day."

Before Lucius could respond, the centurion spoke up.

"The first we heard of this supposed rape was from your emissary, who arrived with the ridiculous accusation a few days ago. We have looked into the matter, and there is no evidence that the attack happened or that any Roman legionary was involved." He paused while the clansmen grumbled loudly at each other. "As for your farmlands, there is nothing we can do about that. We need to feed our troops and are simply following orders from Rome."

A fierce cry in the local tongue sprang from one of the chieftain's bodyguards, inciting all fifteen hundred men to a deep-toned, haunting chant. Lucius assumed it was a call for their death and the death of the cohort. The Britons' horses stomped at the riotous noise and had to be held back from charging on their own.

The chieftain raised his hand and quieted the vicious mob. "As you can see, my men are more than eager to sack your beautiful town and perhaps enjoy a few Roman women in return."

Lucius watched the centurion tighten his grip on the reins.

"This river will run red with Briton blood long before you come close to entering that gate," the Roman officer shouted. "You are facing the best-trained fighting force in the world. Now take your men and return to your tribes before the power of Rome lands upon you."

Once again the Briton war cry was shouted and once again the army of clansmen joined the unnerving chant.

"So be it," the Roman officer shouted. He tugged his reins and spun his horse, but before he kicked it forward, Lucius spoke up.

"Hail, oh great Cadwallon!" Lucius shouted above the thunderous war chants. The chieftain once again raised his hand and quieted his horde.

"What do you think you're doing?" the centurion said through clenched teeth, his back to the clansmen.

"I am saving Aquae Sulis, something you don't seem capable of doing today," Lucius shot back.

"As I said, this is a military matter. Return to your office and leave the battle to those who are trained to fight it."

Even without military training, Lucius knew that the small group of legionaries pissing themselves behind him did not stand a chance against this army of fierce warriors. Although the centurion seemed resigned to a fight, Lucius kept his composure.

"I want a moment alone with these people and I guarantee you this whole mess will be over."

"Are you crazy? They'll lob your head from your body."

Lucius stared hard at the centurion. "If my town is sacked and looted, I will notify Rome immediately that you and your prefect have needlessly caused the deaths of thousands of wealthy Roman citizens. Now ride away and let me handle this."

The centurion glanced over his shoulder. Lucius, too, scanned the Britons. The smirks on the face of the chieftain and his bodyguards betrayed their amusement with the military officer's lack of control of the situation.

"You have until I prepare my troops; then we attack," the centurion said. He galloped away, leaving Lucius alone with the clansmen.

After a few minutes of discussion, Lucius raised his hand in a sign of peace. The chieftain did the same, then spun his horse and rode away down the river bank. He was followed by fifteen hundred Briton barbarians.

Lucius turned his horse and rode back to the Roman ranks. As he approached, the look of bewilderment on the centurion's face was almost comical. Behind the line of soldiers, the nervous townspeople, who had climbed the walls to watch the drama, began to cheer. Their sense of relief spilled over to the legionaries, who realized they would live to fight another day. They, too, erupted in shouts of celebration.

"Hold your tongues, you fucking babies," the centurion yelled. "The next man to cheer gets twenty lashes."

Lucius rode up alongside the officer with a smile. "Why does it always seem to depress veteran centurions to witness diplomacy prevailing over military might?"

The centurion's eyes narrowed with suspicion. "What did you say to them?"

Lucius looked around, then leaned closer to the officer. "We'll talk later," he whispered.

The town gates swung open and a thousand jubilant citizens poured out of the town to congratulate their magistrate. Julia was at the head of the mob, cheering wildly, as her nephew approached the gate. After a brief, insincere protest, she allowed Lucius to lift her onto the back of his horse. She wrapped an arm around his waist to balance herself on the animal's jittery hindquarters. Together they pressed through the crowd and led an impromptu victory parade back into town, waving to the masses as they were followed by the military cohort in smart formation. They traveled slowly down the main street to the Temple of Sulis-Minerva, basking in the adulation of the crowd. Lucius had trouble dismounting in the crush of people. He assisted Julia down and they climbed the steps of the temple, shaking a hundred hands as they went.

"Today we have once again shown these local heathens that Rome rules Britannia," Lucius bellowed so all in the public square could hear. Another round of cheering interrupted him. "Tomorrow I will meet one last time with the barbarians. As Jupiter is my witness, I swear to you that after tomorrow the clansmen will all peacefully return to their tribes." Another roar of approval went up from the crowd as Lucius escorted Julia to their vermilion coach. He motioned to the centurion and the two spoke for a moment before he and Julia disappeared into the opulence of the carriage. Once clear of the town gates on the road to their villa, Julia closed the coach shutters tight.

Lucius lay back on the soft pillows and grinned at Julia, who was flushed with excitement.

"Allow me to commend you on your performance," she said as she crawled across the opening between their two facing seats. Without warning she took his head in her hands and kissed him hard, her tongue parting his lips and probing deep into his mouth. Lucius did not know how to respond. Although she was fifteen years older than he, Lucius still found Julia a remarkably attractive and alluring woman. But what made him squirm in his luxuriously upholstered seat was the thought that Julia was aggressively seducing her own nephew, at least from her point of view. Her right hand slid down his chest and quickly found his crotch. She released his lips and leaned forward.

"It seems to me," she whispered seductively into his ear, "that today's events call for a celebration of our own."

She leaned back long enough to pull the light green stola over her head, tossing it to the carriage floor. She sat naked in front of him. Her breasts were larger and fuller than he had imagined during his frequent nighttime fantasies. Without hesitation, he reached forward and cupped them, kissing them lightly until his lips reached her hardened nipples. Julia began to giggle. Lucius wondered if it was from the physical sensation or from the thoughts running through her devious mind.

"From what I saw, it could not have gone better," she said quietly as he continued to feast. "My plan will set us both up for life."

He lifted his face and looked at her. "Your plan? When did this become *your* plan? Do you have any idea how long I worked to set this up?"

Julia grinned a sly smile and pulled his head back to her breasts. "Oh, what does it matter whose plan, Quintus? It's you that the soldiers saw avert the disaster. And it's your name which will soon be on the lips of the Senate and perhaps Nero himself." The thought seemed to bring her to a new level of ecstasy and she pushed Lucius's head lower as she spread her legs wide and laid back on the soft couch. "On the lips of Nero himself . . . " she repeated in a whisper. She arched her back and enjoyed the remainder of the ride home.

The morning sun sent streams of light through the autumn foliage that overhung the secluded gorge. The rays backlit the five Romans on horseback who waited patiently in the forest a few kilometers outside the walls of Aquae Sulis. The sound of distant hooves echoed eerily against the granite walls of the gorge.

"This had better work," said the centurion who had been denied his battle the day before. Lucius did not bother to reply. The three cavalrymen who accompanied them sat silently on their mounts, their hands red with fresh blood.

Fifty meters ahead, the silhouettes of seven riders turned a corner and broke into the sunlight. The surprise on their faces was evident to Lucius even at a distance—all except for Cadwallon. The clan chieftain kept his stoic look as he raised his eyes from the five Romans to the grisly sight that hovered over them. Lucius watched his reaction intently as the chieftain studied the wooden cross towering four meters above them.

The head of the man hanging from the cross rolled slightly from right to left. Blood pumped from around the large spikes in his wrists, ran down his arms, and painted wide red stripes across his bands of silver armor. The crimson streams merged with the blood pouring from his feet and puddled in a pool of gore at the base of the cross. The irony of the scene did not escape anyone who witnessed it. A Roman legionary, who would normally be hammering the spikes into another tormented soul, was now himself nailed securely to the timbers with his life draining from his body. His swelling face was a deep shade of blue, the effects of suffocation combined with a brutal beating before the spikes were driven.

Lucius's voice broke the silence. "Great Cadwallon, and the lovely Angwen," he began, acknowledging the chieftain's daughter who had accompanied her father at Lucius's insistence. "Last night we continued our investigation into the heinous crime you brought to our attention. This wretched soldier finally admitted to the rape. Please accept our heartfelt apology for his brutal act. We hope you will find the punishment we have imposed befits the crime."

Cadwallon stared at the soldier hanging from the cross, then looked at his daughter. "Is this the dog who attacked you?"

The teenaged girl shielded her eyes from the glare of the morning sun behind the cross. "It's hard to say, Father. His face is so bloodied." She continued to squint at the dying man. Lucius looked at Cadwallon, then back to his daughter. He could sense the cavalry soldiers behind him tightening their grips on the hilts of their swords.

"Yes, I believe that's him," the girl finally said. There was an audible sigh of relief from the soldiers.

"And the land incursions?" asked Cadwallon.

"There will be no further incursions by our soldiers onto your farmlands," Lucius answered.

"And what of the land that has already been taken?" the chieftain pressed.

"I'm afraid that cannot be undone. However, for the next harvest we will divide the bounty from that land evenly with your tribe. This will allow you time to plant your new crops elsewhere."

Cadwallon made a show of considering the offer, stroking his beard as he thought.

"Look again upon this cross," Lucius continued. "It is a gesture of good faith. It shows that we value and respect your people, especially those as beautiful as your daughter." Lucius nodded and smiled at the plump, flushed face of the chieftain's homely offspring.

"So be it," stated Cadwallon. "I will have the warriors return to their tribes. There will be no fighting." The Britons followed their chieftain as he swung his horse around and trotted from the gorge.

Lucius stood motionless waiting for a reaction from the centurion as he watched the clansmen disappear into a cloud of dust.

After a moment, the centurion spoke. "Well, I have to say, that was pretty impressive. You gave them nothing and they rode away happy for it."

Lucius smiled, not so much in response to the centurion's praise but more from the satisfaction at seeing the true target of this ploy fall into his hands. He looked at the centurion.

"It's not always necessary to lose good men in combat to win a battle." He glanced up at the cross. "Sometimes you need only a sacrificial lamb. Now, put that poor bastard out of his misery and let's get going."

"I hope this man's services won't be missed at your villa," said the centurion as one of his cavalry men plunged the tip of his pike into the crucified man's neck, killing him instantly.

"We have many slaves at the villa. One less doesn't trouble us. Especially since he has given his life for such a noble cause."

Lucius wheeled his horse around. "See that your prefect gets an accurate account of what happened here this morning." He spurred his horse into a fast trot toward Aquae Sulis. The centurion ordered the armor removed from the slave and cleaned, and the body and cross buried in the forest.

Julia Melita drummed her fingers impatiently on the soft couch of her vermilion coach. Finally, she heard the distant echo of hooves approaching. The tall thin driver offered her assistance as she stepped from the coach, which had been parked all morning along the roadside in the thick forest north of Aquae Sulis. They both looked up as the seven Britons turned the blind corner and pulled their horses to a stop.

"Did everything go as planned?" Julia asked.

"Yes," Cadwallon replied. "Although your slave did not have to die. I would have accepted your nephew's word that it was done."

"The soldiers would never have believed it. Besides, a slave knows he must give his life for his master if necessary."

"So be it. We have played our part. Where is our payment?"

Julia motioned to the driver, who retrieved a pair of large canvas bags from the carriage and hefted them onto the backs of two of the horses. The animals jittered as the substantial weight of thousands of gold coins was added to their load.

"I thank you for furthering my nephew's career," Julia said with a sly grin. "I hope your next magistrate and his family are as magnanimous as we've been."

Cadwallon smiled back. "I hope the next magistrate is as devious as you and your nephew—and as willing to part with gold to further his ambition."

XX

January AD 66

F OR THE SECOND TIME since joining the ludus, Quintus paraded the circuit of the Glevum arena in the opening pompa. This amphitheater held a special spot in his heart as the place where he had first walked upon the sand. Then he had been a mere kitchen assistant. Now he was a featured fighter. He had decided to wait until the afternoon parade to shed his wool tunic. By then the sun would have warmed the arena to a reasonable temperature on this cold winter's day. And by then he would be ready to become Taurus.

As Quintus marched, he spotted Master Sheng in his yellow robe, sitting with the manager and unctores from the bathhouse. He stopped for a moment and bowed in respect to his tutor, then stepped through a perfectly executed portion of his *wushu* routine. The spectators seated nearby roared their approval. But at this moment, Quintus sought the approval of only one person. Sheng had told him he would be leaving soon to resume his travels across the Empire. Quintus wanted to let his spiritual trainer know he had learned much and was grateful. As he ended his short display, he pointed up to the Easterner, acknowledging the true master in their midst. Sheng nodded with a smile that meant more to Quintus than the old man could ever know.

The pompa wound its way to the editor's podium. The sight of the old Glevum magistrate brought thoughts of Lucius to Quintus's mind. The account of how he had single-handedly averted a disastrous battle at Aquae Sulis had been big news for weeks throughout Britannia. Quintus wasn't sure how he had pulled it off, but he knew damn well there was more to the story than what everyone was saying.

The morning venatio went well for all but one tiro hunter teamed with

Lindani and another venator in a three-against-three lion hunt. The brash young hunter refused to heed Lindani's warning of the stealth and intelligence of the big cats. Impatiently, he charged one of the lions alone with his hunting spear and was quickly overpowered by the three animals. His fellow hunters had no chance to save him, nor were they so inclined, seeing his reckless attitude as a danger to their own safety. The remaining hunter was quick to follow Lindani's strategy of divide and conquer. One by one the lions were separated from their tight pack and eliminated with well-tossed hunting pikes.

Trumpets heralded the end of the noontime break. The tunnel doors swung open and the colorful march of the gladiators proceeded behind the bright yellow banner announcing Petra's familia. The mob was on its feet cheering each fighter as he entered the arena.

"You still have your tunic on?" Julianus asked as Quintus moved past him in the tunnel.

"Give it time," Quintus said with a smile. "You have to pace these things, you know."

As he followed the procession up the dank corridor to the arena, he began to make his mental transformation from Quintus to Taurus. With every step he felt the blood surge stronger through his body. He subconsciously tightened his grip on his sica. His thoughts turned to survival. He would fight hard. He would be victorious. He would survive. He visualized himself at the foot of the podium with palm leaf in hand. He closed his eyes and stepped through the portal onto the sand, feeling the warmth of the sun on his arms and legs. He paused and let out a bellow that startled many of the nervous tiro fighters. The crowd looked toward the tunnel entrance. Quintus placed his fingers into the special seams he had prepared in his tunic and, with another roar, wrenched the cloth apart revealing his massive torso emblazoned with the images of the Minotaur and the Gorgon.

The transformation was complete. He had become Taurus.

There was stunned silence for a long moment, punctuated by screams from some of the female spectators. Taurus struck a pose, then stepped through a few seconds of his Eastern sword exercise, his bright red subligaculum and wide gold belt stark against the earth tones of the arena. A thunderous cheer erupted from the cavea. As he resumed his march he could hear chants of "Taurus! Taurus!" growing in the arena. It seemed his reputation had preceded him, probably carried by the sailors and travelers from the Londinium contest. He watched the faces of the patricians and politicians in the first few rows. All eyes were fixed on his chest and back. He could see some of the women brazenly licking their lips and groping their breasts as he passed, oblivious to their husbands seated next to them.

"Looks like you got the attention you were seeking," came Julianus's voice as he marched up behind Taurus.

"True. But I'm not just bluff. I will deliver for these people."

Julianus nodded as he passed him, a confident smile on his lips.

On this day, Taurus was to be part of a climactic multi-fighter bout that would wrap up the games. He sat along the walls of the holding cells for most of the afternoon. He draped his ripped tunic over his shoulders to ward off the cold winter chill, which seemed magnified by the stone walls. Over the previous winter he had learned the wisdom of keeping his muscles warm before a match, a tip most of the other fighters ignored.

Finally, the call came for the last ten fighters to approach the gate. Taurus was matched against a secundus palus Celtic prisoner named Riagall. The young Roman secured his Thracian helmet and leaned against the tunnel wall, studying his opponent across the walkway. Riagall did not employ the intimidation tactics of Taurus's previous opponents. He was there to do a job and he usually did it well, a fact confirmed by his six wins and three missio. Taurus heard the trumpets and looked toward the gate. The sight of the man who suddenly appeared to his right startled him. A long black cloak, tunic, and boots were topped by a green face bearing an abnormally long hook nose and twin white horns sprouting from his forehead. It took Taurus a moment to realize it was an attendant wearing the mask of Charon, the ferryman of the dead. The heavy hammer he wielded assured that no gladiator would fake death to escape the arena. Charon was a part of all the games in Rome, but appeared only occasionally in the provinces.

Julianus called the men into the arena. Two retiarius dragged their heavy nets through the sand as they lined up against two secutors. Taurus and another thraex faced their murmillo opponents. At the end of the line, two dimachaerii faced off with twin daggers. Julianus yelled for each to stand ready, then gave the "Attack" signal.

Chaos erupted in the arena as the massive battle got under way. While Taurus had sparred a few times in group combat, he was unprepared for the distractions caused by ten fighters in the arena simultaneously. He focused on the Celtic fighter in front of him and unleashed an opening attack. With his reputation for unmatched speed and agility, many in the crowd were watching him. His markings did their job well. He was easy to pick out in the crowd of helmets and flailing weapons. Riagall retreated a few steps then held his ground. The two were still sizing each other up when the net of the retiarius next to them missed its mark and landed partially on Taurus's shoulder, the heavy edge weights leaving a row of red welts. Riagall seized on the unexpected opportunity and delivered a series of lunges at Taurus's chest. Each thrust was parried by the small parmula, but Taurus was forced to retreat. Across the arena he heard a scream of pain as a secutor was pinned to the ground by the points of a retiarius's trident. The crowd's attention turned to that fight and they quickly called for the death of the wounded fighter. He had not put on a long enough display.

As the fights wore on, one by one the gladiators began to fall. The majority were spared for their courageous combat. One of the dimachaerii fell to the sand with both his opponent's daggers imbedded in his torso. His head rose briefly, then fell back lifeless into the sand. As assurance, the attendant dressed as Charon stepped forward and brought his long wooden hammer down upon the man's head, spraying blood and brains in an arc across the sand.

Finally, only the sound of one fight filled the arena. Caught up in the dramatic struggle, the crowd's cheering slowly died away. Even in the cold of the late afternoon, sweat poured down the Minotaur and Gorgon images on Taurus. It had been over fifteen minutes and still neither fighter showed signs of weakening. All of the previous victors, along with those dismissed by missio who could still stand, lined the arena wall and watched the final contest.

Taurus drew strength from knowing that all eyes in the arena were focused on him. With a guttural roar, his sica began to fly at the superhuman speed he was able to summon at will. The blows came from all directions. Up and down. Right and left. Riagall was on the run. He tried to counter each stroke, but the devastating attack opened deep gouges on both his arms. Taurus knew he could deliver a death blow whenever he wanted. Instead, he drove Riagall deliberately backward toward the corpse of the dimachaerus. Unaware of the body, the Celtic fighter tripped and landed hard on his back. Before he even considered regaining his feet, the tip of Taurus's sica was at his throat.

Julianus stepped up and called, "Hold!" Quintus scanned the crowd. White handkerchiefs waved throughout the cavea, showing mercy for his opponent. The magistrate agreed and spared the Celt's life.

Taurus stepped back and flexed for the delighted crowd. The magistrate summoned the five victors to the podium where they accepted their palms and payment purses. The group then did something the crowd had never seen before. With Taurus leading the way, they ran a victory lap as a team, waving their branches proudly to the crowd. Taking the impromptu ceremony a step further, Taurus grabbed the arm of each defeated fighter still standing and raised it for recognition from the crowd. The unusual display of camaraderie incited another wave of thunderous applause and ended the games with a mark of dignity and sportsmanship unheard of in the Glevum arena.

The temperature dropped severely as the sun set beyond the distant bare oak trees that overlooked Glevum's city center. Petra's staff worked quickly, loading the equipment wagons. Many of the fighters were already huddled in their transport carts, trying to ward off the chill. But Quintus had too much pent-up energy to sit still. He paced the line of carts, offering congratulations to the victors and condolences to the losers. As he neared the head of the column he heard a familiar raspy voice.

"That was quite a display you organized out there." Petra stood at the rear of his torch-lit wagon, vapor coming from his mouth as he spoke.

"Thank you, Dominus. It felt good today. Riagall did well. I'm glad he was spared."

"Well, like I said, every one of you that's spared saves me a shitload of money."

Quintus could see that Petra was using the cargo bed of the wagon as a desktop to stack the gold coins he had received for the day's performance. The lanista made a habit of always counting his money before the troupe pulled stakes and left town, although any provincial magistrate who attempted to cheat a man in control of a well-trained troupe of gladiators was flirting with terrible danger. Petra seemed in a good mood after the success of the games, so Quintus decided to push his luck and bring up an issue that had been on his mind for weeks.

"May I speak frankly, Dominus?"

Petra stopped counting and raised a bushy eyebrow. "It depends."

"Well, I mean no disrespect, but you do realize that with the strength of this troupe you should have double or triple the amount of money you're counting there, don't you?"

Before Petra could respond, Quintus took from his belt the small bag he had been tossed by the magistrate, pulled it open, and piled his seven gold coins next to the hundreds already stacked along the weathered floorboard. He looked up at Petra, who was still quietly staring at him.

"We're both ready for something bigger than these provincial arenas. So is Lindani and all the other veterans in our ludus. You have talented trainers like Julianus working with some of the best fighters and hunters in the Empire, and yet we continue to satisfy the whims of small-time politicians and homesick soldiers on the frontiers of the Empire. We are too good for this. All of us."

Petra smiled and nodded, then went back to counting his coins. "So I see the bravado of 'Taurus' now extends beyond the arena. You win a few fights and suddenly you're a promoter and accountant. Is that it?"

"No, sir. I'm just a fighter who's seen many of Nero's games in Rome. There are a lot of fighters and hunters in this troupe I would put up against the best of Rome tomorrow."

"You realize that the Emperor alone controls the ludus in Rome? And when they need more good fighters they turn to the Campania school in Pompeii. Unless there's a sudden call for thousands of gladiators in Rome, they're not going to come to a broken old provincial lanista. That's just the way it works."

"That's the way it works now. Why can't it change? You have great fighters here, Dominus. The time is right for you to make a move. Just like it was right for me to make a move when I joined your school. It's time for the Familia Gladiatoria Petra to make its mark in the Empire. Not out here on the frontier, but in the big arenas of Italia."

Petra continued stacking his coins without a response. After a quiet minute Quintus assumed the conversation was over. He slid his small stack of coins from the cargo bed and shook his head in exasperation. He turned to head back down the line of carts.

"Quintus," Petra called after him. "Don't get your tunic in a bunch. I'm already working on it. Just sit tight and you might get to show off that mosaic-floor chest of yours in Italia someday."

The training field at the Pompeii ludus in southern Italia was crowded as usual with its four hundred fighters and one hundred hunters. Facilix, the lanista, was personally overseeing the training of a promising new secutor he had purchased from the Verona school a few weeks earlier. He noticed his office assistant hovering nearby with a scroll in hand.

"Looks like we need to bail out the ludus in Rome again," he said with a grin to his head trainer, Justus. He waved over the worker with the scroll.

"This message arrived this morning, Dominus. The business manager felt you should see it right away."

The lanista unrolled the scroll and began reading. He could not help but smile, which seemed to pique the interest of the head trainer.

"What is it?"

"Well . . . I'm not sure. It appears to be a challenge from another ludus, near Glevum in Britannia."

"I didn't even know there was a school up there," said Justus as he stepped closer and read over the lanista's shoulder.

"I didn't know about the Glevum school," Facilix replied, "but I've heard good things about the games in Londinium."

Justus began to read aloud. "'The Familia Gladiatoria Petra offers a challenge to the Ludus of Pompeii. We will match the best of Britannia against the best of Southern Italia. The north against the south' . . . Oh, this is absurd!"

"Well, wait a minute," Facilix said. "Think about it. This lanista must have balls the size of melons to challenge the best school in the Empire outside of Rome itself. So either he's a complete fool or he thinks he has some hot-shit fighters in his troupe."

"Oh, come on," the trainer said. "How good can they be, trained in the armpit of the Empire? I'll bet he has nothing but brute Germans and a few wild Celts."

"Maybe so, but it'll offer the Pompeii crowd some fresh faces for a change. The promotional aspects of this 'north-south' thing could be interesting. If nothing else it'll be a cheap way for us to look at some new talent. If we like anything we see, I'll bet we can snatch it up for a few sesterces."

"And who's going to put up the money?" Justus asked, still not convinced. "A big 'north-south' event should have a pretty good payoff. Plus, there's the expense of getting his troupe to Pompeii."

The lanista thought for a minute. "We'll put it back on him. He finds the editor to guarantee our fee and he gets his own troupe here from Britannia. If he can manage that, we're in. What have we got to lose?" Facilix motioned for his assistant. "Get the scribe. I want to send a reply to old Petra right away."

XXI

March AD 66

LUCIUS BURST THROUGH the front doors of the family villa and bellowed Julia's name. The staff in and around the entrance hall scurried to get out of his way as he ran down the corridor yelling.

"Sir, the mistress is taking her morning bath and wishes not to be disturbed." Before the head servant had finished his sentence, Lucius was out of earshot and bounding up the stairs. Without a knock he threw open the door to Julia's private toilet. The sudden intrusion startled her as she reclined in her large marble tub, her maids gently massaging her shoulders and feet. She dropped her legs into the tub with a splash as her attendants naïvely used a large towel to shield her from Lucius's view.

"What is it, Quintus? What's wrong?" Julia asked, panic growing in her voice.

He remained in the doorway, smiling. Slowly, he slid his right hand from behind his back until the scroll it held was in clear view. He watched Julia's eyes widen as she gazed on the Imperial seal that held the parchment closed.

"Leave us!" she said to her maids. The young girls hesitantly dropped the towel and left the room. "Close the door!" she shouted to the last girl, her eyes never leaving the scroll in Lucius's hand.

"This came this morning with the new legionary recruits sent up from Rome," Lucius said as he slowly approached the tub. "Do you recognize this seal?"

Julia nodded as she sat up straight, the water running down her back and breasts. "Well, are you going to open it or are you going to let me die of anxiety?"

Lucius slowly ran his finger along the scroll, breaking the wax seal. He wasn't sure what fascinated him more, the contents of the scroll or watching Julia's anticipation as she licked her lips and began to tremble ever so slightly.

"Oh, hurry up, will you!" she yelled, stifling a giggle.

With deliberate delay, Lucius slowly unfurled the document, paused again for dramatic effect, then began to read aloud.

"'To Quintus Honorius Romanus, magistrate of Aquae Sulis and servant of Rome. The Emperor Nero Claudius Drusus Germanicus congratulates you on your recent success in quelling the barbarian uprising in your district.'" Julia squealed and clapped her hands like a child as she squirmed in the tub. She leaned closer as Lucius continued reading. "'Doing so without the loss of a single life, either military or civilian, is most admirable. You are hereby summoned to Rome to receive a commendation to be presented by the Emperor Nero and to partake in a banquet to be given at the Emperor's Golden House in your honor. May the gods be with you on your journey.'"

Lucius's voice had slowed to a monotone crawl as he read the last few lines, unable to believe the words he was reciting. He sank to the edge of the tub and sat staring at the Imperial proclamation. A giggle rose in Julia, then grew to a loud laugh. The sound was infectious. The smile on Lucius's face also swelled to laughter.

"Put the scroll down for a minute, dear," Julia said as her tittering subsided.

In his fit of rapture Lucius tossed the scroll across the room and raised his arms to the muraled ceiling in victory. Without warning, Julia grabbed him by the white toga and pulled him over the side and into the tub with her. Waves splashed across the floral patterns of the tiled floor. Lucius came up spitting water and laughing hysterically.

"I'm returning to Rome . . . banquet in my honor . . . commendation from Nero . . . " He was unable to make complete sentences as his heart pounded. Julia reached for him, quickly untangling the mass of wet material that floated in the bath water.

"I think you mean *we're* going to Rome, Master Quintus," she corrected.

Her hands worked briskly underwater until she found the body parts she was looking for. "You're not thinking of leaving your Aunt Julia out of this celebration, are you?" Her voice was deliberately pouty and childlike as she began to pump his cock with both hands. "Aunt Julia wants to have a good time in Rome, too." Her left hand moved to his scrotum as her right hand continued stroking faster and faster. "Besides, who would you have to play with if I didn't come along?" The intense pumping of her hand splashed more water across the floor. "Don't you want to make love in the shadow of the Forum?" Her words were working magic on them both and Lucius watched as she repositioned her left hand between her own legs. "Don't you want me at the banquet, which will surely turn into one of Nero's famous orgies?" Both hands were now pumping furiously underwater. "Don't you want to watch all the Senators and their ladies running their hands all over me? Kissing my breasts? Groping at my ass? Pouring wine across my vagina and licking it off?" Lucius moaned loudly. He looked down at the white sperm shooting into the bath water between his legs. The sight also pushed Julia over the edge and she climaxed with a series of convulsions that poured more water over the sides of the tub.

They both laid back in the spacious reservoir, reveling in this success that was beyond their wildest imaginations. Lucius opened his eyes and looked at Julia, who had never taken her eyes off him.

"How can I refuse such an offer?" he said with a smile. "Let's get packed for Rome."

Within seven weeks Lucius and Julia had reached the new harbor at Portus just outside Rome. The sea journey had made Lucius tense. After the events aboard the *Vesta* three years earlier, he would probably never be comfortable on a ship again. He was relieved to be on firm ground. This, combined with the beautiful Italian spring weather, raised his spirits.

The two sat facing each other on satin seats as they rode along the Via Portuensis in one of Nero's State coaches. He watched Julia's contented face as she stared out the window surveying the green countryside, which gradually transformed to congested urban development as they approached the walls of Rome.

They entered the city from the west, crossed the Tiber over the Pons Aemilius, and made their way along the Vicus Iugarius past the Forum toward the new royal palace known as the Domus Aurea, the Golden House. Their progress was hindered only by foot traffic, since State coaches were the only vehicles allowed on the roads of Rome during the day.

"I don't even recognize the city anymore," Julia said as they passed the massive marble temples and the labyrinth of insulae tenements and domus houses. "And I forgot about the smells. There are areas of this city that rival the stench of our horse stables at the villa."

"It looks like the fire leveled most of the older buildings," Lucius said. "Look there. Some of the gutted buildings are still standing." They turned onto the Via Sacra and approached the Palatine Hill.

"Where was your home?" Julia asked.

"Right there, where that open field now sits on the hillside. I knew our area was affected by the fire, but I didn't realize the entire neighborhood was leveled." Lucius tried to seem despondent over the loss, but inside he gloated. There was now no physical reminder of the years he had spent catering to the needs of the Romanus family.

"So how was it serving the Romanus family? Did they treat you well?" Julia asked with nonchalance.

"They were . . . " Lucius stopped. Had he heard her correctly? Had she read his mind? His head snapped around. She was staring at him with eyes two shades darker than before. The smug expression on her face told him that his game was up. How should he react? Should he deny it? He was speechless.

"Surprised?" she asked, the word passing across an evil smile. "Oh, I've been suspicious of your story all along. A crafty mind like yours should know you can't swindle a swindler. You just confirmed my suspicion . . . Lucius." The sound of his own real name coming from her lips sent a shock up his spine. "Besides, you don't really think I'd fuck my own nephew, do you?"

Why was she doing this? Why wait until now, his moment of glory, to spring this on him? He could not sit there deaf, dumb, and blind. He had to say something.

"Alright. So now what? You're going to destroy everything we've worked for?"

Julia glanced back out the window and appeared to casually resume her inspection of the cityscape. "Don't worry, *nephew.*" The last word was enunciated with deliberate exaggeration. "Your secret's safe with me—so long as I'm kept a part of your new lifestyle. I've been looking to harness someone with a political appetite for some time now. We both know that isn't Sextus. But my dear husband made us enough money to put me in the right circles to find someone else." She looked back at him with a sly smile. "Who would have thought he would come in the shape of a shipwrecked slave boy?"

Lucius was reeling. He knew Julia to be manipulative, but he had never imagined her capable of this level of deception. As of this moment, he realized she was a woman to be watched carefully and not to be trusted.

"By Jupiter, look at that!" He heard her excited voice, but it still took a moment to snap out of his mental trauma. He followed her gaze out the window. There, in the middle of a large public square, stood the most majestic statue Lucius had ever seen. It was a mammoth icon, a single male figure atop a square pedestal. The base alone was the size of a large house. Wooden scaffolding still covered the figure below the knees as artists put the finishing touches on the massive pedestal. The coach driver's face suddenly appeared upside-down at the top of the window.

"It is the Colossus Neronis, madam. The Emperor's likeness in a thirty-six-meter-high bronze figure. They say it is larger than the Colossus of Rhodes."

"Well, could it be our good Emperor is compensating for his shortcomings?" Julia whispered to Lucius with a smile. He was not sure how to respond. Was she now looking to trap him into saying something treasonous? His trust in her was shattered and he no longer knew how to react to her. He began to realize how different their relationship would now be.

The coach drew to a stop at the end of the Via Sacra, which wound up the Esquiline Hill to the palace entrance. A slave opened the door and assisted Julia out of the carriage. She stood at the base of a small mountain of marble steps waiting for Lucius, looking elegant in a gold satin palla and matching stola.

"Are you coming, dear? We don't want to keep the Emperor waiting."

Lucius took a moment to breathe deeply and get his emotions under control. He stepped from the coach and looked up at an extraordinary complex of buildings that were, quite literally, dazzling. Surrounded by an artificial countryside setting, the gilded buildings radiated a blinding reflection of sunlight from their white surfaces and golden trim. The marble steps climbed directly into an arched tunnel that penetrated the base of the main domed building. Unfurling on either side of the central edifice were two colonnaded wings that spread for a kilometer each into the exquisite gardens.

They looked up the stairs to where four members of the elite Praetorian Guard flanked the tunnel entrance. An Imperial staff member stepped through the portal and motioned them forward.

"This is it, Quintus," Julia said quietly as they climbed the stairs. "This is what we've worked so long for." It put Lucius at ease to hear Julia use his assumed name once again.

They stepped through the arched portal into another world. Four officials waited to greet them in the cavernous octagonal central hall. The towering domed ceiling, decorated along its edge with colorful murals of an African animal hunt, was open at the apex, allowing both the sun and a cool breeze access to the hall. The sheer scale of the room certainly had the desired effect: making the visitor feel small and insignificant. As they approached the line of officials they could see the opposite side of the octagonal room was open to the main gardens, which contained a vast artificial lake. In the distance, Lucius was sure he saw two giraffes stroll past a waterfall.

The visitors from Britannia were welcomed warmly by the praetor and three other State officials. They were ushered into a large vestibule, equally impressive with its white and gold walls and elaborate murals. Polite applause rose from the dozen or so staff members who were already waiting in the room. The praetor approached Lucius. His lictor, one of his six personal assistants and bodyguards, carried a small oak box.

"Quintus Honorius Romanus, magistrate of Aquae Sulis and faithful servant of Rome—and the lady Julia Melita—we bid you both welcome," he began formally. He opened the box and withdrew a large medallion hanging from a bright red ribbon. "For your dedicated service to Rome in the quelling of the tribal revolt in Britannia, on behalf of our esteemed Emperor Nero, I bestow upon you—"

"Excuse me . . . "

The pompous praetor's face registered indignation as he turned to the source of the interruption.

"I'm sorry, but this ceremony seems a bit rushed," Julia said. "And I don't see the Emperor. The proclamation we received stated that Nero, himself, would present the award to my nephew."

There was silence in the ornate hall as the royal staffers recovered from the woman's audacity. "I'm sorry, madam," said the praetor in a haughty tone, "but the Emperor is not available at the moment. He will greet both of you at this evening's banquet. Now may we resume?"

"No, you may not," Julia said, raising her voice. There was an audible gasp from the lictors and attendants. Lucius felt uneasy, concerned that their first high-level meeting in the Roman political arena would turn disastrous.

"Julia, perhaps you should allow the praetor to resume," Lucius said quietly.

"I will not!" she snapped. "We've traveled for weeks for this presentation. We're not about to be shoved off to a staff member for a paltry ceremony like this. After what this man has accomplished in Britannia, we deserve the attention of the Emperor!"

"And you've got it." The words echoed from the octagonal hall just outside the vestibule. Every head turned as one toward the voice, then bowed toward the marble floor. In the doorway stood the Emperor Nero, his portly body draped with an elaborate purple and gold toga. Behind him hovered a small entourage of guards and assistants, floating like a flock of sparrows matching every move of the lead bird. "I could not help overhearing your disappointment. I was on my way to a meeting with the King of Judea in the dining hall. But you are correct. The affairs of State can certainly wait a while."

Julia was stunned. The volatile temperament of this Emperor was well known throughout his Empire. It flashed through her mind that instead of accolades they might well receive a severe lashing, or worse. She needed to retreat a few steps. "I meant no disrespect, your grace. We were just so disappointed not to be in your noble presence after our prolonged anticipation. I beg your forgiveness." On her last words, she bent far enough forward to offer the plump monarch an ample view down her low-cut gold stola.

Nero's face lit up as he scratched at the sparse beard that wrapped under his many chins. "How can I refuse the appeal of such a persuasive woman who dresses in my favorite color? You remind me of my dear departed Agrippina. She, too, had ways of getting what she wanted."

Julia flushed with excitement at the comparison. "If it pleases your grace, allow me to introduce my nephew, Quintus Honorius Romanus, magistrate of Aquae Sulis. It was he who thwarted the massive rebellion in Britannia."

"Yes, and without the loss of a single Roman legionary," continued Nero, studying Lucius as he spoke. "I've heard the story." He brusquely waved for the award. The praetor grabbed the oak box from his lictor and approached the Emperor. Nero removed the award and laid the red ribbon and medallion around Lucius's neck. "For a job well done, I present you this token of my appreciation."

"Thank you, your grace," Lucius said. "I am here only to serve you and Rome."

Nero smiled and tapped Lucius on the cheek. "You're a good man." The Emperor turned abruptly and walked toward the door, his entourage scurrying close behind.

Julia was suddenly concerned that this would be the only opportunity to make her pitch. They were to be guests at the Imperial banquet that evening, but having never attended such a function, she was unsure of her access to the Emperor. She could not risk losing what might be her only opportunity to address the issue directly with Nero himself.

"Your grace?" Julia called out to his back. Once again the staff members were astonished at her boldness. She dared not make eye contact with the praetor, but felt his enraged stare upon her. Nero stopped in his tracks. She wondered how far she could push her luck.

"I fear the King of Judea has traveled all this way for nothing," he joked to his personal assistant, loud enough for all to hear. "Yes, my dear? What else can the benevolent Emperor do for you?"

"Your grace, based on recent developments, it appears that Rome would do well to have an informed advisor, knowledgeable about the state of affairs in western Britannia."

Lucius jumped in, just as they had rehearsed so many times during the journey to Rome. "The area remains an unsettled province, your grace. As both Julius Caesar and your own step-father, Claudius, learned, the Britons are not an easy people to conquer and rule. As we've just seen, it doesn't take much provocation for the local tribes to threaten revolt. Rome could use someone like myself, with an excellent network of contacts, both Roman and Briton. My advice and recommendations to your senior staff could avert future problems in Britannia and save countless Roman lives."

Nero looked at Lucius for a moment, then waved over the praetor. They huddled for a few minutes, their mumbles echoing off the walls of the vestibule. Julia glanced at Lucius. She saw the lump in his throat as he swallowed, telling her that he, too, was wondering if they had gone too far. The Emperor's voice became louder as he turned and resumed his walk to the dining hall.

"See to it," were his last words before disappearing around a gigantic column. The praetor returned to where Lucius and Julia stood. Julia could tell by his expression that he had not yet recovered from her interruption of the ceremony.

"The Senate and many senior staff have been discussing the issue of the rebellious Britons ever since the Boudicca uprising, which we do not want to see repeated. We must keep our finger on the pulse of Britannia and act quickly to avert any further problems. The Emperor feels you may be of assistance in this matter. He has authorized me to secure your appointment as the Imperial Advisor for Britannia Affairs."

Julia was stunned at the quick decision. A glance at Lucius told her he was equally astounded. They had been prepared for this to be a drawn-out process. But it seemed there were benefits to the impulsiveness of the mad Emperors of Rome. While Lucius stood in bewildered silence, Julia immediately began financial negotiations with the praetor. By the end of their five-minute discussion, she had secured Lucius a salary that was triple his earnings as magistrate, a State apartment overlooking the Forum, and a direct line of access to Nero's senior staff.

As the praetor and his entourage turned to leave, Julia reached for Lucius's hand. She felt it trembling inside hers. She was light-headed but had the presence of mind to realize that, in the span of a few minutes, her life had just changed forever.

• • •

The full moon blanketed the white marble of the Roman Forum in a beautiful blue glow. Two stories above the temples and triumphal arches, squeals of passion flowed from the open balcony doors of one of the State apartments. Julia was in ecstasy. The wine from the royal banquet had helped her lose the few inhibitions she possessed. Atop the overstuffed four-poster bed, Lucius pumped hard against her sweating body. She no longer felt the need to stifle her screams as she had in their midnight rendezvous at the Aquae Sulis villa. Here, there was no husband in the next room, no gossiping servants around the corner. Her cries of passion came faster and louder, until the two fell together in an exhausted heap.

After a few minutes, Julia rose and slipped into a short silk tunic. She stood in the balcony doorway for a moment before stepping out into the night air. The cool breeze was exhilarating against her damp skin. Lucius put his white woolen tunic back on and followed her onto the balcony.

"Well, as disappointing as the award ceremony was, they sure made up for it with the banquet," Julia said, the effect of the wine still causing her words to slur slightly.

"Could you have imagined just a few months ago that one night you would be introduced to Rome's social elite by no less than the Emperor himself?" Lucius asked.

"Imagined it? Yes. Thought it would actually happen so soon? No." She stretched her arms over her head, embracing the night and thinking how right everything had suddenly become in her world. "I don't know who fawned over us more, the Senators, the rich merchants, or those odd and beautiful little sex toys Nero let loose. It's a wonderful feeling being a hero."

Lucius released his gaze from the Temple of Saturn and glanced at her with a curious expression.

She pretended she had misspoken. "I'm sorry. I meant being *related* to a hero." She thumped her finger against his chest. "You, dear nephew, are the true hero." She gave him a smile then quickly changed the subject. "Do you like the way I charmed our Emperor into one of his 'impromptu' lute performances? I did my homework. He loves to be goaded into a performance."

"He seemed very appreciative," Lucius said with a chuckle. "There aren't many who could say they had their breasts groped by the Emperor of Rome on his own banquet couch."

She giggled at the thought. "Oh, probably many more than you think. It did seem to heat up the crowd, didn't it?"

"I think you single-handedly launched tonight's Imperial orgy." Julia let out a provocative laugh. "I know the two dancers who jumped me seemed grateful," Lucius continued through a wide grin. "I think I was their assigned target for the evening. A little bonus from Nero."

"I doubt the Senator and his wife who ended up on top of me were part of a preassigned plan," Julia slurred. "He was certainly no prize package." She paused for a moment, then looked at Lucius with a mischievous spark in her eye. "His wife had a very skilled tongue, though."

The sound of their laughter resonated off the marble walls of the temples. They leaned on the balcony railing and absorbed their spectacular view of the moonlit Forum.

"Imperial Advisor for Britannia Affairs," Lucius said contentedly after a few minutes. He began to mimic the affected speech of the praetor. "'You are to advise the Emperor and his staff on policy and affairs north of the channel—nothing more, nothing less.' What a pompous ass that praetor is."

Julia giggled. She knew she was drunk, but felt it was time to begin giving Lucius some lessons in the politics of Rome. "He's just laying the ground rules early on. Everybody's looking to protect their coveted positions at the palace. Paranoia runs rampant through the Imperial staff. It was like that even with your small staff in Aquae Sulis."

"I can see here it will be ten times worse."

"You need to learn to use that paranoia to your advantage. We must learn quickly who truly has the Emperor's ear and who are the rats that simply scurry in his shadow. You'll need to make a name for yourself—and not just at the Imperial palace. You need to play the mob, just as you did with our little Briton revolt. Those who have the support of the people have the lasting power."

Julia looked back across the beauty of the Forum, but her mind was already pondering the many ways to gain favor with the populace in the political quagmire that was Rome.

XXII

July AD 66

PETRA WALKED HIS HORSE slowly down the dirt road that led to the Italian farming villa of Gaius Tadius Magnus on the outskirts of Pompeii. The hot afternoon sun beat down on his misshapen bald head and combined with the dusty rural roads to parch the old lanista's throat. But knowing he was at the end of his six-week, seventeen-hundred-kilometer journey from Britannia put him in an exceptionally good mood.

He surveyed the low hills that rolled beyond the dozens of tall Italian cypress trees that lined the entranceway. Endless rows of grapevines spread in perfect order in all directions. On the closest vines, Petra could see the green and purple fruit hanging in plump bunches. The urge to jump from his horse and pluck the juicy orbs from their branches was almost overpowering.

Finally, the two-story domus came into view at the end of the road. The villa was alive with hundreds of slaves and staff foremen, some in the fields, others guiding mule carts to and from the winery building behind the domus. Gaius had obviously done well with his business. From what Petra could see, his operation was close in size to the sprawling State-run latifundiums that provided Rome the majority of its wine and produce.

As he approached the house, he was distracted by a group of slaves working the field just in front of the villa. He had passed a few female slaves scattered throughout the fields, but none as striking as the statuesque beauty working the nearby vineyard. The broiling afternoon heat had caused the workers to peel off their woolen tunics and work in their undergarments, the women included. This presented a welcome sight for the occasional summer visitors, especially when their eyes fell upon an auburn-haired goddess such as this. Petra dismounted, his eyes never leaving the glistening near-naked body.

"The sweltering heat of Campania certainly has its advantages." The sudden voice startled the old lanista. He turned and saw the aged face of Gaius Magnus smiling at him.

"You old goat!" Petra bellowed with a laugh.

The two old friends hugged warmly. "Look who's tossing the insults!" laughed Gaius as he pushed back and patted the top of Petra's bald, sunburned head. "You look like the ass-end of a mule, you old fart."

Gaius wrapped his arm over the lanista's shoulder and led him inside the cool villa where an elaborate lunch awaited. It was by far the best food and wine Petra had tasted in the past six weeks, possibly the past six years. After a tour of the winery and olive oil operation, the two relaxed on the broad second-story balcony that overlooked the vast villa grounds. They sat quietly for a while and Petra studied his friend's face. The close-cropped white whiskers of his beard made him look older than Petra had remembered, but the pride in his face as he surveyed his domain brought back the affection and respect he had always held for the man.

"You've done alright for yourself, my friend," Petra said before sampling another of Gaius's five wine varieties.

"Well, I've expanded a bit from that small North African plantation."

"Hey, don't knock it. The proceeds from that farm helped launch our first ludus. Or do you try to forget your days as a part time lanista?"

Gaius laughed as he drained another wine goblet. "Oh, I remember it fondly. But, thank the gods, you were the one who had to deal with the fighters. I was very happy to stay well hidden in the background and supply the finances."

"I'll bet even this vineyard doesn't pay off the way you used to clean up at the El Djem arena," Petra said with a wink. Gaius nodded and smiled. Petra could see that his thoughts were a thousand kilometers away on another continent, two decades earlier.

"There are still a lot of provincials in North Africa wondering how a small-time farmer knew so much about gladiatorial battles," Gaius said. The thought of it brought a loud chuckle from Petra. "I made three times more money on my side wagers than I did on our game fees. I never lost a bet on a fight, and those idiots couldn't figure it out!" He and Petra both broke into fits of laughter.

Gaius called for more wine and Petra let his gaze drift over the villa grounds while he sat back and relaxed for the first time in many months. His eyes sought out the auburn-haired goddess, and he watched as she worked her way down the line of vines, plucking the purple bunches and tossing them into the basket she dragged behind. He also noticed one of the burly male slaves deliberately working his way closer to her. It was obvious that the slave was positioning himself for a pleasant visual diversion to break up the monotony of the day.

"So, you sent me a dispatch and came all the way from Britannia to talk of our old stomping grounds, huh?" Gaius asked.

"Not exactly." Petra took a deep breath before beginning his petition. "It's been a lot of years since I laid out a business offer to you. And you know I would never come to you with anything that I didn't feel was a sure bet."

"Alright," Gaius said as he casually stroked at his beard.

"I've challenged the ludus here in Pompeii to a match. Their best fighters and hunters against mine from Britannia."

"Interesting. What was their response?"

"They've accepted, but they want me to arrange the financing. They say it's too expensive a proposition for them to deal with, mainly because of my travel costs to get fifty fighters here and feed them for the duration. Plus, I'd have to bring them in a few weeks early to counter the effects of such a long trip."

"Well, it sounds novel, to say the least. By why me? My days as a magistrate are over. My replacement at Pompeii should be able to make some political points with an event like this. Why not go to him?"

"I did. I wrote him as soon as I got the reply from the ludus. He's an asshole. He has no vision. He says it's too expensive. He feels his electorate is happy enough with the regular games he sponsors every six or eight months. He sees no reason to spend any more."

Gaius smiled. "Alright, so say I'm not an asshole and I have the vision. What's in this for me?"

"I know the Pompeiian magistrate provides his games free of charge to the public, just as most magistrates do. But for an event like this, don't you think the public would be willing to pay for their seats in the cavea? I know that's not been done in Pompeii, but if these games were promoted right, wouldn't the mob part with a few sesterces to see the most exciting match in a hundred years?"

Gaius continued to stroke his beard, obviously interested by the prospect. "You think you could actually win a match like this? Their ludus is second only to Rome."

"I've got some amazing fighters, Gaius. There's a kid who came in as a volunteer a couple of years ago who's developed an unbelievable style. He's gotten the troupe into a new training system that's not only built them up physically, but bonded most of them in a camaraderie like I've never seen before. *They* think they can win this. So, yes, I think they can, too."

Gaius called for the slave who stood by the balcony door to bring him his abacus and wax tablet. Petra was relieved that he had piqued Gaius's interest enough to engage his intelligent business mind. As soon as the manual calculator was in his hands, the small round stones began clicking. He scratched some numbers into the wax tablet with the stylus and returned to the abacus.

As Gaius worked, Petra's attention was drawn again to the buxom female slave in the vineyard. She continued to fill her basket with grapes and the large male slave continued to creep closer to her side, his attention split between his work and her bare breasts.

"How much do you think you could charge for admission?" Gaius asked as he worked. It took Petra a minute to refocus.

"I'd say thirty sesterces each."

"Too high," Gaius reacted immediately. "Pompeii is a wealthy community, but I don't think we'd fill the amphitheater at that rate."

"Well, then it's going to be tough to make any money on this event," Petra said, disappointment showing in his tone.

"Not if my take comes from more than just admission. If I'm taking all the risk on this event, then I want a cut of all the vending stalls, food sales, anything that's sold on game day. That's *my* audience. My promotion is bringing them to the arena. I deserve a cut of everything they spend that day."

"Well, I've never heard of that being done before," said a skeptical Petra, "but if you can get the vendors to agree, it's an interesting plan."

"They'll agree. Just like you said, this will be the best fight since Spartacus kicked the Roman legion's ass. There will be more souvenirs and trinkets sold than you can imagine."

"And you think that will make up the shortfall?"

Gaius flattened all the rows of his abacus and refigured out loud so Petra could follow. "Alright, your way is simple. I'd pull in six hundred thousand sesterces, but that's assuming I could get twenty thousand spectators to spend thirty sesterces each for admission." His fingers flew again and the tiny stones clicked loudly as they helped him do the math. "My way, I'd charge fifteen sesterces admission, but with my cut of the vendor and food sales . . . making some conservative assumptions based on what I've seen selling at the arena on game days . . . I'd bring in . . . " The stones continued to click until he picked up the stylus and scratched a new figure into the wax. He held it up to Petra, who slowly read the numeral out loud.

"One-and-a-half million sesterces." That was more money than Petra had brought in with his last ten games. "And how would that be split?" he asked quickly.

Gaius smiled as he laid down his abacus and began inscribing on his wax tablet. "Two hundred and fifty thousand for the Pompeii lanista and three hundred thousand for you, the extra to cover your travel costs. I'd hold another fifty thousand in reserve as a bonus for the winning ludus. One hundred thousand will be set aside for the fighters' prize purses. The animals for a typical venatio would normally cost me about one hundred thousand, but let's go for some truly exotic beasts and say one hundred-fifty thousand. I'll need to give the local magistrate one hundred thousand for his gracious hospitality in the use of his arena. Promotional expenses will cost me about fifty thousand. That leaves five hundred thousand sesterces, which is mine. Of course any additional costs will come out of my cut. And I'll guarantee everyone's share from my own personal holdings."

At four times his normal take, Petra was thrilled. But he felt if he did not negotiate one point or another, Gaius would be disappointed in him. "Five hundred thousand is a bit high for your stake, no? I'm thinking more of an even three-way split after expenses."

"But who's taking all the risk?"

"And who's providing the fighters? Without *them*, there would be no games at all."

Gaius raised an eyebrow and grumbled as he reached again for his abacus. Petra smiled and used the opportunity to refill his goblet and check on the vineyard goddess. The male slave was now hovering next to her, his head scanning to check on the position of the foremen patrolling nearby with their long whipping rods. Petra watched as the slave's hand began to casually brush the girl's right breast each time he reached for another bunch of grapes.

"That demon!" Petra laughed out loud as he watched the scene unfold.

Gaius looked up from his wax tablet to see what was happening. "Oh, Claudia . . . She's quite an eyeful, isn't she?"

"Where did you get her?"

"She was arrested for her part in a prostitution scheme set up by her thieving father. He'd been selling her to the local men since she was thirteen and keeping all the money for himself."

"Greedy bastard." Petra was always sensitive when it came to talk of profit from prostitution. He knew that many Roman citizens equated the lanista's job with that of the pimp.

"Well, he got greedier. After five or six years, he also tried blackmailing some of his customers. One of them was a rich friend of mine. He came to me when I was still magistrate and told me the story. So I had her and her father arrested. I turned the father over to my friend to exact his revenge, but the girl I kept for myself."

The two continued to watch the amusing scenario play out in the vineyard. It was obvious from the look on her face that the girl had taken as much harassment as she was going to take for the day.

"She's quite the wild woman in bed and strong as an ox. I put her to work in the fields during the day. But as you can see, she's turned into a distraction for the other slaves. And, by the gods, does she have a temper! Watch her."

The slave groped at her breast once more, then twice. It seemed he had reached her breaking point. She yanked a large bunch of grapes from the vine and shoved them into the burly man's face with enough force to snap his head back.

Petra and Gaius erupted in laughter as the slave scowled at her, grape juice running from his ragged beard. Rather than letting it go, he belligerently reached out and grabbed two handfuls of the girl's sweating breasts. The woman let out a furious cry resembling the banshees of the Britannia moors. She dove at the slave, and the two toppled over a row of staked vines into the rich, dark earth. Her fingers ripped violently at his face between forceful punches to his jaw. Petra and Gaius could clearly hear the blows strike. Petra stood to get a better view. The savagery of the girl's attack hampered the male slave from landing even a single counterpunch. Two of the foremen approached the scuffle but were in no hurry to break it up, enjoying the erotic diversion in the hot afternoon sun. After a few minutes, Gaius called down to them from the balcony.

"Alright boys, the party's over. Send him to the cells and put her back to work."

The two overseers wielded their long wooden rods, whacking once across each back to get the brawlers' attention. Petra noticed that the girl never flinched when the cane struck. She simply stood up, covered in black earth and manure, and victoriously watched her molester dragged from the field.

"You see what I mean," Gaius laughed. "Her scum father was an ex-centurion. He taught her well in self-defense. Plus, she picked up some vicious moves from a street gang she banded with."

"She has the strength of an Amazon, with the fighting spirit of Mars," Petra said as he retook his seat.

"And the body of Venus," Gaius said, smiling as he resumed his calculations. Petra sat back and took another swig of wine, watching Claudia's every move over the rim of his goblet. "I can hear your mind grinding like a wheat mill from over here, Petra," Gaius said without looking up. "What are you thinking?"

Petra paused for a minute then looked at his friend. "I'll tell you what . . . You can have the share of profits you just proposed, but I take the girl. And a horse to get her back to my school in Glevum."

"Ahhhh . . . Yes, she'll keep those fighters of yours happy."

"That's not what I have in mind. I'm going to train her as a gladiator."

Gaius stared blankly at Petra, his mouth slightly agape.

Petra continued, "A woman like Claudia, trained well and fighting half-naked, has probably never been seen in Pompeii's arena. It would assure a full house."

The wrinkles of a smile blended with the age lines in Gaius's face. "You think you can have her up and ready quickly enough?"

"From what I just saw, she already knows how to protect herself. We just need to focus that anger of hers in a better direction."

"But if she's your only woman fighter, and there are none training at Pompeii, who will she fight?"

Petra took his gaze from the vixen long enough to look at Gaius. His only response was a sly smile.

"By the gods!" Gaius said, his eyebrows rising in amazement. "You're going to match her against a man!"

Petra nodded.

"Well, my friend, I know you well enough to know you wouldn't try something like this without the odds stacked heavily in your favor. So, if I played those same odds and placed an additional side wager or two on Claudia, I'll bet I could double my take from the gate."

Gaius let out a loud laugh as he tossed the abacus and wax tablet onto the wooden table. "How can I deny my friend the things that will further his career? And my fortune!" He snatched the goblet off the small table, spilling most of the contents across the stones of the abacus. "Let us drink to this deal!"

Petra was happy to clink goblets and toast the pact. He had been prepared to make this deal even if there was no profit in it, just to introduce his fighters to the bigger Italian crowds. But now he would get all the benefits: a larger audience, a larger arena, a larger fee for himself, and a new fighter who would draw attention to his troupe. The seventeen-hundred-kilometer journey had been well worth his time.

Gaius swallowed what was left in his goblet in one swig. "I warn you, my friend," he slurred. "Be careful of that wildcat bitch. She will cut your throat before you can blink."

Petra watched her easily hoist the heavy basket of grapes onto her shoulder.

"That's just what I'm hoping for, Gaius."

XXIII

August AD 66

QUINTUS AND LINDANI warded off the evening chill with a small fire in the corner of the training field. Quintus looked up at the unusually brilliant blanket of stars above them. He began counting the multitude of yellow streaks left behind by shooting stars.

"The constellation Taurus shines extra bright tonight," Lindani said quietly. "It must have seen Taurus the Bull fight in Londinium again last week."

"What can I say? They keep pairing me up with barbarians. They're all bluff. Can't fight for shit."

"Ah, but you put on a good enough show so the crowd would not stop cheering. I will bet there are still spectators sitting in their seats chanting the wonders of your name."

"Right," Quintus said as he rolled his eyes and laid back to enjoy the celestial show. "But wouldn't it be something to have them react like that in the amphitheaters of Italia, maybe in Rome itself."

"Why must you always worry about tomorrow? Why not think about today and the victories you have had?"

"Because tomorrow is what keeps me going," Quintus replied. "If the appetite wasn't there, I think I'd just lose interest and buy my freedom back from the dominus. But there are still new challenges for me—just not here in Britannia."

Out of the corner of his eye, Quintus saw Lindani suddenly cock his head.

"Well, perhaps this is the dominus finally returning," the African said. "Maybe he has found a way to put you into those big arenas you dream of."

Quintus had not yet heard the horse but knew never to doubt Lindani. As did most of the troupe, Quintus and Lindani assumed the lanista's long unexplained absence had something to do with arranging distant games. Quintus had shared Petra's comment about "already working on it" with Lindani, but nobody else. Perhaps now they would all learn what was happening. They both stood as they saw the attendant raise the timber across the front gate.

"Two horses," Lindani said before the gate was open.

From across the practice field they watched the wooden doors part with a loud creak. Like ghosts from the darkness, two riders were suddenly bathed in the light of the torches that burned near the front office.

"It *is* the dominus!" Quintus said excitedly. "Who's the second rider?"

Lindani did not offer an answer. The cloaked and hooded figure who rode behind Petra dismounted and stood beside the horse. Julianus came through the office door, greeting Petra by grasping the lanista's forearms firmly. Petra ushered both his head trainer and the mysterious hooded figure into his office and shut the door.

"Perhaps the dominus got married while he was away," Lindani said, his white teeth shining in the light of their campfire. Quintus gave Lindani a questioning look.

The African shrugged. "Even under a long cloak I can tell the gait of a female."

Quintus did not get much sleep that night. He was first on the field as the sun crept slowly over the horizon. He and Lindani cut their morning marathon short in order to sniff out any early gossip about the trip or the mystery rider. There was none.

As breakfast ended and the fighters entered the practice field, Quintus was glad to see the podium set up near the statue of Hercules. Petra was going to call an assembly. The anticipation in the troupe was palpable. The fighters hung together rather than split up into their usual training groups. Their hushed whispers of predictions and opinions were barely audible. Quintus could not remember ever hearing the training ground this quiet in the morning, so quiet that every fighter and hunter clearly heard the latch on Petra's office door open. All eyes were on the lanista as he slowly made his way through the milling crowd and onto the small wooden platform. As usual, there was no way to get a reading off his stoic façade. Petra scanned the crowd. There was no need to have Julianus call for order. He already had everyone's undivided attention.

"So, you ladies are probably wondering where I've been for the past three months. Very soon, the best of you will be fighting in the biggest games of your lives." An excited murmur began to grow in the crowd. "Within a month, you will be headed to one of the largest arenas in the Empire. I have challenged an Italian school to a fight, and they have accepted. Soon we leave for Pompeii."

A tremendous roar went up from the practice field. Quintus stood in stunned silence. He closed his eyes and let the feeling of euphoria wash over him like a warm bath. Julianus called for quiet, and Petra continued.

"I will say with certainty that some of you will not return, for you will be facing some of the best-trained fighters in the Empire."

"Bring the heathens on!" Quintus yelled as loud as he could. Again the field erupted in pandemonium. The cheering went on for some time until, instigated by Quintus, it resolved into a chant of "Cassius Petra! Cassius Petra!" For the first time since his arrival at the school, Quintus thought he detected a look of humility in the tough lanista's face.

Julianus tried unsuccessfully to quiet the gathering. An armed guard stepped forward, his hands wringing a leather whip. Quintus watched Petra give a firm shake of his head and the guard stepped back against the wall. Petra raised his hands and his troupe finally settled down.

"Next week, Julianus and I will select the fifty gladiators and venatores who will make the journey. If you're not sure whether you fall into that top fifty, then I suggest you show us something extra this week." He walked toward the edge of the platform, then stopped short before stepping off. "Oh, and one last thing—we have a new recruit."

The statement took everyone by surprise. The ludus was always receiving new recruits, but none of the tiros ever warranted a special mention. Petra nodded toward the back of the training field. "You might want to see for yourself."

Quintus and one hundred and fifty other fighters and workers turned simultaneously, and a gasp came from each throat. Leaning against a column of the portico stood a tall young woman of exceptional beauty and build, her arms folded across the shapely chest that pressed tightly against her beige woolen tunic. The austere look in her green eyes could not diminish the beauty of her chiseled face framed by long auburn hair.

"Allow me to introduce you ladies to Amazonia." Not a single pair of eyes left her form.

"When do we get to wrestle her?" came a voice from the crowd, which prompted loud whistles, whoops, and a string of lewd catcalls. Quintus joined in the laughter, but made no remarks. Petra spoke up again from the podium.

"Amazonia will be training with us beginning today. I will tell all of you right now that I have paid dearly for her. She is my property, as are all of you. I don't want her touched outside the training ring."

Quintus glanced at the men's faces as they examined her body. He knew exactly what was running through each mind: who would be the first to face off against her? Suddenly, everyone jumped at the loud pop of a whip cracking against the wooden floor of the platform. Quintus turned to see Petra standing with the guard's whip unfurled in his hand. He had effectively gotten everyone's attention once again. His voice came slow and deliberate.

"Listen to me closely. If any one of you comes within two meters of her outside the practice field or the arena, you will spend two weeks in the prison cell. That is, once the physician patches you up after Amazonia rips your balls off."

The men laughed at the thought. "It might be worth two weeks in prison for me to get my hands on those titties," said one of the Celtic fighters in a harsh accent. The men around him broke into another round of laughter. Quintus smiled as he looked back to see the woman's reaction to all this. He watched her closely as her green eyes casually scanned from face to face, as if sizing up the entire crowd, one man at a time.

Lindani leaned toward Quintus's ear. "Outside she is like a marble statue, but inside she trembles like a frightened puppy."

Quintus stepped back and looked at his friend. "So now you read women like you read the lions and bears?"

"An animal is an animal, whether on two legs or four."

Julianus's voice bellowed the back-to-work order, and slowly the sounds of the wooden practice weapons once again filled the training field. Amazonia was taken to the palus by an assistant, where she began her training against the heavy wooden post.

Quintus was now sparring against the primus palus fighters. After the most recent Londinium games, he had been promoted to secundus palus ranking. It was only his limited number of arena bouts that kept him from the highest ranking. Everyone at the school, from the head trainer to the lowest tiro, knew he was one of the top fighters in the troupe. Although he was confident of a slot in the Pompeii competition, he still felt it was his duty to put out extra effort for the next week. His sparring matches took on an added level of intensity. His speed and remarkable spinning attacks caused even the seasoned veterans to give ground.

The late morning brought the venatores in from the back field to prepare for lunch. As the group walked along the rear wall, they slowed their pace and eventually stopped to watch a sparring match that was just getting under way. Quintus joined Lindani near the head of the line. The crowd attracted more viewers and before long, most of the back half of the training field had gathered around the murmillo training area.

Amazonia, after just a few hours at the palus, was about to take on her first sparring opponent, a relatively green Briton with one arena win on his record. Quintus had to smile as he watched her trying to secure her helmet, which was obviously foreign equipment to her. A training assistant finally got the helmet in place. Although many of the German, Briton, and Celtic fighters wore long hair, none matched the elegance of Amazonia's auburn locks falling gracefully from the back of her headgear.

Lindani leaned toward Quintus. "So we shall see now what attracted the dominus to this woman," the African said.

"It's interesting that they're going to train her as a murmillo," Quintus said as he watched the trainer give her some last minute pointers. "I guess they feel she needs the larger shield for added protection."

The murmillo trainer called for "Attack." The combatants circled each other cautiously. The Briton, fighting as a thraex, finally made the first move with slices and thrusts easily parried by Amazonia. Jeers came from the crowd, taunting her first male opponent for being bested by a woman. The ridicule forced him into a second attack combination. The trainer shouted instructions to Amazonia, who responded quickly, again blocking each thrust with her large shield and wooden sword. Quintus noticed that the second round of shouts brought Julianus and Petra next to him in the rapidly growing circle.

"Should I send them back to work?" Julianus asked the lanista.

"No, let them watch this. I want them to see that this woman is not one to be fucked with."

Amazonia finally seemed to muster enough confidence to initiate an attack, a short but respectable combination that did little damage. The Briton's immediate riposte gained ground and forced the woman into a swift retreat. His attack ended with a hard slice across her upper left arm, which resulted in a severe welt. The Briton then made his biggest mistake of the day. He laughed at her.

Quintus watched her formidable arm muscles tighten as she increased her grip on the rudis. Amazingly, she tossed her shield aside. A scream of fury that startled everyone on the field radiated from inside her helmet. She raised her sword and let fly a barrage of blows that combined her brief gladiatorial training with her street-fighting savvy. Edge cuts and thrusts from her rudis were mixed with an elbow strike to the Briton's ribcage and a swift knee to the groin. As the desperate man dropped his guard to favor his aching scrotum, Amazonia delivered a spinning kick to his head, knocking his helmet loose. The flying headgear gave the comical illusion that she had actually kicked his head off. Knocked out cold, the Briton fell at Quintus's feet. Quintus looked at Lindani in shock. The entire audience of fighters and hunters was speechless. The only sound for the next few seconds was Amazonia's heavy breathing, an erotic resonance in a most unlikely place.

Quintus looked at the lanista standing next to him. Petra was nodding his head in mock seriousness. "Well, the style isn't exactly by the numbers, but you can't argue with the results," he said without cracking a smile.

Quintus glanced past the lanista to Julianus. The wide grin on the head trainer's face told him everything he needed to know. Obviously the trainer felt his boss had procured another winner. Julianus ordered the troupe back to work, then lowered his voice to speak with Petra. Quintus stepped closer to hear what he had to say.

"That's a maneuver her opponents won't expect or know how to defend against. We need to exploit moves like that—of course, without her tossing her scutum down. I could have her doctore design a special training regimen tailored more to her street style. That'll counter her disadvantage of size in the arena."

Petra nodded. "Good. Do it."

As they stepped away, Quintus joined Lindani, bent over the fallen Briton. Still seeing no sign of consciousness, they offered to take him to the physician's room. The trainer grunted his okay, then returned to working with Amazonia.

"She shows quite a style," Quintus said as he carried the Briton's legs across the field. Hefting the top half of the inert body, Lindani seemed less impressed.

"She is good, but do you think this is a wise idea?"

"Well, the dominus and Julianus see a lot of potential in her. I heard them say so. And you can't deny she'll make our troupe more unique."

Lindani gave a disparaging look. "I think a woman in this environment will cause more trouble than she is worth."

Quintus shrugged. "Maybe. But you've got to admit, she's got a fire inside her."

As practice wrapped in the late afternoon, much of the troupe headed for the latrine before their rubdown and dinner. Lindani was relieving himself at the trough as Quintus entered.

"I just saw Agricola, the physician," Quintus announced to anyone interested. "He says the Briton is still seeing stars and has a massive headache, but he should be fine by tomorrow."

"I don't know," Memnon said, as he stood naked, dumping a bucket of water over his head. "That bitch doesn't fight like us. It's like she has her own set of rules. But I'll show her no mercy if they ever pit her against me."

"You must avoid that wild kick of hers first, eh?" Lindani said, flashing his broad smile.

Quintus approached the trough and slid his subligaculum aside. "What difference, male or female? A fighter is a fighter, right?"

Nobody responded to the question. The latrine suddenly became very quiet. Quintus turned to see what was wrong. In the doorway stood Amazonia. She scanned their faces again. Without a word, she walked to one of the latrine openings, lifted her tunic and sat down. In the silence, the sound of her urine splattering into the stone trough echoed loudly in the room.

One of the Briton fighters began to laugh. "Well, well," he bellowed dramatically. "The tough little lady can drop a gladiator like a drunken child, but she still has to squat to pee."

Men's laughter filled the room, but suddenly became tentative as Amazonia finished and stood up. At almost two meters high, she stood taller than many of the men in the room. She approached her second Briton of the day.

Quintus leaned over and whispered to Lindani. "This should be good."

She jerked up her right hand as a distraction, while her left hand grabbed the Briton's testicles through his tunic and squeezed hard. The man began to whimper like a baby.

"I suggest you learn to respect your fellow fighters. *All* of them. Otherwise there will be two of us in this camp without these nasty things hanging between our legs."

It was the first time any of them had heard her speak since she arrived. The deep raspiness of her voice was almost startling. She gave the Briton's balls a final tug to help make her point, then released her hold and walked toward the door.

Quintus bit his lip and skimmed the faces of the men in the latrine. He saw that they, too, were desperately attempting to hold in their laughter. The Briton caught his breath and looked up from his stooped position at a dozen male faces smiling at him. Quintus could not suppress it any longer, and a quiet chortle resonated from his throat. The sound seemed to push the Briton's humiliation to the breaking point. He charged Amazonia's back. Without thinking, Quintus shouted a warning. But it was unnecessary. Her leg was already on its way around in a spin kick and her bare foot caught the Briton across his face. Two teeth flew from his mouth as he crashed to the filthy latrine floor.

Amazonia glanced at Quintus before she continued her exit. "Thanks, but I can take care of myself."

She walked through the door and headed for the dining hall, leaving Quintus and a group of stunned gladiators in her wake.

XXIV

October AD 66

THE OXEN WAILED LOUDLY as they swung out over the water, dangling from the merchant ship's solid cargo boom. The bellowing grated on Quintus's taut nerves, but most of Petra's troupe watched with amusement as the animals were lowered from the darkening skies into the gaping hatchway in the deck. As their hooves touched the wooden planks inside the aft cargo hold, the oxen once again became placid, unlike the horses and mules who continued to raise a ruckus below deck. The distant thunder only added to the bedlam of noise.

The three-day land journey to the southern Britannia port of Lympne had been uneventful. Now came the portion of the long trip that Quintus feared the most, a two-day sea voyage across the channel to Gaul. Thankfully, Petra had decided on the overland route to Pompeii—southeast across Gaul and down the Italian peninsula. The expense of a five-week sea voyage for fifty fighters and thirty support personnel would have been astronomical. The toll on Quintus's psyche would have been even greater. But since Britannia was an island, Quintus knew that the journey, although shorter, still required crossing the sea.

The ship's crew secured the last of the equipment carts in the hold, and the fighters that Petra and Julianus had hand-selected for the trip began boarding the ship. Quintus's knees shook as he mounted the narrow gangplank.

"Do not think about it and you will be fine," Lindani coached quietly from the walkway ahead of him. "Look at me, not the water." Quintus's head began to swim, and he felt he was losing his balance. He stopped for a second to catch his breath, causing Amazonia, next in line behind him, to run into his broad back.

"Take it easy, will you!" he snapped at her, then walked quickly up the walkway. As he stepped aboard, he turned and caught sight of Amazonia's quizzical expression toward Lindani. The African ignored her and returned to Quintus's side.

"Amazonia!" Julianus called. "Get below deck and try to keep those horses calm."

Quintus watched her climb down the rope ladder into the cargo hold. The sight of the hatch leading to the hold brought terrible memories. He felt Lindani tug his arm and allowed his friend to escort him to a quiet corner of the deck. A light rain began to fall.

"I don't know if I can do this," Quintus whispered through chattering teeth.

"You *will* do this," Lindani said. "Taurus the Bull has met much greater foes and lived to fight another day."

Quintus looked at his African friend, the panic rising inside him. "No, Lindani. I am Quintus, the boy who lost his mother and father on just such a ship. I watched them both die, Lindani." Quintus looked around and saw the old merchant vessel as the *Vesta*. "My father stood right there with his beautiful blue cloak. And my mother floated just there on a piece of the hull. There was nothing I could do to save them." The bulk of his massive body began to shudder and his eyes welled with tears.

"It is only two short days," Lindani said in an optimistic voice. "This storm will pass quickly, and we will be back on land faster than a hunting cheetah."

Quintus jumped as the captain yelled loudly. Two of the deck hands cast off the tie lines and the vessel began to slip away from the dock. Quintus considered sprinting across the deck and launching himself off the bulwark and back onto the wooden pier. Perhaps if Lindani did not have hold of his arm, he would have done it. But, instead, he sank to a sitting position against the stern rail.

The sailors hoisted the foresail, and the ship began to make way slowly through the choppy waters, past the towering lighthouse on the tip of the south breakwater.

Lindani slapped Quintus's back. "That lighthouse is a marvel, eh? One of the deck hands said it is the tallest lighthouse in Britannia."

Quintus stared at the deck without responding. As they cleared the protective harbor wall, the ship began to rock in the stiff breeze. Thunder continued to roll across the dark sky. Quintus's heart pounded faster. Every vivid detail of that horrid night came back to him. The walls of black water rising alongside the ship. The screams of the men as they were washed overboard. The musty fish smell as the rocks broke through the hull. With a groan, he pulled his legs up close to his chest and began rocking.

Once the captain saw his ship through the narrow port entrance, he ordered the mainsail raised, then called out loudly to all eighty passengers. "You are to remain on deck at all times, unless you need to tend the animals. The only exceptions are your lanista and head doctore, who will have berths below deck. This storm should be brief, then you can enjoy your voyage."

The deck hands began stretching rolls of canvas across the deck to provide minimal shelter. Within minutes, most of the eighty passengers were crowded under the makeshift awnings to escape the heavy rain that began to fall.

The horses and oxen settled down once the ship was under way. Amazonia saw no reason to stay in the reeking hold and climbed back up the rope ladder. As she stepped through the hatch, she noticed Quintus, lying alone in the rain near the stern rail. He was curled in a fetal position, secluded from the rest of the troupe behind the equipment crates. Lindani sat nearby like a sentinel, also exposed to the downpour. She walked toward the African hunter, finding handholds as she went to steady herself on the swaying deck.

"What's wrong with him?" she asked.

"He does not like ships. They have not been kind to his family." She gave him a questioning look. "Both his parents were killed in a shipwreck a few years ago," he explained. "He was one of only two survivors."

Amazonia nodded and looked over the crates. She was touched by the vulnerability of this tough fighter who now lay alone on the deck like a frightened child. She moved toward him, but Lindani grabbed her arm. "Leave him," he said.

"Let me go to him. He needs someone to talk to."

Lindani paused for a moment, then released her arm and walked with her around the crates. She sat down on the deck next to where Quintus lay, her back against the stern rail. Lindani sat opposite them, leaning against one of the crates.

"Your parents must have been smart people," she said to Quintus softly in her deep voice.

Quintus opened his eyes and looked up at her through strands of his long black hair, now wet and matted to his face. "What do you know of my parents?"

"I know they taught their child the meaning of confidence and determination."

"I should have done more to help them," Quintus said as he closed his eyes again.

"I'm sure you did everything you could. Some things are only for the gods to decide. Be thankful for the time you had with them."

Quintus stared at her again, and his voice grew in anger. "What do you know about watching your parents die? It's not an easy thing to forget."

"No, it's not," she answered calmly. "I've yet to erase the vision of my mother being beaten to death by a drunken soldier before my eyes. Or the fact that my father was more interested in selling me as a whore than in getting to know me, before he was tortured to death for his blackmail scheme. There are many who have lost their parents to some violent act. But you know what I've learned? That these were fates dealt to them by the goddess Fortuna. There was nothing I could have done to prevent it. That's the lesson you still need to learn."

Quintus rolled over on the wet deck, turning away from her and Lindani. A sudden thunderclap was followed by a strong gust of wind. The mast creaked as the squall attacked the canvas of the mainsail. Amazonia watched Quintus's huge body shudder as the noises grew. He pulled his knees closer to his chin and laid in a tense bundle on the deck.

"I haven't thanked you for your words of support in the latrine on my first day. I appreciated that."

Quintus did not stir. "A fighter is a fighter. We all deserve respect." His voice was flat.

She looked at his broad shoulders. "I've heard about you. They say you may be the best fighter ever to come out of one of the Petra schools."

"You wouldn't know it now, would you?" Quintus replied in an embarrassed, shallow voice.

"Achilles had his heel, Cyclops his one eye," Lindani said. "We all have our vulnerable spots."

Quintus did not respond.

Lindani motioned with his head for them to move away. Amazonia reluctantly followed him back to the crates.

"I think it is best we leave him now," Lindani said as he returned to his self-appointed sentry position atop a large crate. Amazonia felt him studying her as she sat and leaned back against one of the boxes, the rainwater pouring down her tunic. "So why are you here?" he finally asked.

"I was arrested because of my father's blackmail plot. I became a slave for a while in the fields, then ended up here when the dominus bought me."

"That is too bad," he said. "Picking fruit is much safer than facing an opponent in the arena."

"Oh, I'm not sorry about this arrangement at all," Amazonia said with a sly smile. "In fact I've thanked the gods on many nights for sending me along this new path. It's still like being sold as a whore in many ways, but at least now I get to keep some of the money. In all my years as a prostitute, I spent the nights in the best and biggest houses in Pompeii. But the next day, I was always back in my father's filthy, stinking pigsty. It reeked of the wine and beer he squandered all our money on. Not a single sesterce ever came to me. I vowed that someday I would have a beautiful home for myself. The dominus has given me a way to do it, so long as I survive. For me, there's no better motivation."

She watched Lindani intently as he seemed to ponder her story. After a moment, he looked her in the eyes. "You will not make it here. You know that, no?"

She was stunned at the hunter's arrogance. The normally happy and resilient personality she had seen him exhibit at the ludus was suddenly gone. In its place was a scowl and a penetrating stare.

"Really? And what makes you say that?" she replied, doing her best to keep her cool.

"Because this is a world of men. There are bonds of spirit that develop here a female would not understand."

Amazonia stared at the African for a moment. "Do these bonds run throughout the ludus," she asked, "or only between you and Quintus?"

Lindani's expression never wavered as he spoke. "Others have used him to get to where they want to be. That will not happen again."

Amazonia's blood began to boil, but she held her temper in check. "Is that what you think I'm all about?"

Lindani did not reply. His eyes said everything she needed to know. She smiled and stood up. The rain that had gathered in her lap spilled to the wooden deck.

"Not to worry, Lindani. Like I said in the latrine that first day, I can take care of myself."

She found an empty spot under the canvas roof and sat, staring out toward the turbulent sea. She hoped the rain on her face masked the tear that fell from the corner of her eye.

Three hours after leaving port the black clouds surrendered to blue sky, and the seas returned to their normal chop. Amazonia stood at the prow and relished the warm breeze that blew back her long auburn hair. Lindani's words still echoed in her ears, but she pushed them from her mind. She had an arena fight to train for, and she wanted no distractions. A favorable wind filled the sails, and the ship arrived the following day at Gesoriacum, on the north coast of Gaul, ahead of schedule. Amazonia noticed that, even in the pleasant weather, Quintus was the first one off the ship, obviously glad to be done with the sea portion of their long trek.

She accompanied Julianus and his assistants to town to help restock their provisions. Then the caravan of twelve carts and assorted pack animals set off on the southerly road toward Italia. Julianus drove the lead wagon, with Petra seated alongside on the high bench and their horses tied to the rear gate.

Amazonia, Quintus, Lindani, and three other fighters filled the second cart.

Amazonia recognized many of the landmarks as they rode, having recently taken this same route with Petra on her journey to Britannia. She decided traveling by cart was much more comfortable than by horseback, although she looked with envy on the bench that held Julianus and Petra. Before they had left Glevum, the head trainer had managed to secure two padded cushions, which he tied to the wooden seat. While the Roman road network was the best in the world, the hard paving stones took their toll on a rider's backside.

The more she worked with him, the more Amazonia admired Julianus. Had she still been a whore, he was the type of handsome, rugged customer she would have enjoyed. Like Petra, the head trainer was firm but fair. And he had a knack for organization and logistics, especially on this arduous trip. Keeping to a rigid schedule, he saw to it that the group made at least ninety kilometers a day, ticking off the distance using the milestones the legionary construction crews had placed along the roadside. The nights were spent in camps efficiently set up about fifty meters from the road. The soft grass and fresh air provided a welcome alternative to the straw mats of the cramped ludus cells. Each morning Julianus roused the troupe at sunrise, oversaw their ritual morning exercises, then broke them into groups for abbreviated sparring matches.

On their first morning on the mainland, Amazonia had no sooner completed her stretches and fitness training when she heard her name being shouted by the murmillo doctore.

"Amazonia . . . Drusus . . . Suit up now."

Julianus had told her during their restocking trip to town that she would be worked hard in these roadside training sessions. Although he meant it as a friendly warning, she welcomed the challenge, knowing she needed further training if she wanted to impress the crowd in her first match.

In a few minutes she was facing her sparring partner with rudis and scutum shield in hand. Her locks spilled from the wide flair at the bottom of her bronze helmet and rested on the shoulders of her green tunic. She knew there would be no such tunic in the arena. Although she had not yet seen the pompa costume and fighting outfit she was to wear, she was sure there would be no lack of bare skin. Her worth to Petra was obvious, but she was ready to show him, Julianus, and the rest of the ludus that she had a lot more going for her than an ample body.

"Now remember the drills, Amazonia." Julianus personally oversaw her match, ordering an assistant doctore to referee his own Thracian group for a while. "Be on guard . . . Attack!"

Drusus, armed as a thraex, advanced first, slicing right and left to back her up meter by meter. Amazonia was now more comfortable in the headgear and armor. She casually parried the blows and, while she gave ground, she showed no sense of fear or hesitation. When she saw an opportunity she quickly turned the tide. Her blows came swift, each landing with a loud grunt.

"That's it," Julianus said calmly. "Watch your advance. Pace yourself."

The seated fighters waiting their turn to spar shouted encouragement to Drusus. Although they were all a part of the same familia, Amazonia was well aware that the fighters' loyalties always seemed to favor whichever male happened to be facing off against her. Drusus responded by releasing more energy into his sword arm. Amazonia slowed her advance. Drusus went on the attack again, but a quick circular motion from Amazonia's wrist disengaged their wooden blades.

"Nice," said Julianus. "Now lunge!"

Rather than attack with a thrust, Amazonia feinted with a slice to the left. The calculated miss drew Drusus in just where she wanted him. With her sword still pointed toward the grass, he stepped forward. She brought the pommel of her rudis up hard and caught Drusus in the exposed jaw under his facemask. The unexpected move stunned the brawny fighter. As he staggered back Amazonia began her spin. Her foot flew with blinding speed and caught Drusus on the side of his knee. Both legs slid sideways and he went down hard. Before he could look up, Amazonia stood over him, her rudis at his throat. She glanced at Julianus and the murmillo trainer. Both men's faces were aglow.

"You've harnessed her power well, my friend," Julianus said to the trainer. "Good job. Work on her advance a bit."

Amazonia pulled her helmet off and helped Drusus off the ground.

Julianus called to her as he walked away. "Keep it up and you'll be the talk of your hometown."

"I plan on it, Doctore."

Just past Julianus, Amazonia spotted Quintus seated on a low hill watching her, the dappled morning sun throwing spots of light on his painted torso. He smiled and slowly nodded his approval. It was the final bit of affirmation she needed to consider her first roadside sparring match a success.

After seventeen more days of travel, the caravan arrived at the outskirts of Rome. Many in the troupe had never seen such a metropolis and were disappointed they had to travel the ring road, bypassing the city center. Quintus watched intently as the formidable city walls moved past the wooden bars of his cart. On one hand, he yearned to once again see the city of his youth. On the other, he feared the ghosts and memories that might arise would cloud his concentration for the big games ahead.

Julianus gave a tug on his reins and the oxen headed south on the Via Appia, one of the widest and best roads in the Empire. The sights and smells of urban settlement gave way once again to verdant countryside. A day outside Rome, their route began to hug the Italian shoreline, providing spectacular views of the sapphire waters of the Mare Internum. The group stopped for their final provisions at Puteoli on the edge of the Bay of Neapolis, then set up camp along the shore for the last night of the journey.

Looking across the bay waters in the evening twilight, Quintus could make out the hazy outline of the landmark that designated the entrance to the southern Campania region. The summit of Vesuvio loomed over the bay like a stone sentinel.

The following morning, after their workout, the caravan made its way along the shoreline. The cool breeze off the bay subsided as they approached the base of the mountain. After just a few hours of travel, Julianus waved the carts to the side of the road.

"Make camp here," he yelled down the line of carts. "The dominus and I will ride ahead to Pompeii."

The midafternoon heat made the Pompeiian lanista's office uncomfortable. Petra watched the sweat drip from Julianus's forehead, but he knew it had little to do with the weather. The trainer's fist struck the table hard enough to rattle the goblets and utensils left over from the lunch Facilix and Justus had just finished. The Pompeiian lanista and his head trainer seemed unfazed by the outburst.

"This is *bullshit!*" Julianus yelled. "The arrangements were already made." Petra placed a hand on his trainer's arm to calm him. He could tell Julianus saw this last-minute change as a personal insult. It marred the otherwise-impeccable journey his head trainer had planned and executed.

"I'm very sorry, gentlemen," said the Pompeiian lanista, "but I'm afraid it will be impossible to house your troupe here as we had planned. We just made an unexpected purchase of sixty new fighters. We have to house our own men before we can offer temporary quarters for your troupe. You would do the same."

"Not if we had already made a commitment, like you did," said an enraged Julianus.

"Juli, settle down," Petra said. It took effort to keep his own voice calm. He wanted to dive across the table and strangle the Pompeiians more than Julianus did. "Don't worry about it. We'll work something else out." He rose to leave, but leaned down face-to-face with his Pompeiian counterpart as he passed. "Don't think this little stunt is going to disrupt our game plan, Facilix. We will prevail in this matter, and we will prevail in the arena." Petra looked equally hard at Justus, who sat alongside his lanista. The Pompeiian head trainer simply grinned back.

Petra and Julianus turned and walked out the door.

"I can't believe that fucking bastard," Julianus fumed as they rode their horses back through the town gate.

"Juli!" Petra deliberately made his voice stern, although he could not remember the last time he had to reprimand his loyal head trainer. "What's the first thing you always tell your fighters? Isn't it something like: 'Don't ever let your opponent see they've rattled you'?"

Julianus dropped his chin to his chest as they rode on. "You're right. I'm sorry, Dominus. But we have only a few weeks before the biggest fight of our lives. And now we're stranded in the Italian countryside without a training facility, without even a roof over our heads."

Petra kept his composure. He knew he could not afford to show any hint of alarm, even though his stomach was in knots. "Don't worry about it. We have too much to do to start worrying now. Take this road back to the caravan and make camp for the night. I'm going to visit Gaius Magnus. As the game's editor, let's let him earn his cut a little bit."

He spurred his horse down the provincial pathway that led to his friend's vineyard. He glanced back over his shoulder and watched Julianus gallop back along the main road, quickly disappearing in a cloud of dust. Petra knew that his head trainer wanted this venture to be a success almost more than he did. The thought of a long, depressing journey back to Britannia after a humiliating defeat by the Pompeii troupe did not sit well with either of them.

He hoped with all his heart that Gaius Magnus could set things right.

XXV

October AD 66

L ADIES, THERE'S BEEN a slight change in plans," Petra's coarse voice
bellowed just after dawn. Quintus broke from his morning training
and joined the rest of the troupe gathered around the lead wagon where
Petra and another man stood on the lofty driver's seat. He had heard rumors that all was not well with the Pompeii accommodations, which was why
they had been forced to spend another night in their roadside encampment.
The last-minute change had had a visible effect on Julianus, who had become
short-tempered with his assistants and the fighters. Seeing this, Quintus had
grown concerned. He felt he had a deeper stake than the other fighters in this
matter, since it was he who had pushed hardest for Petra to embark on this
venture. But now the twinkle in his lanista's eyes told him their situation was
about to improve.

"Two days ago," Petra continued, "I was told that our temporary quarters
at the Pompeii ludus were no longer available. Personally, I think the stupid
bastards are just trying to rattle us." A sound that was half laughter and half
cheering rose from the group of 78 men and one woman. When it died, Petra
continued. "This is my friend, Gaius Tadius Magnus. He is the editor of these
games."

Quintus led a rousing cheer from the assembled group. Fifty wooden practice weapons were raised in the traditional salute to the sponsor. The older
man with the white beard nodded a "thank you," then waved for quiet and
picked up where Petra had left off.

"I have spoken with the magistrate of Pompeii, and he agrees with me that
our guests from Britannia should not be put at a disadvantage for these his-
toric games. He has graciously granted us permission to use an alternate site

for your housing and training. So if you would all prepare to travel once more, you may follow me . . . " Gaius paused a moment for effect. The troupe leaned forward in anticipation. " . . . to Herculaneum."

Quintus hoped the earsplitting roar from his familia could be heard inside the Pompeii ludus. He, along with every fighter, hunter, and ludus worker, moved with haste to load the equipment carts. Within a few minutes the caravan was back on the road, following Gaius to the nearby town named in honor of the patron god of the gladiator.

"This is a sign!" Quintus yelled from the back of his transport cart. "It's a sign that our god is with us in these games. Not with them in Pompeii, but with *us,* in his own town of Herculaneum!" A defiant roar radiated from all twelve carts.

As the caravan approached the town gate, Gaius turned in his saddle and threw a wink and a smile at Petra, who followed close behind in the lead cart. Quintus began a chant that grew in intensity. "All hail Hercules! Protector of the gladiator! Protector of the venator! Protector of Herculaneum!"

The wooden gate opened as Gaius approached. None of the troupe was prepared for what awaited inside the town walls. As the lead cart entered the Decumanus Maximus, Herculaneum's main thoroughfare, a spirited round of applause flowed from the hundreds of townspeople who had gathered along the street. Local inhabitants, from the youngest children to the oldest patricians, stood in front of the shops and homes that lined the boulevard, waving palm fronds and cheering the visitors.

Quintus watched Petra as he turned and looked down the line of carts. The look of pride on the lanista's worn face made him appear almost noble. Next to him, Julianus smiled and waved to the crowd, obviously in much better spirits than just a few hours earlier.

The procession moved slowly through the friendly gauntlet along the main street. Quintus distinctly heard someone yell for Amazonia, and was even more surprised when he heard one of the shapely young women near his cart call for Taurus. How did these people, 1,700 kilometers from their ludus, know him by name?

All his senses were suddenly assaulted at once. As he listened to their names being screamed, the smells of fish and freshly baked bread floated from the storefronts and mixed with the salty air of the seaside town. Looking down the road ahead, Quintus was struck by the bright orange-red paint that tinted the first story of every building, separating the façades of the lower shops from the equally vibrant pink coloration of the upper apartment walls. Lindani tapped Quintus on the shoulder and used his chin to point at a nearby wall.

"I know," Quintus yelled over the mob's cheering. "They love their colored paint here, don't they?"

Lindani shook his head. "Not the paint. Look at the signs."

Quintus had not noticed the large hand-painted signs that adorned many of the walls. The first one he studied read: "SEE AMAZONIA! THE FEARSOME WARRIOR WOMAN WHO FIGHTS NAKED!" So this was how they knew the names of his familia. The lettering surrounded a picture of a naked woman with gladius in hand who looked nothing like Amazonia, her breasts the obvious focus of the image. He leaned back and looked across the cart at his female fighting companion. Her laughter told him she had already spotted the sign.

"What's it say underneath my magnificent picture?" she asked.

Quintus was taken aback for a moment. It had never occurred to him that Amazonia was illiterate. But, now knowing her background, it was not surprising. "It says you're the fearsome warrior woman who fights naked," he read to her.

"Hey, Amazonia! They're selling your best assets," yelled one of the hunters, which prompted a round of good-natured badgering.

"Look at this one!" Lindani yelled. "Now whose assets are they selling?" Every eye in the cart followed the African's gaze to a new sign, as he read the advertisement out loud. "SEE TAURUS! THE AMAZING PAINTED GLADIATOR WHO FIGHTS WITH THE SPEED OF MERCURY!"

Quintus smiled and shook his head, flattered that the editor singled him out for promotion but grossly disappointed in the quality of the artwork. Not only did the image look nothing like him, but the Minotaur on the drawing's chest paled in comparison to the actual artwork of Lindani and Agricola, the physician.

"I must speak with the artist," Lindani said as he laughed. "I will show him how to design a Minotaur."

"While you're at it, you might want to pose for him," Quintus said, fighting to hold back his own laughter. "Take a look."

Lindani turned to where Quintus pointed. On the wall outside a tavern was a sign promoting: "THE GREAT LANDINI! THE EXTRAORDINARY VENATOR FROM AFRICA!" The only physical features visible on the black blob that was his head were two round white eyes, staring ahead as if in panic. To add further insult, a mischievous graffiti artist had taken liberties with the picture, adding an enormous penis hanging from under the short loincloth. Lindani seemed mortified.

"Hey, Lindani," came Amazonia's sultry voice from across the cart, "now whose assets are they selling? And by the way, if that's an accurate picture, I'll be seeing you tonight after dinner." A chorus of whoops and whistles punctuated her solicitation.

Lindani just stared at the poster and shook his head. "They did not even spell my name right."

"Well, I'll tell you what," Quintus said, holding his side, which ached from laughter. "We'll find out where the artist sits in the amphitheater, and you can fire your first arrow into his painting hand."

"I would very much like that," Lindani said almost too seriously.

The informal parade finally reached the end of the Decumanus Maximus and spilled into a public courtyard called the Palaestra. The square was large, close in size to their own ludus practice ground, and covered with a carpet of blue-green grass. Except for two openings allowing street access, it was entirely enclosed by long beautiful porticos supported by hundreds of white fluted columns of the Corinthian order. The walls of the wide breezeways beyond the colonnade were painted a deep red and richly adorned with murals of various sporting events, some still bearing cracks from the earthquake four years earlier. In the center of the square lay a cross-shaped pool containing a bronze fountain in the form of a five-headed serpent wrapped around a tree trunk.

Gaius, Petra, and Julianus climbed from their wagons and walked back along the line of carts that had followed them into the square.

"Alright ladies," Petra called out with his raspy voice, "this will be our home for the next month." The statement was met with a chorus of cheers.

Quintus jumped down next to the three administrators as Gaius pointed out which buildings were to act as billets for the fighters and workers. He singled out a larger building with an exquisite marble façade as Petra's office and quarters.

"So, what do you think?" Gaius asked with a wide smile. "Will this do?"

"Gaius, I don't know what to say," Petra replied slowly. "This is spectacular."

"I thought you'd like it. Your troupe will have exclusive access to the square for practice every day until the games. There is also another open field the venatores can use. It's a short walk down Cardio Quinque."

In a rare show of emotion, Petra turned and gave Gaius a strong hug. "Thank you, my friend. You will not regret this. We will put your Palaestra to good use."

Gaius addressed Quintus and Lindani as well as Petra. "You can all return the favor by winning these games. I have a lot riding on you boys."

"Only the boys?" came a sultry voice from above. "Do you have no confidence in your own ex-slave, sir?" Quintus stepped aside as Amazonia jumped down from the cartbed.

"Just a figure of speech, Claudia," Gaius said with a laugh.

"Amazonia," Petra corrected him. "That's the only name she goes by now."

"My apologies, Amazonia." Gaius winked at her with a smile. His gaze lingered as she began unloading the equipment. It was clear to Quintus that she had been one of Gaius's favorite slaves, for obvious reasons.

It took only a few hours for the troupe to organize the Palaestra into an efficient temporary ludus, complete with a mess hall, infirmary, unctores room, armory, and staff offices. By the following morning, Quintus and the rest of the troupe were back on the same exercise and training schedule they had worked in Britannia.

As Quintus ran the circuit of the Palaestra with Lindani at his side, he studied the beautiful buildings, which radiated a soft pink glow in the early light. The reality of his situation finally began to set in. He had gotten his wish. He was in Italia, preparing for one of the biggest and best-publicized matches ever held outside of Rome itself. And he would be one of the featured fighters. He thought back to the day he'd sat in the tree at Aquae Sulis with little Decimus, when he saw his future unfurl before him. Now he was living his dream. He would not let his lanista down and, more importantly, he would not let himself down.

Quintus's focus and dedication became the model for the entire troupe, including the veterans with years more arena experience. The lethargic effects of their long trip wore off quickly, and morale was high, due in large part to Quintus's never-faltering enthusiasm. Familia Gladiatoria Petra literally grew stronger by the day.

Two weeks before game day, Petra sat with Julianus on the second-story loggia above the north portico of the Palaestra, drinking wine and surveying his temporary ludus. He had to speak over the sounds of the wooden weapons clashing below them.

"You've done a good job with Amazonia. I'm happy with her progress."

"Thank you, Dominus. She's now sparring against tertius palus-level fighters and holding her own. She even pinned one to the ground yesterday with her rudis in his face."

Petra thought for a minute, then leaned closer to Julianus. "Remember what I said. I don't want anyone from the outside seeing that. That's why I had this viewing balcony closed off to the public." He looked Julianus in the eye and gave him a sly grin. "I like being the underdog. The side-bets pay off much higher that way."

The familiar voice of Gaius Magnus came from behind him. "Two weeks to game day and all you can do is drink wine?" he said with a laugh. Petra turned to see Facilix and Justus from the Pompeii ludus standing alongside the editor.

"Yes, and it's that horse-piss vintage from the Magnus vineyards outside this very town," Petra answered with a straight face. "Allow me to offer you some."

Petra was pleased to see the surprised look on the faces of the Pompeii lanista and his trainer as they gazed beyond the edge of the balcony. "Nice set-up

Gaius put us into here, isn't it, gentlemen?" he said with a bit more relish than he should have.

"Yes, very nice. Perhaps even better than my own fighters have," Facilix said in a scornful tone, looking directly at Gaius.

"With your ludus cells full, we had to make the best of a bad situation," Julianus replied with a smile. There was an awkward silence, until Petra took the lead.

"Let's get started. We have a lot of pairings to do." He reached down by his feet and gathered up the five scrolls which contained the fighting records of each of his fifty gladiators and venatores. He laid the scrolls out on the wooden table that held the goblets and wine pitcher.

The five men spent the next two hours studying and discussing each of the fighters below them, with Justus making copious notes on the record scrolls and on a stack of wax tablets. It had been decided that the pairing of the Britannian and Pompeiian fighters be done by the administrators of the two ludi in advance of the games, to assure the crowd the best possible matches. It also allowed Gaius to have programs made, a luxury in a provincial amphitheater, even one as prominent as Pompeii.

While their responses were honest, Petra and Julianus kept the information on their fighters to a minimum, just enough to arrange a fair pairing. In a ludus meeting earlier that morning, Petra had made it clear that he did not want any extraordinary moves or showmanship on the practice field this day. There was no sense tipping off the competition to any special skills his fighters possessed.

"Now there's a colorful Thracian," Justus said as the evaluations came around to Quintus.

"That's Taurus," Julianus answered. "He will be primus palus soon. He's one of our best. He can be paired against any of your men."

"Well, he'll be primus palus assuming he survives," Justus said casually as he made more notes.

Petra looked across at Julianus as the head trainer grinned. "I think it's safe to say he'll survive," Petra responded.

"And that must be the great Amazonia we've heard so much about," Facilix said. Petra tapped his finger impatiently on the scroll as Facilix took his time inspecting every inch of the female fighter's body. "Gaius, your promotional signs don't do her justice. She's a beauty. Used to belong to you as I recall."

"That's right," Gaius said, "but Petra has found a much better use for her talents. He tells me she's really taken to this life."

"She's a big draw," said Facilix. "We should put her near the end of the program. Keep them waiting." He finally pried his gaze from her body and looked at Petra. "I hope you know what you're doing. She may be good, but she'll be no match for a man."

"We'll see. Just match her appropriately and she'll put on a memorable show for the crowd. She's a tiro, but she's fast. We'll let her fight at quartus palus level. Nothing higher."

"Alright, we'll have some recommendations for you when you visit us tomorrow in Pompeii. Then we'll finalize the program."

Facilix and his head trainer stood to leave. "Until tomorrow then." Petra watched them descend the stairs.

"I don't know if I trust them with the pairings, Juli. What do you think?"

"I'll want to study all their fighters' records tomorrow and watch them train for a while myself. That should keep them honest, unless they falsify the records."

Petra looked to Gaius. "When you were magistrate here you hired his troupe often, so you know his fighters. I'd like you to look over the pairings list when it's completed. If there's anything that doesn't seem right, let me know."

"Not to worry, my friend. Remember, I too have more than a few wagers riding on this game."

Facilix and Justus walked their horses side by side down the Decumanus Maximus on their way back to Pompeii. The lanista watched the sign go by depicting a naked Amazonia.

"Who do you have in mind to fight the woman?" he asked Justus.

"Possibly Savius. I'm not sure yet."

The lanista thought for a while as he rode. "Yes. They should have no problem with that. But listen carefully to what I'm about to tell you." Justus leaned closer in his saddle. "I am not about to earn the reputation of owning the first male gladiator in Pompeii to fall to a female fighter. If a last minute replacement should need to occur in the arena tunnel, so be it. All I know is a loss in that contest shall *not* be on my record." Facilix looked directly into his head trainer's eyes. "Am I making myself understood?"

Justus nodded. "Understood, Dominus. This shall be her first and last time on the sand."

XXVI

November AD 66

I T WAS DIFFICULT TO MOVE in the crush of the twenty thousand spectators that filled the grounds surrounding the Pompeii amphitheater. Vendors sold their gladiator-themed oil lamps, glassware, pottery, and other merchandise faster than the supply servants could replenish the display shelves. Stalls selling miniature statues of the gladiators and hunters in action poses were the busiest. Figurines of Amazonia sold the best, followed closely by icons of Taurus and Vulcanus, the popular local fighter. Gaius had brought in a dozen foremen from his vineyard to keep an accounting of all the souvenirs trading hands. The shady vendors could certainly not be trusted to voluntarily turn over the correct percentage to the editor. To increase his take, Gaius had set up four stalls of his own, selling his wine in souvenir goblets.

Shortly after sunrise the cavea gates opened and the crowd streamed in, scurrying to claim the best of the plebian seats. Fistfights broke out as newcomers attempted to shove their way to the head of a line that had begun forming two days earlier. Legionaries from Campania assigned to handle security quickly brought the scuffles under control. Gaius was not about to have a repeat of the ugly Pompeii amphitheater riot nearly a decade earlier, which had cost dozens of lives.

But the atmosphere on this day was much different. A spark was in the air that ignited a special passion for this fight. Although this was the Pompeiian troupe's hometown crowd, there was still a strong feeling of respect and admiration for the visiting Familia Gladiatoria Petra. A combination of their spirit, their guts, and their tenacity endeared them to the locals. A friendly rivalry had even developed between the residents of Pompeii and those of

Herculaneum who, after a month of hosting the visiting troupe, had adopted them as their own.

The audience could see they were in for a unique spectacle from the moment they entered the cavea. A full quarter of the arena floor had been dug away and filled with water to form an artificial lake. A variety of trees and bushes planted around the waterhole created a dramatic oasis in the sand. Most of the morning discussions speculated on what beasts would soon lurk beneath the water's surface.

A few straggling politicians made their way to the lower seats as a trumpet fanfare from the orchestra announced the arrival of the magistrate. The old administrator entered the podium, stopping periodically to wave to the crowd on the way to his seat. Because he was not sponsoring these games, a fact which he probably now regretted, this would be his only time in the spotlight today.

"Thank you, my friends," he said as loudly as his frail voice would allow. "Today you must save your hurrahs for the man who has put together this noble event for you. I give you my predecessor, Gaius Tadius Magnus!"

The orchestra commenced a stately ceremonial march, and the heavy arena gates swung open at the musical cue. Onto the sand rode a chariot drawn by four white horses and containing a smiling, waving Gaius. The crowd had indeed saved their hurrahs for the editor, and a tremendous cheer erupted from the throng. His successful term as their previous magistrate had already endeared him to many in the crowd, and even those who had disagreed with his policies while in office were his allies today in light of this spectacular presentation.

In the tunnel, the sudden burst of sunlight temporarily blinded Quintus. As his eyes adjusted, he was overwhelmed by the sight of twenty thousand spectators in an amphitheater twice the size of the Londinium arena. He was among the first out of the tunnel, leading the Britannia troupe in their march behind the chariot. Beside him were the other primus and secundus palus veterans, along with the top audience draw, Amazonia. While the men were dressed in their traditional subligaculum, Amazonia wore a sky blue two-piece outfit boasting a tightly tied loincloth and a matching top overlaid in silver mail.

Black boots and a flowing white cape helped punctuate her entrance into the arena, which was greeted by another tremendous roar from the crowd. As they marched side by side, Amazonia's beauty and Quintus's rugged good looks and painted torso seemed to mesmerize every member of the audience, both male and female.

"We seem to be a hit," Quintus said.

"Wait until they see the fighting costume Gaius had designed for me," replied Amazonia. "That should get some hearts beating."

As Quintus expected, the cheering grew even louder as the Pompeiian troupe made their entrance. Chants of "Vulcanus! Vulcanus!" rose from the crowd as the pompa made its circuit. Quintus kept his eye on the man who would be his adversary this day. The senior Pompeiian fighter, a large man with a ruggedly handsome face, acknowledged the crowd's devotion with an occasional pose that emphasized arms the size of tree trunks.

Gaius's horses became skittish as they approached the artificial lake, unsure if an aquatic predator laid in wait for them as they passed. Gaius tugged the reins and steered the team away from the waterhole, stopping in the center of the wide arena. Julianus and Justus arranged the fighters in neat rows behind the chariot.

Quintus continued to study Vulcanus a few rows ahead of him. The man seemed calm and collected. From his body language, it was obvious he was a veteran of many arena matches. In those few moments, Quintus knew this would be his most difficult challenger to date. But he also knew the outcome would be positive.

Gaius raised his arms, and the orchestra segued into an extended, trilling note designed to add tension.

"Fellow Romans and guests," his voice boomed theatrically, "welcome to an epic battle between North and South. The best of Britannia against the best of Pompeii!"

The sustained note became a dramatic fanfare, triggering a thunderous ovation that rolled through the amphitheater. The crowd was not as large as those that filled the huge amphitheater in Rome, but to Quintus's ears, the noise seemed greater. The ovation gave Gaius enough time to dismount and ascend the steps that had been set up leading to the podium. He took a moment to greet the game judges he had appointed. As the cheering subsided, he addressed the crowd and judges alike.

"This contest will be judged fairly. There will be no preference given to the home ludus."

A few boos and jeers came from the cavea, a response that brought laughter from the rest of the crowd and Gaius. Quintus wondered if the jeers were truly good-natured. He scanned the podium and locked eyes with Petra. His lanista radiated a look of pride and confidence. Quintus thought back to their conversation as the carts were being loaded in Glevum so many months ago, where the first seeds of this idea were planted. Now it had blossomed into reality. The orchestra played its final fanfare and, with a nod, Quintus turned and marched from the arena, the proud image of his lanista lingering in his mind.

Cassius Petra's nerves were as tight as a bowstring, but he did his best to convey only confidence. From his seat on the podium, an unusual vantage point for him, he watched his forty-nine men and one woman march back into the darkness of the tunnel. Gaius had insisted that he and Facilix flank the editor's chair on the podium, an honor not normally granted a lanista but offered on this day in tribute to the unique nature of the games. Petra glanced across at Facilix. Although they had worked together in setting up the massive event, he still held little trust for his counterpart.

Gaius stood in front of his elaborate seat between the two lanistae. As the applause subsided he addressed the crowd once again.

"I want to thank each of you for paying fifteen sesterces of your hard-earned money for this special event. These are the most expensive games ever held in Pompeii. I assure you that not one of you will leave here today disappointed. In this morning's hunt you will see beasts that most of you have never seen before. But you did not come to hear me drone on. So I say to you—"

Before he completed his sentence, the heavy wooden doors leading to the arena floor burst open and slapped against the stone wall with a loud bang. The noise startled everyone, including Petra. He watched as a lone slave ran across the sand, yelling dramatically; almost too dramatically, he thought.

"Master, Master! There's a monster in our midst like I have never seen before. It chased me into this arena and traps me here now."

Petra looked up at Gaius who appeared to be only half listening to the ranting slave. The editor glanced at him with a quick wink. Petra looked around the cavea to see who was being duped by the hoax. Their puzzled and shocked expressions told him most of the audience were falling for the prank, despite the slave's terribly overblown performance.

Gaius cleared his throat and yelled back to the man in the arena. "Well, slave, then you shall have the honor of being the first to die in the jaws of the mighty water horse!"

Wild shouting came from the dark tunnel. Suddenly a massive, angry hippopotamus charged through the portal. A collective scream came from the crowd, indicating—as Gaius had predicted—that most had never seen such a huge, ugly creature before. Petra knew this was to be Lindani's prey, but the theatrical entrance was a surprise even to him. The narrow streams of blood running down the beast's sides showed that the animal handlers had done their job in enraging the beast.

The hippo charged at the slave. Its speed belied its tremendous bulk. The screams of the crowd grew louder as the animal opened its gaping jaws and revealed the four dreadful tusks that made it the most feared water animal in Africa. Vile grunts came from the animal as it ran. The slave moved quickly, but in a short sprint it was obvious the hippo could easily outrun even the fastest Greek athlete. With a swipe of its unwieldy head, the hippo knocked its prey to the sand. The slave screamed in terror as the beast grabbed him up in its powerful jaws, the upper and lower tusks penetrating his torso like four razor-sharp swords. The howls of pain ended abruptly as the hippo began twisting his neck and slapping the top half of the man's body onto the ground. With the bloody carcass still hanging like a rag doll from its jaws, the hippo lurched across the arena and plunged into the waterhole, drenching the spectators seated four meters above it. Within a few seconds, only the top of the animal's head was visible above the swells.

Before the shocked spectators had time to react, Gaius was back on his feet beside Petra. "But this beast cannot have all the spoils for himself. He must learn to share. Bring in his companions!"

Once again, the tunnel door opened. A large cart powered by twenty prisoners, ten along each side, entered the arena. Petra could see the terrified looks on their faces even from across the amphitheater. The prisoners were chained to the covered cart to prevent them from fleeing should the hippo decide to claim another victim. Two arena attendants riding atop the wagon prodded them forward with long pokers, glowing red hot at the end.

The hippo kept a close watch as the cart slowly approached the waterhole. The beast raised its head and bellowed, threatening to charge. One of the prisoners closest to the front of the wagon stopped pushing and attempted to hold back the cart. A red-hot poker quickly found his back and left a permanent mark. His agonized scream seemed to momentarily frighten the hippo and it sank again into the pool, its first victim dislodging from the bottom tusks to float facedown in the dark water. The prisoners spun the cart around and backed it up to the water's edge. On the attendant's signal, the slaves moved to the two long rods protruding from each side of the covered cargo bed and began to lift. An unearthly hissing emerged from the cart, followed by five large reptilian bodies, which slid from the bed and splashed into the water beside the hippo.

Gasps again came from the crowd. Petra was surprised that few in Pompeii had apparently ever seen a Nile crocodile. The hungry crocs immediately charged for the body floating in the pool and tore it apart in seconds. The hippo seemed more concerned with the cart than in protecting its kill.

The prisoners, happy to leave with their lives, pushed the wagon from the arena twice a fast as they had brought it in. The wild reaction of the crowd told Petra that the unusual start to the games had just the effect Gaius was hoping for. He would have enjoyed it more himself if his mind wasn't on Lindani, waiting in the tunnel to hunt all of these savage beasts.

Lindani, Quintus, and a top venator from Pompeii stepped aside near the portal to let the cart back through the tunnel. "The water horse is a difficult beast," Lindani said. "I have helped capture a few for the games in Rome. You must move very carefully," he warned the Pompeiian hunter.

"Why not just stall for a while and let the crocs eat the water horse?" Quintus asked.

"These two species respect each other. They live side by side in the great river of Egypt. Crocodiles are not stupid. They know better than to taunt an angry water horse."

"Then give it hell," Quintus said with a smile. "I'm just glad it's you and not I who take on the four-legged opponents."

Lindani grinned as he picked up on their ritual. "And how often do I need to tell you? It's not the legs, but the teeth that are the problem. And there are many, many teeth in that waterhole."

The voice of the arena herald echoing across the cavea interrupted their private little rite. "Gaius Tadius Magnus presents to you the best venatores from both the North and the South—the remarkable Lindani and the masterful Danaos! They will work together and attempt to destroy only the water horse, but not the dragons. The judges will award a point for each hit by arrow or spear, and a bonus of three points to whoever delivers the death blow. Additional points shall be awarded for exceptional moves or style." The herald nodded to Gaius, who stood and bellowed dramatically, "Let the games begin!"

As trumpets blared, the two venatores marched proudly into the arena, spears and bows held high. Lindani attempted to offer some last minute advice to the Pompeiian hunter, but he wasn't sure if his words carried over the trumpets and crowd noise. The heavy wooden door slammed shut behind them, the finality of the sound emphasizing their isolation in the dangerous setting.

They approached the pool slowly with arrows nocked. Six pairs of eyes watched warily from water level as they advanced. The Pompeiian seemed to focus on the hippo, watching the ears twitch, as if convinced the movements would reveal some secret code that would forecast its intentions.

Lindani advanced more cautiously from the opposite side. He was surprised at how close the Pompeiian was getting to the water's edge. The peripheral vision Lindani depended on so heavily in his hunts revealed movement in a crocodile's tail. He shouted a warning. At precisely the same instant a reptilian head shot from the water, jaws snapping at the Pompeiian's bare leg. There was a chorus of "oohs" from the cavea. As with all good hunters, Danaos's reflexes were swift and he jumped back in time to feel only the water spray and cold breath that hissed from the crocodile's mouth. Lindani saw his hunting companion's complexion turn a few shades whiter as the blood drained from his face.

"Be careful, the crocs are very fast," he warned, without taking his eyes from the waterhole. "We must wound the water horse just enough to get him to charge and leave the pool of crocs behind."

Lindani saw his opportunity as the hippo's back surfaced briefly. He fired his first arrow. It struck the beast in the lower back, just above its tail. The animal bellowed. Spray flew from the waterhole as three tons of bulk began to move rapidly. Once again, everyone in the amphitheater screamed, astounded at the speed generated by the four stumpy legs. Although Lindani was the provoking hunter, the hippo charged the closest target, which was Danaos. Lindani sensed this before the animal had left the water and ran toward the hippo rather than retreating. Danaos managed to fire his arrow, striking the bulbous snout of the animal. The shaft buried deep but did nothing to stop the beast. The shot only seemed to enrage it further.

As it left the pool, it picked up speed and within a few seconds trampled over the Pompeiian hunter, crushing one of his legs. Before he went down, Danaos slid his spear from the sheath on his back and managed to bury the point in the animal's belly as he fell. The hippo seemed stunned for a brief second, which was all the time Lindani needed to plow into its side at a full run. It was like hitting a solid wall for the lanky African, but it startled the hippo enough to leave the injured hunter behind and charge Lindani, the spear dropping from its belly in the first few steps. The crowd responded with a deafening cheer. This visitor had just saved the life of their venator. The judges were impressed enough to begin awarding bonus points.

But Lindani had more on his mind than earning extra points. He had a decent lead on the hippo, but the large beast was gaining ground on him. He began weaving from side to side, confusing the animal and keeping it at bay. They ran across the length of the sixty-five-meter arena until, gradually, the hippo slowed to a stop. Lindani turned and faced the beast. The hippo let out another roar of rage. Without flinching, Lindani roared back at the animal, echoing the beast's voice exactly. The amphitheater erupted in laughter as the African enchanted the crowd with an extended display of his animal mimicry.

As he taunted the hippo, Lindani kept an eye on Danaos. He had hoped the distance would allow the injured hunter time to crawl to safety. Even across the wide arena he could see the man's left leg was a bloodied pulp below the knee. But instead of crawling away from the pool of hungry crocodiles, Danaos sat up and pulled an arrow from his quiver, nocked it, and lined up on the hippo. Lindani saw the move for what it was: an attempt to draw attention away from the visiting hunter and earn points for the home ludus. He also knew the decision was a foolish one.

"No! Do not fire!" he yelled just as the missile flew from the bow. It took a full two seconds for the arrow to fly the length of the arena. It struck just behind the hippo's front leg, but did not have the power to penetrate to the heart. The animal spun, now delirious with rage, and focused on Danaos. Sand flew as the stubby legs began to carry its massive weight back toward the injured hunter. Anticipating what was about to happen, Lindani launched into a mad dash after the hippo. He reached over his shoulder for his hunting spear, while considering how to steer the hippo's path. With three mighty leaps he was alongside the accelerating animal. He planted the butt end of his spear into the sand and used his momentum to catapult himself into the air. He landed hard on the back of the galloping hippo. The beast hardly noticed. Lindani brought the long pole forward and repeatedly whacked it hard against the left side of the hippo's face. The enraged animal charged on, focused only on finishing off the aggressor who had now attacked it three times. Lindani dug his heels into its soft wet sides to stay upright, his long beaded braids slapping against his neck in beat with the galloping rhythm. Unable to withstand the constant beating, the hippo's head slowly began to turn to the right as it ran, causing its path to curve in the same direction. Finally its head turned beyond the point where it could see what was coming, and the galloping hippo became disoriented. It did not see the large crocodile which had crawled from the water, attracted by the scent of blood streaming from Danaos. The hippo's two front legs struck the reptile and collapsed. Its giant nose plowed into the ground, throwing Lindani into the air.

He seemed to fly for hours. He could see the oasis pool coming toward him, the yellow eyes watching his every move. As hard as he tried, he could not change his arc of travel. It became all too obvious that he was going to strike the water. His bare feet began kicking before he hit. He landed with a thud and a splash, half submerged in the waterhole. His kicking feet came down on the snout of a crocodile. The reptile snapped but could not get a grasp on the moving appendage. Lindani scrambled from the water, badly cut but with all his limbs intact.

The hippo had regained its feet and was once again charging the Pompeiian hunter. Lindani sprinted after it, snatching his spear from the sand as he went. Danaos had already loaded another arrow. He took careful aim at the beast's head as it charged directly at him. He drew back the bowstring and fired. The shaft penetrated just below the left eye, causing the hippo to toss its head. But still the animal kept coming. Lindani was now alongside it. His arm drew back as he ran and, with a rapid snap, he threw the spear with all his might. The metal tip pierced the tough hide between the ribs, just behind the first arrow Danaos had fired from across the arena. The spear traveled much deeper than the arrow and struck the animal's heart. With a tremendous roar the hippo reared its head back then dropped into the sand, plowing to a halt barely a meter from the wounded Pompeiian hunter. Danaos's hair blew back as the beast's final breath exploded in his face.

It was the cue for the mob to go wild. Never had they seen such speed and daring in a hunter. They chanted Lindani's name, to the obvious chagrin of Danaos. Lindani looked every bit the embattled victorious hunter as he stood bleeding at center stage, breathing heavily in his golden-yellow loincloth and beaded headband. He was proud of his performance but also sympathetic toward his competitor, who squirmed in agony as he was placed on a stretcher by the arena attendants.

Gaius shouted his own accolades from the podium and tossed a substantial purse of gold onto the sand. Lindani retrieved the reward and bowed toward the podium. To the side he could see Petra cheering enthusiastically, a sight few had ever witnessed. The stretcher team hefted Danaos off the sand and began moving toward the tunnel. Lindani stepped in front of them and took the wooden handles from the front litter bearer. He left the arena honoring his fallen comrade by bearing his stretcher. He had already won the crowd's respect for his courage, now he won their hearts for his humility.

• • •

The following teams of venatores slowly worked their way through four of the five crocodiles. It had been decided to leave one alive as an added danger to the afternoon gladiator bouts. Zebras, antelope, boars, a cape buffalo, an auroch, and a lion were all dispatched with skill and daring by hunters from both schools. At the end of the morning venatio, the points were tallied and Gaius announced a virtual dead heat, with the Pompeii school in the lead by only a few points.

The lunch period featured a few trained animal acts. It was kept short due to the full agenda Gaius had prepared. Only the patricians and politicians dared leave their seats for the break. The plebeians in the higher tiers stayed put, afraid of losing their place to one of the hundreds still waiting in line outside the arena. Gaius would not have been happy with the dozens of spectators who used his souvenir goblets as portable toilets in order not to visit the latrines.

It took only a half hour to rake the puddles of animal blood under fresh sand and unfurl the wool canopy that would protect the audience from the afternoon sun. The orchestra commenced a second ceremonial march, and the gates swung open to reveal the gleaming armor of the gladiators. Standard bearers carrying the yellow banner of Petra's ludus and the blue banner of the Pompeii troupe led the procession, alongside two trumpeters with their circular cornu horns. The fighters were arranged in the order of their bouts, marching side by side with their opponents. Tension built as each pair entered the arena, the mob anticipating the final four warriors. Fifty, sixty, seventy colorful combatants passed through the portal. Finally, greeted by the loudest cheering of the day, the top champions emerged.

Mixed within the primus palus fighters were two of the biggest draws, although strictly speaking neither had yet to earn the top ranking. Amazonia was a vision of splendor as she stepped onto the sand. Her prediction of the crowd's reaction to her fighting costume proved accurate. A golden waist-chain hung loosely over her emerald green loincloth. Above it shone a nude torso, glistening with the body oil that had been liberally applied by the luckiest of the unctores. A crown of three gold horns adorned her head and a brown fur cape billowed behind her, framing her muscular body. Her well-developed bare breasts quickly became the focal point of the entire parade. Most of the shocked audience considered Gaius's claim of presenting a naked female gladiator to be nothing more than hype, but once again their favorite ex-magistrate had followed through on a promise. Marching alongside Amazonia was Savius, the quartus palus fighter the lanistae had agreed upon as her opponent. His only right to walk among the top fighters in the pompa was his fate in being paired against one of the biggest crowd pleasers.

A break in the procession separated the final two competitors from the rest of the field. Arena workers ingeniously used large bronze sheets to reflect daylight through the tunnel, dramatically silhouetting the two consummate specimens who stood in the portal. The beams of sun backlighting them seemed even brighter in the shade of the arena's awning. The musicians played a special fanfare as Taurus stepped from the tunnel, shoulder-to-shoulder with Vulcanus, the hero of Pompeii. The Minotaur and Gorgon stigmates, accentuated by a liberal amount of body oil, worked their magic on the crowd. The two headlining fighters posed and flexed for the crowd, then joined the slow-moving procession.

Amazonia heard Taurus come up behind her. "Play to the crowd," he quietly coached over her shoulder. She smiled to herself, knowing how unnecessary the suggestion was. To her it seemed only a few days ago that she was slaving in a local vineyard and whoring in the local bedchambers. Now she was the center of attention; the envy of half the women in the cavea and the fantasy of every man. Reveling in the cheers of twenty thousand fans chanting her name came close to the few sexual climaxes she had achieved with her favorite customers.

"Now you know why I'm here," Taurus said from behind her. "There is no greater pride or sense of belonging for me than the moment I step onto the sand of the arena." She suddenly understood that sentiment. It was a feeling that could be described a thousand times, but never truly grasped until experienced for one's self. "Of course an outfit like that helps to get the crowd going, too," he continued. She could hear the smile in his voice. She kept her eyes on the cheering fans as she walked, speaking over her shoulder.

"I'm only giving them what they want, just as I did when I was my father's whore. Only this time, the money is mine."

From the podium, Petra watched twenty thousand heads follow Amazonia's every move. *If you think this is good, wait 'til you see her fight,* he wanted to shout. But he remained quiet, reveling in his decision to pluck her like a perfect grape from Gaius's vineyard. As if reading his mind, Gaius turned and smiled at Petra.

"A wise move, my friend. Very wise."

The procession steered clear of the artificial lake and its sole resident. Julianus and Justus arranged the fighters in tight formation before the podium. As the music ended, the trainers gave the signal and eighty polished weapons were raised as one. "Hail Gaius Tadius Magnus," came the deep chorus of voices. "We who are about to die salute you."

Petra leaned forward to see the reaction. The look on his friend's face was a combination of shock and gratitude. Petra knew the salute had only been offered to the Emperor Claudius, but he and Facilix had decided to have their men surprise the popular ex-magistrate with the honor.

"I wasn't aware you had your eye on the principate," said the old magistrate seated next to Gaius, with more than a trace of jealousy in his voice. Petra had to stifle a laugh. Gaius cleared his throat and stood.

"Fellow Romans and guests! The judges have scored this morning's hunt in slight favor of Pompeii." He was interrupted by clamorous applause. "Had it not been for the African's remarkable performance, our home team would be well ahead. But so be it. Today's challenge will obviously be decided with the gladiators." He addressed the fighters directly. "May Hercules protect all of you, and may he help our judges to fairly and honestly present us a clear victor today. Each triumphant fighter shall receive twenty pieces of gold, whether or not his ludus is declared the overall winner." The announcement brought gasps from the audience and smiles to the faces of the gladiators, who normally fought for a quarter of that amount. "And the victorious lanista shall receive a bonus of fifty thousand sesterces." Again the mob reacted. The amount was fifty times the annual salary of a Roman legionary and more than most wealthy business owners profited in a year. Petra was still amazed that he had managed to put such a project together, but to be reminded of the possible payoff was like remembering a long-lost love.

"Doctores, clear the arena and let the fights begin!" Gaius yelled.

The forty Britannia gladiators turned with military precision and marched back toward the tunnel. Watching their proud and determined bearing from on high, Petra felt his chest swell; but whether it was pride or a deep breath of apprehension, he could not tell. He suddenly wondered which of the gladiators before him would not be returning to Britannia. He knew it happened every time he supplied fighters for the games. But this time it was different. These were the best of the best, and there was not one he felt was expendable.

The sound of Taurus's voice suddenly rising above the din of the cavea broke him from his fatalistic thoughts.

"Who will win these games?"

"Familia Gladiatoria Petra!" came the chorus from his comrades as they marched across the sand.

"How will we win these games?"

"By being the best!"

"Why will we win these games?"

"Because we are the meanest motherfuckers in the Empire!" The final answer was followed by a coarse battle cry that resembled the screams of the Celtic tribes. The Pompeiian crowd cheered the visitors' spirit. Petra sat back and offered a brief prayer to Hercules.

For the entire afternoon, the audience was treated to some of the best fighting ever witnessed in their arena. Even many of the early bouts, featuring the tertius and secundus palus gladiators, had the crowd on its feet. Because of the caliber and tenacity of the combatants, virtually all the fights ended in missio, and both fighters were allowed to return to their ludus alive. One of Petra's retiarius lost his life to a devastating slice from a Pompeiian secutor. Another provocator from Facilix's troupe stepped too close to the oasis pool and was snatched by the four-meter crocodile and drowned. His opponent walked away with twenty gold pieces he had hardly earned. Two midafternoon group bouts saw a close split between ludi—eight victories for

Britannia and seven for Pompeii. Both Julianus and Justus were kept busy as referees, but neither required the use of the rod to goad their gladiators into battle. Their fighters were more than ready to fight.

As the games went on, it became obvious that both teams were remarkably well-matched. The point tally fluctuated. Just as one ludus pulled ahead, the other would dip into some hidden reserve and equal the score.

By dusk, with only three fights remaining, the Britannia troupe had managed to gain a slight lead over the Pompeii troupe. The setting sun caused a hold in the action while the awning was drawn back and torches lit around the arena. The games were supposed to have ended by sunset, but the bouts were running longer than anticipated, neither team's fighters willing to give up points by faltering or capitulating. Gaius wisely insisted on installing the giant torches. He had had a strong feeling that these games might run well into the night.

Finally, the trumpets heralded the resumption of events. As their names were called, two primus palus fighters, Valentinus from Petra's familia and Paris from Facilix's familia, rose from the wooden benches in the holding area and walked up the entrance tunnel. Although the games were almost over, the staging area and tunnel were still bustling with activity.

Quintus and Amazonia found a quiet corner where they stretched their muscles to stay loose and to keep their nerves in check. Quintus made a point to isolate Amazonia from the other fighters. He knew the last thing she needed now was to be distracted. She had added a padded manica to her sword arm and a short metal greave to her left leg. Petra had given her a woolen scarf to tie around her chest outside the arena. The distant clashing of swords and screams from the crowd echoed down the tunnel, creating an eerie resonance that seemed to grate on her. Quintus watched her eyes, which continued to glance toward the tunnel.

"Don't let your nerves control you," he said. "I made that mistake on my first bout and was lucky to escape with my life." Amazonia nodded but did not respond. "This Savius you will fight," he continued in a low voice, "remember that Julianus said he appears to have weak vision in his left eye. Stay to his left and you'll have the advantage."

"I know, I know," Amazonia replied. "We've gone over this a million times. I'm ready. Just let me get in the arena."

The arena manager called for the next two fighters. "Amazonia . . . Ursus . . . Stand by the gate."

Something about the order caught Quintus off guard. He jerked his head up and looked at Amazonia.

"Ursus? You're to fight Savius." He looked beyond her and watched a stout fighter stand and walk toward the tunnel entrance. "What's happening? Who is this Ursus?"

"I don't know," Amazonia said, shrugging casually. "But I'm ready to kick anybody's ass right now. Just put me in that fucking arena. I can't stand this waiting anymore."

"Let's go!" yelled the testy arena manager. "The fight on the sand is winding down."

Amazonia casually untied the scarf and tossed it on the floor, then picked up her helmet. Quintus walked with her toward the tunnel. "Amazonia, be careful. They've changed your opponent. Something's up." The arena manager suddenly stepped in front of Quintus, blocking his path up the tunnel.

"Why don't you mind your own business, pretty boy?" he growled into Quintus's face. "You have your own fight to worry about."

Quintus knew then that this had been a pre-arranged substitution. Surely the dominus would not allow the match to go on. He stared into the manager's eyes for a moment then returned to the staging area.

Amazonia was cool and focused as she walked up the tunnel side by side with her new opponent. She glanced over at him to see who she would soon be killing. The scarred, bearded face of an ugly Thracian grinned back at her. He made a point of lowering his eyes to study her bare breasts, which bounced as she made her way up the slight incline of the tunnel.

"What's the matter, asshole. Never seen a pair of tits before?"

The Thracian's grin took on a more evil look as they reached the arena gate. "This is going to be more fun than I imagined," he said, then placed his crested helmet on his head. The scars on his body and his confident attitude told her that this man had seen arena combat many times before. Petra's order that she would not fight higher than quartus palus level had obviously been ignored. Her nerves began to tingle as she donned her helmet, but she forced herself to focus.

The wooden doors in front of them swung open, and Valentinus, from Petra's familia, was carried through the portal by two arena workers, a large gash across his abdomen. He groaned and rolled his head to the side. Amazonia looked out into the arena, now bathed in orange torchlight, and watched the Pompeiian fighter receive his reward.

"Britannia's fallen behind again," said the arena manager who had hobbled up next to her. "Let's see what you and that beautiful body of yours can do to earn some points, honey." She would have loved to bloody her gladius with the imbecile's guts, but she held her rage for the arena.

The herald announced the next bout. "From the city of Pompeii, but fighting now with the troupe in Britannia, Gaius Tadius Magnus presents to you the radiant Amazonia!" She stepped forward onto the sand and raised her sword. The oil and sweat on her naked torso reflected the flickering flames of the torches. The crowd reacted with cheers, whoops, and catcalls. She knew the catcalls would stop once they saw her fight. The herald continued. "Her opponent from Pompeii, fighting as a thraex, is the great Ursus!"

Petra jumped to his feet on the podium. He made his raspy voice heard over the crowd. "Gaius, that's not her opponent! What's happening here?"

Gaius checked his program. Petra reached around and pointed to Servius's name. Gaius raised his hand, and the herald shouted an authoritative "Halt." The fighters had walked to the arena center, but were stopped by Justus and Julianus before the first blow was struck. Petra could see that Julianus, too, realized something was wrong when the unfamiliar, bearded fighter entered the arena.

Petra and Gaius looked at the Pompeiian lanista seated across from them. He was huddled with one of his attendants. "Well, Facilix, what's the meaning of this?" Gaius asked.

Facilix waved the attendant away. "I've just received word that Savius became ill this afternoon and had to be replaced."

"What?" Petra yelled. "This is bullshit. I've never seen a fighter replaced for becoming ill. *Most* gladiators are ill before a fight!"

Facilix shrugged and put on a face that said "It's out of my hands."

Petra could hear the crowd near the podium becoming restless. "What is this Ursus's ranking?" he yelled across the podium at Facilix.

"Not to worry. He's also a quartus palus fighter."

Petra looked at Julianus on the sand in front of the podium. The trainer shook his head. It was obvious from the mannerisms, body language, and scarring that Ursus was higher in ranking than Amazonia's original opponent.

A murmur was beginning to grow in the cavea. A spectator in the plebian seats shouted, "Let them fight!" The fickle crowd was obviously not picky about who Amazonia faced in battle. They just wanted to see her naked body embroiled in sweaty combat. The cry quickly became a chant that filled the arena. "Let them fight! Let them fight!"

Gaius leaned over and spoke to Petra in a low voice. "We both have an interest in seeing Amazonia survive her first arena battle, but it doesn't take much to get a riot started in this amphitheater. I suggest we let her fight, my friend. Otherwise there's no telling what this mob might do. I think Amazonia can take care of herself."

Petra looked at Julianus in the arena. He knew his trainer was wrestling with the same impossible dilemma.

"Let's go!" Amazonia yelled over the chanting crowd. She rocked side to side and slapped her gladius loudly against her large shield. "What difference whose balls I cut off? Let's do this!"

Julianus smiled. He looked back at Petra and gave a nod.

"Fine," Petra said. He leaned forward, looking past Gaius, and snarled at Facilix, "But if she's killed, you and I are going to have a little talk."

"Let the fight begin!" Gaius yelled. The roar from the crowd was deafening.

XXVII

November AD 66

Fighters, be on guard!" Julianus shouted. He looked into Amazonia's visor. "Be careful," he said quietly, then dropped his arm. "Attack!"

Ursus lunged first with a well-executed combination. Amazonia's reflexes were perfect, blocking each strike with her scutum and gladius.

"Good work," Julianus yelled. "But don't stay on the defensive. Attack!"

As she did in her sparring sessions, she followed her doctore's instructions well. She sliced upward with her short sword, backing her opponent up and giving herself room to work. She took a deep breath and advanced with a series of cuts and thrusts, punctuated with a lightning-fast jab with the round pommel on the handle of her sword. The blow connected with Ursus's throat. He gasped and gagged for air, the ugly sounds reverberating inside his helmet. Although he never lowered his guard, Amazonia knew she had connected. She smiled to herself as she heard him gagging. The sounds boosted her confidence to match her showy bravado. She saw Ursus's arms grow tense, and she readied herself for another onslaught.

He came at her harder than the first time, his sica slashing from right to left, then left to right. She used her shield well, protecting her vulnerable spots until she saw an opportunity to counterattack. She spun quickly and went for his legs, but the seasoned gladiator saw it coming and jumped over the slashing blade. She raised up and advanced on him, beating hard enough with her gladius to force a retreat. Every step forward she took brought a louder cheer from the crowd. She assumed it was more a reaction to her bouncing breasts than to her gaining any advantage in the bout. She ended her advance with a second spin, this time bringing her leg up to connect with the Thracian's square parmula. Her unusual move caught him totally unprepared and the small shield flew from his hand and landed behind him near the waterhole.

Ursus seemed stunned and was slow to react. His uncertainty allowed Amazonia the luxury of time. She glanced at the lost parmula in the sand behind him. But something even more interesting caught her attention. The large gray crocodile had crawled from its private pool and now lay in the sand not far from the shield.

"Come on, Ursus, do something!" Justus yelled, working as the second referee. "Back her up, then retrieve the parma."

"Yeah, come on, big boy," Amazonia taunted. "Who's the big shot now, huh, numb nuts?"

"You have the advantage," Julianus yelled to his female fighter. "Use it!"

Before Ursus fully recovered, Amazonia struck again. She unleashed a blistering attack, forcing him to retreat farther. Ursus did a remarkable job of blocking her surprisingly powerful blows using only his sica.

"You're sending him right back to his shield," Julianus warned.

"I know what I'm doing," she yelled back. "He's . . . about . . . to meet . . . a little . . . dragon," she blurted, the words coming between each stroke. She feinted low to force him to lower his sword, then spun as fast as she could. From deep in her lungs came the ferocious banshee cry, startling Ursus, Justus, and most of the spectators. Just as she did on her first day at the ludus, she brought her bare foot around with blinding speed and caught her opponent hard on the side of his head. His helmet flew high enough to clear the retaining wall and land in the second row of the cavea. The local politician who caught it seemed afraid to look inside, fearing the man's head was also sitting in his lap.

But the bearded, disheveled head was still affixed to the Thracian's body, which teetered backward and landed hard beside the waterhole. Amazonia watched the crocodile finish her job for her. The lizard lurched forward and grasped the dazed fighter's head in its jaws. As it usually did with large prey, the croc went into a death roll. The Thracian's fragile neck bones were no match for the four-meter reptile. As the croc rolled, the loud snap could be heard halfway up the cavea. There would be no need for the attendant dressed as Charon to be sure this fighter was dead.

The amphitheater erupted in pure pandemonium. Julianus grabbed Amazonia's arm and lifted it in victory. With her other hand she ripped the helmet from her head and let out another banshee cry, driving the audience to an even higher level of frenzy.

She looked toward the podium and saw Petra and Gaius both on their feet, screaming with the masses, while Facilix stared in disbelief as the crocodile continued to chomp down on the crushed skull of his fighter. Amazonia stepped away from the waterhole as an enraged Justus smacked the croc with his long rod and pulled the mangled body a safe distance away. Two arena attendants took it from there and dragged it through the Porta Libitensis, the Gate of Death.

Amazonia approached the podium. A green palm and a good-sized leather purse struck the sand at her feet. She lifted the coin purse first.

"That is well deserved, young lady," said a jubilant Gaius. "It's obvious you are better suited for the arena than for picking grapes in my vineyard. May you have a long and successful career in the arena." She looked up into his compassionate eyes, and for one brief second Amazonia again saw herself as the pitiable orphan Gaius had helped rescue. "Good-bye, my child," he said with a smile. "May Hercules protect you."

Amazonia smiled and bowed to him. "Thank you," she mouthed, then walked from the arena, her hand clutched tightly around the bag of gold.

Quintus hated arenas with full wooden doors rather than open-frame gates at the tunnel entrance. He could hear the crowd going wild but could not tell for whom they were cheering. Finally the door opened and relief enveloped him like the glowing light from the torches. Amazonia was approaching the portal, her arms raised and a wide smile on her face. Someone seated above the tunnel entrance yelled loudly to her.

"You're wilder in the arena than you were in bed, Claudia!"

Quintus assumed the man was one of her old customers.

"Those days are over, Nepos. And if you ever call me 'Claudia' again, you won't have a dick left to amuse your new harlot." Everyone in the section broke into laughter, including her old customer. They cheered her noisily as she stepped into the tunnel.

"Since you're coming in alone, I take it you handled Ursus well," Quintus said.

"Let's just say he got a closer look at that croc than he ever expected." She leaned her head to the side and looked past him. Quintus turned to see the monstrous form of Vulcanus, outfitted as a hoplomachus, approaching the doorway. "Go kick this brute's ass so we can take our money and go home."

Quintus felt like a proud older brother. Amazonia had returned to her hometown and, in one evening, showed the population that she was no longer a whore or a vineyard slave. She had emerged as a new hero.

"Taurus! Vulcanus!" yelled the arena manager. "Stand by the gate and wait for your introduction." The manager shook his head in disbelief as he watched Amazonia drop her helmet and unfasten her manica. "I don't know how she did it," he said to the two remaining gladiators, "but Amazonia's win has tied the point tally. In fact, Britannia might be ahead because they probably gave her extra points for dropping Ursus into the croc's jaws. It looks like you two will decide this. Pompeii's victory is up to you, Vulcanus."

The Pompeiian fighter ignored the slimy coordinator and continued to stare into the orange glow, awaiting his name. Quintus studied his opponent's face for a moment, seeking any trace of concern. There was none. The torchlight shimmered off the man's close-cropped blond hair as he leaned forward and placed the large bronze helmet on his head. The blue and black design on his small round parma shield matched the cerulean hue of his subligaculum.

Amazonia leaned toward Quintus. "Use the waterhole to your advantage," she whispered. "Try to back him up in that direction." He nodded, then secured his glistening red-plumed helmet. He stood tall, taking deep breaths, which made the Minotaur on his chest appear to snort as it readied for a charge. He was already well into the mental transformation from Quintus to Taurus when the herald made the final introductions of the evening.

As they stepped onto the sand, a tremendous wave of sound assaulted Taurus. He glanced at the cavea and saw the entire mob on their feet, hands punching toward the stars in beat to a chorus of "Vulcanus! Vulcanus!" Taurus would have preferred to hear his own name but, oddly, he drew strength from the chanting. He saw it as a personal challenge to leave this arena with the crowd chanting his name rather than the hometown hero's. He thought about the sound of it. He visualized it happening. And he set his mind to make it so.

They reached the center of the sand and turned to face each other. He embraced this opportunity to single-handedly change not only his own fate, but that of his lanista, his doctore, and the rest of the top fighters. He knew winning this single bout would put them all on a new level. They would finally have the biggest arenas opened up to them, perhaps even Rome. With such an awesome burden, he wondered how many of the other fighters—even the primus palus fighters—would want the responsibility of standing there at that moment. Probably not many. But it was the way Taurus liked to work. He once again had control of his own destiny.

"Gladiators, be on guard!" Julianus yelled. Both fighters tensed their arms, crouched slightly, and got ready for the signal. Taurus glanced quickly toward the artificial oasis off to his right. The crocodile was back in the water, its two evil eyes watching their every move.

"This is for the entire match," Julianus said. The statement was meant for both fighters, but he looked directly at Taurus's visor. The trainer raised and dropped his arm. "Attack!"

Taurus moved first, his sica coming down quickly on his opponent's round shield. Vulcanus parried each slice and thrust with textbook precision. Within the first few seconds, Taurus realized he was correct earlier when he sized this man up as his most difficult opponent yet. Vulcanus went on the offensive, backing Taurus up a few steps and drawing a small amount of blood as his gladius glanced off Taurus's square parmula and nicked his leg.

Taurus did his best to maneuver the Pompeiian into a position that put his back to the waterhole. But Vulcanus was not cooperating. For many long minutes, the two battled forward and backward, but the Pompeiian was careful to keep his eye on the oasis and not allow himself to get trapped between the water's edge and Taurus's sica. Taurus became so focused on trying to maneuver his opponent, he was sacrificing his usual fighting style.

"Come on, Taurus, come on!" Julianus yelled as he circled the fighters. "Stoke it! Come on!"

The words jolted him back to his normal fight plan. On his next advance, the speed of his sica increased significantly. Vulcanus's air of confidence appeared to wane as Taurus's weapon became a blur. The parries blocked the flying sword more by luck than by deliberate placement. The lengthy attack was finally consummated with a rapid spin that turned the Minotaur stigmate on Taurus's chest ever so briefly into the Gorgon. A sudden yell and flash of red told Taurus the spinning slice had at least partially connected with flesh.

"Watch yourself, Vulcanus!" Justus yelled. "Don't get sloppy. The reputation of our ludus is on the line here. You'd better not fuck up!"

The Pompeiian grunted. He came back at Taurus hard and fast with a ferocious barrage of blows. While the Pompeiian's speed could not match his own, Taurus got a taste of what it was like to be on the receiving end of a fast, vicious assault. He gave ground and circled around, looking for an opportunity to turn the tide. He continued to anticipate where each stroke would land. His sica or parmula was always there, ready to parry. But the assault continued.

"Careful!" Julianus warned.

Taurus took another step back and suddenly felt the sand turn wet. The waterhole! He had allowed himself to get trapped, exactly as he had planned to trap his opponent. He heard the water rustle behind him and knew that the croc was on the move. He dared not turn to look or Vulcanus's gladius would surely slice through his neck. The screams of the crowd, at a fever pitch from the beginning, rose even higher. He knew he had only a millisecond to counterattack or be dragged to his death by the terrible lizard. He dug deep and willed power to his sword arm. It responded. Once again his blade turned to a smear of silver. Vulcanus retreated a step. It was all Taurus needed. He jumped sideways and heard the loud pop of the reptile's jaws snapping shut just centimeters from his right leg. With a loud howl, he advanced on Vulcanus, forcing him back two meters, then four, putting as much distance as he could between his legs and the jaws of death.

"Do not fuck this up!" Justus screamed at his retreating fighter. "Either kill this man now or spend a month in the prison cell. Do it!"

Now it was Vulcanus's turn to draw on some unknown force. He seemed to absorb power from Taurus. The Pompeiian's retreat slowed and suddenly his gladius seemed to fly from all directions at once. Again, Taurus had his parmula in place to block each stroke, but the sheer strength in the blows forced him back once more.

"Watch the water," Julianus warned. "Don't get trapped again!"

Taurus tried to move sideways, but Vulcanus managed to herd him toward the crocodile like a shepherd moved his flock.

"You want me in the water?" Taurus suddenly yelled through his visor. "Fine, let's go!" He began retreating, closing the distance to the waterhole more rapidly as he allowed himself to be beaten back. Vulcanus picked up speed as he charged forward, keeping up the relentless attack. Ten meters closed to nine, then eight. The croc opened its jaws, waiting for its prey to simply stumble inside. Faster and faster Taurus retreated toward the deadly pond.

"What are you doing? Be careful!" Julianus screamed.

Taurus had no choice but to guess at the distance. If he felt the sand go wet, he knew all would be lost. He increased his speed of retreat. Vulcanus was with him step for step. He pounded against Taurus's sword and shield. Six meters shrunk to five. The croc hissed. Taurus used the sound to gauge his distance. Four meters, three . . . Now!

As Vulcanus came with the next thrust, Taurus knocked the blade aside with his sica and dropped his shield. He grabbed his opponent's sword arm, fell to his back, and used his momentum to pull Vulcanus onto his raised feet. Taurus flipped him up and over his own prone body. The hoplomachus came down with a splash. He was in the water right next to the crocodile. The reptile seemed as shocked as Vulcanus and every other person in the amphitheater. But it recovered quickly and jerked its head to the side, clamping its jaws down on the upper half of Vulcanus's right arm. The croc pulled him deeper into the pool. The Pompeiian fighter and all twenty thousand spectators screamed in terror. Both referees stood in shock as the hero of Pompeii slipped under the water's surface. Julianus looked at Taurus, as he stood up and pulled the helmet from his head.

Taurus studied the rippling water where the croc had floated. He had achieved the result he hoped for, but something was not right. He suddenly realized he did not want the match to end this way. His opponent was far too good a fighter to be condemned to a criminal's death by a beast. Taurus flipped the curved sword over in his hand and held it like a long dagger. He took two long strides forward and dove into the oasis pool.

On the podium, Petra jumped to his feet. Next to him, Facilix had already sprung up as he saw his prized fighter dragged underwater. Both lanistae watched as white foam and furious splashes obscured the battle that commenced underwater. A leg broke the surface, kicking wildly before it splashed back under. Then an arm marked with a band of stigmates held the sica aloft. The point pierced the water's surface in a violent downthrust, once, then again. Billows of red clouded the artificial lake. The choppy surface smoothed to low swells, and the screams of the crowd died to soft murmurs. Nothing stirred in the pool for what seemed an eternity. Petra held his breath. The lanistae looked at one another, wondering if they had lost their premier fighters. In spite of all the missios, this would then prove to be a costly event. A shout from the crowd brought Petra's attention back to the pool. Bubbles broke the water's surface, followed by Taurus, his long black hair covering most of his face as he gasped for air. Petra took a step back and dropped into his seat with a sigh of relief.

Taurus drew a deep breath and shook the water and wet hair from his eyes. He scrambled toward shore, dragging the limp body of Vulcanus under his arm. He pushed the body up on the sand and pulled the helmet from his opponent's head. Behind them, the carcass of the crocodile floated to the surface, Quintus's sica buried deep in its neck. The Pompeiian's right arm showed bloody, ragged channels left by the croc's teeth. Cuts and gouges also marred the artwork across Taurus's chest. Roughly, he rolled Vulcanus onto his stomach and began pounding on his scarred back. The slap of the harsh punches echoed in the silence of the arena. After the third hit, Vulcanus coughed loudly and vomited a sizeable amount of red water.

The silence was shattered by an earsplitting roar from the crowd. Taurus stood and retrieved the gladius which lay nearby in the wet sand. He straddled Vulcanus, placed the tip of the sword against the back of his neck and looked toward the podium for a mandate.

The crowd's roar became a chant of "Missio!" and white handkerchiefs fluttered throughout the cavea. Gaius pulled the white cloth from his toga sleeve and waved it twice across his chest. The mob erupted like a volcano.

The bout was over; the games were at an end. The herald stood to make the official announcement of what everyone already knew. "With a point tally of 177 to 175, Britannia wins the games!"

Taurus reared back and, with a growl, threw the gladius to the ground. Iron sank into sand and the sword stood like a defiant monument at his feet. His growl became a scorching yell, releasing the store of energy he still held in reserve. His arms stretched toward the dark sky, then curled under into a triumphant display of his physique. The raw power of his form was enhanced by the streaks of blood that dripped down his massive torso and partially cloaked his Minotaur.

From his left he saw gleams of orange light reflecting off polished metal. His troupe had lined the wall near the tunnel portal to watch the final battle. Now they shared in an arena celebration that was remarkably spirited, considering the defeat of the home ludus.

Julianus slapped his back. "I think the editor is waiting for you."

Taurus approached the podium. To Gaius's left he saw Petra, uncharacteristically cheering along with the mob. "That was for you, Dominus," Taurus yelled. "Your courage gave us strength."

"Well put, Taurus," Gaius said as he waved to quiet the crowd. "Your lanista had much to risk with this event. He might have returned to Britannia a laughing-stock. But now that I have seen his fighters work, I know why he had the courage to risk his reputation. You and your troupe are among the best we have ever witnessed here in Pompeii."

Taurus raised his hand and caught the leather prize purse Gaius had tossed to him. The weight told him it was indeed more reward than he had ever received in the Britannia arenas. The bag was followed by a laurel wreath rather than the standard palm leaf, a special honor awarded only to the best of the best in arena combat. Attached to it was a large medallion of gleaming metal.

"That's solid gold," Gaius said. "I had it specially poured for the victor of the final fight."

"Thank you, sir. I am honored."

He raised the laurel high as he walked across the sand. The chant of "Vulcanus! Vulcanus!" that had assaulted his ears when he first entered the arena now changed to a thunderous mantra of "Taurus! Taurus!" The sound was different than he had imagined it when he visualized his victory moments earlier. It was sweeter.

It took an hour for the spectators to clear the amphitheater. The celebration in the Britannia holding cells went on long after that, although the sounds were muffled to Petra. He and Julianus had sequestered themselves in a side room to count their fee and bonus, not so much out of distrust of Gaius as to revel in the highest take they had ever earned in a single day.

Gaius had sent wine and ale to the staging area, and Petra could hear his troupe making the most of it. More than a dozen local women had bribed their way into the rooms and were engaged in a variety of private celebrations with the fighters and hunters. Amazonia had called her old customer, Nepos, down from the cavea and smuggled him into the cell for herself.

Petra separated out the first two thousand sesterces he counted. "This is yours, Juli," he said, pushing the large pile toward his head doctore. "You've more than earned it."

Julianus's eyes were wide with disbelief. Petra knew very well that this was more money than Julianus was paid in a full year. Before the trainer had a chance to respond, a voice came from the doorway.

"Take it, Julianus, before the old bastard changes his mind." Gaius had a wide grin on his face and a twinkle in his eyes. Petra knew the look well. His friend had either just collected the payoffs from his side wagers or had seen his receipts from his wine stalls. Either one would have made any Roman a happy man.

"I'm sure this hoard pales in comparison to *your* take today," Petra said with a wink.

"It was a good day for all of us," Gaius replied. He sat on the bench across from Petra. "And I'm not sure it's ready to end yet." Petra looked up from his gold coins and Gaius went on. "I just met with Facilix and Justus. They want to talk with you."

Petra glanced at Julianus. The trainer's face reflected the same suspicion he felt inside. But after a moment, the trainer shrugged. "Let's hear what they have to say." Without a word, Petra nodded to his friend to bring them in. As Gaius left to retrieve them, Julianus lifted a wooden chest from the floor and began clearing the gold coins from the bench.

"Hold on, Juli," Petra said. "Let's leave it out so our friends from Pompeii can see what they lost." Julianus grunted a laugh and restacked the coins he had pulled down.

Gaius reemerged through the doorway with the Pompeiian lanista and trainer in tow. Petra impassively continued counting his gold coins. Both he and Julianus remained silent.

"That's quite a troupe you have there, gentlemen," Facilix said. Petra and Julianus did not respond. "You should be proud of Amazonia. She did very well . . . " Facilix paused for a moment, then continued. " . . . even with the change in pairings."

"We hope Savius is feeling better," Julianus said, the sarcasm dripping from his voice.

"Yes, well . . . " Facilix stuttered. "Perhaps we should come right to the point and discuss more pleasant matters." He motioned to the trove of coins laid out on the bench next to Petra. "Today, between your fees, travel expenses, and bonus winnings, you've brought in three hundred fifty thousand sesterces. Correct?"

"That's about right," Petra said without looking up, still suspicious of the Pompeiians' motive.

"That's not a bad haul for a provincial lanista. But, granted, you are not the typical provincial lanista. You worked hard to get where you are. You're ambitious. You're smart enough to hire the right people, like Julianus here . . . "

"Look, Facilix," Petra interrupted, "did you just come down here to jerk me off or do you have a point?"

Gaius shifted and drummed his fingers on the wooden bench, filling the uncomfortable silence.

"Right . . . " Facilix continued. "I'm prepared to offer you five times that amount right now to buy all of your surviving fighters. That's one million, seven hundred fifty thousand sesterces."

Petra continued to count his gold pieces, making sure the expression on his face never changed. Other than the clink of the coins, the only sound in the cramped room for the next few seconds was a small mouse scurrying across the straw-covered floor. Gaius sat quietly, smiling as he observed from his side bench. Petra could feel everyone's eyes upon him. Although he allowed no outward signs, the lanista was silently recovering from shock. The amount he had just heard was taking a while to sink in. It was more money than he could spend in a lifetime, let alone the fifteen or twenty years he probably had left. It would be a retirement fund that surpassed his wildest imagination. It would allow him the freedom to travel the Empire in his golden years, staying and eating in only the finest establishments. It would provide for everything a retirement could be. There was only one problem. He was not yet ready to retire.

"No thanks," he said, never looking up at Facilix.

Julianus's gulp of air was audible from across the room. Facilix cleared his throat before he spoke. "Did I hear you right? Did you say, 'No thanks'?"

Petra finally looked up from the coinage. "You heard me right." He let a moment pass for effect, then continued. "But I'll tell you what I will do. I'll take your one million, seven hundred fifty thousand sesterces to become an equal partner in the Pompeii school and bring my fighters with me. I'll continue to supply the school with more top gladiators and hunters by bringing them in from my schools in Africa and Britannia, at preferable rates, of course. I get one-quarter of your future winnings until you've recouped your investment. Then I get half. With the addition of my fighters, you know you'll be able to more than double your fees."

Facilix nodded quietly for a moment, then turned to the man still drumming his fingers on the bench. "You've taught him well, Gaius," he said to the sponsor, who seemed to be enjoying the negotiations more than a theater performance.

"No, I think not," Gaius said with a laugh. "There's not much I could teach this man when it comes to managing a successful ludus."

"I thought you would want to retire," Facilix said to Petra, "but I see you want to stay in the business."

"It's my life, it's my blood, and it's all I know in this world," Petra responded in his worn, gravelly voice, which seemed to make the statement that much more poignant. He studied Facilix's eyes and could almost hear the abacus in the Pompeiian's mind clicking.

"It'll take too long to recoup that investment if I'm sharing profits," Facilix said finally. "One million sesterces."

With talent like Taurus, Amazonia, Lindani, and the other top fighters, Petra knew Facilix would be getting a bargain at that rate. Taurus alone could bring in four hundred thousand sesterces should Facilix ever decide to resell him someday.

"One million, seven hundred and fifty thousand," Petra responded, not wavering from the original offer.

"One million, five hundred thousand, and we can celebrate this deal as complete."

"One million, seven hundred and fifty thousand, or I head back to Britannia with my fighters in the morning."

Facilix conferred quietly with Justus, then looked toward Gaius rather than Petra. "Your friend drives a hard bargain. But I can see why you continue to gamble on him and his troupe. They're good people. Stubborn, but good." Facilix finally looked at Petra. "The deal is done. The ex-magistrate is our witness to the terms. I'll have my scribe record the deal for signatures in the morning. You'll be paid then. Congratulations, you're now a partner in the best privately owned ludus in the Empire."

Facilix offered his arm. Petra looked at it for a moment and considered refusing it, but realized it was a bad way to start a new partnership. Yet even as he grasped the lanista's forearm and shook on the deal, his heart told him to beware.

XXVIII

December AD 66

THE BALCONY of Lucius and Julia's State apartment provided the perfect vantage point to view the Imperial festivities, high above the crush of the ten thousand people who mobbed the Roman Forum below. Purple and red banners fluttered in the cool December breeze, which carried the melody of an orchestra along the length of the Forum. A bright sun kept the temperature mild while it glistened off the gold bunting that hugged the temple columns.

"This is quite a send-off," Lucius said, seated comfortably on a padded bench next to Julia. He eyed their guests, the Senator Publius Nestorius Nerva and his wife, Drusilla, who quickly agreed. Drusilla selected another morsel from the elaborate food platter that had been laid before them and offered a portion to her husband. Since Julia's carnal encounter with them at Nero's feast on her first night in Rome, both she and Lucius had made it a point to remain close with the powerful couple.

"The Emperor doesn't take his entourage to Greece everyday, Quintus," Drusilla said in a comically mocking high-society accent. "Our resourceful Senators felt it only wise to send him off in style." She smiled at her husband, who took the jab with a laugh.

"Do you know what happened to the Senators who didn't vote to provide Caligula with an elaborate send-off when he left for Capri?" he asked.

"What did he do, force them to fuck his whore sister?" Julia asked. Drusilla spilled her wine as she laughed.

"No, nothing that awful," Publius said with a chuckle. "He forced them to fight as gladiators at his next arena games. I prefer to do battle with words, not swords, thank you. I was happy to vote for whatever funds were necessary to send him to Greece in style. He may be gone for six months or more, you know."

Lucius was surprised the Emperor would undertake such a lengthy trip so shortly after completing his spectacular new palace. He glanced over the balcony wall as the Imperial procession began moving down the center of the Forum. Hundreds of Praetorian Guards in their brilliant gold armor marched just behind the standard bearers and were followed by horses and oxen adorned with flowers and red sashes. The Emperor's personal servants and staff came next, many weighed down with heavy litters of golden accouterments that would never be used during the trip. Across the Forum he watched the Emperor himself, dressed in his favorite colors of gold, white, and purple, step into a golden chariot. A skilled driver handed Nero the reins, then ducked behind the front bulwark of the chariot, remaining on board in case the horses got too frisky for the Emperor to handle alone.

"I guess he's practicing for the games," Publius said. Laughter crept into his voice as he went on. "You know, he sent word ahead to Greece that not only were they to organize a special Olympic games in his honor but that he fully expects to be invited to take part in the games himself." His giggling was infectious and soon all four were snickering as he spoke. "He says he won't leave until he's won a chariot race!" This brought bouts of laughter. "Can you imagine Nero's fat ass being dragged around the circus for seven laps? Those poor horses. What I wouldn't give to see that!"

Tears of laughter ran down Lucius's cheeks, but he was careful not to say anything slanderous about the Emperor. His episode with Julia six months ago as they arrived in Rome had taught him to trust nobody.

There was a light knock on the door of the bedroom suite. Lucius yelled for the caller to enter. A slave hurriedly carried a paper scroll to the balcony. "This just came for you, sir." Lucius took the scroll, and the slave stepped back, straining his neck to steal a peek at the Imperial procession moving past the balcony, until he was waved away by Julia.

"Ahh, it's from Virilis, the new magistrate at Aquae Sulis," Lucius said. "Let's see what he has to say about our old hometown."

Lucius had spent most of his time in Rome establishing an efficient communications network with all the magistrates in Britannia. Monthly reports were now required from each region, keeping Lucius informed on the latest news from the Isles.

"The local clans have been quiet lately," he read to Julia, then glanced up with a smile.

"You just need to know how to treat Cadwallon and his band of heathens, that's all," she said with a straight face.

"It seems our textile business is doing very well," Lucius continued. "Sextus is expanding into the shop next door at the baths." He scanned over news about a tax collection issue and the state of the treasury, then spoke up as he read the final item. "This is interesting. It seems the lanista at the Glevum ludus took his fifty best venatores and gladiators—including a woman!—to Pompeii. He writes: 'This has caused much grumbling among the troops of Legio II Augusta stationed near Aquae Sulis. They wonder when their next games may come. It is also of concern to me, since I would like to sponsor these games, but I am left with no primus palus fighters in my region.'"

"Those Pompeii games just happened a few days ago," Publius said. "I hear the mob considered them the best games ever held outside of Rome itself." Lucius slowly rerolled the scroll as the Senator went on. "They billed it as a North versus South grudge match, and amazingly the troupe from Britannia won. Apparently they had three outstanding performers—a Thracian painted with a Minotaur who calls himself 'Taurus,' an African venator who rode and killed a mad river horse, and a rather beautiful woman gladiator named Amazonia. They say she fought naked."

"Now that would have been something to see," moaned Drusilla quietly as she licked her lips. Lucius had lost interest in the pageant just beyond his balcony and focused on the arena news.

"I know this lanista," he said. "A man named Titus Cassius Petra. I worked with his staff to set up my games at the Aquae Sulis arena."

"Well, I'm afraid your successor won't have the pleasure of his services like you did," Publius said.

"Why not?"

"My sources tell me that he consolidated his best fighters into the ludus at

Pompeii, and he himself is now an owner and manager there. He's sending back an assistant to run the Britannia school."

Lucius was now totally unconcerned with the festivities in the Forum. He could feel Julia's eyes on him as she tried to read where his mind was heading. A loud cheer from below caught the Senator's attention.

"Ahh . . . the mob's insatiable appetite for games," Publius said as he scanned the lively crowd. "It's what draws our own Emperor to Greece, although theirs are so much tamer than ours."

Lucius looked up at the Senator. "How long has it been since the people of Rome have had games?"

Publius thought for a minute. "Oh, perhaps six months or so. Just before you arrived, the Games of Flora were held. It was just an excuse to persecute more Christians. He still blames them for the great fire, you know. But the mob loved it. They consider it their *right* to be supplied with arena spectacles now. The games are power incarnate, which is why in this city they've come under the control of the Emperor himself." He turned and looked back out over the crowd. "Yes . . . Where would a Roman be without his precious games?"

"And how long did you say our esteemed Emperor will be away in Greece?" Lucius asked. The smile on Julia's face told him she had finally caught up with his train of thought. The Senator was right behind her.

"Perhaps six months, perhaps eight. Who knows?" He smiled at Lucius. " . . . And with Nero gone for so long, who will be sponsoring the games?" Lucius smiled back at him. Drusilla was now the only person on the balcony still watching the Forum parade.

Julia sat forward and picked up the conversation. "You know, our games in Aquae Sulis were very successful, Publius. We have a history with this lanista who's now the talk of the Empire. Perhaps we should contact him again. Sponsoring games would be a nice gesture and a way to introduce ourselves to the people of Rome."

Lucius's heart beat faster as the plan came together in his mind. The knowing smile remained on the Senator's face as he sat quietly for a moment, stroking his chubby face. "On occasion, Emperors do share the hosting of games with other sponsors, even though technically the hunters and gladiators at the Rome ludus belong to the Emperor. It might be possible. Of course, you realize that the games of Rome are on a much, much larger scale than those in the provincial arenas."

Lucius looked at Julia, then nodded. "Bigger arenas mean bigger games. We're aware of that," he said to Publius. "What would be our first move?"

"I suggest you wait a while and see the mood of the mob. How much longer might they go without their treasured games? Pace yourselves. Wait for public sentiment to head in that direction. Then make your move."

Lucius was already considering how he might speed up that process. The cheers and screams of the mob below rose to a crescendo as Nero passed, waving from the back of his chariot. The Emperor looked up and smiled at the quartet on the balcony, who waved back enthusiastically.

"Good-bye, your grace," yelled Julia. "May your songs and athletic prowess show those Greeks where the true cultured society exists in this world." Nero smiled and waved to her. "And whatever you do, don't hurry home," she said quietly enough for only Lucius to hear.

The rowdy taverns of Rome were busier than normal that evening, many of the patrons looking to gossip and poke fun at the Emperor's upcoming exploits in Greece. An unfamiliar figure walked quietly into one of the larger taverns along the Alta Semita in the northern part of the city. He ordered wine from the attractive maid behind the worn marble counter, then found space at a long wooden table in the center of the bar. Since the moment he slipped through the door, he had been eavesdropping on every conversation he could. The topic of most discussions eventually centered on the recent Pompeii games. Information on the fighters, much of it wildly exaggerated, flowed among the patrons and resulted in spirited debates.

"Well, I've just come from Pompeii," said the stranger loudly enough for all at his table to hear. "This hot-shot lanista, Cassius Petra, has been bragging that his fighters are ready to take on the Imperial School of Rome itself." The statement brought vulgar howls of protest from the drunken crowd. "You know, perhaps we should set up our own grudge match right here in Rome," the stranger continued. "Let's see what this asshole and his troupe of whores can do against *our* men." A befuddled chorus of "Yeahs!" went up across the tavern. "Perhaps Petra's naked bitch will fight for us!" The statement brought even more cheers. All eyes and ears were now turned on the boisterous center table, just as the stranger had planned. "I say we demand these games. Then we'll see once and for all who trains the best fighters and hunters in the Empire!" A deafening cheer erupted in the tavern that could be heard blocks away. Gamblers began waving coins at the tavern bookmaker, who was already working to establish odds on the fight. After a few minutes, the bookmaker looked up and shouted to the crowd.

"Wait a minute! With Nero gone, who'll sponsor these games?"

The stranger barely heard the bookmaker's question and the muttering that followed as he stepped out the door and headed down the dark alley.

Throughout the next few weeks, the same scene was repeated in taverns, brothels, and markets throughout Rome. As in the tavern on the Alta Semita, the seed was planted, but the sower left the bush to bloom on its own.

A naked Lucius descended the ten steps into the warm water of the tepidarium pool at the Baths of Agrippa. He always enjoyed this interlude between the steaming water of the caldarium and the cold water of the frigidarium. He joined the small circle of Imperial staff and advisors near the east end of the pool. After a few minutes of casual conversation, he leaned back and relaxed, studying the towering columns supporting arches and skylights forty meters above the huge public pools. The combination of green and white marble throughout the baths, accented with gargantuan bronze statues and mosaic sea serpents swimming along the floors, gave the building a look of whimsical fantasy. Throughout his earliest years in Rome, he had often wondered what the insides of such buildings looked like. But a household slave boy was never given the opportunity to enter and find out.

"Ah, Quintus, they said I'd find you here," Publius said as he approached the pool. "Amazingly enough, people all over the city are calling for games—a match with this new Pompeii lanista who says his troupe is ready to take on the Imperial School. I wonder where the fuel for that idea came from?"

Lucius smiled up from the warm water before he replied. "Well, with that bigmouthed lanista, it was just a matter of time before the idea of an Italian grudge match surfaced."

"Yes, quite," said the Senator, obviously not convinced. "The subject came up before the Senate this morning. They were reluctant to allow any games in the Emperor's absence at first. But once I told them that you were willing to personally sponsor such a spectacle and it wouldn't cost the State a single sesterce, they were much more interested."

The advisors who floated beside Lucius gave a cheer that caught the attention of the other bathers. Lucius could not be sure if the hollow echo of their congratulations was from the marble bath surfaces or the shock that suddenly overtook him.

"Publius, may we speak in private?" Lucius asked, the shakiness in his voice evident even to himself. He swam to the steps and called for a towel boy. He wrapped the white cloth around his midsection as he hustled the Senator across the wet floor and into one of the many side halls.

"Are you crazy?" he said, exasperated. "Do you have any idea what that will cost me?"

The Senator thought for a moment, then replied calmly, "Well, you'll be limited to one hundred pairs of fighters and fifty hunters. Only the Emperor can sponsor shows with more. I'd say—including the animals and the costs of the arena support staff—probably about a million-and-a-half sesterces."

"What?" Lucius's throat closed and the word came out an octave higher than normal.

"Of course, it could be a bit more, depending on how many fighters you sentence to death. You'll need to compensate the ludi for that."

Lucius stared at the Senator, speechless.

"I warned you that games in Rome would cost more than provincial games," Publius continued. "You said you were aware of that. 'Bigger arenas mean bigger games,' I think you said."

"Yes, but I meant I would *contribute* to putting on these bigger games, not bear the full burden myself."

"I see," Publius said. "I'm sorry. I guess I misunderstood. I thought you and Julia were offering to fully sponsor the games. That's the way I've already presented it to the Senate and that's the way they approved it. It's the only way they would have agreed to games in Nero's absence anyway."

Lucius was in a daze. He looked at the floor as if hoping for divine inspiration from the sea serpents.

"Look," Publius said, "the State-sponsored games are free, but since you're doing the population such a welcome service with this match, I don't think the crowd would mind parting with a few sesterces to see such a wonderful program. That's what was done in Pompeii, and I hear the editor made a handsome profit."

Lucius looked up. He could feel both hope and color returning to his face.

Publius smiled. "While the Emperor's away, let's say we treat Rome like a province for a few days, eh?" He slapped Lucius on his bare back as they returned to the tepidarium. "Cheer up, Quintus. You're about to become a very popular man in Rome."

Lucius's hand was shaking as he pushed past his personal guard and opened the door to his State apartment. He passed through the vestibule, rehearsing the careful wording again in his mind. But as soon as he saw Julia in their bedroom, just coming in off the balcony, all pretense left his mind. She was too sharp. There was simply no way to dance around the truth with Julia.

"I can never get enough of these beautiful Roman sunsets," she said as she closed the louvered doors and turned to him. "What's wrong?"

He attempted a smile. "I met with Publius today. He got the Senate to approve our games."

Julia beamed and broke into a fit of giggling laughter. "That's wonderful news! Oh, I know just what I'll wear. That long beige tunic with the deep green satin palla. That looks stunning together. We'll need to do an invite list for our guests on the podium." She drew in a long breath. "By the gods, do you realize we'll be sitting in the Imperial box in Rome's arena?" Her breath drew deeper and she clutched at her chest. "Do you realize," she almost whispered, "that I will be sitting in the seat once used by Agrippina herself?" She sank slowly to the edge of the bed and looked up at Lucius with suspicion in her eyes. "So what's the problem? Why aren't you happy about this?"

He decided to just come out with it and get the bad news over. "We have to pay for the entire thing ourselves. Publius estimates it at a million-and-a-half sesterces." Before she had a chance to react, he quickly followed up with the only positive qualifier. "He did say that we could probably charge admission to recoup some of the money."

Julia lapsed into another giggling fit, making Lucius wonder if she'd lost her mind. She finally caught her breath.

"Oh Lucius, Lucius, Lucius . . . " He hated when she used his real name, especially when she did it to be condescending. "Don't you realize cost is a low priority when the social and political stakes are so high? This is an investment in our future. Besides, I can spend my money however I wish, and I can't think of anything that I'd rather spend it on."

"And what about Sextus? Don't you think he might have a different opinion?"

"Sextus is too busy with his textile business to bother with this. Besides, I helped build that little empire, so as far as I'm concerned, it's just as much my money as his." She grabbed the front of Lucius's toga, and drew him down beside her on the bed. "We have games to plan, young man. First tonight's, then the ones in the arena."

Quintus joined Lindani, who was already seated in the dirt near the small stage of the Pompeii ludus. Their new school was bigger and better equipped than the Britannia ludus, but Quintus missed the inspiring statue of Hercules that no longer overlooked their assemblies.

"What's this all about?" Quintus asked.

"Some message from Rome, is what I hear," Lindani replied.

Quintus looked around the grounds. He estimated about five hundred people sat waiting for the announcement, five times the number of fighters at their old Glevum school. Although the two troupes were into their fourth week of joint training, the Britannia fighters tended to stick together. Tension still simmered from the Pompeii games and hindered a smooth integration of the two schools. The fact that enough cells suddenly became available to house the new fighters was proof enough that Facilix and Justus had deceived them earlier. It was an insult that was not easily forgiven. Tension often boiled over in sparring practice. A bout did not always end when the trainer called "Halt," and the combatants frequently needed to be physically separated by the doctores.

Quintus had tried to do his part to get the two troupes better integrated. He offered fighting tips to some of the tiro fighters from Pompeii. He worked with the Pompeiian armorers to reconstruct many of the weight-training contraptions he had designed in Britannia. As each was completed, he volunteered to show any interested fighter how to use the devices, but few Pompeiians took him up on the offer. Loyalties to the original troupes were steadfast. Quintus wondered if this merger was ever going to work.

Finally the door to Facilix's office opened, and he and Petra emerged. Petra had been given an office next to Facilix, but the two lanistae had been together, discussing this announcement, since the dispatch arrived. They walked across the field and stepped up on the low stage. Quintus hoped that what they were about to say would help bond the fighters into a single cohesive unit. Facilix allowed Petra to make the announcement.

"There is news from Rome that you should all hear." His scratchy voice carried clearly to the lowest tiros seated in the back. "Word of our performance last month spread quickly to Rome. We are apparently the talk of the town." A low murmur grew to a loud cheer. Petra waved for quiet. "Somehow, word got round that I've been challenging the Imperial School of Rome to a similar match. I offered no such challenge. But a response came yesterday anyway. They accept. In a few months, you will be fighting in Rome." A thunderous roar erupted from the assembly, loud enough to startle passersby and business owners outside the ludus walls.

Quintus and Lindani were among the loudest. "We'll show the Emperor where the best fighters are trained," Quintus yelled, "and it's not in his Imperial School!" This prompted a new round of cheering, both teams on their feet as one. It took longer for Petra to settle them down the second time.

"Unfortunately, the Emperor will not be seeing you fight. He has gone to Greece to see a different sort of games." The crowd became hushed for a minute, until Lindani broke the curious quiet.

"Who, then, is sponsoring these games?"

Petra looked toward Lindani. "It's someone who has sponsored our fights before in Britannia." He took a deep breath, then focused his eyes squarely on Quintus. "It's a new Imperial advisor and his wealthy family from Aquae Sulis." Quintus's jaw dropped open before Petra even finished. He knew what was coming.

"His name is Quintus Honorius Romanus."

XXIX

April AD 67

I T HAD BEEN FOUR YEARS since Quintus had seen Rome. Now, from the bed of his transport cart, he watched intently as the majestic Circus Maximus passed by. The long caravan of 25 carts and assorted oxen, mules, and horses had entered through the Porta Capena, the city's south gate, and was proceeding along the Via Triumphalis. The usual ban on wheeled vehicles in daylight hours had been lifted temporarily to allow the citizens to witness the arrival of the visiting fighters from Pompeii.

"Is it as you remember?" Lindani asked, staring up at the massive buildings.

"Some areas, yes, but most, no. It looks like the great fire did more damage than I imagined."

They were interrupted by yelling from the congregation lining the street. Most of the spectators offered up friendly applause mixed with good-natured jeers, but the more rabid fans hurled everything from venomous insults to rotten vegetables.

"Not exactly the welcome we got in Herculaneum, is it?" Amazonia said, dodging a flying egg.

"Welcome to the big city," Quintus replied. "Things are different here."

Lindani pointed out more hand-painted wall signs advertising their big two-day event. It was being promoted as "The Rome vs. Pompeii Challenge." As in Herculaneum, each ad heralded a specific fighter or hunter.

"At least they have spelled my name correctly this time," Lindani said.

"And nobody has altered your anatomy," Amazonia added with a wink and a sexy smile.

Much to Quintus's chagrin, each sign included the line "Presented by

Quintus Honorius Romanus" in large red letters.

The procession turned left onto the Via Sacra, heading toward the Campus Martius. A few fighters in the cart excitedly pointed ahead. Quintus strained his neck and caught a glimpse of Nero's Domus Aurea, the Golden House. The afternoon sun reflected brightly off the white marble walls and gold-leafed ornamentation, producing the intended heavenly appearance. Quintus studied the grounds of the palace, then suddenly realized where he was.

"By the gods, I used to live there," he said, a tinge of disbelief in his voice. Everyone in the cart looked at him.

"You used to live *there?*" Lindani asked, pointing at the Golden House.

"Not in that palace, but my villa used to be just there, beyond the giant lake in that park."

The setting brought a wave of emotion on Quintus. Vivid memories replayed in his mind of his beloved mother and father, and of Aulus, his friend and protector from whom he learned so much. He could picture the villa that used to sit on the hill, recalling every detail—the sound of the atrium fountain as it echoed off the colorfully muraled walls; the smells of the fresh breakfast bread his mother would lay out for the family; the look of the yellow sunlight as it stole through his window each morning and crept across his bed to force open his eyes. But the pleasant memories were tarnished with thoughts of Lucius, although the visualization of him dressed again in his olive drab slave tunic brought a grin to Quintus's face. As he watched the hill pass, his mind went to that day, at that very place, when he and Lucius tangled in the garden fountain over the broken toy boat he had so cherished. Without realizing it, his hand went to his side and thumbed the outline of the tiny terra-cotta boat captain he still carried in his leather pouch. And now, once again, the bastard was sponsoring games in which Quintus would fight. How had he ended up in Rome? And in such a high position?

Commotion rose again in the cart as they approached the Campus Martius. Just beyond the Capitoline Hill, the outline of the Amphitheater of Taurus came into view. As the contours of the impressive arena materialized, so did Quintus's realization that he had come full circle. He was about to fight in the very amphitheater where he had sat as a child with his father and watched the gladiators. He was about to fight in the largest arena of them all. The thrill and anticipation was almost overwhelming. Yet deep inside there was heart-ache, as he thought of the people from this place he had loved and lost.

The troupe was housed in the barracks of the Ludus Magnus, which adjoined the amphitheater. This time, there were no petty squabbles over not enough room to quarter the visitors. The procurator who ran the Imperial school was too sophisticated for such foolishness. All one hundred twenty-five fighters and hunters from Pompeii were easily accommodated at the ludus, which housed and fed an average of two thousand fighters on any given day. The three days leading up to the games were spent on the ample practice field and in the small arena built within the walls of the ludus. A few hundred elite citizens were allowed to view the sparring matches from the tiered seats surrounding the practice arena.

The evening before the games brought the usual pre-fight banquet, although the Pompeii troupe had never seen such a large public turnout. It seemed half the population of Rome wandered freely about the ludus training field and the Campus Martius. Quintus sat with Amazonia and Lindani at a long wooden table with veterans from both the Britannia and original Pompeii troupes, including Vulcanus who had acquired—the hard way—a lasting respect for Quintus. The fighters from the Familia Petra and Familia Facilix were finally beginning to mingle now that they needed to work together against a common foe. But while the mood was light, there was not the festive party atmosphere that had permeated the Herculaneum banquet.

For the most part, Quintus enjoyed meeting the spectators and discussing technique with the more learned of the fans. But he was getting tired of answering questions about his stigmates. An hour into the feast, he had already explained to more than fifty people that the markings did not come off when he sweated. He did not mind, however, reviewing that fact once again with the two attractive females who squeezed their way onto the wooden bench alongside him. The girls spent the next few minutes tracing their fingers along the designs, a practice Quintus never discouraged so long as the fingers belonged to young ladies. He used the opportunity to turn the questioning around.

"So tell me about the editor of these games," he asked, "this Quintus Honorius Romanus. What do you know of him?"

"Well, I heard he single-handedly crushed a rebellion by a fierce Briton tribe," one of the girls answered, never taking her eyes off the black-ink Minotaur on Quintus's chest. "As a reward, they appointed him Imperial Advisor for Britannia Affairs."

The second girl leaned in closer and glanced around to see that no one else was listening. She spoke in a sultry voice. "It's also widely known that he enjoys the company of his own aunt, and I mean for more than just social gatherings. They even live together in a single bedroom, according to some of the slaves in the State apartment."

"So they live in a State apartment?"

"Yes, the big one along Clivus Sacer that overlooks the Forum."

Quintus was surprised. The building was less than a kilometer from the site of his old villa. It was fascinating how some structures were leveled in the fire while others just a few blocks away were left untouched.

"Is he well-respected in Rome?"

"He's gaining a reputation as a real political animal," said the second girl, while her friend continued to trace her finger around the stigmates. "He and his aunt know who to fuck to get ahead."

Her friend giggled then looked into Quintus's eyes. "Speaking of knowing who to fuck, why don't you come join me and Panthia for a while in the barracks?" Her hand had now moved off Quintus's chest and on to her friend's. She rubbed and squeezed Panthia's breasts and both women gave him an inviting smile. "We know the perfect room," she said. "We've used it before, but never with such a fine gladiator."

Quintus considered the offer, but before he could respond, the moment was ruined by the ranting of an obnoxious lout who had parked himself across the table next to Amazonia. The drunken fan was loudly making a similar offer to Amazonia, but the female fighter was ignoring him, trying to eat her dinner. Quintus saw the drunk's hand slip under the table, then watched Amazonia's eyes widen. She spit a mouthful of pheasant back onto her metal plate and threw down the roasted carcass. Her oily hands disappeared between her legs. Quintus switched his focus back to the drunk as his face contorted from a look of devilish lust to one of profound pain. From under the table, Quintus heard the unmistakable sound of a cracking finger bone, followed by a howl that startled everyone within a twenty-meter radius of the table. Quintus stood, looking to defuse the situation quickly.

" . . . And that's how she does that move!" he said with a loud laugh. "Amazing, isn't she? Run along now, dim-wit, before she shows you her deadly spin kicks." He smacked the drunk hard enough in the side of his head to let him know his time at the table had expired. The drunk took the hint and stumbled off, holding his limp right hand under his left arm.

"I'm sorry, ladies," Quintus said to Panthia and her friend, "but I'm afraid I need to speak with my colleague here for a moment. Please excuse us." He motioned with his head for Amazonia to follow him.

"You'd better behave or you'll be facing lions tomorrow instead of a fighter," he said quietly as they walked toward the dark side of the ludus grounds. "Romans don't take well to visiting gladiators assaulting their citizens."

"So I'm supposed to sit there and quietly eat dinner while he finger-fucks me?"

Quintus laughed. "No, you're right. He deserved it." They walked on toward the gate opposite the amphitheater. "There's tension in the air tonight," he said. "I think we all know we'll be up against some tough fighters over the next two days. And I can tell you from experience that the Roman mob likes to see blood spilt, so fight hard tomorrow."

"It wasn't long ago you were part of that mob calling for blood," Amazonia said. "Now you're on the other side of the arena wall."

The roar of a lion being loaded into the holding pens broke the quiet darkness near the arena gate. Quintus leaned against the wooden lattice of the fence and looked up at the Amphitheater of Taurus across the walkway.

"One of my favorite memories of my father was sitting in this arena, watching a naumachia and a bridge fight between two top gladiators. That night, he took me to an Imperial banquet on a barge right there in the flooded arena. As long as I live, I'll always remember that day." He felt if he stared at the arena façade long enough, he would see through it to the very seat in which he sat. "I remember a man behind us saying that I should be teaching the fighters instead of watching them because I was able to predict everything that happened."

"And now here you are."

"Here I am, back to fight in the same arena." He finally broke his gaze from the structure and looked down at the stone street. "I wish my father was here to see this."

He could feel Amazonia staring at him. "Do you really? Or do you simply wish you could see him again?" Quintus did not answer. "How do you think a parent would feel sitting in the cavea knowing that, with a flick of a blade, their son—or daughter—could be lying dead in the sand? Could you watch your son do what we do? In my case, I doubt my father would care, so long as he didn't wager too much money on me. But in your case, I'll bet your father would much rather see you a successful merchant than an arena hero."

Quintus thought about her words. "I needed a new family," he said after a while. "I had nothing left. That's what drove me to the arena. That, and the pride in having the mob cheer for me."

"You don't need to justify it to me," Amazonia said. "You forget that I'm here for the same reasons, although the money probably means more to me than to you."

Quintus turned away from the gate and looked at her. "You're right. It's best to let the memories drift on their own current than try to steer them where they don't belong." He studied her for a moment and unexpectedly saw a more delicate woman. Perhaps it was the glow of the torches against her auburn hair. Or was it the sense of understanding in her eyes? A quiet moment passed. Then a sudden vicious image of the two of them facing off in an arena, weapons in hand, flashed through his mind like a lucid nightmare. He turned away quickly.

"Thank you for listening," he said and stepped from the gate.

She paused a moment, then followed him. They walked quietly back toward the pool of torchlight at the center of the ludus grounds. The shouts from a group of arena workers caught their attention as they passed a dark walkway leading to the loading area. At the end of the alley, silhouetted against the open lattice of a wooden gate, stood Lindani. Beyond the gate, six animal handlers were herding a group of lions and leopards into their cells, prodding them with long poles through the cage bars. Lindani appeared to study each animal, especially the lions. Quintus and Amazonia approached him from behind.

"Do you think the lanistae were paid well for this fight?" Lindani asked without turning around. Quintus could never understand how the African always knew what was going on behind him.

"I'm sure Lucius has my aunt paying the lanistae extremely well for a real spectacle. Why?"

Lindani finally turned from the loading area and looked directly at Quintus. The seriousness of his tone was uncharacteristic for the confident African. "Because I do not know how many of the venatores will survive these next two days." He looked back toward the loading activities. "These are the most vicious animals I have ever seen. The animal procurers of Rome know how to mistreat the beasts so they put on the best possible show. That is good for the crowd, but bad for the venator. A legionary once told me the cats used in Rome are not merely starved, but are trained to attack and devour humans. The handlers use Christians and other criminals as training bait and food."

A wild roar from the caged catwalk interrupted Lindani. One of the largest and angriest of the male lions had spun and grabbed at the pole that prodded his flanks. The worker desperately tried to untangle his wrist from the leather strap at the end of the pole, but not before the lion had his arm. With a quick snap of its long incisors, the lion cleanly ripped the man's arm from his body. The scream of the worker carried to the ludus banquet, inducing lewd comments and riotous laughter among the patrons. Lindani simply turned and looked at Quintus, his point graphically proven.

"Well, perhaps now you'll want to fight the two-legged animals, like we do," Quintus said with a sympathetic smile. "Don't worry. A few well-placed arrows and they'll be falling like rain on the sand." A loud cheer came from the banquet. "Come on, let's finish our meal." He wrapped an arm over the African's shoulder, and the three walked down the dark passageway together.

They turned the corner in time to see the ludus procurator on the small torch-lit stage complete his introduction with the words: "I give you . . . Quintus Honorius Romanus!" Quintus stopped in his tracks. He stared from the darkness as Lucius stepped onto the stage to the cheers of the crowd. Once again, his lifelong enemy had materialized from the shadows and reentered his life. Lucius stood waving, flanked by Petra, Facilix, and Tiberius Lupus, the Roman procurator. As Tiberius applauded, his face suddenly registered alarm. Quintus followed his gaze and saw an enraged Julia waiting impatiently for her introduction. Tiberius quickly stepped forward before Lucius began speaking.

"My sincerest apologies. May I also introduce the lady Julia Melita, the cosponsor of our games."

Julia smiled and dipped her head, reveling in the loud whistles that greeted her semisheer yellow stola. Quintus was pleased to see Lucius give her an annoyed look for stealing the wind from his sails. It seemed their partnership was getting a bit competitive. Lucius finally raised his arms to reclaim the crowd's attention.

"Welcome to the banquet of the Rome versus Pompeii Challenge!" A chorus of cheers rose from the crowd and continued as Lucius skillfully roused the attendees, instigating a cheering match between the supporters of the Rome troupe and the Pompeii troupe.

Quintus remained in the shadows, blending in at the periphery of the crowd. Lindani and Amazonia stayed close by his side. Quintus was again astonished at the change in Lucius. Not only was he physically bigger, but he radiated an even stronger sense of self-confidence than he had as the Aquae Sulis magistrate. His brown curly hair was still closely cropped in the traditional Roman fashion. His phony smile and persuasive voice now had the power to captivate a crowd. He appeared every bit a leader, a refined patrician, and a master politician.

" . . . And may Hercules watch over each of you," Lucius concluded in a booming voice. "May he protect the bravest of the men . . . and women . . . " He paused for the expected laughter. " . . . and grant the people of Rome a glorious two days of games."

The applause was loud and lengthy as he and Julia stepped from the stage. The Pompeiian lanistae cheered loudest of all, and Quintus could understand why. Although Petra saw the greed and evil in Lucius, business was business and Petra could not overlook the vast amounts of money he had made off Lucius's rise to power. The substantial fee of six hundred thousand sesterces being paid to the Pompeii ludus, combined with the winner's bonus of another two hundred fifty thousand, would make this a lucrative trip for Petra and Facilix.

Lucius and Julia slowly made their way through the crowd, smiling broadly and treating total strangers like they were long-lost relatives. While Lucius focused on the Roman citizens at the banquet, Julia quickly became distracted by the hard bodies and earthy rhetoric that surrounded her.

Quintus watched as Lucius drifted closer and closer. He considered confronting him there and then. After all, he now had little to fear from these two. He had become one of the most popular fighters in the Empire. There was little chance the lanistae, or the public, would stand for him being accused as a runaway slave or horse thief. He was simply too valuable. He stood his ground. But as Lucius approached, a change began to come over Quintus. Ghosts conjured in his mind. He suddenly saw himself as a slave once again, shoveling horse dung in the Viator stables. He remembered Lucius belittling him in front of the staff and family. And he heard Lucius speaking of Quintus's parents as his own. The final thought brought a rush of adrenaline he had felt only in the arena. He knew the feeling well. Taurus was emerging.

Lucius was only five meters away now. Quintus's fingers curled and his sweaty hands turned to potent fists. His breathing became labored. He struggled to control himself. Part of him considered the dire consequences of harming the editor of Rome's games, while another part prepared to wrench arms from sockets. Did he really want a confrontation here at the ludus? Was this the right place? Or the right time? Lucius reached out to touch hands with the old matron standing beside him. Quintus battled to control his rage. To control Taurus. But it was a battle he feared he might lose. Lucius said a few words to the old woman, then got ready to move on to the next handclasp. That would be Quintus. Sweat poured. His heart pounded. His blood raced to saturate every muscle in his body. He began to shake uncontrollably. In a final desperate moment, Quintus's mind sought to command Taurus's feet. *Turn and walk away.* He stood frozen for another instant, then miraculously, he felt his legs begin to move. One step, then another, away from Lucius.

He passed Amazonia and Lindani, and realized they had been watching him. Lindani said nothing, but Amazonia followed him. "The Fates have brought you two back together. Why not face him now and get it done?"

"Leave me," Quintus said as he continued walking. "I can't do this now." His pulse began to slow and his mind cleared.

"Why not? He wouldn't dare challenge you tonight, especially here. You're surrounded by friends, tough friends. He knows he'd have a hell of a fight on his hands."

Quintus stopped for a moment and turned to look back at Lucius. The master politician was still shaking hands, a phony smile etched into his face. Quintus took a deep breath and looked at Amazonia's strong eyes. "No. The time is not yet right for this. I'll know when it's the right hour to face that spineless bastard."

Lindani stepped forward and took hold of Amazonia's arm as Quintus turned and walked into the darkness.

Lucius spotted the auburn-haired beauty he was seeking. She stood with a thin African, staring into the darkness.

"And you must be the great Amazonia I've heard so much about," he said as he approached. The statuesque warrior turned and faced him. The soft shapely curves of her back and hips gave way to a harsh scowl. Lucius was taken aback for a moment, then applied his counterfeit smile. "I'm looking forward to watching you fight tomorrow," he continued. "I hear your wardrobe is truly something to see." He allowed his gaze to drift off her face and linger on her chest.

Amazonia stood stone-faced. "Yes, well, my fighting wardrobe has been known to give men erections. But that's assuming you have a prick to begin with." She flashed a condescending smile at him and walked away.

Lucius was stunned for a moment and looked at the African, who shook his head and shrugged.

"Women—what are they good for, eh?" the black hunter said, then turned and followed Amazonia toward the ludus cells.

Lucius was left standing awkwardly alone, puzzled at what had just happened. A familiar giggle caught his attention. He looked across the crowd to his right and caught a glimpse of Julia, arm-in-arm with two large gladiators, headed toward the barracks. He shook his head and smiled to himself. It looked like his "aunt" would be making the most of her visit to the Ludus Magnus this evening.

XXX

April AD 67

D EATH HAD COME EARLY to the Amphitheater of Taurus on Day One of the Challenge. Shortly after sunrise, three spectators had been trampled to death as the gates swung open and a mob of thirty thousand tossed their tokens at the guards and rushed for the best of the plebian seats. But within a short time, the casualties had been forgotten as the music of the water organ lent a cheery note to the orchestration that accompanied the grand pompa. Two-hundred-and-fifty gladiators and venatores began their march around the circuit of the arena. The anticipation of the fighters was dwarfed by the expectation of the crowd, many of whom had traveled from Pompeii and Herculaneum to cheer on their home team.

From down the long, dark tunnel, the colorful parade looked to Quintus like a giant mythical snake winding its way between the dozens of trees and boulders that the harenarii arena attendants had placed randomly in the sand for the morning hunts. About thirty meters ahead of him, Lindani stepped into the sunlight, directly behind the banner bearers and twin trumpeters with their cornu horns. With his bright red tribal robe, dark skin, and colorfully beaded hair, the African easily stood out from the crowd of fifty hunters. The Pompeiian supporters began chanting his name. The mantra was soon taken up by the entire cavea and echoed down the long tunnel. Even at this distance, Quintus could see Lindani's radiant smile beaming in return.

As usual, the loudest cheers were reserved for the gladiators. The Pompeiian trainers, Julianus and Justus, stepped from the dark tunnel. The cheering of the visiting crowd was barely audible at first over the jeers of the local fans. But as the tertius, secundus, and finally, the primus palus fighters emerged, the jeers turned to applause from the entire crowd. The ovation grew louder as

Amazonia stepped onto the sand a few meters ahead of Quintus. He watched through the portal as she turned and looked up into the cavea, a clear look of awe in her emerald eyes. How else could she react? he thought. Only her second time in the arena and she already stands in the largest amphitheater in the Empire.

Amazonia looked spectacular in her new parade costume. Her long hair was gathered atop her head with a wide gold band, then fell across her shoulders, which were adorned with spiked leather shoulder pads. Her breasts were covered by golden plates held in place with a delicate alloy chain. A leather and gold belt sat low on her hips, crowning a tight red subligaculum. As she began her march, the supple steps of her bare feet and long athletic legs gave the illusion that she floated above the sand.

Then Quintus stepped through the portal. He knew the Minotaur on his chest would identify him to the crowd, but he did not expect the riotous response that rose from the cavea. Obviously, his reputation had preceded him. Rome's spectators knew their games well. They appreciated a talented fighter, just as he had done when he sat in this amphitheater. He scanned the packed seats of the cavea, letting the encounter sink in for a brief instant. It was the moment he had dreamed of.

He stepped forward and followed the serpentine path of the parade, stopping periodically to glide through a portion of his *wushu* sword exercises to thrill the crowd. As he approached the northwest corner of the arena, he looked up toward the spot where he and his father last sat all those years ago. He wondered which of the thousands of faces looking back at him sat in those same seats. The sudden intensity in cheering startled him from his thoughts. The Roman fighters had entered the arena. The crowd chanted an assortment of names with energy over and over. Quintus heard the name "Spiculus" shouted especially loudly. He remembered that this was the popular hoplomachus he had cheered that day with his father. Now he stood alongside the same warrior in the arena.

The last of the gladiators wound through the trees and boulders until the home team was absorbed into the large square formation that had assembled in front of the podium. The praecone, the narrator of the day's events, waved for quiet.

"Gentlemen, ladies, guests from Pompeii, and fellow Romans . . . I bid you welcome to the Rome versus Pompeii Challenge. And I present to you the editor of these great games . . . the Imperial Advisor for Britannia Affairs, Quintus Honorius Romanus . . . and his special guest, the lady Julia Melita."

As the orchestra began a new fanfare, the gate at the north end of the arena rose and four zebras galloped onto the sand, their striped heads adorned with brilliant red feathers. The team pulled a golden chariot driven by a muscular Nubian. Flanking the driver stood Lucius and Julia waving to the crowd as the trained zebras pulled them around the arena. Julia's green palla blew out dramatically in the wake of the chariot.

Quintus watched intently as his aunt and his mortal rival bowed from the bed of the swift vehicle as the Nubian skillfully drove it among the rocks and trees. The crowd's response was impressive. It appeared Lucius had once again managed to advance his career another rung up Rome's political and social ladders.

Suddenly, from the open tunnel poured more than one hundred slaves, running in waves toward the marble wall in front of the podium. As the chariot began its last circuit, a group of the largest slaves dropped to their hands and knees in a perfect line leading toward the wall. A second wave of bulky men jumped on the backs of the crouching slaves and maneuvered into a similar position. The activity continued until the acrobatic slaves had constructed a human staircase from the arena floor to the podium five meters above.

The chariot driver timed his final circuit to end as the last body dropped into place. Without the slightest hesitation, Lucius stepped from the chariot onto the back of the lowest slave. Holding each other's hand firmly, he and Julia stepped from one bare back to the next, ascending the podium wall. The crowd went wild, thrilled at the unique commencement. Quintus could not help smiling as he watched the stunt, seeing himself as the first poor slob in Lucius's human ladder.

The two popular editors reached the top slave then stepped across onto the podium. They were warmly greeted by Senator Publius Nerva and his wife, Drusilla, along with the dozen other personal guests they had invited to share the podium, each a current or potential political ally. As the slaves disengaged from the staircase and ran toward the tunnel, Lucius waved the thirty thousand plebeians and fifteen thousand patrician spectators to silence.

"Hail Nero, the honored Emperor of Rome!" he bellowed loudly. The crowd echoed the homage. "The great Nero, through the voice of the Senate, has been kind enough to allow me to sponsor this match for you, the citizens of Rome, between the Imperial ludus and the new ludus of Pompeii. Now, without further delay, I pronounce this Challenge open. Let the games begin!"

Julianus and Justus gave the signal, and the gladiators and hunters in the arena raised their weapons in salute. All except for Quintus. He found it simply impossible to raise his arm in salute to this editor. He stared at Lucius and Julia as they settled on the podium, then turned with his troupe to march back to the tunnel.

"Look, there's the fighter with the Minotaur and Gorgon markings," Julia said giddily as she carefully surveyed the largest of the glistening bodies before her. Lucius was preoccupied with another minor dignitary looking to be seen with the game's editor.

As the hulking fighters marched away, Julia turned to find the seat she had been craving so long—the chair of Agrippina. She could tell right away that neither of the two vacant chairs in the center of the podium were meant for royal bottoms.

"We felt it wise to replace the chairs," Senator Publius said. She realized the disappointment must have been evident on her face. "The Emperor would not look kindly on staff members using his throne and guest seat in his absence."

Julia gave a tentative smile, then sat on the mahogany backless chair that had been set upon the riser. She bit her lower lip to calm her anger. The orchestra struck up another fanfare, and the praecone stood to explain the scoring system.

"For the hunt, the rules are simple: one point for each animal killed, an extra point if done in some extravagant manner, two points lost for each hunter killed by an animal. Workers spaced throughout the cavea will keep a tally for their designated hunter, then send a runner to the scorekeeper's table with the results after each event."

The gate was raised again and forty venatores marched into the arena, stripped of most of their clothing. The Pompeii hunters wore a simple red loincloth; the Rome hunters wore a similar garment in bright blue. The nearly naked bodies helped to take Julia's mind off the chair incident. She watched as the hunters took up positions around the arena, some on the ground, some in the tree, and some atop the massive rocks.

Lindani selected a boulder near arena center. During the pompa, his trained eye had already selected the spot that would provide the most commanding overview. He drew one of the thirty arrows jammed into his oversized quiver and took practice aims at the variety of kill zones he spotted. He then laid out his ten special arrows. Their flat metal tips looked more like miniature crescent blades than standard arrow heads.

The musical conductor got a nod from the games manager stationed near the gate. The orchestra launched into a lengthy selection that would provide an exciting musical background throughout the hunt. The heavy doors to the holding area were thrown open and, with a series of whoops and hollers, a stampede of more than two hundred animals streamed into the arena. Gazelles and antelopes leaped and darted between the boulders. Red colobus monkeys ran for the trees. Wild boars charged the few hunters on the sand. Zebras galloped across the sand in a frenzy. And a dozen ostriches pranced back and forth across the long oval of the arena.

Lindani made the first three kills. He had already anticipated where the first of the panicked animals would run and had his sights set early. He dropped a gazelle with an arrow through the heart, then knocked two of the monkeys from a tree twenty meters away. Within seconds there was a mass melee in the arena. Arrows and hunting spears flew in all directions. Many of the early shots went wild. Some ended their flight in the audience; one imbedded in the arm of an old man who could not move fast enough to get out of its path.

Lindani stayed focused, his eyes and mind racing to select the next target from his high perch. His peripheral vision caught one of the large boars chasing a Pompeiian across the sand. Even at a distance, he could see the saliva running from the beast's tusks. He took aim, hoping the hunter did not suddenly change direction and wind up with Lindani's arrow in his side. Had the hog been chasing a *Roman* venator, Lindani would have let it make its kill first then dropped the beast. But a teammate was a different story. He let the arrow fly and caught the boar on the side of its head, stopping its charge but not killing it. In less than a second he had another arrow nocked and killed the hog with a shot to its right side.

Cheers arose for a Roman hunter who was doing a remarkable job of chasing a zebra at full gallop. The hunter's long legs enabled him to keep pace with the animal for the few seconds it took to hurl his spear. The striped head dropped into the sand, and the zebra flipped onto its back in the last moment of life. The flamboyant Roman hunter jumped onto the beast's belly, made a thrusting motion toward the carcass with his arm, and let out a warbling howl of victory, obviously his trademark based on the rabid response from the audience.

The scene lasted only seconds, but it was enough to get Lindani's heart racing. Like any champion, he hated to see himself bested by an opponent. He reached for one of his special crescent-tipped arrows, his eyes searching for the nearest ostrich. A pair of the ungainly birds were crossing his path about 25 meters to the right. He swung around and drew back his bowstring. He sighted down the shaft with the deadly crescent razor aligned horizontally. In a split second his mind calculated their speed, their gait, the weight of this special arrow, and his firing distance to determine the length of lead. The bowstring rolled from his fingertips. The arrow flew. A millisecond later the crescent razor struck the long neck of the lead ostrich just below the head. The tiny head sprang from the body as the serpentine neck began to flail. But the body continued to run on, not a step or two, but meter after meter across the sand. The site of an immense headless bird running crazily through the sand sent a wild cheer through the cavea.

Lindani nocked another crescent arrow and let it fly toward the second ostrich. This shot showed the first was no lucky accident. Two headless birds now ran across the sand, their overworked hearts pumping spurts of blood from the cleanly cut neck ends. The first ostrich finally dropped, while the other ran blindly into the thick trunk of a poplar tree, knocking a colobus monkey out of its branches. Seeing where the bird was heading, Lindani was already prepared for the collision. Before the monkey hit the ground, it was pierced by one of Lindani's pointed arrows.

Knowing he had scored extra points with all three hits, Lindani took a moment to raise his arms and bow dramatically atop the boulder. With all eyes on him, he made a show of taking a deep breath and pausing to gather himself. His right arm then became a blur, pulling arrows from the quiver at his side and firing them faster than seemed humanly possible. Every shaft struck an animal and either dropped it in its tracks or wounded it seriously enough to be finished off with a second shot. Like their Roman venator hero, Lindani also had a trademark move and saw a perfect opportunity to introduce it to the Roman audience. He drew back hard, until his bow appeared ready to snap under the strain. The arrow flew from his fingers, pierced the left side of an impala's neck, exited its right side, and struck a gemsbok that had been running alongside it. Both antelopes dropped as a pair. Again, the crowd went wild.

With the number of targets dwindling, the African spent the few remaining minutes of the hunt decapitating more ostriches, a sure crowd-pleaser that meant double points for his team. The hunters scoured the field of carcasses for movement. There was none. One by one they raised their weapons in victory. Only one Pompeiian hunter had fallen dead, impaled on the twisted horns of an enraged eland. Other than a few cuts and bruises, the remaining 39 venatores had escaped remarkably unscathed. Lindani was suspicious. These tame beasts were not what he expected from the bloodthirsty Romans.

The musicians wrapped their musical accompaniment, and Lucius stood to wave the hunters to the podium for their rewards. From his friend's experience, Lindani knew this man's history and the way he operated. His suspicion grew. The other hunters were jumping from their boulders and trees and approaching the podium. Lindani held back for a moment, his eyes glued on the mischievous smile across Lucius's face. His intuition tingled. Something was wrong. His mind flashed to the night before. What happened to the other, much more deadly, animals he had watched the workers unloading? In an instant, he realized what Lucius had planned.

"Gather your arrows and spears," the African yelled from the boulder.

Many of the hunters stopped and looked back at him. "Something is not right. I feel it. Gather your weapons." Lindani jumped from the boulder and began pulling arrows from the carcasses around him and restocking his quiver. A few of the Pompeiian hunters followed his lead.

Lindani glanced at the podium as he worked feverishly. The expression on Lucius's face suddenly changed. Lucius looked toward the arena manager, still standing quietly at the arena doors, and nodded. The doors were again thrown open. This time the arena workers concealed themselves behind the open doors, up against the marble wall.

Every hunter froze as a terrible roar echoed from the tunnel. The smart ones ran immediately for the boulders and trees, while the others stood in dumb shock, foolishly thinking their hunt was over. Lindani was back on his perch with almost as many arrows as he had started with, although the new shafts and feathers were sticky with blood. He had also managed to retrieve three hunting spears and set them at his feet on the high rocks.

Within seconds, a mass of one hundred deadly cats streamed into the arena. Venatores ran in every direction, some looking for weapons, others scrambling up trees and boulders. Many in the crowd screamed, urging their favorites out of harm's way. The slower hunters were tackled by lions, leopards, cheetahs, and black panthers.

Lindani looked first for any beast attacking a hunter in a red loincloth. There were many. His previous night's assessment of the unusually fierce nature of these cats proved accurate. It took three arrows to dispatch the first lion alone. He worked quickly, firing with as much power as he could will into his right bowstring arm.

There was a loud yell from the branches of the poplar tree that adjoined his boulder. Lindani knew that leopards climbed trees almost as easily as monkeys, but he had never seen one claw its way up a trunk as quickly as the one beside him. The spotted cat was after a young venator attempting to use the branches as sanctuary. Lindani spun and fired an arrow. The shaft pierced the leopard's neck. It screeched a terrifying high-pitched scream, clamped its jaws on the leg of the trapped venator and promptly died, rolling from the branches. Even in death, the cat refused to release its long canine teeth from the man's leg. The hunter soon had the full weight of the dead cat hanging from his left limb, ripping the skin open and pulling him from the branch. To Lindani, although the cat was dead, its spirit was still very much alive, and it was determined to drag this hunter into Hades with it. The man could no longer stand the pain and released his hold on the tree, falling into the death pit below. In seconds, he was ripped into four large pieces by the waiting lions, their black manes rustling as they fought among themselves for the tastiest morsels.

Lindani knew that male lions usually stood back and waited for an easy kill such as this. They were, therefore, not as dangerous as the females. But he took advantage of the opportune targets below him and easily dispatched the four cats. The growl from behind told him that he had made a mistake. He glanced over his shoulder into the evil eyes of a titanic lioness who had quietly leaped up the back of his boulder. This was the stalker and killer he should have been concerned about. He cursed himself for being so stupid. He knew he could not take his eyes from the beast to look for the hunting spears. She would be on him before he looked back. He slid slowly to his left a half-meter. He watched the lion's tail carefully, waiting for the sign of attack. The twitching stopped. The lion leaped. Lindani was already falling flat onto his back. The jolt of hitting the hard rock jarred the air from his lungs. His hand reached for the spear that he knew in his soul had to be there. The feel of the pole was a sign from the gods he would live. As he had done once before with the mad bear in Aquae Sulis, Lindani aimed the metal tip at the underbelly of the charging lioness. The cat's momentum drove her onto the spear. Lindani's arms tensed and lifted the lion up and over his body. The screaming, impaled cat was vaulted over the front edge of the boulder and onto the pile of male lion carcasses in the sand below.

In a second, Lindani was back on his feet, his bow in hand and his eyes searching for the next target. He focused again on the cats attacking the Pompeiian hunters. One by one he picked off the beasts with hits to the neck or flank. He was running low on arrows. Luckily there were only a few cats left alive. One of the last, a fierce black panther, was rolling through the sand in a violent struggle with a Roman venator. Other hunters in blue had come to his aid, but the thrashing had enveloped the pair in a cloud of dust. The man screamed for help. A comrade ran forward and thrust with his spear just as the panther spun the pair again. The spear tip pierced human flesh on the man's back, adding to his agony.

Looking down from the boulder, Lindani had a better angle on the action. "Stand aside!" he yelled as he nocked his last arrow. It seemed an impossible shot, but there was no other option. Lindani watched and waited, the tip of his arrow following every move in the struggle. The pair rolled again. There was a flash of white flesh, then a flash of black. Lindani fired. The cat screamed as the arrow punctured the back of its neck. The metal tip penetrated the cat's airway and emerged from its throat, stopping its travel just a few centimeters from the hunter's face. A drop of blood ran from the tip of the arrow and struck his nose. Then the panther went limp. The Roman hunters stepped forward and lifted the dead cat off their badly mauled comrade. The arena went quiet as they huddled over him. Within a few seconds, the man was on his feet, supported by two teammates. He looked up to the high rocks above him and raised his bloodied arm in salute to Lindani. A resounding cheer erupted from the cavea. As in Pompeii, once more the African made the crowd his own by rescuing one of the locals.

The last of the cats fell and the hunters slowly made their way across the sand. Many seemed tentative, fearing yet another surprise waiting for them behind the tunnel doors. They all kept tight hold on their weapons. Rather than watch the doors, Lindani kept his eyes on Lucius, looking for any more signs of trickery. There were none. Lucius motioned the fighters forward, and they gathered in two groups before the podium. There were six venatores missing from the Roman team and two from the Pompeiian team.

"Did you enjoy that little surprise?" he yelled to the hunters with a smile. "We needed a little excitement for the crowd. You handled it well. You are all true heroes, the best in your field."

The runners had arrived at the scorekeeper's table, and the results were passed to the praecone who announced: "After our first venatio event, the score stands at Rome: 157 points; Pompeii: 215 points." The cheering of the Pompeiian fans and hunters was mixed with the jeers of the Roman fans.

Lucius addressed the hunters in the red loincloths. "Congratulations. That's quite a lead to take so early." He began throwing the money purses from the podium, then spotted Lindani near the back of the group. "Ahh, our African friend. Your skills with the bow are even more impressive than we witnessed at Aquae Sulis. According to the tally, you killed more beasts than anyone today." Lucius tossed him the largest of the venator purses. "Well done."

Lindani bent to retrieve his reward bag but said nothing. Again, he locked eyes with Lucius and refused to relinquish the stare. He was happy to see the action once again had an effect on the spineless bureaucrat. Lucius squirmed and spoke quietly to Julia, then tried to force Lindani away with a brush of his hand. The hunter stood his ground and remained in place for another moment. Lucius quickly nodded to the herald, who ordered the arena cleared and announced the next event. Lindani smiled as he strolled from the sand.

The rest of the morning was filled with smaller hunts, a bull fight and a few beast-on-beast fights, the bloodiest of which pitted a bear against a lion. The animals were chained together and prodded with burning torches to make them fight. The carnage did nothing to affect the point tally of the Challenge, but provided the mob with one of their favorite novelty exhibitions.

As the sun and temperature climbed, the vellarium was pulled into place, providing welcome shade to most of the cavea. An orchestral fanfare signaled the gladiator matches, and one hundred fighters emerged from the tunnel to make their circuit of the arena, each paired with his adversary. The lanistae had decided to hold Amazonia for the final fight of Day Two, so she did not participate in the afternoon pompa. They had also decided that Day One needed a sensational climax to assure a full house on the second day. For that, they would pit Taurus against Negrimus, one of Rome's most popular fighters.

It seemed to Quintus that the cheering could be heard across the city as he and Negrimus appeared in the tunnel portal to join the pompa. But mixed with the applause he could hear gasps of shock from the Pompeiian fans seated near the portal. They obviously recognized the Minotaur design on his muscular chest. But he knew they did not expect the weapons, for this day he was outfitted to fight as a *retiarius*. He wore no helmet. Instead, a leather headband held back his long black hair. In his left hand he carried a metal trident, the three polished prongs presenting a menacing appearance. He adjusted his pugio dagger, which was tucked securely in the bronze belt that wrapped the top of his blood-red subligaculum. Draped over his right arm hung his weighted net, and around his neck, a small good-luck charm hung from a thin strip of leather.

Beside him stood Negrimus, armed as a secutor. He carried a large blue rectangular shield and a gladius. The short dorsal fin atop his streamlined helmet completed the look of the fish-man, whom the retiarius would attempt to ensnare in his net and spear with the weapon of Neptune, god of the sea.

Quintus raised his trident in salute to the crowd, then stepped onto the sand as part of the parade. He had visualized his fight—and his victory—in the tunnel. He had become Taurus. With the boulders and trees now removed, he and the other marchers hugged the arena wall, affording the crowd a close, unobstructed view.

"Let's go, Taurus!" came a familiar voice from the cavea. "If you could do it as a thraex, you can do it as a retiarius!" Taurus scanned the crowd for a recognizable face. He spotted it in the second row where Gaius Magnus, the Pompeiian editor and friend of Petra, cheered him on. He acknowledged the support with a smile, but wondered if Gaius's optimistic statement was true. Could he win as a retiarius? It was a style in which he was tested during his earliest days in the Britannia ludus. Although he did well, Petra and Julianus had decided he would do better fighting as a thraex. But after his victory in Pompeii, he had wanted to broaden his horizons. Julianus argued that he was possibly the best thraex in the Empire. Taurus remembered his own response well: "Then allow me to begin training to be the best *retiarius* in the Empire as well." A brilliant sparring match with net and trident just one week later convinced both lanistae and head trainers to honor the request. The versatility could only increase his value to the school. And he knew he was good. Very good.

"Let me see you work, Taurus! Do it for me!" yelled a young woman a few seats to the left of Gaius. Taurus dropped the net and obliged, anxious to get as many in the crowd cheering for him as possible. He stepped through a brief portion of the new *wushu* exercise he had developed. His fast, graceful movements were even more impressive with the long trident than with the

Thracian sica. The pole flew from a tucked position under his arm into a variety of thrusts and lunges, then became a double-sided threat as he advanced rapidly, swinging both the pointed and flat ends of the trident. He raised the weapon above his head and it virtually disappeared as it spun faster than the eye could follow. As quickly as it had turned to a blur, it reappeared, neatly tucked once again under his robust arm. The spectators above him erupted in wild applause. Taurus retrieved his net with a flourish and took a short bow.

Apparently not wanting to appear intimidated, Negrimus leaned back and belted out a blustery theatrical laugh that further inflamed the crowd. Taurus glanced at his opponent as they resumed their march and was sure he detected a trace of anxiety in his eyes. The unexpected reaction gave Taurus the extra boost of confidence he needed for his first retiarius battle.

As they passed the podium, Taurus gazed casually at the opposite tiers of the cavea, never making eye contact with either Lucius or Julia.

"They say this Taurus was part of the Britannia troupe," Julia said, "but I don't remember anyone looking like that fighting in our Aquae Sulis games." Her breathing quickened as she carefully studied the artwork on Taurus's massive chest.

"And you would certainly have remembered a specimen like that, no?" Lucius said.

She finally broke her gaze from the fighter and saw a smile cross Lucius's lips. Julia responded with a devilish grin of her own. "Perhaps you could persuade the lanistae to introduce me after the program."

The music and herald signaled the start of the afternoon matches. With the best of Rome, Pompeii, and Britannia competing, the quality of combat, even in the earliest bouts, was far superior to the provincial games Julia was used to. Solo fighters were followed by a five-against-five brawl, then a chain-match where two fighters were anchored together by neck shackles that restricted their movement and forced nonstop, close-quarter combat.

As the afternoon wore on, Julia noticed that the Roman crowd was more bloodthirsty than the Aquae Sulis crowd had been. A gladiator truly had to fight hard and aggressively to be spared if he fell. While she certainly enjoyed the near-naked powerful bodies in physical contact, the abundant bloodletting and stench of death, combined with the unseasonably warm weather, began to sicken her. She waved her perfumed white handkerchief under her nose and distracted herself by watching the crowd. As she observed the cavea, she spotted an unusual seating arrangement that seemed unique to Rome's amphitheater. Many of the women were seated in the laps of their male companions rather than on the wooden benches. The harder the fighters fought, the louder the crowd screamed, and the more these women bounced and cheered in their neighbors' laps. But their screams were much more than cheers for the fighters. It suddenly became as clear as night air to Julia. These people were enjoying sex during the gladiator bouts.

She focused on a young couple very near the left side of the podium wall. As the next fight built in intensity, the look on the woman's face became flushed, then contorted with passion. Her lover's hands reached around and groped her breasts, which were bouncing violently under her tunic in time to her grinding. Her cries were inaudible over the cacophony of noise in the cavea, but her message was unmistakable. Her eyes were fixed on the fight. Julia glanced back and forth between the action in the arena and the action five meters from her in the seats. The more heated the fight became, the faster the woman pumped on her lover's lap. The Roman fighter advanced, drawing blood. The woman bounced more frantically. The fighter knocked his opponent to the ground with a crashing blow, and the woman's screams grew loud enough to be heard by Julia. The Pompeiian fighter was sentenced to death. The woman cried out. "Yes! Yes! Kill him! Yes!" The Pompeiian assumed the position of honorable death and the Roman drew back his gladius to deliver the death blow. The woman's eyes widened with expectation. Her pumping grew frenzied. The gladiator thrust his sword into the back of the man's neck. The woman slammed her body down hard on her lover's lap. The look of ecstasy on both their faces made it clear they had timed their climax perfectly.

The woman climbed from her neighbor's lap, sweat running from her face and arms, body fluids dripping from under her short tunic. She caught sight of Julia's stare and returned a roguish smile and a wink. Julia flushed and dropped her gaze to her own lap. It was then she realized her hands were nestled between her legs and the tunic under her green palla was damp. She glanced around to see if anyone else had been watching her spy on the couple. Everyone's attention seemed to be on the arena. She relaxed and waited for the next bout.

Petra paced the labyrinth of halls near the cells as the muffled crowd noise from above rumbled through the stone passageways. It had not been a good afternoon for the Pompeiian ludus. Their early point lead was slowly eroded by the power and confidence of the Roman fighters. More importantly, the disappointing performance of many of their tertius and secundus palus fighters had resulted in more death sentences than he had anticipated.

The lanista approached his counterpart, Facilix, seated on a nearby bench, wringing the program in his hands until the scroll turned to pulp. "Our fighters seem intimidated by the Romans," Petra said.

Facilix shook his head. "I don't know why I let you talk me into this."

Petra felt the hairs on the back of his neck rise as he looked down on his new partner. "Nobody twisted your arm, Facilix. You smelled the money just as sweetly as I did. We need to speak with our doctores tonight. We need to get our fighters better focused for tomorrow."

As if to punctuate his sentence, a wild cheer floated down the tunnel and word passed among the fighters that Rome had just taken the point lead, with only three matches left in the day.

Petra sat down next to Facilix and remained motionless as the results of the next two bouts were shouted down the tunnel. Two of their top fighters, Priscus and Valentinus, had both fallen to their Roman rivals. Petra thanked Hercules that both had fought well enough to be spared by Lucius and the crowd.

He looked up as Quintus and Negrimus brushed past and headed for the portal. The determined, confident look on his young fighter's face told him that he had already made the mental transformation to Taurus.

"Do you still think it was a good idea to let him fight as a retiarius today?" Facilix asked. "We desperately need this win."

"If Juli felt he was ready, that's all the reassurance I need," Petra replied, hoping with all his being that the head trainer was correct.

XXXI

April AD 67

WITH THE MOST DRAMATIC musical introduction of the day, the herald announced the final bout. Quintus stepped through the portal and onto the sand, flanked by Negrimus. He strode to the center of the arena with confidence, acknowledging the roaring ovation with a wave of his trident. Once again, he was put in the position of safeguarding the pride and reputation of his ludus. It was a privilege he treasured.

He faced his opponent and readied himself physically and mentally. Julianus leaned forward and spoke quietly.

"We can't win this today, but we can get back in the running for tomorrow."

"I know," Taurus replied, never taking his eyes from Negrimus.

"Don't make me regret telling the dominus that you're ready as a retiarius."

Taurus looked at the trainer. He suddenly realized how unusual it was to see the doctore's face in the arena without looking through the screen of a visored helmet. "Let's just do this thing," he said with a smile.

Julianus smacked his hands together loudly. "Be on guard!" he shouted to both fighters. He dropped his arm. "Attack!"

Negrimus was first on the attack. He charged with a fast combination of cuts and thrusts. Taurus knocked each blow aside with the metal pole of his trident. He gave ground quickly, which was common for a lightly armored retiarius. But Taurus always hated giving up real estate. He used the early retreat as a ploy to get the secutor moving forward quickly. He then suddenly planted his foot and looked for Negrimus to close quickly into the points of his raised trident. But the secutor's experience against retiarius fighters was evident. He turned sideways to narrow his profile, and the tips of the trident slipped past harmlessly.

Taurus crouched and shook the net bunched in his right hand. The lead weights that edged the one-meter-wide rete clicked and jingled as his hand rattled back and forth. In a flash, he swung the net at the Roman's legs, looking to trip him. Again Negrimus was wise to the move and hurdled the obstacle. Taurus feinted with the trident, then swung the net again. Again the secutor jumped. Taurus used the momentum of the weights to bring the net high, and in the blink of an eye, his arm thrust forward and the net was in flight. The sudden move seemed to surprise Negrimus, but he managed to angle his shield up in time. The weighted net scratched across the smooth metal surface and slid harmlessly to the sand. Before the secutor counterattacked, Taurus jerked the leather cord tied to his wrist and, as if by magic, the net flew from the sand and was back in his hand. But Negrimus was again on the attack.

Taurus anchored his trident tips in the sand to help absorb the shock of the gladius blows. He made a show of concentrating on the placement of the pole to parry the thrusts, while his right hand worked surreptitiously to ready the net for another toss. His arm sprang forward like a catapult and again the rete was in the air. This time it snagged the Roman's helmet and shoulder. Taurus pulled hard to throw his opponent off balance. But with a swift dip of his head and a blindingly fast slice of his gladius, Negrimus freed himself from the tenuous hold. To Taurus's horror, the secutor had also managed to sever the retrieval cord tied to his wrist.

"You won't be seeing that rete again," Negrimus growled as he flew into another attack.

"That's alright," Taurus answered. "I won't be needing it." He grabbed the trident like a staff. Taurus detected the same concern in his opponent's eyes he had seen during his *wushu* display for the crowd. As with his Thracian sica, the trident became an extension of his arm.

"Do it, Taurus! Stoke it!" Julianus yelled as he refereed the action.

Both ends of the metal pole became a blur. Taurus advanced on his opponent and for the first time that day, Negrimus retreated. The trident was impossible to follow. Taurus struck the Roman hard in the arm, then in the leg. The crowd noise became deafening. Rarely had a retiarius advanced like this on a heavily armored secutor, especially one of Negrimus's caliber. A sudden flash of the trident points cut a gash in the secutor's sword arm. His quick glance to check the wound's severity was all the time Taurus needed to dive for his lost weapon. He somersaulted through the sand and came up holding the net. Before Negrimus could close the distance, Taurus had the net swinging in the air. As a feint, he thrust hard with the trident, then released the rete. This time the net found a solid target, blanketing the secutor's body. Taurus gathered the edge quickly as Negrimus leaned back, pulling the webbing taut. The secutor's right arm was still free, the gladius swinging wildly to keep Taurus at bay. The match became a tug-of-war. The net webbing stretched to its limit. Taurus looked for a safe opening to drive home the triple points of the trident. He lunged forward with a mighty thrust. The metal tip clanged against the scutum. He withdrew and thrust again. The gladius knocked the trident aside. Taurus pulled tighter on the net, dragging his opponent closer one centimeter at a time. The muscles in his arms strained under the pressure. Suddenly the net went slack. The loss of resistance made Taurus stagger backward. Negrimus was charging him. Taurus could feel himself going down. He knew he would be dead if Negrimus landed on top of him. He dove sideways and used the force of his fall to hurl Negrimus past him, using the net like a giant slingshot. Both gladiators hit the sand. The crowd jumped to their feet. Taurus was up first, his trident slippery in his hand from the mixture of sand and sweat. Negrimus was half clear of the net, but his shield was hopelessly entangled. Taurus charged. The three points of the trident drew closer to their target. Negrimus released the shield handle and slipped free. Both fighters knew that a secutor with no shield stood little chance against the length of a trident. Negrimus had only one option. With a bloodcurdling scream, he charged Taurus. There was a collision of metal and flesh. A spray of blood flew through the air, but neither fighter showed pain. Negrimus tried desperately to lock himself to Taurus, using his arms, legs, and gladius. If he could keep Taurus in close quarters, he would be clear of the metal prongs at the far end of the trident. But Taurus had anticipated this tactic. He grasped the pole with both hands and once again used it as a staff. Both ends were a smear of metallic reflection that struck flesh once, then twice, and again on the side of the neck. Purple welts appeared. Negrimus staggered. Taurus knew then he had won. He spun the pole again and knocked the sword from the Roman's hand. The blurring motion came to a sudden halt as he locked the weapon under his arm and thrust forward with a booming yell. Two of the three metal points drove into the secutor's right foot, pinning it to the ground. He screamed and fell backward. Almost before he hit the ground, Taurus was on him, the pugio dagger held firmly in his left hand. The point pressed hard enough under the secutor's chin to draw a trickle of blood. Negrimus raised his finger in a plea for mercy. Julianus stepped in and grabbed Taurus's hand. The match was won.

The two combatants and the referee scanned the cavea. All three were surprised to see so many thumbs turned down. Taurus heard the vanquished gladiator whisper a despondent "No." Then one by one, white cloths appeared throughout the amphitheater. Taurus looked across the arena toward the podium. Lucius was studying the crowd and considering his verdict. The noise was almost unbearable. Taurus assumed those with their thumbs turned felt their fighter should have easily beaten a new retiarius. But others obviously wanted to see their hero fight another day. Lucius finally brought up his arm and waved a white handkerchief across his chest.

"Missio!" Julianus yelled. Taurus felt Negrimus's tense muscles relax and heard him breathe a sigh of relief. The unmistakable sounds of taunts and ridicule mixed with the cheers that reached the arena floor.

"Just get that fucking trident out of my foot," Negrimus said through clenched teeth.

Taurus obliged, jerking quickly on the metal pole. The secutor bit his lip until it bled, but did not scream. He stood and limped across the sand under his own power, roughly pushing away the harenarii who had scurried across the arena to help him.

Taurus had won the match, but he felt he had yet to win the crowd. Despite a gash across his leg, he swung the trident over his head and stepped through another incredible exercise of speed and agility. The few jeers still resonating from the mob began to subside. They watched in awe as the painted fighter controlled the trident with what was surely some form of magic. The faster he moved, the louder the choir of voices grew. He spun the staff to a halt in a stance worthy of a marble statue of Hercules, then dramatically flung the trident into the sand. The crowd bellowed their appreciation.

"Quintus . . ." Julianus said to him over the crowd noise. The name jarred him for a moment. He looked at the trainer. " . . . I think it's time you finally said hello." Julianus nodded toward the podium and smiled. "You two have some catching up to do."

Quintus knew he was right. He had delayed the inevitable, but now the time had come. He walked slowly toward the podium, buoyed by the adoration of the crowd. He looked from side to side, partly to acknowledge the chant of "Taurus! Taurus!" that had begun, and partly to delay making eye contact with Lucius and Julia until the last minute. Would Julia even recognize him as the hapless stable slave she had once owned? Would Lucius recognize him as the master he had once despised?

He reached the base of the podium and looked up. He stared for a moment into the eyes of the man who had stolen his life. Lucius squinted slightly, as if trying to place a face from his distant past. But before he could say anything, Quintus called out loudly.

"Oh, great Quintus Honorius Romanus . . . Before you honor me with the palm, I wish to first honor you."

With a puzzled expression, Lucius looked toward Julia. But Quintus could see that her eyes were locked firmly on his chest. He reached up and slid the good-luck charm from around his neck. "It is my gift to you."

He tossed the tiny icon up to the podium.

Lucius caught the icon and looked down at his hand. What he saw confused him. Why would this gladiator give him a terra-cotta figurine? The gift made no sense. But then, like recalling a horrible phantasm he wanted so badly to suppress, he recognized the gift for what it was. He suddenly saw the entire boat, sitting on the breakfast table in a villa garden not far from where they now sat. He threw the figure back with a yell, as if it had burned a hole in his hand. The sudden noise made Julia jump.

"What's wrong? What was it?" she asked.

Lucius never heard her. He watched the gladiator retrieve the figure from the sand and slip it back over his head. "But you wanted it so badly back then," the fighter yelled up to him. "I thought you would still enjoy it." The bloody gladiator stared him in the eye, grinning a triumphant smile. "I beat you, Lucius. You forced me here, but I overcame it, and I beat you."

Lucius squirmed in his seat. He prayed he would wake at any moment from this nightmare, like he had done so often before. But this time it was no nightmare. He could feel Julia staring at him. He turned slowly and looked into her wide, questioning eyes. He saw her shiver.

"Quintus," was the only word he said.

Julia's head snapped back to the sand.

"You've been so preoccupied with studying every detail of his chest," Lucius sneered, "you've not even looked at his face." He could see it all come flooding back to her as well. The close-set brown eyes and long lashes, the round face with a hard jawline, the handsome smile. It was most certainly Quintus.

"What's wrong?" Quintus called to him. "Am I not to be awarded the palm before my adoring crowd?"

In his shock, Lucius had grown oblivious to the mob. He scanned the questioning and impatient spectators near the podium and decided he had better proceed with the ceremony. Even in his panicked state he knew insulting an arena hero could ruin the goodwill he was looking to establish with the games.

"Forgive me . . . Taurus," Lucius stammered loudly. "I must have mistaken you for another. Please accept the victory palm and this gold as my congratulations for such a wonderful performance."

Quintus watched Lucius's hands shake as he fumbled with the change purse and awkwardly tossed the rewards into the sand. He felt himself smile. Lucius's trembling fingers then covered his mouth as he sat mute, staring down at him.

But Quintus was in no hurry to leave. He was amused that he had flustered Lucius so dramatically. He watched the tittering, mumbling, and dubious glances his rival received from the others on the podium, especially the Senator and his wife seated alongside him.

"Thank you, sir," Quintus finally said. "I shall honor the name of Quintus Honorius Romanus this night as I worship our god Hercules." With a broad smile Quintus raised his prizes toward the crowd, inciting another round of loud applause and cheering. He threw Lucius one last triumphant look, then turned and walked toward the tunnel.

He heard the praecone's final announcement of the day as he crossed the sand. "The Imperial ludus leads the Pompeiians by just under one hundred points." The crowd responded with the expected cheers, but Quintus cared little about points at this moment. "The tally will continue tomorrow. Be here to witness the conclusion of the Rome versus Pompeii Challenge. And join me in praising the Imperial Advisor for Britannia Affairs, Quintus Honorius Romanus, and the lady Julia Melita for their generosity in sponsoring these spectacular games. May the gods be with them!"

Yes, Quintus thought with a smile, Lucius looked liked he could use some divine direction right about now.

Neither Lucius nor Julia were there to hear the herald's blessing. Lucius had dragged her from the podium and headed into the private tunnel behind the royal box used by the Emperor to come and go during the games. Senator Nerva and his wife attempted to follow.

"Quintus, what was all that about? Who's 'Lucius'?" the Senator asked.

Lucius was still trembling with fear and rage. He snapped viciously at the Senator, "He's nobody! Now please use the public entrances like everyone else and leave us alone."

Shock registered on both the Senator and his wife, but Lucius hardly noticed.

"Quintus!" Julia yelled. "What's gotten into you? I'm so sorry, Senator, Drusilla. Please accept my apology on behalf of my nephew . . . ," she looked hard at Lucius, " . . . who appears to have sat through too much violence today."

"We can see the two of you need to be alone to discuss matters," the Senator said in an indignant tone.

"Yes, we were going to invite you to our home for a private banquet this evening," said Drusilla, equally offended, "but we can see you're not in the mood." The couple left Lucius and Julia alone in the empty tunnel.

Lucius felt he was about to explode. He began ranting the second they disappeared, his high-pitched voice echoing off the stark walls. "After all these years, what evil god has brought that fucking bastard back into my life? He plagued my nightmares. Now he plagues my life. What are we going to do?"

"Will you calm down!" Julia shouted. "You're ruining everything we've worked so hard for."

"Me? It's that . . . that . . . *gladiator* who'll ruin everything for us. The great *'Taurus'* is the one you should be concerned about." He lowered his voice to a frantic whisper. He pulled her close and spoke directly into her face. "He knows too much. He can bring us both down."

Julia stared at him for a second, then burst out laughing. "Are you serious? Even if he's stupid enough to try to sell a far-fetched story like that, who'd listen? Who would believe a common gladiator over an Imperial advisor?"

"But he's *not* a common gladiator. You saw the way he fights out there. He had everyone behind him, even the ones cheering for Rome. That type of gladiator can wield power. Not just with a sword, but with words."

Julia looked at him blankly. He could tell she simply was not grasping the gravity of their situation.

"Damn it to Hades, woman, will you listen to me? Suppose he's called on to bed down with some high-ranking couple tonight. You know it happens all the time with the top fighters. It happened with *you* last night, didn't it?" Julia averted her eyes to the stone floor. "Suppose he begins planting this story into the ears of some high-placed women. He knows enough details of my life to make it convincing enough to raise some eyebrows and get people talking. And what about his father's old friends and business associates? They might not recognize him at first, but he *is* Quintus Romanus. He'll convince them of that with just a few words."

The look on her face finally began reflecting comprehension, but she quickly shook it off.

"How can he be a threat?" she asked, the condescending smile returning to her face. The smirk was beginning to infuriate Lucius. "Look, he proved a few minutes ago that he's the most powerful man in that arena. He basked in the glory of the crowd. So why should he pursue this? Why would he put this fame and glory at risk just to cause you trouble?"

"Because I ruined his life!" he hissed through clenched teeth. "In the course of one day, I sent him from a life of luxury to the life of a horse-stable slave. He had a fortune to inherit and now he lives in ludus cells and kills people for a living. What do you think? Are those enough reasons for revenge? And by the way, he would not be causing *me* trouble, dear Aunt, he'd be causing *us* trouble. If I go down, you go with me."

Her smile had faded, and Julia stared at the wall. Lucius could see her mind was racing with the horrible possibilities.

"It's making sense now, isn't it?" He grabbed her arms and forced her to look at him. "If he talks, you can forget Roman society, forget your view of the Forum, and get ready to return to the textile business in the shithole of the Empire."

Julia winced visibly at the thought. "Perhaps you're right," she said after the briefest minute. "Maybe we should play things safe and be sure he's silenced. Then this sordid past of yours will be over and done with for good. What do you have in mind?"

As she spoke, Lucius was already drafting a plan.

XXXII

April AD 67

I T TOOK MORE THAN three hours to clear the darkened amphitheater after the final bout. Many of the spectators tried unsuccessfully to bribe the guards into letting them spend the night in order to hold their choice seats for the next day's games. Most simply left dejected; others needed to be forcibly removed. A cleaning crew of slaves picked up the remnants of food and garbage. Some were assigned to clean bodily fluids and human waste from the seats and floor with buckets of reeking water.

Near the deserted podium in the flickering light of a single torch, Cassius Petra tapped his foot impatiently. Sitting in the dark cavea with Facilix and Tiberius Lupus, the procurator of the Roman ludus, was grating on his nerves, especially with so much work to do.

"The games resume tomorrow morning, and we have to sit here waiting for these two assholes," he fumed.

"Careful how you speak of our editor, Petra," warned Tiberius. "Roman politicians have long memories when it comes to those who defy them."

"Well, what do they want of us at this time of night? Don't they realize what needs to be done before morning?"

"I don't know," Tiberius said as he watched the last few slaves wiping down the seats. "I just got an urgent message for us to gather here and wait."

Knowing the real story behind Lucius and his impersonation of Quintus, Petra had little patience with the scheming deviant. Now having to sit and wait for the swine just increased his loathing of the man. Finally, he heard footsteps echo in the tunnel behind the podium. Lucius and Julia stepped through the archway and onto the podium. Both showed calm, pleasant smiles.

"Thank you for joining us, gentlemen," said Lucius. "So sorry to keep you waiting."

"This better not take long," Petra said brusquely.

Tiberius gave him a hard look and spoke in a more conciliatory tone to the financial backers of their games. "What Petra means is that we have a great deal of work to do and many wounds to mend."

"Well then, I'll come right to the point," Lucius said. "I want to make a change in tomorrow's games."

Petra glanced at Facilix and rolled his eyes. Late changes in the middle of games was an eccentric annoyance tolerated only from an Emperor. Private editors were rarely afforded such whimsy.

"Day One was so successful, we feel we need a more dramatic finale for Day Two. I want to put the best gladiator and the two best venatores—one from each school—in the arena together to fight against twenty lions."

The lanistae looked at each other in shock. "Primus palus gladiators do not fight animals," Petra said, barely holding his temper. "Venatores fight animals."

"I'm sorry. You misunderstand me," Lucius replied. "The gladiator will not be fighting at all." He looked at each of them and grinned a shrewd smile. "The gladiator will be tied to a post. He'll be the ultimate bait. This is a test of the hunters' skills, not the gladiator's."

Petra was dumbfounded. Facilix and Tiberius seemed more puzzled than before. "Why use a gladiator?" Tiberius asked. "Why not put a slave in with the hunters?"

Lucius broadened his smile. "Because it's good showmanship. Who would the crowd rather see in peril? A simple slave? A virgin? A Christian? If the hunters lose, what's the cost? Just another slave. No, to really get the crowd behind the hunters, the venatores must be forced to protect someone the crowd really cares about, one of their heroes. Say, the big winner of today's games . . . Taurus."

Petra immediately saw the plan for what it was. He had heard enough. He stood up to leave, but Facilix and Tiberius remained seated. After a second, Facilix said, "You do realize he's my best fighter?" Petra bristled at the

Pompeiian's reference to *his* fighter when discussing Quintus. "This man will be very expensive bait."

Julia picked up the discussion. "We're well aware that this will cost us more. We'll pay you one hundred thousand sesterces each for the services of the two hunters. If either hunter dies, we'll pay another fifty thousand to the appropriate lanista. If Taurus dies, we'll pay another two hundred and fifty thousand to the Pompeii school."

Facilix and Tiberius looked shocked at the unexpected windfall. Petra could clearly see where this was headed. "Absolutely not," he said hastily, then turned to leave.

"Hold on, Petra. I think this is worth considering."

Petra knew that amount of money would pique the interest of his new business partner. He stopped and looked Facilix in the eyes. "You're not actually considering this bullshit?"

Facilix did not reply. The distant look in his squinting eyes told Petra he was busy running calculations.

Tiberius suddenly stood up. "Well you can count me out, although I thank you for the very generous offer. My upside in this deal is only one hundred fifty thousand sesterces. I'm afraid that's not enough for me to put my best venator on the line. And, going up against twenty lions, I'm afraid the odds just wouldn't be in my favor." He looked at Facilix, who still seemed to be running calculations in his head. "But I don't know . . . If I had four hundred thousand hanging in the balance like you do, Facilix, I'd certainly be considering this deal." Tiberius brushed past Petra with a smirk and left the podium.

Facilix looked at Julia and counteroffered. "I'll provide one hunter for one hundred fifty thousand sesterces, plus fifty thousand extra if the hunter is killed. Of course, by himself, he goes up against ten lions, not twenty. And we're paid three hundred thousand extra if Taurus dies."

Before Julia could respond, Petra dove at Facilix and grabbed the front of his tunic. "Are you insane? You're risking two of our best men on a stupid publicity stunt!"

"Yes, a publicity stunt that could wind up paying us a half-million sesterces! Come off it, Petra. You know damn well that we can buy twenty more good fighters for that kind of money. How much did you pay for Taurus, anyway? I'll bet my soul it wasn't close to the three hundred thousand we'll get if he dies."

Petra released his hold, and the Pompeiian dropped back into his seat. Petra's mind raced. He was not about to say that he had only paid one hundred sesterces to a pair of thieves for Quintus. But he had to talk Facilix out of this decision. Should he tell him the true reason Lucius came up with this bizarre idea? Should he explain that the person sitting in front of him was not really Quintus Honorius Romanus? How would Lucius react if he did? Lucius and Julia held the purse strings. If there was a scandal because of what he said now, the Pompeii ludus would surely not be paid for these games. It would mean a black mark against the new combined school. Then Facilix would probably come after him for the lost revenue. Petra could lose his ownership stake in the ludus. No, he could not risk all this for the sake of a single gladiator, even if that gladiator was Quintus. Petra glared at Lucius and Julia, but spoke to Facilix.

"You'd better start planning how you'll spend the money, Facilix. I have a strong feeling that Taurus will not be leaving the arena alive tomorrow."

The pleasant smile on Lucius's face disappeared. He swallowed hard, then looked at Facilix.

"Your terms are acceptable to me, if they suit my aunt," he said, obviously looking to close the deal before they changed their minds.

"I accept as well," Julia said quickly. "We'll modify your contract when we return to our apartment this evening."

Petra had no choice but to put his faith in Lindani. Only the African's hunting skills could keep his best fighter alive.

Like the other Day One fighters, Quintus was annoyed that he had been roused in the predawn hours just to march in the opening pompa for Day Two of the Challenge. Now, back in the staging area under the amphitheater, he was looking forward to the walk back across the Campus Martius for some relaxation time at the ludus before the journey back to Pompeii.

"We put in our time yesterday and emerged victorious," he said to Lindani. "You'd think they'd let us sleep a bit this morning."

Lindani nodded and walked away. He sat alone on a bench in a side cell. After a moment, Quintus moved across the crowded, dark room and joined

him. A gloomy atmosphere seemed to hang over his friend. Quintus wondered if it was just the musty air in the cell, still ripe with the stink of sweat
and blood from the previous day's action.

"What's wrong with you? You haven't said a word all morning."

"It is nothing. I am worn out from yesterday's hunt." Lindani forced a
smile, but it was easy for Quintus to see it was not one of the African's usual
flashes of cheerfulness.

"You're coming back with me this afternoon to cheer Amazonia from the
tunnel, right?"

"Of course," Lindani answered, then turned away.

Before Quintus could press him further, the arena manager's voice
boomed.

"All Day One fighters and hunters, line up for the walk back to the ludus.
Now!"

Quintus stood and joined the line that filed out. As he reached the manager, the gruff overseer dropped the long leather handle of his whip.

"Not you. You're staying put," the manager said.

"What? Why?" Quintus asked.

"Your lanista will be down to talk to you. Take a seat with your friend in
the cell."

Quintus had assumed Lindani was in line behind him but instead found
him still seated alone on the wooden bench. He had never left it to line up.
Quintus returned to the cell and hovered over his friend. "What's going on,
Lindani? You know something."

There was no response from the venator.

Amazonia passed by the bars of the holding cell as she was changing from
her parade costume to her fighting armor. She stopped when she saw the two
occupants. "What are you two still doing here? You don't trust the Day Two
fighters to win this thing?"

"We'd love to leave you to it, but they won't let us go," Quintus said. He
studied Lindani's impassive face as the hunter sat quietly. "It seems our
friend here suspects something, but he's not talking. He's been like this all
morning. It's like his animal senses are telling him something."

He left Amazonia to her preparations and joined Lindani on the bench. After a short time he heard Petra's voice asking for them. As soon as the lanista appeared in the doorway, he could tell something was terribly wrong.

"I have news, and you're not going to like it." Over the next few minutes, Petra laid out their impossible task for the afternoon.

"Tied to a post! Ten lions! *What kind of bullshit is this?*" Quintus was furious.

"This is suicide, Dominus," Amazonia protested, standing in the doorway.

Quintus paced the cell. "Don't you see, this is just Lucius trying to get rid of me again to protect his little fantasy world? And now he's dragging Lindani into it."

As he said his friend's name, he stopped pacing and looked across the cell. Lindani slowly raised his eyes to Quintus.

"You knew about this," Quintus whispered. *"You knew about this!"* he yelled as he sprang toward the bench. Petra and Amazonia grabbed his arms before his sizeable fists reached Lindani. "You didn't tell me, you bastard! How did you know about this?"

"I told him!" Petra yelled as he struggled to hold Quintus back. "I felt he needed the time to prepare, so I told him last night. He's your only hope for survival."

The look in Lindani's eyes melted Quintus's rage. The African's voice came softly. "What difference if you had known last night or right now? At least you had a few more hours of peace. There is nothing you can do to challenge the Fates."

Knowing this benevolent, unassuming man would probably not see another sunrise because of Lucius's twisted plans, Quintus once again turned his wrath toward Petra. "You're going to let that bastard get away with this? This is nothing but a plot to kill me! And in doing it, he's probably going to kill Lindani, too!"

"Don't you think I realize that?" Petra fired back as he pushed Quintus onto the bench. He looked around and lowered his voice. "How can I explain such a ludicrous story to my new partner? And if I did, do you really think we'd be paid for these games after causing the editor so much trouble? What happens to our ludus then? Facilix is already counting all the extra money the scheming bastard is throwing at us to make this happen. I had no choice."

"Yes, but Dominus—" Amazonia began, but Petra cut her off.

"Look, like it or not, you are all my property to do with as I see fit. Now you'll do as I say or you'll feel the whip."

Even as the harsh statement left the lanista's mouth, Quintus knew he did not mean a word of what he said. Petra looked down at the cold, stone floor.

"Look, Quintus, you'll have the best venator in the Empire at your side," he said in a low voice. "I don't agree that it's suicidal. I think you two can do this."

"Well, there's not much I'll be doing tied to a fucking post."

Petra did not make eye contact with him. "I'm sorry. May Hercules be with you." He walked out the cell door. There was silence in the room.

"So have you used the extra time to figure this out?" Quintus finally asked Lindani. Quintus could not tell if the young African was in a state of shock or already mentally rehearsing every shot he would fire at the lions. He hoped it was the latter, for both their sakes.

"When I was a child in my village in Ethiopia, the Axum chief recognized that I was the chosen one. I had the gift. I knew the animals. He told me that someday this power would lead me to good. When I was arrested during the Roman hunt, I thought he was wrong. The power only led to evil and suffering. But now I know the Axum chief was right. This is the day that the power will lead me to good. I have closed my eyes and watched the cats many times in my mind since last night. I have devised a plan of attack, and a second to bolster the first." Lindani looked up at Quintus. "I swear to you, my friend, by all the gods in both our heavens, that I will not let you die today." There was a passion in his eyes that Quintus had never seen before. It should have brought him comfort, but deep inside Quintus knew that Lucius would not allow him to escape the arena alive.

"I accept your pledge, my friend, and I thank you with all my spirit. But let me say this: Should the beasts disagree with your pledge, do not feel guilt or shame or remorse. I know that you will have done everything in your power to try to save me. You may not realize it, but you *are* only human."

Lindani gave his friend a broad smile. "That is not what my elders told me. We shall see."

XXXIII

April AD 67

THE MORNING HUNTS were well under way, but on the podium, Lucius's mind was elsewhere. Now that the plan was in place to rid himself of Quintus, he was able to settle down. He looked at the empty seats where Senator Nerva and his wife had sat on the previous day. He realized what a blunder he had made in snapping at them in his rage. The point of the games was to advance his political stature, not destroy it. He wondered how long this wound would take to heal. Julia's distant voice broke the spell and answered his question.

"Oh, I'm so glad you're here. We were beginning to worry. Quintus . . . Publius and Drusilla are here."

Lucius rose quickly and hugged Drusilla. He clasped forearms with Publius as the Senator cleared his throat before he spoke.

"Yes, well, Drusilla and I weren't sure if you wanted us here today. After yesterday . . . "

"I'm so sorry about that episode," Lucius said with as much sincerity as he could muster. "I'm afraid I was just not myself yesterday. Perhaps some of the shellfish on the food platters didn't agree with me."

"We were hoping that the two of you would join us after today's games," Julia said. She batted her eyelashes and dropped her voice to a sensual whisper. "We have a most interesting private banquet planned, if you know what I mean."

Lucius watched Drusilla's eyes light up and an impish smile cross her face. "We'll count on it," she said without hesitation. They took their seats as two venatores finished off four large bears they had been battling for almost fifteen minutes.

By the end of the morning hunt program, Rome was still ahead in the standings, but their margin had been cut to only 27 points. Trained monkeys and acrobats provided the crowd with some lighter entertainment during the midday break. Lucius ordered the vellarium roof pulled into place, shading the spectators from the unseasonably fierce heat.

The afternoon pompa brought the gladiator pairings onto the sand. Amazonia was, once again, the center of attention. This was her first appearance in Rome nude. Other than the white padded manica on her right arm and her single golden shin guard, she wore only a tiny triangular metal plate at her groin that had no visible means of support. Lucius unconsciously licked his lips as he watched her play to the audience. The response was overwhelming. A few female gladiators had fought in Rome before, but never looking like this. It was the difference between a musk ox and a supple gazelle.

As Amazonia approached the podium, Lucius heard Julia's voice in his ear. "Now aren't you glad we threw in the extra money for her? Perhaps we should see if she's available for our little party tonight. I'm sure Drusilla would enjoy that."

Lucius looked at the Senator's wife and saw her mouth open ever so slightly as the naked fighter passed. He made a mental note to speak with the lanistae about it.

As the pompa concluded, Lucius nodded to the herald, who announced the first bout. In a moment, the afternoon matches were under way. The quality of the combat was as good the second day as the first. Blood stained the sand as the point tallies increased. By late afternoon, the Pompeiian fighters finally overtook the Roman school by winning a prolonged ten-gladiator bout. As with the Pompeii games, the final few battles would decide the entire Challenge.

The crowd waiting outside for the occasional seat that came free got updates from an urchin who shouted the results of each match over the top wall. Their frustration at missing the final critical bouts while standing in the broiling heat finally boiled over. They stormed the gates and filled the stairs and aisleways of the entire cavea. Lucius discussed the situation with the guards, who advised him that it was safer to have an overcrowded arena than a riot on his hands. He agreed and allowed the gate-crashers to stay.

All eyes were focused on the arena as the pressure of the close point tally, combined with the almost unbearable heat, pushed the last few fighters to the breaking point. While the fabric roof provided shade from the sun, it also acted as a pot lid, trapping the body heat and steaming stench of the dangerously overcrowded cavea. The foul odor mingled with the reek of offal and guts, which were ineffectually raked under the surface of the sand after each bout. Every spectator in the choice patrician seats near the arena wall had their perfumed handkerchiefs in hand to mop the sweat and mask the vile smells.

But on the podium, Lucius had become too keyed up to notice any of it. The final bout featuring a naked Amazonia was about to begin, followed by his surprise added attraction, which would rid him of his worries once and for all.

Amazonia stood in the tunnel and watched the current fight on the sand through the latticework of the gate. The fighters' fatigue was evident to her even at a distance. She had seen each of the fighters who were not carried through the Porta Libitensis—the Gate of Death—return to the staging area drained of all energy.

"Be wary of the heat," Quintus said, suddenly standing at her side. "Don't burn yourself out too early. When it gets this bad, you need to pace yourself."

She studied his drawn face for a moment before she spoke. "Why are you concerned about me? With what that bastard is throwing at you and Lindani, you have more important things to think about."

"I'm trying not to." The tone in his voice told her he held little hope of survival.

"Lindani is the best. You know that. If he says you won't die, believe him."

They both looked back down the tunnel to Lindani seated against the far wall. The African's eyes were closed, and there was a look of pure serenity on his young face. Amazonia knew the strength of this man's bond with Quintus, and knew nothing—animal or human—would ever break that bond.

"Believe in him," Amazonia said.

"Don't think about this," Quintus replied as he turned back to the arena battle. "You're up next. Concentrate on your fight."

They were joined at the gate by Amazonia's opponent, a burley Germanic hoplomachus with more hair on his torso than the bears from the morning hunt. He looked down at her and smiled, revealing his four remaining brown teeth.

A scream from the crowd brought her attention back to the sand. The Pompeiian fighter had taken a bad slice to his left leg and dropped. The mob granted him a missio, but the fall put Rome solidly ahead in points. As the praecone announced the tally, Amazonia knew she would not only have to win the fight, but put on an amazing performance. She placed the heavy helmet over her head and secured the strap. Finally, the last two fighters of the day were called forward by the herald.

"Remember the heat," Quintus called out as she marched to arena center.

Her naked body was already dripping with sweat as she lined up to face the German. She heard Julianus whisper the same warning to her.

"I know, I know. Let's get going."

She shifted from side to side, waiting for the signal. Her mind alternated between thoughts of Lindani and Quintus, and her strategy for the fight. Her opponent was armed with a thrusting lance, a weapon she had sparred against only a few times. Behind his small, bowl-shaped parma she saw the point of a dagger, his secondary weapon. She studied the tip of the spear as it swung lazily above the sand. She noticed he did not wear any manica padding on his arm, apparently his way of telling the crowd he was not concerned about strikes from a female opponent.

"Attack!" shouted Julianus. She had not heard the order to be on guard and was taken by surprise.

Her opponent lunged first. His spear tip glanced off the top of her scutum and punctured her left shoulder. The audience cheered what they saw as a quick final victory for the Imperial ludus. But the sting of the sweat flowing into her wound provided a constant reminder not to let her guard down again. The next two thrusts from the lance landed harmlessly on her shield, giving her time to plan her attack. She brought her gladius down hard against the mahogany spear pole, pushing the deadly point toward the sand before she advanced, swinging quickly and accurately. Her sword tip glanced through skin and hair on the German's lance arm, leaving a shallow gash that oozed blood. The barbarian seemed to hardly notice. He stood his ground and lashed back, using the spear tip to both thrust and slice. Amazonia retreated to gain some working distance. She took a deep breath of humid air and launched another attack. She let out a scream and used both her gladius and scutum as offensive weapons, swinging both in swift controlled arcs that put her opponent into retreat. The blistering attack ended with a spin kick to the head. But the Roman trainer had done his research and warned his fighter to expect the move. The German ducked and Amazonia's foot flew harmlessly past his helmet. She came full circle and was surprised to see the barbarian already in mid-thrust with another lance attack. Sheltering her body behind the large red scutum, she parried each jab effectively. As his attack began to falter, she again filled her lungs with the steamy air and went on the offensive. This time her kick was delivered low, and she connected hard against the German's left leg. He staggered but kept his feet. She spun a second time and hit her original target, smashing the bottom of her foot into the side of his helmet. Again the German wavered but remained standing. She was stupefied. She had never seen an opponent withstand two powerful spin kicks and simply shake it off. Her frustration turned to rage and a wailing banshee cry filled the arena. The crowd responded. She began pounding away at the hairy barbarian. Her gladius met his parma again and again as she advanced on him. She struck at his knees with the bottom of her scutum. She spun again and landed a kick to his right shoulder. She continued to press hard, taking shot after shot with sword and shield. But the German never faltered; he simply continued to parry effectively and give ground.

Mixed somewhere between the crowd noise and her own labored breaths echoing inside her helmet, she heard Julianus's voice. "Slow down! You're draining yourself!" he yelled. But by then it was too late. The inside of her metal helmet suddenly felt like a bread oven. Her head began swimming with the effects of heat stroke. She began to panic. The German seemed to sense it and made his move. His mild defensive parries turned into a solid counterattack that stopped her in her tracks. He advanced on her, jabbing hard with the lance. Her arms were growing weak and, combined with the shoulder wound, she could barely hold up her scutum any longer. He jabbed at her face to force her to keep the heavy shield raised. Then he unexpectedly dropped the lance tip low. Her reaction was slow. Too slow. The deadly point pierced deep into her left thigh. She screamed and fell backward. In a second the German's repulsive body was straddling hers. He tossed his lance aside and drew the dagger from behind his shield. Before Amazonia could react, the tip of the thin blade was at her throat.

Julianus grabbed the German's wrist before the barbarian pronounced a death sentence of his own. Amazonia was frozen with fear. The point of the dagger felt like ice against the burning skin of her neck. Sweat stung her eyes, which were locked open in sheer terror. She could hear the echo of her heart beating inside the steaming helmet. She knew she was about to die.

Through her visor she saw Julianus look up toward the mob. Between the vertigo caused by the heatstroke and her wildly racing heart, she suddenly felt everything around her slow to a dreamlike pace. She looked over Julianus's shoulder to the cavea section above her. White handkerchiefs fluttered in slow motion, mixed with thumbs pointed downward. She twisted her neck to look toward the podium, the dagger point cutting the skin under her chin as she turned. Her eyes settled on Lucius. She watched his head move ever so slowly as he scanned the mob, milking the final judgment for every second of drama possible. She wanted to throw her sword at him. *Get on with it, you gutless bastard,* she thought. *If I'm to die here, then let it happen.*

Lucius's arm suddenly sprang forward waving a white cloth.

"Missio!" yelled Julianus, louder than usual.

The roar of the crowd wrenched her from her daze. She realized her opponent's grimy free hand had been groping her bare breasts as she lay under him. Julianus roughly yanked the barbarian's arm, forcing him off her. The German pranced away, accepting the adoration of the hometown crowd.

Julianus tried to help Amazonia to her feet. But her dizziness had subsided and was now replaced by rage. She roughly shrugged off her trainer's support, removed her helmet and threw it hard against the arena wall. She watched the German strut around the sand, basking in the victory cheers. He had won the day for Rome. But what infuriated her was that she had allowed him to do it with cunning rather than strength. While he conserved his energy in the stifling heat, he had successfully drawn her into a fury that sapped her strength by the second. It was a hard lesson she would not forget.

She limped toward the gate and saw Quintus watching her. His face showed relief, but she continued to feel only frustration and anger.

"Don't worry about it," he said with a wink. "You're alive to fight another day. That's all that matters."

Amazonia pushed past him and dropped onto a bench in the tunnel. The ludus physician arrived instantly with a bronze needle, flax sutures, and his crushed cabbage-and-egg-white liniment. She felt the sting of his needle piercing her flesh—a just penance, she thought, for her stupidity.

Two guards rushed past her bench and flanked Quintus, each grabbing a muscular arm. She suddenly remembered Quintus's fate and cursed herself yet again for allowing her blind rage to cloud reality. She was about to speak, but the gate opened and in an instant he was gone.

Lucius's heart pounded heavily in his chest, not for the dramatic victory of the German barbarian, but for the secret event still to come. The praecone standing beside the podium waved his arms and shouted the final tally: "With a score of 989 to 981, Rome wins the Challenge!" The thunderous cheering seemed to rattle the arena. Lucius was in his glory, waving and bowing to the euphoric crowd, Julia at his side. He took a quick moment to throw the German fighter his prize purse and round laurel, then returned his attention to the mob. He knew he had accomplished his political goal with the games when many of the dignitaries made it a point to animatedly congratulate him, more to be seen with him by the jubilant masses than as a genuine compliment. Senator Nerva and Drusilla were among the first in line. But Lucius had other thoughts on his mind.

He noticed some in the crowd were beginning to move toward the exit tunnels. He quickly nodded to the praecone, and the herald called to the crowd.

"Gentlemen, ladies, guests from Pompeii, and fellow Romans . . . Our generous editor and his special guests invite you to remain in the amphitheater for an extraordinary final event."

Those spectators who had seats, reclaimed them. The remainder of the overflow crowd sat once again in the stairways and aisles. Workers rolled back the vellarium, finally releasing the heat and stench, and bringing a welcome breath of fresh air back to the amphitheater. An expectant quiet fell across the arena. Lucius stood to take over the announcements himself.

"In honor of Rome's spectacular victory in the great Challenge, I have prepared a special treat for all of you." He looked toward the orchestra, which struck up a refrain of the exciting hunt theme. A service gate opened and one of the towering boulders that had been used in the morning hunts was dragged back onto the sand. A single bare tree trunk had been added to the pinnacle of the rock three meters above the arena floor. As the boulder reached the center of the ring, Lucius nodded to the arena manager standing at the main gate.

The wooden barrier rose and, flanked by two guards, Quintus entered the arena. As soon as the crowd recognized the stigmates, a deafening roar erupted from the cavea. But the gladiator's entrance was much different from his previous appearances. Gone were the flamboyant flexing and dramatic demonstrations of his *wushu* exercises. Instead he looked defeated, his face cast down toward the sand as he walked. The cheering subsided and was replaced by a curious murmur.

"As you can see, the great Taurus joins us again." Lucius's voice boomed. He paused and savored the anticipation of what he was about to witness. "But today things will be different. Today his life will not be in his own hands, but in the hands of the best venator in the Empire. I give you the astounding . . . Lindani!"

The crowd sprang to life once again as the African stepped through the portal, his golden-yellow robe billowing in the late-afternoon breeze. He held a thick hunting spear in his right hand and a bow in his left. The leather quiver slung over his shoulder was packed with twenty arrows. Petra had petitioned for more, but Lucius ordered no more than two per lion. Lindani crossed the sand and stood quietly next to Quintus, his dejected attitude also beginning to perplex the crowd. Lucius continued his vigorous presentation. "Today this great hunter will hold the fate of this conquering gladiator in his hands. It is the ultimate test of skill. Should the hunter lose his battle, then Pompeii shall also lose its top fighter."

Rather than the wild applause Lucius expected, the murmurs and mumbling grew louder. Everyone on the podium seemed to sense the tension. He overheard the Senator's words to Julia. "I hope he knows what he's doing. The Roman crowds don't like to see a hero who's fought so well sacrificed unnecessarily—even if he is from a provincial ludus."

Lucius was alarmed by the few catcalls that came from the cavea. But he was not about to allow a fickle mob to alter his own fate. He ignored the jeers and nodded curtly to the two guards. They gave Quintus a shove.

Before Quintus moved, he looked at Lindani.

"Remember what I said. No matter what happens, this is not your fault."

Lindani shook his head and repeated his vow. "You will not die today." His white teeth suddenly shone through smiling black lips.

For an instant, Quintus saw a glimmer of hope. "I'm just glad it's you who fight these four-legged beasts and not me."

Lindani's smile broadened. "And how many times must I tell you, it is not the number of legs that is the concern, it is the number of teeth."

"The gods be with you, my friend." Quintus turned and walked toward the back of the boulder. Once again, as he had in the tunnel, he searched inside for the inspiration to convert himself to Taurus. But it was not there. He was about to be placed in a deadly position where he would have no control over his own destiny. It was a situation he detested. He glanced at Lucius, smiling from the podium. It was the same sneer he had seen on the bastard's face as Quintus cleaned the horse stables at his uncle's villa.

The guards followed him up a craggy area in the rock surface and pulled him against the tree trunk. As they bound his wrists with heavy rope, the jeers and whistles from the mob grew louder. The workers finished their tasks and left Lindani and Quintus alone in the arena.

Quintus stared at Lucius. Perched atop the boulder, he was almost eye level with his adversary on the podium. "You think this will end it, Lucius?" he called across the opening. "This is only the beginning." Lucius's smirk quickly disappeared.

"Bring on the beasts!" Lucius screamed, then dropped into his chair.

The hunt music once again poured from the orchestra. From the gate below the podium Quintus saw flashes of beige and white as ten immense female lions fought to get through the portal. Screams came from the crowd as cat after cat entered the arena. Quintus thought he had mentally prepared for this moment, but the size and speed of the lions sent a shock through his system. With sudden terror he realized he was not behind the safety of a wooden gate for this hunt. There was nothing between him and these ten man-eaters. Nothing except a single African hunter. As the cats spread out, his eyes flashed to Lindani. What he saw startled him even more than the lions.

Lindani stood perfectly still. His eyes were closed. Quintus shouted to him but could not break the trance. He struggled against the ropes but, even with his potent strength, the bonds held fast. He looked again at Lindani, praying silently for the African to open his eyes and fight.

Lindani's tall thin form wavered slightly, first to the right, then the left. He felt the Axum spirit enter his body. Suddenly, as if pushed over, he broke into a rapid sprint. He ran parallel to a group of four lions, easily keeping pace with them as they hugged the arena wall. His spear sprang from his hand with a lightning-fast flick of the wrist, and the first lion plowed into the sand, dead. Before the cat hit the floor, Lindani had his bow at the ready with an arrow set in place. Without losing a step he began unleashing a torrent of arrows. The second and third lions dropped together. The fourth continued on with two arrows imbedded in its right side, blood streaming down its beige fur. It ran for another ten meters than stopped in its tracks and reversed direction, looking unsuccessfully to escape its assailant. With his animal-like reflexes, Lindani stopped at precisely the same instant and followed the cat back to the left, never allowing an extra meter to grow between them. A third arrow finally dropped the cat back near its three companions. Lindani kept up the blistering pace, his eyes scouring the arena for the six remaining lions. A shout from Quintus caught his attention. Two of the animals were attempting to leap up the smooth front face of the boulder. One succeeded.

Quintus saw the lion grow in his field of vision as it clawed its way over the rounded edge on the front of the boulder. Once it got all four legs under it, the lion charged. Quintus tightened his arms against the rough wood of the tree trunk to support his weight. As the cat leaped he brought both legs up high and kicked. His bare feet caught the lion in the chest and sent it hurtling back over the edge. Before it hit the sand, the animal had one of Lindani's arrows imbedded in its head. The jolt against Quintus's legs felt like a hammer blow against the bottom of his feet. A loud scream from the audience, mixed with a caustic growl from behind him, took his mind off the numbing pain. One of the deadly cats had found the easier path up the back side of the boulder. Quintus could see Lindani was preoccupied with another lion trying to come up the front. In seconds, he felt the cat's hot breath behind him against his hands, then a swipe of its powerful claw against his forearm. He instinctively spun his body, painfully grinding the Gorgon on his back against the coarse tree trunk. But the move only managed to bring his left arm closer to the lion. The animal raised up on its hind legs and sank its canines into Quintus's powerful bicep. His howl of pain must have gotten Lindani's attention, for Quintus felt the breeze of an arrow pass his face and heard it slam into the lion's neck. The beast tried to roar in defiance, but a wet gurgling sound was all that emerged. The cat's reaction freed Quintus's arm from its jaws, leaving four deep puncture wounds. A second and third arrow followed a split-second apart, and the lion finally fell dead at the base of the tree.

Seeing the large cat drop at Quintus's feet, Lindani turned his attention back to the menace in front of him. Even after the third arrow, the fierce animal refused to die. He reached to draw a fourth from the quiver and his fingertips verified what he already knew. He only had two arrows left. He fired one of them into the brain of the stubborn beast before him. It finally dropped into the sand, blood flowing from the wound in its head. He nocked the last arrow and glanced up at Quintus. None of the three remaining lions were on the rock with him.

Lindani's senses tingled. There was danger behind him. He glanced over his shoulder and saw one of the lions charging him from behind. He knew this probably meant the other two were lying in wait. He had witnessed the tactic often with lions on the Ethiopian plains. If he ran in the direction the cat was chasing him he would be herded like a dumb zebra into the kill zone. He had already made one mistake with the lions the day before. He was not about to make another.

He sprinted away from the boulder, concerned about leaving Quintus temporarily unprotected, but a move necessary for his own survival. He circled wide and spotted the other two cats at the backside of the boulder waiting to ambush him. Both heads snapped around as they realized their prey had not cooperated. They turned and charged across the arena toward him.

Lindani saw the dreadful situation all too clearly. He stood with one arrow loaded, none in his quiver, and three lions charging him from two different directions. The closer the lions came, the louder the mob screamed. Lindani's mind calculated his options. There were not many. It was time to execute his back-up plan. He raised his bow and drew back the arrow. He aimed at none of the charging beasts.

As the arrow's intended direction of flight became obvious throughout the amphitheater, a cacophony of noise assaulted Lindani's ears. A massive wail erupted from the mob. He clearly heard Petra's raspy voice among the throng. He heard Amazonia scream from the tunnel. He heard Lucius's voice cry out with lust, "Yes! Yes! Do it!" *It is not what you think,* he wanted to scream back at them. But he was too busy zeroing the point of his arrow on Quintus's back.

XXXIV

April AD 67

AMAZONIA COULD FEEL the tension rising in the amphitheater as the growing crowd noise traveled down the tunnel. She roughly pushed the physician away as he applied his ointment to her freshly sutured thigh and ran up the tunnel. The scene that revealed itself through the wooden grating defied description. Lindani had his bow pulled tight, the arrow tip aimed squarely at Quintus tied to the tree on the boulder. Totally helpless behind the gate, she could only scream.

Quintus saw the panic on the faces in the cavea. He saw Lucius's eyes widen with delight as he screamed. What he could not see was Lindani and the remaining lions behind him. A low branch prevented him from sliding around the tree. He suddenly heard Lindani's voice carry over the roar of the crowd and lions.

"Do not move!"

Quintus knew better than to question his friend. Although he could not see what was happening, he followed Lindani's instructions explicitly. He froze. He did not blink. He did not breathe.

As the arrow left the bow, the screams in the cavea startled Quintus, but he forced himself not to flinch. It took two full seconds for the arrow to travel the 35 meters to its mark. Quintus felt the metal tip of the arrow strike. His hands suddenly fell to his sides. He was free. Lindani's shot had split the rope that bound him to the tree. A roar unlike any heard in Rome shattered the sky above the arena. The entire cavea, including Lucius, was on its feet.

Quintus spun full around in time to see one of the cats pounce on Lindani.

In a second, Quintus leaped from the high boulder. As he fell, he felt the warrior spirit surge inside him. He knew exactly what he needed to do. His fate was back in his hands. He visualized three dead lions at his feet. Before he struck the sand, he had become Taurus.

He let out a fierce growl that startled the two lions charging from behind the boulder, forcing them to change direction. He sprinted across the sand toward the tangle of beast and hunter. The lion was fighting to get its jaws onto Lindani's neck. The young African's hands were covered in blood as they held tightly to the cat's jowls, depriving the beast of its target for a few critical seconds. Taurus leaped on the animal's back, knocking the wind from Lindani. He reached over the lion's head and grasped its muzzle in his right hand and the skin under its chin in his left. There was no question in Taurus's mind who was stronger, he or the lion. He felt the strength of Hercules in his arms. Holding firm, he engaged every muscle in his body to pull the beast back and increase the distance between Lindani's face and the lion's fangs. But as the lion was wrenched backward, it struck out with its powerful claws. Its right paw connected hard with the side of Lindani's head. The sickening sound was like a thick pole hitting a melon. Over the lion's shoulder, Taurus saw Lindani's head snap to the side. Then the hunter laid motionless.

Taurus slipped his left arm around the lion's neck. He yanked the muzzle hard to the right and heard the cat's neck bones snap. He released the head and the beast fell to the floor, its tongue flopping grotesquely into the sand. He looked at Lindani, but the hunter was as still as the dead lion next to him. Taurus's mind began to contemplate the worst scenario imaginable. But before he could reach out to touch his friend, a scream from the crowd reminded him there were still two more lions to deal with.

He spun and saw that both cats had resumed their charge. Looking frantically for a weapon, he quickly realized his only protection in the entire amphitheater was the hunting spear embedded in a carcass across the arena. He took off running but sensed it was a wasted effort. The spear was behind the two remaining lions. How could he possibly outmaneuver the two agile beasts? He ran toward the arena wall. If nothing else, he could try to draw them away from Lindani's body. But out of the corner of his eye, the blur of another person dashing across the arena gave him renewed hope. He heard a voice yell to him.

"I've got it! I'm closer!"

Amazonia saw the lion's paw strike Lindani's head from her position at the tunnel entrance. Her heart sank. She knew Quintus would be devastated if his closest friend was killed by these beasts. In amazement, she watched Quintus snap the lion's neck with his bare hands. She knew that kind of strength could only have come from Taurus.

Her eyes flicked back to the two remaining lions just as they sprang from their crouched position into a full-tilt charge. Her feeling of helplessness was overwhelming. She could no longer stand behind the safety of a wooden gate while Taurus and Lindani were torn to pieces at the whim of a madman. Something had to be done.

"Open the gate!" she screamed at the burley attendant standing next to the wheel that raised and lowered the portcullis-style grating.

The man laughed at her. "With two lions loose out there! You must be crazy."

She grabbed a gladius from the weapons box beside the doorway. She considered running the fat worker through with it but did not have the time. She tossed the sword on the floor, then dropped to her knees and tugged at the heavy gate. The fresh stitches in her thigh ripped open as her muscles strained to lift the wooden grating. It finally rose just high enough for her to drop and roll under it, grabbing the gladius as she went. Her naked body became clothed in a thin layer of damp sand, except for where the blood flowed freely down her left leg.

Quickly assessing Quintus's intentions, she sprinted toward the hunting spear protruding from the dead lion. It was only ten meters from the tunnel entrance.

"I've got it! I'm closer!" she yelled. But her voice attracted more than Quintus's attention. One of the lions split off from its charge toward Quintus and came at her.

"Be careful!" Quintus yelled.

She was at the spear in seconds. She pulled hard at the stout wooden handle, and the weapon popped free of the carrion. Behind her she could hear the thundering feet of the lion even above the rising screams from the crowd. But her first concern was to get a weapon to Taurus. Taking on a lion barehanded from behind was miraculous, but head-on would be suicidal. She looked to her left and saw him zigzagging toward the boulder, trying to outmaneuver the enraged beast.

"Take the spear!" she yelled as she blindly hurled the pike in Taurus's direction, hoping it landed within reach. The momentum of the toss spun her around until she faced the charging lion. She was shocked to see that the cat was in midair, hurtling straight at her. She flipped her gladius from her left hand to the right as she dropped to the sand. The lion could not correct its path of flight and overshot its victim. As it flew above her, she slashed at its underbelly. The frightening scream and sudden gush of blood as it landed near the wall told her the sword had found its mark.

But the wound was not severe enough to drop the beast. It spun in the sand and growled at her, close enough for the hot, reeking breath to blow back her auburn hair. She jumped up and prepared for a second attack that, thankfully, did not come. The lion sprinted off along the arena wall.

"Protect Lindani!" Taurus yelled.

She was relieved to see the hunting spear in Taurus's hand, its sharp point keeping the second lion at bay. She ran across the sand to where Lindani lay and carefully cradled the hunter's bleeding head on her good thigh. There was no reaction from the African.

The lion approaching Taurus swatted at the hunting spear and growled in frustration. Taurus's attention was split between the menace in front of him and the one he knew was somewhere behind. He glanced toward the large boulder in the middle of the arena floor. If he could back up to that, it would afford at least some protection against a rear attack. He worked his way slowly toward the rocks, glancing over his shoulder to be sure the pathway was clear. The screams of the crowd told him something was happening. He continued to glance around him, retreating more quickly toward the rocks. The beast in front of him grew more bold and tried to charge past the spear. But Taurus's reflexes were as good with an animal as with a human opponent. The spear tip was already in place as the animal charged and the point pierced the lion's shoulder.

He glanced back and could see he was almost at the boulder. His back would soon be protected. But the rising screams from the cavea told him something was still not right. From the corner of his eye, he could see Amazonia jump up thirty meters away waving her gladius.

"Above you!" she yelled, cupping her hands to her mouth. "It's up on the rock!"

He glanced up in time to see the second lion snarl at him from the top of the boulder two meters above. Its four long canines gleamed in the afternoon light. What he did not see was the paw of the first lion in front of him, which lashed out the moment he looked away. The claws caught him on the side of his leg, and he went down. The crowd and Amazonia screamed in unison. Taurus caught his breath as the lion on the sand charged. He tried to get the flailing spear to cooperate, but it seemed an eternity before the sharp tip was pointed once again in the right direction. The beast's charge was a blur of beige fur and white teeth. But the spear became a blur of mahogany. It dropped into place in time to pierce the lion's chest. The cat reared back with a howl. It pulled itself free of the spear and ran off.

Still on his back, Taurus had a perfect view of the second lion as it crouched to launch itself off the boulder. Rolling away was not an option. The cat would be on his back in a second. With an intimidating roar, the lion leaped. But rather than seeing the gleaming canines falling at him with the speed of an arrow, another image suddenly appeared in Taurus's mind. He saw Lindani in battle with the bears in the Aquae Sulis arena. He realized that the African hunter's final move in that battle was what would save him now. He jerked the bloody spear tip up to a vertical position and braced for the impact. The lion landed on him with a scream. But the spear did its work. The metal tip punctured the belly of the beast and exited its back just below the shoulder blade. The rear legs, dangling just centimeters above Taurus's face, jerked in spasm. A torrent of warm blood ran down the thick pole and covered Taurus's hands, arms, and chest. He pulled the pole to the left and the lion toppled into the sand.

Taurus stood and let out a howl of pent-up nerves and adrenaline. The crowd was in a frenzy. He looked up into the eyes of Lucius. The look on the cowardly bastard's face was a mixture of awe and rage. Taurus envisioned climbing the podium wall and strangling him in front of thousands of spectators. But a sudden rise in the screams of those spectators slapped him back to reality. The last lion! He had forgotten there was still another beast to deal with. He spun in time to see the giant cat charging Amazonia.

He grabbed the spear that protruded from both sides of the dead cat at his feet. But even with the extraordinary strength in his two massive arms, the stubborn animal refused to relinquish the weapon easily. A high-pitched scream radiated across the arena floor. Taurus had heard it before. It was the banshee cry of Amazonia.

The naked female warrior stood guard over Lindani's inert body. She watched the lion carefully as it approached. The white fur of its chest was stained red with a ribbon of fresh blood. The wound only seemed to enrage the animal, its movements now swift and jerky, its ferocious roar coming more frequently. Without prelude, the lion charged. Amazonia tightened her grip on the gladius. As the beast launched from the sand, she began the swift spin that had become her trademark. Her scream of power and rage filled the amphitheater. Rather than connecting with her foot, she used the momentum to bury her sword up to its hilt in the lion's flank as it flew past her.

The animal hit the sand next to Lindani then, remarkably, sprang up and resumed the attack. Although stunned at the cat's resilience, Amazonia's survival instincts took over. She dove for the hilt of the gladius that projected from the animal's flank. The cat growled and sprinted off before she could touch the weapon. Circling around, the lion prepared for another charge. Amazonia stood and placed herself between the lion and Lindani's body.

"It's not going to happen, baby," she purred at the cat. "If I have to strangle you with my bare hands, so be it. But you're not getting any closer to this man."

She and the lion faced off. Amazonia hunched and shifted her weight side to side. Her muscles strained under the tension, causing the open wound on her thigh to throb. But the pain was the last thing on her mind. Every nerve of her body tingled. The cat growled and crouched.

"Come on, asshole. I'm ready for you," she whispered. Although she held no weapon, there was no doubt in her mind that she would kill this cat. She had to. For Quintus.

The cat leaped. She extended her hands as if they were her own claws. The rows of dagger-like teeth flew closer. The cat's roar turned to a sudden scream, almost human in its sound. It arched its back and twisted its head. The noise in the amphitheater became deafening. Then the cat fell at her feet, a mahogany hunting spear wobbling in its back. Even in its death throes, the lion grabbed for her leg. She jerked the gladius out of its flank and drove the wide blade into the cat's neck. Finally, the beast gave up its spirit. Amazonia looked up to see Taurus approaching.

"I could have taken him," she said over the frenzy of the mob. She hoped her bravado masked her relief. As Taurus stepped next to her, she watched the manic look dissipate in his eyes and his heaving chest settle to controlled breathing. As often as she had seen it, the transformations between Taurus and Quintus always intrigued her.

Quintus smiled. "Sorry to steal your moment of glory. Just didn't want any more marks on that stunning body of yours."

As he spoke, she saw that his attention was focused behind her. The look of concern and compassion in his eyes tore at her heart. He passed her and knelt beside Lindani.

The African's eyes remained closed, but his lips began to move. His voice came weakly. "The lion is no match for the claws of Amazonia, no?"

Quintus let out a short laugh, mixed with a heavy sigh of relief. Amazonia knelt alongside him, and they sat Lindani up slowly. "You saw all that?" she asked.

Lindani's eyes fluttered open and he pressed his hand to the side of his head. Blood trickled between his fingers. Quintus ripped a length of woolen material from his red subligaculum and wrapped it around the hunter's head.

"I saw enough to know you were very foolish." Lindani looked up at Amazonia. The benevolence in his eyes was much different than the harsh, suspicious look he had given her during the sea voyage to Italia some months back. "Why do you take on a lion to save a skinny hunter who has treated you unfairly?"

Amazonia smiled. "Because I realized the skinny hunter was just protecting his friend the best way he knew how. Anybody with that kind of loyalty deserves better than getting gnawed on by a damn cat."

Lindani's teeth showed brightly and he began to cackle, until the pain in his head caused him to wince. Quintus and Amazonia bent over to lift him from the arena floor and carry him back to the staging area.

"No," he said quietly. "Allow me to walk from the arena. I can do it."

Amazonia smiled at Quintus, and they helped Lindani to his feet. Although obviously in agony, the African hunter walked proudly between his two friends. As they traveled the length of the arena, Quintus looked up into the cavea and saw only jubilant, adoring faces. The intensity of the cheering had not diminished.

"The home ludus may have won the games," he said, "but it appears we have won the crowd."

As they reached the gate, they raised their arms once more in salute to the Roman crowd. The response was thunderous. Quintus looked toward the podium to toss Lucius one last victorious smile. But the two seats on the royal riser were empty. Lucius and Julia had left the games.

XXXV

April AD 67

THERE WAS PANDEMONIUM deep under the cavea as Lucius ran wildly through the animal holding area. The arena manager, chief animal handler, and Julia were having a hard time keeping up with him as he wound through the dark labyrinth of cages. His manic shouting echoed against the mossy stone walls and barely carried over the muffled cheers from the amphitheater above.

"By the gods, if you don't send another beast into that arena you'll be fed to your own animals in the next games! Do you hear me?" He violently rattled the bars on one of the empty cages to make his point.

"I've told you we have no more animals to send," the handler said. "We have nothing left."

Lucius was livid and looked for something to throw. He lifted a piece of chain from the floor and flung it against another empty cage with a high-pitched scream. He ran frantically to the adjoining cellar to see for himself.

"Liar! What are those then?" Lucius hollered, pointing to three black bulls standing in a corner cage. The huge animals had an unusual crop of curled hair between their long horns. Painted markings adorned their faces and flanks. Lucius's yelling was making the animals nervous. They began pacing and spinning in their cramped cell.

"Sir! Not those!" the manager pleaded. "They are to be sacrificed to Pluto next week."

"Not anymore. Now they will be used in this arena to gore the great *Taurus*." He drew out the name like a whining child. The bulls snorted loudly and began smacking their long horns into the metal bars of the cage.

"I cannot do that," the manager said stubbornly. "It will invite the wrath of the underworld gods." He motioned to his assistant to fetch the guards.

"Fine," Lucius screamed, "then I shall do it myself."

"Quintus! Stop this now!" Julia demanded. Lucius roughly pushed past her. He reached through the bars, pulled the metal pin from a gate and swung the cage door open.

"No!" the arena manager yelled, hysteria rising in his voice. "You idiot, that's the wrong gate!"

The bulls were now in a full state of panic. The open gate provided a welcome escape path. Before Lucius could correct his mistake, the bulls burst through the doorway and into the corridor used by the handlers. Julia screamed in terror. She, Lucius, and the manager pressed against the bars as the powerful animals dashed past them. Had Lucius opened the left gate instead of the right, he would have sent the animals toward the arena. But now the three bulls were headed into the corridors used by the animal handlers, who were already scattering, trying to outrun the beasts in the narrow hallways. Lucius heard the screams and shouting grow louder as more and more workers found themselves in the path of the frantic bulls.

The arena manager was in shock. "That corridor leads to a public passageway. You've just sentenced dozens of spectators and workers to death."

Lucius felt he was going mad. In a few moments, his life had gone from glorious to hopeless. He looked at Julia, speechless.

"We'd better get out of here," she said in a voice that demanded obedience.

Amazonia bit down on a piece of wood as the ludus physician peeled back the puncture wound in her leg with his metal hooks. For the second time in a day he had to clean the sand from her wound. Lindani laid on the table next to her, the physician's assistant wrapping clean bandages around his head. From a nearby bench, Quintus watched Amazonia's contorted face and wished he could take the pain on himself. The four holes in his arm, caused by the lion's canines, had already been cleaned and bandaged. Although his bicep still throbbed with pain, he was sure it was nothing close to what Amazonia was feeling.

Without warning, a handful of arena workers burst into the gladiator holding area screaming about bulls. Everyone was puzzled until a few seconds later when a massive black bull charged into the room, throwing benches and tables everywhere. As fast as it appeared, it was gone, vanishing down another hallway to wreak havoc elsewhere in the amphitheater. Screams from the spectators began filtering down the tunnel.

"What's going on?" Quintus yelled to one of the workers.

The exhausted animal handler could barely speak after being chased for three hundred meters through the bowels of the amphitheater. "The editor . . . Romanus . . . let bulls loose . . . tried to get them . . . into the arena."

Quintus looked at Lindani and Amazonia in disbelief. "That bastard just won't give up!" He leaped to his feet.

Agricola, the head physician, was helping Amazonia back onto her table. "Be sure you see to her and Lindani before they call you outside to help the trampled civilians," Quintus said as he ran past.

"Where are you going?" Amazonia yelled.

"I need to pay Lucius a visit."

The rampaging bull had triggered a surge of adrenaline that recharged Quintus. He hustled down the corridor, through a broken door, and out into one of the main spectator entrance tunnels. The cavea was in chaos as tens of thousands of spectators tried to escape the three angry bulls, which had spread out across the amphitheater.

Quintus shoved his way toward the podium area. As he turned the corner, he ran into Petra and Facilix coming the other way.

"Where's Lucius?" Quintus yelled.

"I don't know," answered Petra. "We're looking for him ourselves. He still owes us half our money."

"Who's Lucius?" Facilix asked. "I thought we were looking for Quintus?"

"I'll explain later," Petra said.

The screams in the walkway suddenly became louder. The three men jumped back around the corner as one of the bulls gored and trampled its way past them, its horns saturated with blood.

"After causing all this, I'm sure the coward has left the amphitheater," Quintus said. He could see enlightenment on Petra's face.

"I wondered how these bulls got loose," he said. "They were intended as a surprise for you, weren't they?"

"I'm looking to pay the bastard a little visit right now to discuss that matter."

Petra grinned. "Fine. But we get our money first. How are you going to find him?"

"I know where they live. One of the Roman girls told me the other night at the banquet. They're in the State apartments, not far from here."

Lucius shoved his personal guard aside and burst through the door of their apartment, more frantic than he had been in the animal cells. Julia was right on his heels.

"What are we going to do?" he screamed as he slammed the door behind them. He was seething with rage as he paced the foyer. "This will ruin everything. And he's still alive! After all that, the son of a bitch is still alive!"

"Shut up!" Julia screamed. "Will you please shut up for two minutes and let me think?" Lucius was startled by her anger. But deep inside he was encouraged. Perhaps she would take care of this mess. Yes, perhaps "Aunt Julia" could somehow fix everything. The thought settled him down.

"Maybe we could pay off the arena manager to keep his mouth shut," Julia thought out loud. "Blame the mess on some stupid animal handler or arena slave."

The thought of the arena manager suddenly struck Lucius as funny. As hard as he tried, he could not stifle a small snicker. Julia looked at him, disbelief on her face. For reasons he could not understand, this struck him even funnier, and his snicker turned to a laugh.

"Did you see the look on the manager's face?" he said in between gulps of air.

"You find this funny? Are you out of your fucking mind?"

The more she yelled, the funnier he found their situation. His mad laughter filled the foyer in which they stood.

The sound of the door being kicked in behind them made Julia scream. It swung hard against the wall, tipping over a small table and smashing the black vase that sat on top. Lucius's cackling came to an abrupt halt. He stared in shock at Petra and Facilix standing in the doorway. His guard lay unconscious on the floor behind them. He wondered how the lanistae had tracked him down so quickly.

"I think you owe us some money," Petra said. "Somehow you left without paying us the balance of our fee."

"Perhaps it was in all the confusion with your bulls," Facilix added.

Julia nonchalantly moved to the tablinum, the small office within the apartment. Lucius continued to stare in silence at the two lanistae while she pulled a strongbox from a hidden compartment in the wall behind the desk. She returned with five bulging purses and handed them to Petra. He untied the string on each to check inside.

"There's more than enough gold there to cover your fee," Julia said with an indignant air. "Now get out."

Petra nodded to Facilix. They moved toward the door, and Julia stepped forward to shut it behind them. Petra turned unexpectedly and grabbed her arm. Lucius moved to help her, but Facilix stepped into his path and stared him down. Petra put the tip of his crooked nose up against Julia's.

"Listen, woman. If I ever have the displeasure of doing business with the two of you again, you can be sure it will be on different terms. If any of my people had been killed in that little stunt you pulled, I'd be here with a gladius, and your guts would be on this floor."

Julia seemed shaken but remained defiant. "You've gotten your money, lanista, just as we said. Now leave."

Petra grinned at them both. "I'll leave, but I think there's someone outside who wants to say good-bye."

Lucius followed the two lanistae to the door in order to bolt it. He wanted no more surprise visitors. But as he reached for the metal pin, Quintus stepped from around the doorframe. Lucius let out a squeal as he came face-to-face with the painted head of a Minotaur. Quintus's marked torso, still stained with blood, looked even more intimidating up close than it appeared in the arena.

"Hello, Lucius . . . Aunt Julia." Quintus nodded politely to both of them, but Lucius could clearly see the pent-up rage in Quintus's eyes.

• • •

Quintus watched with amusement as Lucius began to back away from him, his face contorting with tension.

"By the gods, he's here to kill us!" Lucius shouted.

He turned and ran deeper into the large apartment. Quintus was right behind him. Julia chased after them both, screaming for calm. Lucius slammed doors as he ran, trying desperately to slow his pursuer down. Quintus shoved at the bedroom door before it was locked, knocking Lucius to the floor on the other side. He stepped through the doorway and looked down at the man who had turned his life upside-down. He felt the adrenaline rush that signaled his transformation to Taurus, but through clenched teeth he fought to keep his lethal alter ego in check. A quick death for Lucius would be too easy.

"I would have been happy to go my way after yesterday's fight. I just wanted you to know I was still around, that's all. But you had to try to kill me and my innocent friends any way you could." Quintus stepped forward. "You should have let it go, Lucius. I had no intention of making a stink over your little swap job. But now, you've almost killed a good friend of mine, and I can't let that go." He reached for Lucius.

"No, Quintus, don't kill him!" Julia screamed. Lucius whimpered and cowered against the bed. "We can work something out," Julia said. "I'll buy you from the lanista, then let you go. You'll be free."

Quintus turned and looked her in the eye. "You knew about this little charade of his all along."

Julia stared at the floor. "Not at first, but I eventually saw through his story." Her voice reflected a hint of shame, but to Quintus it was just another performance. "I knew you were my nephew," she continued, "but Lucius had aspirations. I knew if we worked together, we'd both get to where we wanted to be in life." She looked up at Quintus. "I didn't mean to hurt you. I can make it right. Sextus and I will get you out of that filthy ludus and set you up with enough money to live the rest of your life in luxury."

Quintus smiled at her in pity. "You just don't get it, my lovely aunt Julia. I *want* to be there. That's my family now. I love my new life . . . " He glanced back at Lucius. " . . . even if it was forced upon me." Lucius curled into a tighter ball as Quintus stepped forward. "But this bastard needs to be taught a lesson."

Quintus lifted a trembling Lucius from the floor by the front of his white tunic. Quintus was surprised to see a grin grow across his enemy's face. Lucius suddenly snickered, then laughed loudly as he hung suspended from Quintus's sizeable arm.

"Go ahead and kill me, Quintus," he screamed. "But I want you to know something first. Your buffoon of a bodyguard . . . Aulus? For a strong man, he was remarkably easy to drown. I only had to twist that broken arm of his a little as I held his head under." Lucius threw his head back in another fit of mad laughter. "He was the most ineffectual bodyguard ever!" He abruptly stopped laughing and looked directly into Quintus's eyes. Quintus could feel his captive's hatred burning into him like a hot iron. "He certainly didn't help protect you from me, did he?"

Quintus's blood raced. The flush of heat that assaulted his face was like a blast from a furnace. He drew back his arm and punched Lucius in the jaw, knocking him unconscious. If he had not held Taurus in check, he knew he would have beaten the bastard to death on the spot. Instead, he tossed the inert body on the bed and pulled both ends of the forest-green bedsheet over him.

"What are you going to do with him?" Julia asked in a panic.

Quintus ignored her. He hoisted the package on his shoulder and walked to the balcony. Without hesitation, he casually threw Lucius over the railing.

Julia's heart stopped as she saw Lucius's body disappear over the railing into the late afternoon light. She ran to the balcony and looked over the edge, fully expecting to see a blood-soaked bedsheet on the pavement of the Roman Forum two stories below. Instead she found a transport cart parked below the balcony. Lucius's wrapped body lay in a thick pile of hay on the rear cargo bed. The African hunter stared up at her from the driver's seat, his head bandaged and his white teeth gleaming like the marble of the surrounding temples.

She looked at Quintus standing next to her on the balcony. "Where are you taking him?"

"Back to where he belongs. And if you're smart, you'll go back to my uncle where you belong and forget this last year ever happened."

"The Praetorian Guard will hunt you down. He's an Imperial advisor, you know."

Quintus shook his head and stepped over the railing. "After what he did at the amphitheater today, you think any politician will support this madman again? I think they'll be happy to have him simply fade away unnoticed. Good-bye, Aunt Julia."

Quintus jumped off the balcony and landed in the hay next to Lucius. Lindani snapped the reins, and the two horses pulled the cart out from under the balcony and across the wide Forum.

Julia Melita closed her eyes and listened as the sound of the horses' hooves on the stone pavement faded away to silence. Tears streamed down her cheeks. She began considering the best transportation route back to Aquae Sulis. She had never felt more alone in her life.

As they rode along the Vicus Iugarius, Quintus pulled the white tunic off Lucius. He yanked him to a sitting position and tugged a dirty olive-drab rag over his head. Although Lucius was still unconscious, Quintus spoke to him as if he was fully alert.

"Do you remember this scene, Lucius? Something just like it happened about four years ago. Except now the roles are reversed once again. I told you the tables would turn. I told you to keep looking over your shoulder and one day I'd be there to avenge what you've done. Well, here I am, asshole. Say good-bye to your life of luxury."

The sight of Lucius dressed once again as the slave he was, helped to calm Quintus's pounding heart. The bastard's defiant glee over Aulus's murder was just one more reason for Quintus to hate this wretched scum with all his being. But knowing what was in store for Lucius made letting him live seem worthwhile.

Within minutes, they approached the Amphitheater of Taurus and the Imperial ludus complex. The pathways throughout the Campus Martius were a disaster. Bleeding and trampled spectators were still being attended to by physicians. Smashed vendor stalls and broken merchandise littered the area for a half-kilometer. The amphitheater grounds would take weeks to clean up.

Petra and Julianus approached Quintus as soon as the cart pulled into the busy ludus practice field. Dozens of oxcarts were being loaded with equipment and personnel.

"Did you take care of business?" Petra asked.

"It's wrapped up and ready to go, Dominus," Quintus said with a nod toward the cargo bed. "And, Dominus . . . " Quintus wondered for a moment if he should share the news with Petra, then decided his lanista had every right to hear it. After all, he had once known Aulus as well as Quintus did. "It seems Aulus did not die by accident in the shipwreck." He said no more but knew the message was clear.

Petra looked silently at the bundle on the cart bed. "I'll keep that in mind," he said as he walked away.

Quintus and Lindani stepped from the wagon and climbed into another transport cart. Amazonia was already stretched out in the back, her wounded leg heavily bandaged with wine-soaked linen.

"How's it feel?" Quintus asked as he settled in next to her.

"Well, I won't be wrapping it around any Roman studs for a while, but I'll live."

Past the wooden bars of his transport cart, Quintus watched Julianus drag the bundle of forest-green silk from the cargo bed and slide it through the door of an enclosed wagon, which already held five slaves and three boxes of supplies. He locked the door and climbed up onto the driver's bench alongside another ludus worker. Petra approached and raised his arm to Julianus. The head trainer grasped his forearm and smiled.

"I want you to bring us back some decent fighters," Petra said. "I'm looking to you to replenish our ranks in Pompeii."

"Count on it, Dominus. I'll see you in eight months with some new talent."

Petra glanced through the small window on Julianus's wagon, then looked across at Quintus and smiled. "Oh, and be careful with that package in the back," he yelled up to the trainer. "We can always use the extra help in such an isolated location." Julianus nodded as he turned the oxen around and headed out the gate toward the cargo port at Ostia.

Petra stepped to the cart that held Quintus, Lindani, and Amazonia. "I want you three out of here now," he said. "We'll catch up in the morning along the Via Appia." Quintus caught a wink from Petra. "So you finally got to fight in Rome."

"Yes, and I always knew it would be memorable."

"Oh, by the way . . . " Petra added as he began to walk away. "Congratulations. You're now primus palus."

They were words Quintus had waited years to hear. There was not the pomp or ceremony he had dreamt of, but the words came just as sweetly to his ears. He looked at Lindani, whose wide smile was in place.

"So our little kitchen assistant has done well for himself, eh? He will now see the world from the top of the ladder."

The driver snapped the reins, and the cart rolled through the gate and turned south. Quintus watched Julianus's wagon head west, silhouetted by the setting sun.

"So tell me, Lindani," he said, "what are summers like in the provinces of North Africa? You think it's a climate that will suit Lucius?"

Lindani stroked his chin in mock seriousness. "Well, it is not bad for those who are born there, but I do not think it would be to a Roman's liking."

Quintus smiled to himself as he watched Lucius's wagon get smaller on the horizon. "Especially when he's spending his time cleaning latrines as a ludus slave," he said quietly.

"Damn," Amazonia replied with a sarcastic grin. "Is there a worse job in the Empire?"

Lindani's white teeth showed brightly. "Not that I am aware of."

Quintus watched the dark silhouette of the Amphitheater of Taurus grow small and disappear over the Palatine Hill. It was a day he would relive often in his dreams. He thought about who had helped him most on this journey to his true calling. Was it Petra and Julianus? Or was it Master Sheng, his tutor in the ways of *wushu*? Perhaps Aulus? Or his two closest friends, Lindani and Amazonia?

No, deep inside he knew the answer. It was Caius and Politta, the father and mother who had been taken from him at such an early age. It was they who had given him the strength and judgment to overcome the obstacles the

Fates had thrown his way. He was smart enough to see that now. He still cursed the name of Neptune whenever he thought about that horrid night at sea. But somehow he knew his father was in the cavea this day. And his mother waited for him just over the next hill. He wrapped his fingers around the terra-cotta figure that hung from his neck. He knew they would protect him for the rest of his days on the sand of the arena.